FOR THE LOVE OF OIL

J. SERVAIS

For the Love of Oil is a work of fiction. References to real people, events, establishments, organizations or locales are intended only to provide a sense of authenticity and are used fictitiously. All other characters, incidents and dialogue are drawn from the author's imagination and are not to be construed as real.

FIRST EDITION

Printed in the United States of America

ISBN: 0-9896377-2-7
ISBN-13: 978-0-9896377-2-5

DEDICATION

This book is dedicated to all men and women who lost their life while drilling or producing oil and gas.

TABLE OF CONTENTS

ACKNOWLEDGMENTS

My deep respect goes out to all women taking care of the family while their men are away from home earning a living in the oil and gas industry.

Part 1: War and Freedom

Chapter 1

It was as if the great river had torn the country in two, forming a natural barrier between war and freedom, delaying the Allies from liberating it in its entirety. While the southern part of The Netherlands had regained its freedom, the part that lay north of the Rhine River was still occupied by German forces. Here, the Gestapo continued carrying out unexpected raids in cities and villages to arrest adult men, who were deported to Germany and forced to work in factories to produce weapons to sustain its war. The Allies bombed those factories, and thousands of people lost their lives.

It was no wonder that men and women from the North continuously tried to cross the dangerous battle zone along the Rhine to be free, away from the hated Germans, find jobs and start a new life in the South.

In Ootmarsum, a small village north of the Rhine and just four miles from the German border, Mark Oolderink spent his time hiding. Most of the days he hid in the forest, where he and his two friends had dug a secret and well-protected hideout close to the village. They only came out in the evenings to see their family and obtain food.

They ran the risk of getting arrested and deported to Germany, so they planned their journey to freedom.

Knowing that his parents would never agree to his plan, Mark left them a letter in the hideout, where they were bound to find it.

Armed with a compass, the three men walked across the country at night, and slept in the woods during daytime. The war seemed to have descended all around them, especially when they came close to the battle zone near Arnhem, where fighting was particularly intense. They knew that this would be the most dangerous part of their journey, so they moved with care until they found a safe place to cross the river.

Here the German presence was not that strong and the ever-searching lights were seen less frequently.

At first, Mark intended to take his backpack, which contained an extra sweater and some food, but he noticed that he had to dive several times in order to avoid the search lights. He decided to leave his backpack behind and only keep his compass. He advised his friends to do the same, but they insisted on taking everything with them.

They lowered themselves into the water, which was far colder than expected, and the strong current surprised them. Mark was a good swimmer, but halfway across the river he felt completely exhausted and was forced to float with the current, back into the war zone. He had to make the decision to float back or risk drowning by swimming against the current towards freedom. Barely able to hold his head above the water, he called out to his friends, but he could not see nor hear them.

He chose to swim for freedom, but in his weakened state, he did not have the strength to dive and avoid the searchlights scanning the river's surface.

The cold water chilled him to the bone, and exhaustion took hold of him.

He could feel the icy waters close above him.

Suddenly he felt firm ground underneath his feet, which gave him the energy he needed to resurface. He swam, he crawled, and he clutched his way to the shore, where he fell asleep, completely exhausted.

When the sound of gunfire woke him, he did not know how long he had lain there.

He crawled towards the forest by the river, where he covered himself with leaves to stop from shivering. He had no idea if his friends had returned back to shore, or whether they had swam their way to freedom.

When he reawakened, the air around him seemed to be filled with the sound of gunfire, low-flying airplanes and bombs exploding in the distance. There was no way of knowing where the frontline was. That night he walked on, and in the morning came across a farmer's barn where he found some old clothes.

During the day he slept, and after three nights he arrived in Maastricht, the most southern city of Holland.

Cold and hungry, he knocked on several doors in the Jeker valley, named after a small river originating from Belgium. Much to his relief, a family with two young children opened the door and let him in. He told them of his escape and asked if he could stay until he found a place to live, and they offered him food and a bed in the attic.

The father worked as a cook in the army. He told Mark that if he wanted a job to join him in the morning, as the army was looking for recruits.

Both men got up early and walked to the army base. Mark went to the recruitment office and after a medical test he was selected for a three-month training program to join the military police. That same day he moved into the recruitment quarters where he was given a bunk to sleep and his uniform.

In the evening, he visited the family telling them of his good fortune, and thanked them for their hospitality.

Most of his military training took place around a hill called the St. Pieter near the Jeker valley, just outside Maastricht.

One day, as the recruits prepared to make a wet crossing through the Jeker, Mark noticed a girl leaving the house next to the river. Briefly, their eyes met. He had never seen anyone so beautiful, and found it hard to concentrate on the exercises for the rest of the day.

The following Sunday he walked down to the Jeker and sat down in the grass next to a steel pedestrian bridge. For an entire hour, he observed the house by the river, families crossing the bridge on bicycles and farmers crossing the river with their horse and wagon returning home from church for lunch.

But there was no sign of the girl.

Finally he decided to walk up to the house and knocked on the door. The same girl opened and she was even more beautiful than he remembered.

'Could I please use your water pump?'

'Of course. You must be very thirsty. I watched you sitting there for more than an hour. Wait here. I'll get you a cup.'

'No thanks, I can drink out of my hands.'

After a few pump strokes, he drank the fresh, cold water and washed his face.

'Thank you. My name is Mark. Would you please walk up the St. Pieter with me?'

She blushed, which suited her very well, Mark thought.

'I have to ask my mam and dad. I'll be back in a minute.'

She closed the door, and after a moment she was back with her coat on. 'We have one hour because at three I must be back home. My relatives are coming over for coffee and vlaai. Do you know what vlaai is?' He shook his head.

'It's a pie made from a special kind of dough with fruit or rice. It's a specialty of this area.'

'Can you bake vlaai?'

'Not yet. My mam still has to show me how.'

They walked up the small steep stony path until they reached the top of the St. Pieter. There they found a bench near St. Mary's chapel overlooking the valley.

'I love this place,' she said. 'And I hope I never have to leave it.'

'What's your name?'

'Jessica. But they call me Jess. I was named after my grandma.'

'My name is Mark. I was very lucky to escape from the north and just joined a three-month training course to become a member of the military police.'

They talked for an hour. She told him that she was the youngest of three girls and that she assisted her mam at home or on the plot of farmland that her dad leased.

'Our income depends on the yearly potato and vegetable harvest,' she told him.

'It's hard work. The whole family has to walk for an hour every morning. Then we work the whole day, apart from lunch of course. We usually don't return until late in the evening to prepare dinner. We always go to bed early. And on Sundays we go to church, and sometimes our relatives visit for coffee.'

Neither of them felt any rush to return. They walked as slowly as they could.

As they walked, he noticed that she was limping, and asked what happened.

'It's a strange story, but I'll try to explain. As kids we got up to the usual stuff, like pulling door bells and quickly disappearing. Or we made secret hideouts, smoke self-rolled cigarettes and got sick. One day we played with a group of girls and boys near the river, when a Gypsy woman walked up with a basket to wash her clothes.

'She limped and walked with the aid of a cane. One of the boys thought it would be funny if we girls took her cane. They selected me, but I refused. They then gave me the choice: do it or be banned from the group.

'We live in a very isolated place here, and the group was very important to me, so I chose to do it. I walked up to the woman, who was busy washing, and took her cane that she had left on the riverbank. I ran back, and we watched as the woman finished her washing, searching for her cane. She knew that we had something to do with it, so she shouted at us to return her cane.

'None of us did. She had to walk without it. We all saw that it was difficult for her to walk.

'When she limped by, she looked at us intently. "One day," she said, "whoever took my cane will remember this day."

'In the years that followed, one of my legs kept getting shorter and that's why I limp.'

They walked up to the house where her dad was waiting on the bench next to the front door. Mark apologized for being late and introduced himself. He didn't leave until he obtained permission to see Jess the next Sunday.

That week, he could barely concentrate, and his instructors warned him several times that if he didn't focus he would have to stay at the base, and clean toilets, during the weekend.

The warning had its desired effect, as he desperately wanted to see Jess again.

Sunday morning he walked along the river and knocked on the door. Every time he saw her, he discovered something new. She invited him for lunch and introduced him to her mam and sisters.

They had lunch at a big round table. Her dad cut tough-crusted, homemade bread, and there was cheese or homemade marmalade. He decided to select the cheese, but he found the smell awful, reminding him of very sweaty feet. He could barely finish his sandwich.

Jess glanced across, smiling. 'Don't you like it? It's called Rommedoe. It's a specialty of this area.'

Slightly embarrassed, he told her that he would rather have marmalade on his next sandwich.

After lunch her dad took off his hat, rested his head on his arms and took a short nap on the table while the girls cleaned up and washed the dishes. Her mam sat down on the couch and asked if Mark would also join them for coffee. He hesitated, feeling slightly uncomfortable, but accepted the invitation.

After Jess finished the dishes they went outside and walked to the steel bridge, lowering themselves onto the supporting beams just above the water's surface so no one could watch them.

He told her about his family in Ootmarsum and their grocery store, and his wish to return home after the war. He told her how his mam would take care of the store while his dad left early in the mornings with horse and wagon to sell groceries, fruit and vegetables to the local farmers, that his dad was getting older, and he thought of talking to his parents about taking over his dad's work.

While he talked, she moved closer to him. As her skin brushed against his, he felt his heart pounding. For what seemed to be an eternity, they looked each other and kissed for the first time.

During the following months, Mark passed all his tests and was stationed in Maastricht. Every weekend Jess showed him different parts of the city, and they cycled through the surrounding villages.

Chapter 2

After a long and tough battle near Arnhem, the Allies finally succeeded in liberating the north at a great loss of lives on both sides. The Dutch celebrated their newly found freedom for three whole days.

Many of those who had escaped to the South returned home. Others stayed, in the towns and villages that had welcomed and helped them making a new start in life during the war. Mark wrote his parents, assuring them that he was fine. They wrote back straight away, asking him to come home. His family had been worried sick and they desperately wanted to see him.

Mark and Jess agreed that he should return home as was expected of him.

They promised to write each other, and to experience how life would be without each other.

After three months Jess decided that she wanted to see Mark, because she missed him terrible, and asked her parents' permission to visit him. They understood how she felt and Mam helped her pack.

The next morning she left home with enough money for a return train ticket to Oldenzaal. It was the first time that she visited another part of Holland, and she felt exhilarated to see Mark, enjoying the trip immensely, arriving at Oldenzaal in the afternoon.

Outside the train station she asked a woman how to get to Ootmarsum.

'You'll have to walk as there is no bus or other transport available, but I can show you the way.'

After they had walked for ten minutes, the woman inquired after the reason of her visit. Jess explained that she wanted to surprise her friend who she had not seen for a long time. The woman asked her the address, and Jess told her that the family owned a grocery store.

'I know that place because that's the only store in the village.'

While she was giving directions, a farmer passed by with his horse and wagon. In a dialect that Jess did not understand, the woman asked him if he could give the girl a ride to Ootmarsum, and told him to stop at the grocery store.

The farmer reined in his horse and agreed to take her to the next village. After placing her luggage on the back, he helped her up and climbed back on the driver's seat next to her. Spurring his horse on, he asked her a question, but she simply could not understand him, just as her mother had warned her she wouldn't.

The dialect from the province Twente that he spoke sounded like an entirely different language to her.

Instead of attempting conversation, she kept quiet, enjoying the ride through the surprisingly flat countryside. It was so different from where she was born. The landscape from her province Limburg was far hillier than this.

When they arrived in Ootmarsum the farmer helped her down, handed her the suitcase and directed her to the grocery store. Feeling nervous, she entered the store, where a young woman asked her if she could be of any help.

'I'm looking for Mark,' she said uncertainly.

'Then you must be Jess,' the woman said to her in plain Dutch, and she walked up to her and kissed here on both cheeks. 'Mark told us so much about you. He is right. You are beautiful! I'm Wilma, Mark's sister-in-law. I help out in the store. Come, let me carry your suitcase and introduce you to Mother.'

'Is Mark here? Could you please tell me where I could find him?' Jess asked excitedly.

'Oh! I'm sorry, but he is out with his dad. They should be on their way home now.'

'Can you tell me which way I should walk so I can meet him? I dearly wish to see him.'

Wilma laughed and took her outside, where she gave her directions. Jess left the suitcase in the store and started walking until she saw a horse and wagon coming her way. She stopped, shielding her eyes against the setting sun when she saw him and started running.

Mark jumped off the wagon and caught her mid-air when she jumped into his arms, covering her face with kisses.

'Jess! It is so good to see you,' he murmured into her hair. 'To hold you at last. But what on earth are you doing here?'

'I could not stay home any longer. I missed you too much,' she said, clinging on to him.

His dad stopped the wagon and looked at her. 'Now, you must be Jess. Welcome to our village. I'll go ahead and drive home to tell mother that we have a guest. Take your time. You two will have a lot to talk about,' he added with a grin.

Mark took her hand and they walked on, unable to take their eyes off each other.

The village of Ootmarsum consisted of one main road with houses on both sides. The church, which was built of large sandstone blocks, stood at its center. Jess noticed how the people stared at her.

Mark smiled. 'It's a small village, Jess. Everyone knows each other here. You're a stranger. Tomorrow people will visit the store to ask my mam who you are, and what you are doing here.'

She laughed. 'What will she tell them?'

'Just that you're visiting for a few days.'

She looked at him in disbelief. 'Well if you want me to go, I'll leave.'

He laughed. 'You know I don't want you to go. These past months I've been asking myself what's important for me in life. When I saw you running up to me I suddenly realized how much I've missed you. And how much you mean to me.' He stopped, took both of her hands in his and looked suddenly very serious. 'I know now that I want to be with you for the rest of my life.'

Jess felt tears fill her eyes as she looked at him. 'And I'll go wherever you go.'

He took her face in both hands. 'So be it, then.'

They walked on, arm in arm, through the village until they reached a small alley that led to the barn in the backyard. The stables and the main house were attached to the store.

His dad was still busy unloading the wagon and Mark showed her how to take care of the horse. When they were nearly finished, his mam came into the stable. She kissed Jess three times.

'Welcome, my dear. It's wonderful to meet the woman who took care of our son in Maastricht. You've made a different person out of him.'

Jess blushed. 'I fell in love with your son. That's the reason why I'm here.'

While they talked, Mark finished helping his dad. Together they went into the house where she met Mark's brother, Bart, and his two sisters, Hannie and Truus.

The sisters prepared the meal and set the table. While they ate, Mark's sisters told her that they were both engaged and hoping to get married within the next year. Both their fiancés had been deported to Germany, where they worked in factories for the last four months of the war. They had just returned home last month and found jobs at a cotton factory in Oldenzaal. The girls worked as nurses in the hospital, to which they cycled six miles every day.

After dinner Jess helped to clean the table and wash the dishes. Truus told her that their fiancés would visit that night to play cards. Both men arrived at eight and Jess was introduced to Truus' fiancé, Wim, and Albert, who was engaged to Hannie.

Wilma taught Jess how to play rummy, and after a few trial games, they played cards, sang different songs, exchanged stories, and told the latest jokes. Jess thoroughly enjoyed herself, as she was not used to this kind of spending time together. Her own family life consisted of little more than working, sleeping and eating. Sundays was filled with going to church and relatives visiting for coffee.

When the clock chimed ten, the girls asked their parents if it would be all right to go outside and have some privacy with their fiancés before they left. Mother told Jess that she could share the bedroom with Truus.

After she said goodnight, Mark brought her suitcase upstairs and asked if she would like to help him the next day.

'Yes, I would love that.'

'You'll have to get up early, as I have to take care of the horse at six. At seven I load the fresh supply of fruit and vegetables onto the wagon. My mam always prepares lunch and breakfast. We eat on the road.'

They went downstairs, where Mark told his dad that he could sleep in because Jess would like to join him the next day.

'That's fine,' his dad said. 'I'll get up early anyhow to show Jess how to load the groceries. That way you can prepare the horse and wagon.' And with that, his parents went upstairs.

They were alone at last and started kissing. Mark's hand strayed towards her breast, fondling her. But when he began to unbutton her blouse, she stopped him.

'Don't, Mark. Please don't. I truly want to make love to you. Really I do. But I promised myself that I would not give myself to anyone before I got married. Do you want me to break that promise?'

He hesitated for a moment, feeling lustful, but he ended up kissing her.

'No, I would like you to keep that promise. We'll just have to get married, but I don't know if I can hold out for much longer. I desperately want to make love to you, Jess,' as his hand strayed again. 'I have longed for you so long, but will respect your decision.'

They went upstairs, and after one more kiss they walked to their bedroom. "Did you enjoy the evening?' Truus asked eagerly as Jess slipped underneath the bedcovers next to her.

'Oh, Truus, I absolutely loved everything. I never expected to be welcomed in such a warm way. I loved the way your mother and father accepted me.'

'I think they know you're the reason that Mark changed. He went from being a boy chasing girls, always trying to find excuses not to help at home, to a responsible young man who suddenly started taking life seriously.'

Jess could feel herself blush, and fell asleep with a smile on her face.

The next morning Mark gently kissed her awake, telling it was time to get up.

He shaved while she washed her face, and together they went downstairs to find his father waiting.

'Good morning, Jess. I hope you had a good sleep? Come to the store with me and I'll show you what to do while Mark takes care of the fruit and vegetables.'

They moved from the kitchen into a small corridor that led to the shop. He switched on the lights and handed her a list that was hanging on the door. 'This list shows the groceries we have in the store and the amount we like to take with us on the wagon. You check the items low on stock and write down the total number you require from the store.

They went to the barn, where Mark's father pulled on a cord that lifted the plastic covers off the wagon. Jess noticed that wooden crates were stacked in an angle and that one side of the wagon was for fruits, and the other side for vegetables. Above the crates was a separate storage rack for groceries. He handed her the list and pencil and she wrote down the required groceries. He also showed her the trolley to transport everything from the store to the wagon.

Mark was loading the fruits and vegetables when they returned with the groceries. After they loaded everything they went to the kitchen, where mother was preparing sandwiches and coffee.

'Good morning, Jess. Would you like a cup of coffee?'

'Thanks Mam, we are late and have to go,' Mark told her. As he took the basket with sandwiches and coffee.

Father took the horse and wagon out of the yard, while mother kissed Jess, wishing them a lovely day.

It was a twenty minutes' drive to the first farm. Mark told her to wait while he went inside to ask for the shopping list. After several minutes Mark emerged from the farmhouse, with a woman at his side.

'Hello!' she said with a smile. 'So you're Jess! It's good to meet the girl Mark has found so far away from home and everyone seems to be talking about! Mark, please select the fruit and vegetables, then Jess can help me with the groceries.'

Mark laughed. 'Jess, you can help, but don't tell her too much!'

As Jess did what she was told, the woman asked her how and when she had met Mark, and how long she intended to stay. Wary, Jess told her as little as possible. There was no doubt that any news would go around town in no time.

She was relieved when Mark came to her side and offered to give her a hand filling the baskets.

'Mark, we are doing fine, and Jess was a great help,' the woman said.

He took the two baskets and before the woman returned to her kitchen she said, 'I do hope to see you again by the end of the week, Jess. Thank you for your help. Oh, and I love your accent.'

'How do you get paid for the groceries?' Jess asked as they walked back to the wagon.

'We keep a record of all deliveries in the shopping book. By the end of each month they pay us or deliver goods such as potatoes, fruit, vegetables or corn. This is how all farmers pay their bills.'

Once they had climbed back onto the wagon, Mark clicked his tongue and the horse moved on. Before they stopped at the next farmhouse, they ate a sandwich and drank coffee.

'People in this town don't lock their doors. If no one is around I just take the basket and grocery booklet from the kitchen. Then we select the items ordered, return the basket to the house and sign off at the bottom of the page.' He smiled. 'But if the farmer's wife is home, she will usually ask for any news or gossip.' He looked at her with a grin. 'I think that you'd better prepare yourself. I have a feeling that every woman around here may want to see you because they know that we met in Maastricht. They're bound to be curious, because you're the hottest news in town.'

Jess was thoughtful for a moment. 'Do you want me to tell them that I'm your girlfriend or that we're just friends?'

Mark threw her a shy glance. 'You can tell them that we're about to get married, if you want.'

Jess felt her face go scarlet and wrapped her arms around his neck. 'That's exactly what I want, and that's what I'll love to tell them.'

From that moment onwards, Mark would go inside every farmhouse to return with the farmer's wife and introduced Jess as his fiancée.

At noon Mark stopped for lunch and selected a beautiful spot next to a small river called de Dinkel. He handed her a plaid from the back of the wagon and fed the horse. Jess spread the plaid on the grass, unpacked the lunch basket, and watched him while they ate their sandwiches.

'If we want to spend the rest of our life together, where will we live and how can we make a living?'

Mark took her hand. 'My dad told me that he wants to stay home because he is getting old. I want to ask him if we can split the profit of the store and the wagon sales between him and my brother. Then we may have sufficient money to live. I would also like to rebuild the barn into a small home for us and will discuss this with my parents tonight.'

After they finished their lunch, they lay down, side by side, enjoying the warmth of the sun. He looked at her, grinning. 'Let's go for a swim,' and started taking off his clothes.

Jess blushed as he stripped down, naked. 'Do you mean to swim here, naked?'

'Oh yes. We always swim here naked. No one ever comes here at this time.'

Jess looked around hesitantly. Shyly, she slowly started to remove her clothes.

Mark watched her and smiled. 'You know, I fell in love with your beautiful face, your eyes and hair. But I never knew that you had such a perfect figure. You've got beautiful legs, a delightful bottom and most of all, breathtaking breasts. I always dreamt about a woman like you, standing in the sun, just as you are now. Let's go for a swim, because I have to cool off.'

They raced to the embankment, where they jumped into the cool water, enjoying the tug of the strong current. Standing in the shallow waters, Jess put her arms around his neck. He moved closer, and she found that the coolness of the water had not affected his arousal at all. She enjoyed the way he pressed himself against her legs, the way he gently stroked her breast.

They remained that way for a while, their hearts racing. Then he picked her up and walked to the blanket, where they made love until they were completely exhausted. They dozed off until Mark could feel his horse's snout nuzzling his face. He lay on his side, watching Jess in her sleep and thought that he had never seen a more beautiful woman in his life.

He kissed her awake, went for another swim, and they made love again.

Jess kissed him one final time. 'You made me break my promise,' she said with a satisfied smile. 'But I have no regrets. I'll make love to you any time. Now let's go for a last swim and dry in the sun before your customers start wondering what's keeping you.'

They walked along the riverside until dry enough to get dressed.

After stopping at the last customer they returned home, getting back just before the sun disappeared behind the trees.

'Mark. This was the most beautiful day of my life. I enjoyed every second of it. Please let's do it again tomorrow.'

'We will, but I first have to discuss a few things with my parents.'

Father was already waiting on a bench outside the shop, and mother was waiting for them with dinner.

Quickly they brought the horse in, parked the wagon in the barn, washed their hands and went to the kitchen, where Bart and Wilma were waiting. The gorgeous smell of food was mouthwatering, and they quickly took their seats at the table.

Mother threw them a knowing glance. 'You two look happy. Are you hungry or prefer to wait?'

'No Mam, we're starving. Let's have dinner!' Mark said.

Mother served them a feast: fried potatoes with fresh salad mixed with sliced tomatoes, cucumbers and a dressing of sweetened vinegar. Throughout the week, there was no meat on the table. Potatoes, salad or beans were served for dinner at most families in this village. Father said grace, thanking the lord for the day and the food they were given, and then they ate.

Mother asked Jess how her day had been. 'It was lovely. I'm just happy to be with Mark and help wherever I can.'

Mark glanced at her, betraying his nervousness. 'Dad, there's something I've been meaning to ask you.'

'Well, go ahead, Mark.'

'Jess and I have known each other now for nearly a year. We don't want to live apart any longer. We want to get married and start a new life together. I was wondering…Would it be possible to take care of the customers outside the village and split the profit?' He spoke quickly now. 'And I was thinking, we could modify one side of the barn and create a small bedroom, kitchen and living room for ourselves? That is…with your permission, of course.'

His parents looked at each other. It was a while before either of them spoke.

'Well, actually. I've already discussed this with your mother. We did notice that you changed, and that this relationship is serious.' He cleared his throat, a small frown on his forehead. 'You know Bart is the oldest son. I don't have to tell you that according to local tradition, the oldest son usually takes over the house, farm or business. We have two families living off the proceeds from the shop. These are hard times, Mark. With the war just over, there aren't any jobs. We have to barter goods to make a living. What we make is barely enough to provide for two families, we can't support another.' He downed the remains of his milk. 'In the near future Bart has to take care of the wagon sales, Wilma has to run the shop and we help them wherever we can. I wish things were different, but there's no other way. However, I would like to make a proposal.' He wiped his mouth with the back of his hand. 'If you really want to get married, we suggest you combine your wedding with that of your sisters. Then we will cover the costs. And you have our permission to modify the barn to create a home for the two of you.'

'I talked about a job with one of our clients,' he went on. 'He can arrange for you to work at the cotton factory. For now, that's all we can do.'

Mark glanced across at Jess, and then looked back at his dad. 'I'd like to have my own business. You know that. But I respect your decision. Jess and I will have to discuss and decide what we want to do.'

An uneasy silence filled the kitchen. Mark felt disappointed. He knew that tradition played a strong role in the lives of families in Holland. But should the oldest son always continue the family business, or the person who is the most motivated, and best suited for the job? But he kept his thoughts to himself.

They quickly cleared the table, after which he and Jess went for a walk. They walked hand in hand and did not speak for a long time.

Mark finally broke the silence. 'I would love to have my own business, but it's just not possible. We have no money. Still, I really want us to get married. I think we accept my parents offer for a joint wedding, and to modify the barn so that we have a place of our own.

'But I will look for another job. I'd hate to work in the cotton factories, where it's hot and without daylight.' He fell quiet, somber now.

'I could work,' Jess offered. 'I always assisted my parents in the house, and on the land.'

Mark thought about it for a while. 'Maybe we can find a family that needs someone to take care of their children, help in household, that sort of thing. We can ask Wilma. That's what she did before she married my brother.

'Jess, there is one question I have to ask. The first time we went for a walk you mentioned that you love the Jeker valley and never wanted to leave. Now we're making plans for you to settle here, away from home and family. Is that really what you want?'

Jess looked up at him. 'I broke a promise because I love you. You are the most important person in my life. I cannot ask my family for money, because they just have enough to survive. This is the only chance we have of being together. Let's just stay here and accept all the help we can get. I will talk to Wilma to see if she can help me to find a job.'

Mark kissed her and whispered in her ear, 'Right now all I want to do is go back to the riverside and make love to you.'

She kissed him. 'Don't be silly. It's too far. Can you ask your father if I can help him deliver the goods until I find myself a job? Then you and Bart can start modifying the barn.'

It was getting late and they went back to the house. Mark told his parents that they gladly accept their offer of the joint wedding and barn house, but he will only take the job at the cotton factory if nothing else was available.

The following weeks Jess helped out with loading and delivering the groceries while Mark and Bart modified the barn into a cozy place with a living and bedroom, a separate kitchen and toilet. In the evenings they painted the rooms. As soon as water and electricity was connected, they painted an old wooden bed that they found in the attic.

Once they finished, Mark lifted her up and carried her into what would become their home, and kissed her. 'This is all I can offer you for now, Jess. I hope that this small home will bring us happiness.'

She looked around. 'I quite like it. It's a place of our own, Mark. Don't worry. Wilma found two families that need someone to clean and take care of their kids. I start next week. Then we'll have some money to buy the things we need.'

'So when are you going to tell your parents that we're getting married?'

'I sent them a letter after we made love for the first time by the river. I wrote that I found the man I want to spend the rest of my life with. I will write them this week as soon as we know the wedding date. That way they can prepare themselves. They've never travelled outside of Maastricht you know.'

Mark felt a sudden peace come over him. 'Shall I get some blankets from the house and sleep here tonight?' he asked.

'I would like that, but only if your parents don't object.'

'Let's go to the house and ask them.'

But father was adamant. 'We understand that you wish to be together, but we live in a small town. Tradition dictates that you live separately until the day you get married.'

Mother disagreed. 'Come on, dear. Think back to the time when we were young. Don't you remember how we agreed to get married, and lived in your rental room from that day on? I told my parents that I was living at the nurses' ward.'

Father grinned at his wife. 'All right, I get the message. You have our blessing. So go ahead, take all you need from the house and we will handle town gossip as it comes. We'll have to set a date for the wedding for you and your sisters this week and I suggest we plan it for this summer.'

'Thank you,' Mark said. 'I know this goes against tradition. We really appreciate this and promise to be careful in order to avoid gossip.'

They went upstairs, quickly gathered what they needed for the night, said their goodnights and hurried to their new home. Within seconds Jess closed the curtains and lit the candles in the living and bedroom.

'If this is the first night in our own home, then let's make it our wedding night.

'I always wanted this to be a romantic moment. So, Prince Charming, any ideas?'

'Yes. I suggest you take off your clothes, and we can check if the paint on the bed is dry.'

'No. That's cheap. I want to be overwhelmed with kisses, I want a special massage and…'

He stopped her with a kiss, picked her up and placed her on the bed. He began to kiss her feet, moving up ever so slowly, and by the time he was halfway up her body she was so overwhelmed that she begged him to make love to her. They did so for the better part of that night.

The modified barn worked out so well, that Bart and Wilma asked Mark to assist and modify the other side, as well, so that they could live there. Within three weeks they had created a similar home.

Jess found work in the village looking after the three children of the local doctor, aged between three to seven years old. The doctor and his wife had a combined medical and veterinarian center and hardly any time left to take care of the children and household chores. Jesses started work at seven, preparing breakfast and getting the children ready for school. She cleaned the house, made lunch and dinner, and got home at six to help unload the wagon.

Chapter 3

The following weeks, Jess, Hannie and Truus prepared for the wedding, which was scheduled to take place in two months' time. They decided to hold the joint ceremony on a Sunday, so that no one would have to miss a day's work.

Mother was very busy sewing and fitting the wedding dresses and suits, while Jess wrote to her parents that they could stay in the barn houses.

After discussing their finances, Mark finally relented and took the job at the cotton factory, simply because there was nothing else available. He left every morning at five with a special bus that picked up factory workers from different villages and returned home around three in the afternoon.

It was hard and hot work coloring the big rolls of cotton, but with their combined income, they managed to have enough money for a living. As the wedding day drew closer, mother finished all the bridal dresses.

With meat and flour still rationed by the government, father had to barter with the farmers for meat, flour and cheese for the wedding. For lunch they opted to bake fresh bread for sandwiches topped with ham and cheese, meatballs with potatoes and fresh salad for dinner, and Jess and her mother would made apple vlaai for dessert.

According to local tradition, neighbors decorated the front door of the bride with spruce leaves a week before the wedding. They also attached a sign with well wishes for the newlywed couples, framed with red and white paper flowers, as well as decorated the door of the grocery shop. Custom dictated that the bride had to provide a corn jenever with a stifling forty percent alcohol percentage. The strong beverage set the right mood, and inevitably all the men ended up drunk, causing severe hangovers the next morning.

Jess' family arrived three days before the wedding, and all the women kept busy preparing food and making corsages for the guests. Everyone was so busy with the preparations that the last evening was there before they knew it.

The men moved all the tables and chairs they borrowed from neighbors into the backyard to form one long table. The next morning they all woke up at five, so that the women could fix each other's hair, and the men could set the table and prepare breakfast. By nine everyone was dressed and ready.

The weather was excellent, and father had arranged for three horse-drawn carriages to transport the couples and parents. The rest of the wedding party followed the carriages to church on foot.

The church was full with people from the village and surrounding area.

It seemed that everyone wanted to attend this special ceremony: three couples getting married in a joint ceremony. It was something people had never witnessed before.

The ceremony was kept simple. Each couple had to come forward for their vows and exchange of wedding rings. After the ceremony everyone, except the married couples, left the church and formed two rows. As the couples came out of the church they had to walk between the two rows of people, who clapped and cheered for them.

Passers-by stopped in the streets and congratulated the newlyweds until the carriages brought them back to the shop. The rest of the day they feasted. The couples were given wedding gifts and had their pictures taken. They all sang songs, and each newlywed had to suffer listening to embarrassing anecdotes told by some relative, usually accompanied by raucous laughter.

It turned out to be a perfect day, which ended in Mark's parents asking Jess to call them Mam and Dad.

By three in the morning, Mark and Jess finally went up to Mark's old bedroom, because their barn house was occupied by Jess' relatives from Maastricht. They kissed each other good night, wishing that they could make love in their own bedroom. No wonder Bart and Wilma had moved out. There was absolute no privacy sleeping next to your parents with only a thin wall.

Jess tossed and turned and could not sleep. After one hour she woke up Mark and told him that she had missed her period, and thought she was pregnant.

He embraced her, delighted. 'Jess, this is just wonderful. I'm becoming a dad! I think that the first day at the river or first night in our home was our wedding night.'

Too excited to sleep, they discussed this miracle that would change their lives forever. At six they went down to the kitchen and prepared breakfast for the whole family. Mam was the first person to come down.

'Up so early, you two? My goodness. Is anything the matter?'

Mark blushed, and told her what happened.

Mam looked at them and smiled. 'Maybe it's just the stress of the wedding. And if it isn't, then you didn't stop to think of the risk when you made love. Anyway, you're married now.'

Encouraged by Mam's down-to-earth response, Jess told her parents that she might be expecting while they sat on the bus to the train station in Oldenzaal.

She said goodbye to them with pain in her heart.

The next day Mam arranged for a doctor's appointment. Two days later the doctor confirmed that Jess was two months pregnant.

When Mark returned from work, Jess waited for him with a cup of tea.

'We only just got married, Mark,' she said with a frown. 'And you're about to become a father. Everything is happening so fast! We did not save any money to pay for doctors and other expenses.' She fell silent. 'Mark, for me it's like a dream come true. I know we discussed this, but is this really what you want?'

He took her into his arms. 'It's not only your dream, Jess. From the moment you came running at me I knew that I wanted to start a family with you. But yes, we do have to think about money. I asked my boss if I can work more hours in the factory, and that's possible.' He suddenly frowned. 'But you won't be able to continue to work after you have our baby, and we can't support a family just on my salary. Bart and I were raised partly by my grandma, as Mam had to work in the shop while Dad was doing deliveries. I know that you want to raise our child, but I see no other option than ask my parents if they can help. I think they are desperate to know your test results so let's go to the house.'

When they entered the kitchen, Mam was preparing dinner and Dad was setting the table for four. They smelled erwtensoep, a soup made of peas, pork and potatoes that they both loved. Mam looked up as they came in.

'We already thought you'd come over to tell us the result. Would you like to join us for dinner?' she asked.

'Yes, thank you,' Jess said, grateful. 'We'd like that very much.'

Before they said grace, Jess told them that they were about to become grandparents.

They both became very emotional as this would be their first grandchild, and Dad insisted on getting a bottle of wine from the cellar.

'We only drink wine at very special occasions. I think this occasion is as special as they come. Let's drink to you and to the baby. That it will be born and live in good health.'

Once the initial excitement died down, they enjoyed a leisurely dinner and discussed practical matters, such as what to do about the doctor's fee and the extra cost of having a child. As they could not afford to pay rent anywhere else, Mark asked if they could stay at the barn house. He recently increased his working hours from twelve to fifteen a day, and worked weekends cleaning and servicing machines. Still, he barely made enough to cover the bills, and said that Jess would have to continue her work, which faced them with a dilemma.

Mam laid a hand on his arm. 'Mark, there's no need to ask. Of course, I will take care of the baby while you're both at work. Besides, you won't have to buy anything for the baby because I kept everything from when you and Bart were born.'

After the men cleared the table and the women finished doing the dishes, Mark and Jess went home feeling grateful and relieved.

'Jess, did you ask the doctor if we can make love while you're pregnant?'

She laughed, took his hand and guided him to the bedroom. Then she lit a candle and lay down on the bed, where she slowly started to undress. By the time she took off her bra, Mark was already at her side, stroking her body lovingly.

The months flew by. In her few spare hours, Jess unpacked the boxes stored in the attic and took what she needed for the baby's first year. She painted the crib, dresser and playpen blue.

'Why blue?' Mark asked her.

'I had this dream. I dreamt that I would never have any children. So I prayed to our holy mother, Mary. I promised her that I would dress my child in blue for nine whole years if she would grant me a healthy child.'

'But blue is a boy's color. What if it's a girl?'

'It's a boy,' she assured him.

A few months later, Jess gave birth to a healthy baby boy. They called him Rob.

As from this day, Bart and Wilma took over the shop and moved into the main house, while Mam and Dad moved into the other barn house.

Marks sister Hannie and her husband moved close to the German border, where they started a grocery store with the financial help of her husband's parents.

Truus and her husband moved to The Hague, where they started a furniture agency.

Grandma took care of the baby while Jess worked, and Dad helped out in the store.

Mark and Jess did discuss birth control, but decided that their wish was to have another child, so they accepted the fact that this meant hard work and long hours to get by.

Chapter 4

The post-war years were difficult for Europe. With hardly any jobs available, poverty was everywhere, and the damaged, war-torn continent had to rely heavily on help from the U.S.A.

It was U.S. General George Marshall who visited Europe and saw that without the support of his country, Europe was in danger of falling in the hands of Stalin's Soviet Union.

Named after him, the Marshall Plan provided struggling European economies with billions of dollars to rebuild their infrastructure, which slowly led to new business opportunities and jobs.

The store did well and expanded, and both his sisters saw their businesses grow with each passing year. Hannie was blessed with two children, and the children's clothes they no longer required were passed on to Jess and Mark.

When Rob was three years old, Jess became pregnant again. With the barn house becoming too small for them, the time had come to find another place to live.

Dad found them a three-bedroom house with a small living room and a tiny kitchen, right next to a dry cleaning service. They could stay rent-free, under the condition that Mark would take care of all repair and maintenance issues.

They accepted the offer gladly. The following week they moved into their new home, only to find that the dry cleaning machines were run at nighttime.

It took them many sleepless nights to get used to the endless noise, but with his room right next to machinery Rob never did get used to it.

All their spare hours went into painting and repairs. There was a leak in the hallway, so whenever it rained they had to place several buckets on the floor. Dad helped them out where he could.

The last two months of pregnancy were hard on Jess. Her back hurt and she had difficulty walking. The doctor suggested adding an extension to the heel of her left shoe; so that both sides of her body could share the extra weight she was carrying. She agreed, but would return after the baby was born to discuss other options, as she yearned to get rid of her limp and walk normally.

They finished the other bedroom just on time when Jess delivered a baby girl, whom they named Agnes.

Jess hated the house. It was noisy at night and quite dark, the only daylight in the cramped living room coming from a single window facing the street. With the lack of windows and ventilation, it was also quite damp and moldy.

On the other side of the street lived a couple that owned the bakery in the village. Their unmarried daughter, Ineke, was of the same age as Jess, and their son Johan assisted his father in the bakery. He was a handsome young man, and also the first person in town with a car, which made him the most sought-after bachelor in town.

In the evenings when Mark had to work late shifts, Ineke would join Jess while grandma taught them how to knit sweaters, socks, scarves and gloves. Within a few weeks they had learned to knit, enjoying each other's company, and became close friends.

Also Johan came over, under the pretext of taking his measurements for a sweater.

From that day forward Johan became a regular visitor, with Jess enjoying both his company and his attentions. She especially loved it when he would take them for a drive around town.

It wasn't before long that Dad told Mark about the gossip in town. He wasn't happy with the situation at all. He worked two shifts a day, as well as the weekends to support his family, while Jess was driving around with the most desirable bachelor in town.

When he brought this up, she became angry. She told him that she could live in the dark, moldy house, take care of the household and two children without complaint, but that Ineke was her best friend, and if that included being friends with Johan, he just had to live with it.

The next day she went to the doctor and asked him what could be done about her limp. The doctor advised her to see a specialist at the hospital in Oldenzaal.

There she was told that it was possible to place an extension into her hip that would enable her to walk normally. Jess was very pleased and they agreed on the operation date. When she told Mark of her plans, his reaction was not at all what she had expected. He said that he did not want her to have the operation and that he had accepted her limp since the day they met. He explained that people hardly notice that she limped with the heel extension she was wearing.

Jess was furious, and it was their first big argument since they got married. She went against his wishes and proceeded with the operation.

The operation should have only lasted two hours, with her to return home the following day. But things turned out differently. A rare infection took a hold of her, so she had to stay in hospital for weeks. During the years that followed, she had several difficult operations, until the specialist finally decided to remove the extension from her hip. Her heel extension was installed once more, but she was unable to walk without a cane.

While Jess was in hospital, Mam took care of Rob and Agnes. During the holidays she put them on the train to Maastricht, where Jess' parents would wait at the station to collect them. The children would help their grandparents gather potatoes and fill baskets with vegetables to be sold at the market.

At home, there was no money for sweets or fruit. But their grandparents' house stood alongside a large fruit orchard with plums and pears. Rob and Agnes had never tasted these fruits. Every day they crawled underneath the fence to eat as much as they wanted.

One day, while lying in the tall grass and eating pears, they were surprised by the sound of a large mowing machine. Rob ran to the fence, but Agnes remained where she was, too frightened to move. The mower kept moving towards her, and Rob dashed forward in front of his sister, upon which the machine came to a shuddering halt, just inches removed from where he stood.

A shocked farmer stepped down from the machine. 'What in blazing hell are you two doing in the orchard?' he demanded.

'Sorry sir, we've never tasted pears and plums before,' Rob said.

'It's alright,' the man said, still shaken. 'You just saved your sister's life. I'll tell you what. You two can come and go as you please, but let me know when you're inside the orchard.' Relieved, he took them to their grandparents and told them what had happened.

It was Dad who suggested visiting his sister Hannie. Mark had not seen her since she left town, and after completing his early Sunday shift, he took the bus to Nordhorn, a city just across the German border. He got off the bus at the border and noticed a large grocery store. His sister was waiting and she greeted him with hugs and kisses.

'Mark! It's so good to see you. How are you? Come; let's go inside to meet the rest of my family.'

They entered a newly built house attached to the store, which was closed as it was Sunday. He shook hands with his brother-in-law and met their two children, a boy and a girl.

After Hannie had taken the kids upstairs for their afternoon nap, she told Mark that Dad had spoken to them about his situation. She knew that Mark had to work long hours, and that he hardly had any time with his family. She also heard about the gossip that surrounded Jess and Johan.

'Listen, Mark. We want to expand the grocery section, and are building an additional vegetable and fruit store. With the big price difference for basics such as coffee, cheese, butter, vegetables and fruit between Holland

25

and Germany, lots of Germans come to our store. The business is growing so fast, that we need someone to drive to the vegetable and fruit auctions early in the morning to buy and thereafter sell these products during the day. Would you like to work for us?'

Mark hesitated. He didn't want to have anything to do with Germans, because he just didn't like them. Wartime occupation had been hard on the Dutch. Many Dutch families lost relatives and nearly everything they had, so most people hated the Germans.

But he would be his own boss, and could work with vegetables and fruit, which was something he had always wanted. He would not have to work at the weekends; there would be no more night shifts, and the salary they offered was much more than he earned now, so he realized that he had to get over the German hurdle.

He gratefully accepted the job, and asked them when to start. Delighted, they explained that a secondhand truck was just purchased, and that someone at the auction would assist him to buy the required vegetables and fruit. There was only one issue: the new vegetable and fruit store required another two months before its completion.

Mark thought about it and suggested that in the meantime, he would set up a stand on the sidewalk to sell the fruits and vegetables. They all agreed, and he would be paid as from that week on.

The next day he quit his job at the factory without a single regret, as he had always hated it. Then he visited the council's housing office, not only because he could now afford a decent home, but also to create some distance between Jess and Johan. He was granted a family house in a more remote part of the village, and they could move in as soon as the housing site was completed.

Part 2: The Worker

Chapter 1

Rob remembered that his mam was in the hospital for a long period and that he visited her every Sunday. His grandparents had looked after him and his sister Agnes during that time.

He remembered how they lived in that dark, damp house, with the constant noise of those infernal machines, always running, rattling and hissing at night.

That his dad was hardly ever home and always at work.

He remembered how his dad took him for a swim one day in the canal close to the village. While he was playing in the water, his dad had moved away, joining a woman in the water near him. Rob watched them as they laughed, how he reached out and touched her. After a while he looked again and found that his dad had disappeared and the woman was gone, too.

Bewildered, he looked everywhere but could not find them. He cycled home where he checked the barn for his dad's bicycle. But it wasn't there: he still hadn't returned, so he went back to the street corner to wait for him. When his dad finally came, Rob noticed that he avoided his look and they cycled home in silence. Somehow he knew what had happened, but he didn't understand because he thought his dad loved his mam.

Rob never told a soul about what he'd seen. From that day on, the respect for his dad was gone, and he felt that they would never become close again.

He thought of the constant arguments between his parents and his efforts to protect his mam.

Those efforts would only result in a beating, either with a belt or a mattenklopper, a whacking device used to beat the dust from rugs. And every night he would masturbate in order to escape the ceaseless noise, and the real world, until he finally fell asleep.

Already as a young boy he felt responsible for his mam and sister.

Each morning he ignited the stove to heat the kitchen before his mam and sister woke up. He prepared hot water and porridge for breakfast, and listen to the radio.

He remembered well how rich he felt when they got their first radio.

The first news bulletin he heard was about Captain Carlsen of a ship called the Flying Enterprise. In severe weather conditions, the captain refused to leave his sinking ship until all his crewmembers were rescued. He felt responsible for his men and would not admit defeat because he believed his ship could be saved.

Excited and with interest, Rob listened to the daily broadcast, admiring the captain for his bravery and ethics.

When he came home from kindergarten, he would help Mam or play with his sister.

The clothes he wore were always secondhand. Only at Easter Mam would make a new shirt and a pair of pants for him, as they couldn't afford anything else.

Each Sunday morning the church square would fill with horse-drawn carriages belonging to farmers who attended church and socialized in the café afterwards.

Most of them returned home drunk, ate lunch and slept throughout the afternoon. After everyone had left church, he would crawl underneath the benches to search for coins until the pastor finally caught him and told his dad.

He remembered eating homemade bread with marmalade for lunch, and beans or potatoes with vegetables for dinner. Only on Sundays did they have meat, which consisted of meat leftovers pressed together into sausages distributed by the government to families with a minimum income.

The first time he tasted chocolate and sweet milk powder was when an allied soldier gave it to him. The American and Canadian men, who had risked their lives to free Europe and left so much of their friends in graves scattered throughout Europe, were finally going home. The soldiers came from Germany and passed through his village on their way to Rotterdam, where they boarded the ships bound to their home countries.

One of the soldiers in the back of the truck threw his daily ration tin to him.

The tin contained chocolate and milk powder, which he shared with Mam and sister.

Only on Saturday evenings he and his sister would get a glass of lemonade. In order to prolong the enjoyment, they would sip the lemonade and spit it back in the glass. As there was no money for sweets, Rob would pinch walnuts from the mayor's garden, until the police finally caught him. As punishment, he had to write one hundred lines, stating that he was not allowed to steal from the mayor.

The neighbor wondered why his strawberry plants never bore any fruits, until he caught Rob one day with a long stick, picking the strawberries from underneath their fence.

Then one day, Mam told him that they would move to a new house without noise and with windows that could open. On a bitter cold day, with snow blasting through the streets, Rob helped his dad transport what little they had onto horse and wagon and moved into their new home.

Chapter 2

Living in the new house was like living in a castle. The council estate was built along four streets, housing about a hundred families. There were four houses to a block, with every two houses sharing a small covered entrance, and a passageway between each block.

They lived in a corner house, where everyone had their own bedroom—with windows—and one bathroom with a shower and sink. There was no mold, and everything smelled clean and fresh.

In the old house they only bathed once a week using a large bowl of water heated on a stove that was mixed with cold water. After Rob and Agnes washed first, their parents washed themselves. Now they had a bathroom with hot, running water, an unaccustomed luxury for everyone.

Rob started elementary school, but his first day at school was a great disappointment. The classroom was divided into a left side for boys wearing expensive leather shoes and a right side for boys with wooden shoes.

Playtime was no different. Rich boys played with boys wearing shoes, while the poor boys with wooden shoes played together. The teachers did nothing to encourage their mixing.

His first morning ended in a fight because Rob, eager to go home and hungry for lunch, did not wait for the 'shoe side' to leave first. He was given a thorough beating by the doctor's son, who made sure the 'rules' were clear to him once and for all.

Rob came home with a swollen lip. He lied to his mam, telling her he had slipped while playing. It never occurred to her that he might have gotten into a fight, knowing he would never hurt anyone.

He always ran home from school for lunch. He loved coming home for lunch, as Mam always made pancakes or French toast with sugared cinnamon to surprise him.

She meant the world to him.

He soon discovered that the 'shoes' played soccer in a village team with specially made leather soccer shoes, uniform shirts and a real leather ball on a proper grass soccer field. He played soccer in the street wearing wooden shoes with a self-made paper ball tightly wrapped with rope.

After school he would help Mam assemble small medicine boxes. While he would press the box frames from the precut cardboard sheets and fold the boxes in place, she would glue on a label. Together, they made thousands of these boxes.

With the money she made, Mam slowly furnished their home.

Not surprisingly, the doctor's son turned out to be a bully, who made everyone follow his rules in and outside the classroom. Rob was given a beating almost every day, probably because he was taller than the rest. Rob accepted this as part of his life, and he hated school.

One day he came home to find Mam crying. She told him that her best friend Ineke got married, and that she had moved to another city. One week later Ineke's brother, Johan, arrived in a fancy car to pick up Mam to visit Ineke. Rob took an instant dislike to him, and when the car moved off, he ran after it until all the muscles in his sides ached.

Days later, he discovered a secret hiding place that contained letters from Johan to his mam, but he was too scared to read them. Everything made him feel sick to the stomach. Things got worse when Mam took them to visit their grandparents in Maastricht. For the first time, he got to ride with his sister in Johan's car.

But that was also the last time. He told Mam that he did not wish to sit in his car anymore because it made him carsick. He simply did not understand. Mam should be with his dad, not with Johan. He remembered one of his classmates telling him that his father lived with another woman, while his mother was left with the children.

Rob was terrified that the same would happen to his family.

Word about his parents' odd relationship must have spread in the village, as one day, the doctor's son made a cruel remark about his mam. That did it. Rob exploded in anger and gave the doctor's son such a beating, that things changed from that day forward.

His teacher punished him by hitting him with twenty hard, painful strokes on the fingers with a wooden ruler. He instructed him to go to the doctor's house and apologize for beating their sun. Rob didn't understand. His teacher had never made the doctor's son apologize to his mum for beating him up every day.

The doctor's wife opened the door, beat him around the ears and told him never to touch her son again. He left, his face swollen and red, but never told anyone what happened. From that day on, he was the leader of the class, and the 'wooden shoe side' always left the classroom first. He was no longer the boy who never hurt anyone and got beaten every day at school. Those days were over.

Still, he was a loner all those years at elementary school. After school he rushed home to help Mam or play with his sister, rather than spend time outdoors with the boys from school.

Music and reading were important and helped him to forget his troubles. They enabled him to float away to a dream world, away from his ordinary life.

He joined the church choir. A boy from his street taught him to read music and how to sing the songs that were sung in church. His favorite song was Ave Maria by Mozart.

Whenever he and his mam assembled medicine boxes, he would fiddle around with the radio controls, always searching for different frequencies.

He wanted to hear music that differed from the standard harmonica and guitar music that was always played on the Dutch and German channels. He discovered a U.S. channel created for American and Canadian soldiers stationed in Germany, and heard Mahalia Jackson singing 'He's Got the Whole World in His Hands' for the first time. He loved it and thought that this music, which they called gospel, came from another world.

He had the same feeling when he listened to Louis Armstrong, who played a completely new kind of music called jazz. Than he heard Bill Haley, playing and singing his rock and roll music.

But Dad would not allow this kind of music when he was home, as the vicar had said that it was a sin to listen to such music and believed that it might have a bad influence on youngsters. The vicar visited families in their homes, telling couples to have more children, how to raise them and to visit church daily and twice on Sundays. And his parents listened most of the time.

Reading became more important to Rob than learning. The teacher confiscated several of his library books when she discovered he was reading books during class.

He began to dislike the long hours they had to spend every day assembling the boxes. He started looking for work at the farms and was hired to work in the fields after school and summer holidays. After a few weeks he made enough money for them to stop making those damned boxes.

During his last holiday of elementary school, he worked at a farm harvesting potatoes where he met a girl named Gertie. She told him that her family had just arrived in Holland from Indonesia, and that she was living on his street.

The following four weeks, the two left home at five in the morning to cycle to the farm. They harvested potatoes side by side, ate their sandwiches in each other's company and came home late in the evenings.

It took Rob only one week to understand that he was in love for the first time in his life. While biking home he told her that he wanted to marry her, and inspired by her stories of the country where she was raised, to live in different countries.

But on their last holiday at the farm, she told him that her parents wanted her to concentrate on school. Because girls and boys went to separate schools she was not allowed to see him anymore after school. They promised each other to meet again after they finished their education and get married.

Every morning he watched her pass his house from the bathroom window.

Rob wanted to quit school and start working, but his parents insisted that he had to complete his basic education. Because he promised Gertie to finish his education, he finally accepted. His next school was in Oldenzaal, one hour bike ride each way, so a large group of boys and girls would gather daily to ride to and from school.

While working at one of the farms, he met his Uncle Bart, who was delivering groceries. His uncle told him that if he needed a job to come and see him, knowing that he needed the money. He explained that they had no children and needed somebody to assist in the grocery store and take care of the horse in the evening.

Rob was at the store every day, and he liked the work and enjoyed grooming the horse. Sometimes his uncle would even take him horse riding. However, his school marks did suffer from the working hours, and every year he just made it to the next grade.

He had been working at his uncle's store for three years when a bus stopped in front of the store, and several big colored men walked in. Rob felt as if his heart had stopped beating and thought he was about to faint. He couldn't help but just stare, as one of the men who entered the store was none other than the great Louis Armstrong.

He had recognized him straight away. His aunt and uncle sometimes took him to the movies, where they always showed the news before the main feature. One evening they showed Louis Armstrong playing jazz in New Orleans. He never believed that it would be possible to meet someone like him in real life. Louis Armstrong and his band members were on route to play for the U.S. troops stationed in Germany.

As his uncle and aunt did not speak a word of English, they left it to him to serve one of his all-time favorite jazz musicians. Rob was terribly nervous and fumbled with his English, but he would remember forever the words that Louis said to him: 'You are doing very well, my son.'

The first time he left his hometown was on a school trip by train to Artis, the zoo in Amsterdam. He had never been on a school trip previously for the lack of money, but this time his uncle paid for the trip. He loved the train ride, hanging out of the window until another train passed, leaving him covered in smoke. It was then that he knew for certain that he wanted to travel the world, and not to live in his hometown for the rest of his life. His dream was to live in the U.S.A.

Chapter 3

By the time he was eighteen, his aunt and uncle had taught him all he needed to know to serve clients and how to purchase the goods required for the store. When necessary, he would take his uncle's place visiting farms to deliver groceries or buy potatoes and vegetables. They also taught him everything he needed to start his own store and finally asked him if he would be interested in taking over the store, with their financial support.

They agreed to discuss the matter again once Rob had completed his mandatory eighteen-months in the army, which would start the following month.

The next day he went to Gertie's house, confident that he was now in the position to offer her a future. She came to the door to tell him that she was seeing someone who owned his own store in the next village and could provide her with more security.

He stared at her in disbelief. He could feel that same pain and sickness rise up inside of him as when his dad disappeared with that unknown woman, and when he had chased Johan's car with his mam inside. He turned around without saying a single word. The nights that followed were sleepless and tormented.

He was desperate to leave his hometown.

After three months in the army, he was selected to become a sergeant. He progressed greatly, until he injured his knee while running down a hill during a training exercise. He had knee surgery, but was unable to walk for two months.

With field training no longer a possibility, he was trained as a cook instead, which made the rest of his military service easier by working in the kitchen of the officer's mess.

He enjoyed coming home on weekends, bringing fillet steaks that he cut and prepared for his mam. She had never tasted anything that delicious in her life.

These weekends he stayed home with Mam and his sister, whom was becoming quite a young lady and about to finish school. She told him that she met a German boy whom she liked very much.

Rob frowned. This was a time when boys and girls could not cross the border because they had no passport.

If a boy wanted to visit a dance hall on the other side of the border, he would have to take the smuggler route used to smuggle cigarettes, cheese and butter into Germany. Young men were warned to stay on their side of the border when it came to courting girls. Agnes' boyfriend had already been given several beatings. Rob told her to be very careful, because Dad absolutely hated the Germans.

One weekend Rob decided to visit his uncle's store and see his dad at work. It was a warm, sunny day so he took the bike road through the forest. He was only halfway there when he heard a noise. Following the sound, he first could see a steel derrick of at least a hundred and fifty feet high. As he moved closer, the noise grew louder. He stopped at a large open space where he observed a traveling block that was moving a pipe up and down inside the derrick. When the block went up, the engines made a roaring sound. There was a man working on a platform halfway up the derrick who was busy disconnecting a long pipe from an elevator, storing the pipe inside a racking system. There was a second platform twenty feet above ground level with men working on it.

Warning signs indicated that he was not allowed to go inside the fenced area. For more than an hour he stood outside the gate, fascinated by the dynamics and the sound of engines and steel. He knew then that he wanted to work in such an environment.

The gate opened and a man walked up to him, somewhat suspicious. 'Can I help you in any way?'

'You wouldn't be looking for workers, by any chance?'

The men looked him over with scrutiny. 'Ever worked on a drilling rig before?'

'No, sir. I've never seen anything like this. It's fascinating, that's for sure!'

'We don't hire people here. To apply for a job, you'd have to visit the company's headquarters in Germany, near Hanover.' The man wanted to leave but hesitated, and turned back. 'Would you like a tour around the rig?'

'Yes, please! I'd like that very much.'

The man took him into his office, saying that he was Hattenberg Oil's representative and a drilling supervisor. Rob listened as the supervisor explained how it all worked. An oil company would first assign a firm that carried out seismic measurements in the area to locate formations that might contain oil or gas. If these results were favorable, the company would then decide to drill an exploration well to confirm such a presence, and hire a drilling contractor that provided a rig and drilling crews. Such crews consist of roustabouts for general maintenance work, roughnecks to work on the rig floor and drillers to operate the drilling machinery and equipment. Mechanics and electricians serviced and maintained the drilling machinery. A tool pusher was in charge of the drilling crew to ensure that his crew carried out the drilling operation according to the drilling program issued by the oil and gas company.

He drew a diagram, showing Rob that drilling for gas or oil was just like pushing a reversed telescope with different diameters into mother earth.

After this basic introduction on drilling operations, the supervisor handed Rob safety boots and a hardhat and they started the tour around the rig.

They put on ear protection before they visited the engine room. Here, Rob met the mechanic and electrician responsible for maintaining the engines and ensuring continuous electrical power distribution for the drilling operations.

He then visited the mud tanks, where the supervisor explained how the mud pumps extracted the mud through suction and built up pressure to circulate the mud through the drill pipe and the drilling bit. He explained that the mud had to cool the bit and circulate the formation samples to the surface and showed him how the mud returned over a number of screens separating formation samples and mud. He was then taken to the rig floor where the driller had just stopped the mud pumps. Rob was introduced to the driller who showed him the different gauges and handles, the stop and start controls and everything else he wanted to know. After he witnessed how a new drill pipe was connected to the drill string, and drilling operations resumed again, he was shown the geologists' core lab where formation sampling took place to compare and correlate the rock samples with the available seismic data.

The tour around the rig lasted almost two hours. Rob thanked the drilling supervisor enthusiastically, leaving only after received the address of the company headquarters in Hanover.

It wasn't only the fascination Rob had felt that led him to make the decision to work on a drilling rig. There was more. In October of 1963 an accident happened at one of the coalmines in Germany, where water and mud had flooded into the mineshafts, trapping the miners working below. In order to rescue the men a drilling rig had been used, like the one he just visited.

This rig had drilled holes inside the mineshafts, after which the miners had been lifted out in capsules. It had been a difficult operation, but they managed to rescue a hundred men, some of whom had been trapped for more than two weeks. The whole rescue operation had dominated the national news for weeks, and it made a lasting impression on him. After watching this rescue on TV and meeting the person who showed him the rig, he was determined to do everything to become a drilling supervisor.

When he returned home, the first thing he did was find a German road map. Then he called his superior officer to ask for a few days off to look for a job.

The following morning he applied and received his passport, and took the train to Hanover. When he arrived at Hattenberg Oil's headquarters, he was told at reception to wait while the lady called the Human Resources department.

In the waiting room he watched television. There was a news broadcast showing a man giving a speech, and he was immediately fascinated by what he heard. The speech was impressive and the words touched him. He had never seen anyone so charismatic. The man spoke about his dream: a dream about a free world where white and black people lived together. The narrator announced his name: it was the new elected President of the U.S.A., John F Kennedy. He felt that the U.S. should be very proud to have such a man as its president. This man seemed unafraid of tackling the difficulties between the two nuclear power nations or the racial issues in his country.

An elderly man came in and introduced himself as the Human Resources Manager. After inviting him into his office, he asked Rob the purpose of his visit.

When Rob told him about his visit to the rig and that he would like to work in such an environment to become a drilling supervisor, the man looked at him with interest.

'Do you have any experience working on a rig?'

'No, I don't.' He gave the man a brief summary of his work experience and said that he would be released from military duty in three weeks' time.

'Sorry, can't help you,' the man said. 'We don't hire anyone without drilling experience. You might want to inquire with this contractor we use for rigging up and down drilling equipment and derricks in Holland. Perhaps they've got work for someone like you. Get some experience and come back, if you're still interested,' he said as he handed him the address.

To his surprise, Rob noticed that the company was located in Oldenzaal.

'Thank you for your time,' he said, whereupon he left feeling disappointed.

The very next day he visited the company in Oldenzaal, and was hired to work on one of the construction teams as soon as he was available.

When he finished his military service two weeks later he called the foreman, who told him that he would be picked up for work on Monday.

Chapter 4

Uncle Bart and Aunt Wilma were disappointed at his decision. They had hoped that he would take over the store one day. Still, they were supportive, and assured him their offer would always be available if he ever changed his mind.

On Monday morning he was picked up by a van at five o'clock, and by the time they picked up a total of eight men the crew was complete.

The drive took nearly two hours, and most men slept.

He couldn't help feeling anxious, not knowing what to expect.

When they arrived at a drilling location near Alkmaar, he saw another company van that had delivered the crane driver and his crew. Large steel parts and structures surrounded him. The foreman told them they first had to assemble the crane, and introduced Rob to the crew, explaining that he was new to the job. He assigned another man from his village to show him what to do.

He was shown how to select a steel sling to lift crane sections until the crane was ready to lift loads. Most of the work consisted of selecting steel slings to lift heavy equipment from one place to the other, and that different slings were used according to the weights to be lifted.

His colleague told him that they had rigged down the derrick and drilling equipment and transported everything to this new location, where it had to be rigged up again.

Once the bottom part of the steel derrick structure, the engines, mud pumps and tanks were in place, they started to build up the derrick. The crane picked up one derrick section, whereupon someone climbed up to guide, connect and bolt the next higher section.

Whenever a section was completed, a ladder was placed on the outside of the derrick to reach the top of that section. At a hundred feet a working platform was mounted for the derrickmen who had to connect or disconnect the length of pipe from the lifting elevator.

After one week of lifting loads with the crane at ground level, Rob asked the foreman if he could climb along the bracings and ladders into the derrick to see how that work was carried out. Permission was granted, and he stayed there the whole day to watch the men at work. He had no fear of heights and liked the work.

A week later he became part of the rigger crew specialized in rigging up and down derricks and received a pay raise.

He spent two weeks working twelve to sixteen hours a day, after which the crews went home Fridays to return again on Monday. The money he made was very good, and most of it was going to his mam while part of it was used to obtain his driving license.

He liked the work, the crew he worked with and the fact he was home after two weeks work.

While driving home one weekend, the foreman informed the crew that they would have to work overtime to dismantle a rig that was recently rigged up.

After they arrived at the location, only the upper part of the derrick was visible.

A large crater had swallowed up the lower derrick structure. He was shocked to learn that someone had made a mistake and an eruption took place.

They dismantled the upper derrick sections, but it was impossible to reach the lower section that had sunk deep into the crater. Weeks later, he heard that they had filled up the crater with cement.

A year later he witnessed how one of his workmates fell down through the grating of a lower platform that someone had forgotten to bolt down. His mate fell from a hundred feet, and was killed instantly.

The incident gave him nightmares, in which he dreamt that it happened to him.

He no longer felt safe and finally quit his job.

He contacted Hattenberg Oil in Hanover and made an appointment with the Human Resource manager. During the interview, he learned that the firm belonged to a large shipping company called Wedel Shipping, which purchased a small local oil and gas company Hattenberg Oil that owned drilling rigs to drill wells and work-over rigs to repair producing wells. The reason was to cut costs on fuel and lubricants for their shipping fleet. Oil and gas was discovered in the Hannover area, and the company had extended its search for oil and gas into various countries, including Holland. He explained that apart from drilling personnel, the company sometimes hired drilling engineers and supervisors to drill and produce these wells, and Rob had two options to gain entry into the drilling industry.

His first option was employment with a drilling contractor to learn the job from scratch as a roustabout and roughneck for a period of about four years, after which he could work as a derrickmen, assistant driller and driller. After fifteen years he might then become a tool pusher, who was the person in charge of a drilling rig.

The other option would be to start with an oil company to become a drilling engineer or a drilling supervisor. He would have to start as a trainee to get experience with the drilling crew and follow courses to reach the drilling supervisor level, which would take him about ten years to complete.

The difference between the two options was that if he chose to work as an engineer or supervisor, his company would pay money into a pension fund during a forty-year period. If he opted to become a tool pusher, he would have to set aside money for his retirement.

Because during his first interview Rob made a good impression on him, and he was determined to become a drilling supervisor, the Human Resources Manager was willing to offer him the trainee job. For Rob, the choice was simple: he was extremely interested in the trainee job to become a drilling supervisor. After one more interview with Werner Brandt, the operations manager he was hired.

He started his trainee position on one of the company-owned land rigs, drilling near Hanover. Here he became a member of the roustabout crew, carrying out maintenance work and transporting all kinds of equipment to and from the rig floor.

After one year one of the drillers asked him if he would be interested to work on the rig floor. This was where the actual drilling operations took place, something that appealed so much to him the first time he visited that rig. He did not have to think about it and started the next day as a member of the drilling crew.

His first job was to handle the big rotary tongs that connect and disconnect the drill pipes. After the driller operated the tongs to break the connection, Rob had to open the lower tong while keeping the upper tong in place. While standing on the rotary table, the driller operated a switch, causing the rotary table to turn. Before Rob knew what happened, he was thrown against the railing of the rig floor and badly bruised his hand.

No one had warned him not to stand on the rotary table that was rotated to unscrew the pipe: he had to learn this the hard way.

He learned how to make 'mud' and to repair and operate the mud pumps. He also learned how to throw the spinning chain to rotate the pipe before it was made up with the rotary tongs.

Everyday something new happened, and he thoroughly enjoyed it, working weekends and holidays: guarding the rig or servicing the machinery.

He wanted to make as much money as possible, so he would never be poor again. Once a week he wrote Mam, sending her money to support the family.

He wanted her to know that he was doing well, and asked her to let him know anything that was happening at home or in his hometown.

She answered every letter, bringing him up to date on all the events in Ootmarsum, informing him who was getting married, gave birth or passed away.

After six months he finally returned home for Christmas.

He took Mam Christmas shopping, something she had never been able to afford before, and bought himself a secondhand car, in which he took Mam and Agnes to visit his grandparents in Maastricht.

He had to get used to the discipline at work, of following orders without asking any questions and just doing the job as he was told. The drillers and tool pushers were influential, and could make or ruin his career.

Rob had to work hard and perform menial tasks such as polishing their boots or washing their cars after normal working hours.

Once he was accepted by the crew, he began to realize the importance of teamwork. He noticed that they all watched out for one another to avoid accidents.

The best teams were those who had worked together for years, and these men often became best friends.

He learned the importance of storing tools, drill pipes and casing joints in neat rows and that a clean, organized rig was a safe place to work.

But there was also another side to the life that these men lived. Several of the married men had affairs when they moved from place to place, inevitably causing breakups and divorces. Based on what he saw around him, as well as his own past experience, he vowed that he would never get married.

But still, he was a man. In Hanover he met a girl living on the other side of his boarding house. Her sister was dating one of the crewmembers, asking Rob to join them to the disco downtown. After a few weeks and numerous visits to the disco, he had sex for the first time in his life.

It felt as if his sexual floodgates had opened, and he wanted more. From that moment on, he dated, explored, made love to and used every woman he could lay his hands on.

Within a three-year period he worked himself up from roustabout to derrickmen, the person who handles the drill pipe at a hundred feet in the derrick.

He was soon promoted to assistant driller and was taught how to operate the drilling machinery and instruments.

Punctuality became his friend, and he liked the clean and precise working ethics of the Germans.

He also got drunk for the first time in his life drinking German schnapps with his crewmembers. Sick and with a huge hangover the next morning, he promised himself never to drink such strong liquor again.

One of his duties was to complete the daily report detailing the work the drilling crew carried out. He found that the drilling, mechanical and electrical departments made precise reports of the work that was carried out, so that anyone reading the reports could understand exactly how the job was done and any mistake or accident could easily be traced.

In his off time and between shifts, Rob spent long hours reading the drilling reports to learn how each specific sequence or operations took place.

In the Tool Pusher office he discovered a shelf full of manuals on drilling procedures, specifying how the operations should be carried out. It was obvious that no one ever looked at these manuals, as there were no recent updates and the pages looked like new. This struck him as odd. He therefore copied important sections relevant to his job, and compared these with the daily reports, discovering the crew did not always follow the procedures as described in the manuals. Even the drilling engineers and tool pushers appeared to be taking shortcuts in their work, with accidents and mishaps as a result.

While drilling by far the deepest oil well in Germany, he met a Hungarian geologist, Laslo, whom he often visited at work. He was specialized in evaluating formation samples of deep wells. Taking note of Rob's interest in his work, he shared his knowledge on the different formations through which they drilled, teaching him a great deal. As driller and future drilling supervisor, Laslo felt that it was important for Rob to understand that both pressure and temperature could vary according to formation, and that movements of the different formations could affect both pressure and temperature. The deeper the wells were drilled the greater and less predictable these effects could be.

It was interesting for Rob to learn from him that drilling vertically through formations containing oil or gas only yielded limited production. If the technology became available, he should be thinking of drilling horizontal wells into these formations, so that they could drastically increase oil and gas producing rates.

Another idea was fracking, which had been used for years in different formations, could be applied in shale formations. These formations were known to contain gas and could increase the production rate considerably. One of the advantages was that shale was often found at shallow depths. But that these fracking operations should be very carefully planned and executed, as there was a risk of channeling to the surface, which could be dangerous. They would have to ensure that the casing and cement were thoroughly tested to the maximum pressure before any fracking could take place.

He cautioned Rob to always find the right balance: treat Mother Earth carefully and you could tap into her oil and gas resources, but safety always comes first. His warning indicated if he didn't operate with care, a roaring, destructive monster could be unleashed.

He loved to listen and discuss his ideas, but the discussions always ended with a subtle warning. The German company accepted him for his expertise, but the Germans never really accepted him as one of them. The point he made was clear: his career developments within the German company would have its limits.

While driving back from work to his boarding house, he was shocked to learn of John F. Kennedy's death. With anguish he listened as the news broadcaster announced that the president of the U.S. was shot in broad daylight while visiting Dallas. Stunned and confused, he wondered if the mafia was responsible for his death. Why shoot the president of the U.S.? Was it about politics, a play for power? It occurred to him that the power might not lie with the freely elected president, but where the big money was.

Shaken, he went to the nearest hotel and watched the tragedy repeated on television. It sickened him to his stomach to watch the president die in the arms of his wife.

Chapter 5

After four years of working on the rig, the Human Resources Manager called and asked if Rob would be interested in studying at a college in Clausthal-Zellerfeld. The college was financed by the oil industry, and provided a two-year specialized training program for supervisory functions. Apparently Rob's ethics and determination had earned the respect of the manager, who felt he deserved a chance to reach his goal.

Rob was flattered, but worried that his knowledge of the German language wouldn't be good enough, especially when it came to learning the technical terms.

But the HR Manager insisted that he consider it, emphasizing that this was a one-time opportunity. Besides, based on Rob's German proficiency, he expected no problems, and this training course would be a future requirement to become a drilling supervisor.

Within a month, he started his training program.

At college, Rob learned details about the history of drilling:

- The very first oil well was drilled in China in 347 A.D using drill bits attached to 800 feet of bamboo poles.
- The first 'modern' oil well was drilled in Asia, east of Baku in 1848.
- The first well in North America was drilled in 1858, in Ontario, Canada.
- The first U.S. oil well was drilled in Titusville, Pennsylvania.
- The first offshore drilling operation took place in the Pacific Ocean in 1896 from a standard cable-tool rig.
- And finally, the first German well was drilled in Wietze near Celle in 1920, where a museum now stands showing both old and modern drilling technologies and how oil is produced.

He attended classes during the day, and worked on his homework and projects until deep in the night. At the boarding house he shared a room with Dieter, a German who worked in the oil and gas production fields for years and wanted to become a production supervisor. Dieter would often help him with the technical German terms, and they became close friends.

They complemented each other well. Rob preferred to drill the wells, and Dieter's preference was to produce and refine oil and gas for consumer use. They learned the oil and gas dictionary explaining the language and equipment used to drill and produce wells and shared their experiences. When Dieter got married, he asked Rob to be his best man.

Rob also learned how the drilling industry was organized. He became familiar with terms such as lease purchases, drilling permits, and how drilling contractors were hired against market rates. He learned how drilling teams consisted of people with different operational and engineering backgrounds. Each oil company had its own in-house engineers, and contracted third parties with specialized knowledge for different operations such as cementing, logging, and numerous other tasks to drill and complete the well. Oil companies greatly depended on the expertise of their drilling staff, especially on that of the drilling supervisors, whose job it was to communicate with the drilling team on a daily basis.

He also learned that the industry's labor market fluctuated. Sometimes an excess of personnel was laid off during low periods created by the oil price, while at other times there may be a worldwide shortage of experienced drilling personnel, supervisors and engineers.

Oil companies would often hire tool pushers and young engineers to fill these vacancies, and assign them to work with the most experienced drilling supervisors and engineers to learn the job as fast as possible. Their technical and theoretical knowledge had to be continuously updated as he now experienced at college.

Still, the quality of drilling supervisors and engineers was mostly based on years of experience drilling different wells around the world.

One area that interested Rob most was how to make previous valuable drilling experience available to him and future drilling supervisor in the quickest time. Could they avoid continually reviewing endless drilling reports and procedures?

He wrote down every step he carried out to complete each operational sequence, taking special note of each accident and mishap that occurred during these various drilling sequences.

He realized that drilling contractors and other third parties also relied heavily on company procedures and the experience of onsite supervisors. These companies compiled their own standard procedures and instruction manuals, but often the essential information was difficult to find or disregarded.

He realized that safety departments managed all safety information, and detailed accidents information was stored in separate filing systems. It just didn't make sense to him.

Fluctuating market situations also had an effect on safety. Unfavorable market conditions, such as a low oil and gas price, led to large numbers of experienced staff layoffs, or companies hired less experienced—and cheaper—personnel that required continuous supervision, with an increase in risks and accidents as a result.

He studied every day until early in the morning, eager to become the first Dutch student finishing the college with good grades, and hoping to become a certified drilling supervisor.

He decided to write his final paper on 'bit' selection to drill deep wells into high pressure and high temperature formations, visiting several drilling bit manufacturers to discuss with specialists the problems associated with drilling into deep formations.

He visited three of the deepest wells drilled at that time in Germany to compile important information. One of these wells was drilled at a sixty-degree angle, and as this closely approached the Hungarian geologist's idea of horizontal drilling, he made sure to obtain all the details.

Chapter 6

Rob got his Master's degree in Drilling Engineering, and Werner Brandt offered him a job on one of the contracted rigs in the Saudi desert, to continue his training program.

He packed his bag and departed from Amsterdam's Schiphol airport, and said a brief prayer before takeoff.

His mam was worried so she made him make a promise to say a prayer 'with God,' before any start or landing so that someone would be watching over him.

It was on the first flight to Riyadh that the captain announced Martin Luther King's death; he had been shot. Rob remembered one of the famous reverend's speeches about a dream that he once had. That one-day, his four young children would live in a nation where they would not be judged by the color of their skin, but by the merit of their character. He also recalled one of his memorable sayings, that 'one has a moral responsibility to disobey unjust laws'.

He felt the same sympathy, respect and admiration for King as he did for Kennedy. Both men had such charisma! Still he could not help but feel that the events that were taking place were not what they appeared to be. Who were these people, to kill this great man? Did these men believe that they formed some kind of obstruction? Where they madmen? Men lusting for power, Ku Klux Klan or companies pulling their deadly strings and money always prevail?

He became aware that a man seated on the other side of the aisle was observing him constantly. When they exited the plane in Frankfurt, he proceeded to the transit lounge, where the man approached him.

'Are you Rob Oolderink?'

'Yes?'

'Oh, good. I got a message from my company secretary. She said that a new assistant driller would be on this flight. I'm Harry and the driller they've assigned you to work with. Happy to meet you, Rob. I look forward to working together.'

They boarded a non-stop flight to Riyadh after which a DC 10-charter plane took them in a low flight over the desert before landing. Arab drivers drove them to the campsite in a Land Rover.

Harry introduced Rob to the contractor tool pusher, who took him to the drilling supervisor, an American.

'Welcome to the desert, Rob. My name's Dave,' the man said with a lazy Texan drawl. 'They told me you're one of our trainee drilling supervisors and that you'll be working as an assistant driller on this rig. If you have any questions or need advice please let me know. My door is always open at any time. Good luck!'

'Thank you Dave, I'll remember that.'

The tool pusher showed him around the campsite, which consisted of six very large transport skids with living quarters mounted on them. Another housed the kitchen, mess room and bar, while the last two skids served as electrical power supply, a hospital, radio and cinema. Finally, he was shown his caravan, with bed and bathroom. The local staff was accommodated in big tents located next to the campsite.

Rob took an instant dislike to Harry. There was something unsettling about him that he could not quite explain.

One day Harry and his crew were assigned to prepare a new drilling location, because the present well was nearly completed. Two trucks were loaded with living quarters, water tank and a Caterpillar tractor. One of the trucks could be modified into a small crane to lift loads. An interpreter joined them to make contact with the local sheikh and his tribe.

The new drilling location was a two-day drive away, bringing them deep into the desert. After arriving they started work by equalizing the drilling site with the Caterpillar tractor and built up the camp.

When the first derrick sections arrived, Rob noticed that they were stacked horizontally on the truck. Each derrick section consisted of two large beams with bracings between them. Rob had to stand on the back of the truck, attaching the sling to lift the first section off the truck.

The all-clear sign was given for the crane to start lifting, but then something went wrong: one of the bracings got caught in the second section still stored on the truck.

Horrified, Rob looked up and saw the second section coming at him. He just managed to jump clear before the heavy steel structure landed right next to him.

He realized that he had been standing in that spot just a second prior.

With his heart still racing, it occurred to him that this wasn't the first time he had such a close call. He had fallen thirty feet down from the derrick and sustained plenty of bruises, but nothing serious. The second and third time he fell twenty feet from the rig substructure while rigging up, yet both times he was able to stand up and continue work.

He was sure his mam prayed for him every day and someone was watching over him. Thankful, he prayed to the holy Mother Mary every night.

The next day Harry, the interpreter and Rob visited the sheikh of the local tribe.

They negotiated the use of his men as general workers while drilling in return for canned food, goats, tools and water.

Once the negotiations were completed successfully, the sheik invited them for dinner. They sat around a campfire with a goat turning on a spit with a large heap of cooked rice in their midst. The interpreter told them to wash their hands in the small bowl of water next to them, and to use only their right hand to eat, as the locals used their left hand for cleaning purposes, there being no water or toilet paper available.

When the meat was ready to eat the eldest member of the tribe cut the pieces and heaped them on top of the rice. As guests of honor, Harry and Rob were offered the goat's eyes. The interpreter told them to take one eye each, mix it with a portion of rice until a small ball was formed and eat it.

Rob's stomach nearly turned. But it was dark, with only the moon, the stars and the campfire to light the night. He could not see if Harry ate his eye, but he quickly pushed it back into the pile of rice and only took a ball of rice.

After dinner, they were served dates and figs with sweetened, strong coffee brewed in a copper pot. Once they finished eating, the other tribe members had their share of the meal, after which part of the remaining food was first given to the dogs. The leftovers were for the women, which for Rob was a clear indication of how little these people valued their women.

The following evening Rob and Harry watched the sun set on the dunes, turning them a deep, burnished red. Rob was entranced by the sight, and taken completely off guard when Harry touched his crotch and suggested they shower together. Horrified, Rob realized that his intuition had not failed him. Harry was a homosexual. Rob firmly declined the offer, barely unable to conceal his disgust.

He was undecided on whether to report the incident to the tool pusher, unsure if Harry's work experience would be of more importance to him than Harry's sexual preference. He chose not to report it. From that day on, both men carried out their work, but kept their distance, and Harry refused to share any practical advice or operational experience with Rob to support him.

From assistant driller to manager level, it was mandatory to update well control training. These courses were held each year, and failure to pass the final test would jeopardize employment.

In order to train personnel how and what to do in case of different well control situations, the company used a dry well near Hanover, where they left a small rig for simulated training purposes. Each well control situation could be simulated, and every man was taught how to make the correct calculations and take the necessary steps to avoid and control any type of well control situation.

Rob followed this course every year, and was always relieved when he passed the final test. Still, he felt that practical experiences should be transferred from the supervisor to his subordinates, until they were ready for promotion.

With no practical experience support from Harry, Rob had to rely on his previous work experience, the drilling sequences he created, and by reading old well reports and procedures.

He frequently asked Harry for information and practical tips, but Harry refused to provide any assistance.

Dave, on the other hand, was very helpful, but he had to limit his visits as Harry did not like it.

In his spare time he assisted the mud engineer, who taught him how to analyze the mud properties, such as weight and viscosity. He showed him how to create a thin mud cake filter to control the amount of water entering the formation, and which chemicals to use in order to change the viscosity, weight or any other properties that were required to drill through the different formations without any problems.

He became specialized in dealing with mud and often replaced the mud engineer while on leave.

As time went by, he noticed that Harry had become quite friendly with the local tribe boys. These boys were aged between ten and fifteen, and hired to clean the living quarters and campsite. They looked like gorgeous girls, with shiny dark hair, brown eyes and long lashes. He had watched them enter Harry's caravan, and knew that they spent time with him.

Homosexuality seemed to be rife in this part of the world. In the campsite and desert towns, he regularly saw men walking hand in hand, and even witnessed them making love outside the campsite.

One day Rob visited the souk to buy gifts for his mam and sister before his flight home. His crew had taught him some basic Arabic, so he understood when a local asked him how he was doing. He answered in Arabic, saying that he was fine. The Arab then fell in step beside him, and suddenly grabbed for Rob's crotch. Rob used all the Arabic swear words he knew, upon which the man finally walked off.

The most shocking experience was when he opened a tent to collect one of his crewmembers and found the man having sex with a goat.

After the tool pusher finally caught Harry in his caravan with two naked local boys, he fired him. With Harry gone, Rob was promoted to driller.

Rob always warned his crewmembers to be aware and prepare for the dangers of the job and to follow the sequences as prepared by him. He was very strict to avoid any risks at the job.

His work schedule consisted of four weeks on the rig, followed by four weeks of leave, making good money during that period. After having saved enough money, he bought a plot of land in Germany, because land was cheaper there. He wanted to design and build his own house, which was something he thought would never be possible. Now one of his dreams became reality.

After he returned to Saudi, he found that the rig had suffered a blowout. It turned out that an inexperienced driller had forgotten to fill the hole with mud while pulling the drill string out of the hole. The column of mud was continuously reduced while pulling the pipe and not sufficient anymore to control the mounting formation pressure.

The remaining mud and pipe were blasted out of the well. Gas escaped and a massive explosion was the result.

The crew had managed to escape just in time, but the rig and equipment couldn't be salvaged: everything was burned to the ground. A specialized firefighting crew was flown in to extinguish the fire and install a wellhead cap to stop the well from flowing.

By the time Rob arrived, a second rig was in place to drill a relief well. This was a delicate operation, as they had to find the center of the damaged well at a depth of five thousand feet.

Rob felt downright miserable at the sight of the enormous damage that had been done. Not only did they suffer severe material damage, the explosion also had a catastrophic impact on the environment.

All this because of one stupid, human mistake. This fundamental warning was emphasized over and over again at the well control course: Keep the hole filled with mud at all times! It took them three months to partly clean up the mess and regain control over the well.

He wrote to his mam once a week, and was always excited to receive news from home. Because regular mail took too long, the letters were posted and collected by men coming and going on leave.

One day he received a letter from Agnes. She wrote that she was expecting a child from her German boyfriend, Klaus. They were planning to get married as soon as possible, but she knew that her pregnancy would cause a scandal, as the whole town would talk about it. But the biggest problem was how to tell Dad, because he hated the Germans.

When Rob returned home, he went to visit his Uncle Bart, explained Agnes' predicament and asked him for help. Uncle Bart went with them to break the news. Predictably, his father was livid. Uncle Bart tried hard to placate him, but he hardly listened. Then his uncle finally lost his temper.

'Get over it, Mark. These things happen!' he shouted at his brother. 'Fuck the scandal! Since when do you ever worry about what people think? Instead of sulking, you should be happy to become a granddad. I never had any children. I would swap places with you any time to have what you've got. We've tried to have children for years. And look at you! Think! You're about to have a grandchild!'

After several weeks of grumbling, Dad had no choice but to accept that his unmarried daughter was expecting from a German.

Agnes and Klaus had no money and no place to live. Fortunately, Klaus worked in the home building industry. Rob suggested building a house on his property, and offered to finance the materials. The next eight months, Rob and Klaus worked hard on weekends, holidays and his time off to build the house.

Once Agnes and Klaus moved in, Rob purchased another piece of land in the same village and Rob asked Klaus if he would assist to build a single-story house in return for his investment. Klaus agreed and Rob took a mortgage.

In less than a year they completed the second house and he created a separate living and bedroom for himself. He asked Mam if they wanted to move in with him because he knew that it was difficult for her to climb the stairs in their home. She agreed, and they moved in. He bought Mam the first television in town, enabling her to watch movies and shows, something that she had never watched before.

With his dad planning to retire soon, the issue was raised of what would happen if Rob ever got married. Would they be able to stay in the house? Rob made an appointment with the public notary to formalize that they could remain in the house incase Rob would get married as the house was big enough for two families. After all, he had built this one-story home also with his mother in mind, and he had no intention of getting married. Living together was convenient and the main purpose for all concerned, so they signed the agreement.

The following years he was hardly ever at home. When on leave he travelled widely, and slept with as many women as possible to make up for the time lost in the desert. He drove a nice car, had a job that provided him with both status and money, was quite tanned, so he had no trouble attracting women, often dating—and sleeping with—several at a time.

Chapter 7

He had become an expert in onshore drilling operations, and was always trying to get the job completed safely and in the shortest possible time.

He always experimented with different pump volumes and pressures, rotary speeds, and the weight that was applied on the drilling bit, until he finally found the optimal and ideal parameters for drilling different formations.

But offshore drilling increasingly got his attention. New technologies such as used to drill offshore wells interested him, so he read all the literature that was available.

One day he called the Human Resource Manager and asked if it was possible to get offshore drilling experience. The manager explained that the company owned and operated various drilling rigs that functioned as training facilities, and one of their most valued drilling contractors provided the drilling personnel to drill the wells. One of these training rigs was a semi-submersible rig, commonly known as a semi and used to drill in deep water. These rigs floated in the water and were towed by tugboats to new drilling locations. The semi was kept on location by anchors throughout the drilling operation. He told him to discuss his request with Mr. Brandt the Operations Manager.

A week later Mr. Brandt called and asked if Rob would like to work on a semi to gain offshore experience.

One month later, Rob became assistant drilling supervisor on one of the first semis near the Shetland Islands. He boarded the semi and watched the anchor handling vessels and the crew struggling to set the anchors.

In wind force five lashing at the aft deck, the anchor crew continued to work as the waves crashed over the sides, connecting cables and running anchors. It was an awesome and somewhat frightening sight. The men finally managed to secure the semi with eight anchors.

It was his job to plan the drilling operations. He developed a planning system by summarizing all drilling sequences with a seventy-two hour timeline and supervised the drilling operations during the night. He had to call the drilling supervisor in case anything happened that was beyond his knowledge or expertise.

During his first week he was confronted with high wind force dangers. The high winds experienced in this area made it necessary to secure everything. Yet on that day, the wind force had torn a board loose from the helicopter deck, falling down on a roustabout working thirty feet below on the main deck. The board hit the man on his neck and killed him instantly.

Helicopters were used to transport the crew from the airport to the rig.

Most helicopters were equipped with wheels to maneuver on land, but some had steel landing gear for improved stability while landing. Rob had only been on the rig for a month when he witnessed how a helicopter with steel landing gear tried to land in stormy conditions. The pilot tried to maneuver the helicopter onto the transport carriage that could then be moved into the hangar for service. But things went terribly wrong. Only one section of the landing gear landed on the transport carriage, while the other side slipped, dragging the full weight of the helicopter to one side. It caught fire and exploded on the deck.

But by far, the most dangerous operation to him was saturated diving, a technique that allowed professional divers to reduce the risk of decompression sickness, commonly known as 'the bends'. Divers lived in a pressurized environment such as a saturation system or pressure tank for a prolonged period of time so that their bodies could acclimatize to the pressure, enabling them to adapt more quickly to the depths. For weeks divers were kept in such environments, after which they were decompressed at surface at the end of their dives.

These divers were extremely well paid for this type of work, but Rob was surprised by the number of young men willing to risk their lives to perform these dives. It wasn't just the decompression that posed a risk to their health. Sometimes divers never resurfaced. Accidents while handling the equipment under water were a regular occurrence or the strong currents would drag the divers away.

Working on the semis posed another serious risk. One night, while enjoying the fresh air on deck, Rob noticed flashing lights coming straight for the semi. He reported this to the first mate, who immediately sounded the alarm: a tanker or container ship was heading straight for them. Frantically, they tried to find a radio frequency to contact the approaching ship to implore it to change its course. All personnel were ordered to the life boat stations as the lights came closer. With bated breath, they listened in the control room, but still, no contact could be made. All that they could do now was shoot emergency flares and pray that they would be spotted in time.

Then suddenly the ship changed course, veering away from the semi with only a hundred yards between them.

The incident was reported to the coast guard, but the semi captain was convinced that the container ship had been moving on automatic pilot. The ship probably traveled this route frequently and did not expect a semi at this location.

Accidents happened on a regular basis, and anyone unable to work was replaced. Most of these accidents took place on the rig floor while throwing the spinning chain, operating the rotary tongs to connect and disconnect the drill pipes, or diving.

Very little was done to prevent these accidents from happening again. Everyone in the business regarded the dangers as a professional risk. It was a risk that many were willing to take, as the job was well paid.

While on board the semi, Rob made it his priority to become immediately familiar with the shortest escape routes. He took these routes several times at night time and fog conditions. It was important for him to find his way to the life boats or the lowest point of the semi in case of a fire, blow-out or any other of the dangers that faced them.

But working on a semi was completely different, and it took Rob over a year before he read through all the drilling procedures and was able to operate the complicated air and hydraulic operated heave compensator located under the traveling block used to drill and carry out operations while the semi moved up and down in the heave, to understand the anchors tension system and learn how to safely land the blowout preventers (BOP) on the seabed. He worked long hours, changing the procedures into various drilling sequences. He made checklists for all sequences and included any accidents or human mistakes that occurred in the past. He did everything to avoid these mistakes from happening again and every crewmember was instructed to study the sequences before they carried out any job.

He changed the complex drilling procedures into simple drilling sequences that were more accessible to the crew.

A recording system was in place that recorded the time required to drill one feet of formation, the number of rotations per minute, the time it took to move the pipe in or out of the hole, the pump pressure and many other variable factors. These recorders were located on the rig floor, in the drilling contractor's offices and at the company's office.

The recording system enabled Rob to keep an eye on each operation, but the recorders had a time delay. He asked himself if it was possible to produce a real-time recording system to react in time to avoid drilling problems.

Then the first woman trainee engineer arrived on the semi. A woman on board was, until that moment, considered to be asking for problems and bad luck.

Most men on board would shave just before going home and watched porn twice a week to find out if everything was still in working order.

A separate living quarter was placed on the semi, and from the moment the woman set foot on board, life on the semi changed. All men suddenly started shaving and changed their clothes daily. The rig store never sold more after-shave and deodorant. While the men were watching porn, the woman knitted a sweater for her husband. It was a change for the better, and Rob decided that if he ever were in charge of a rig, women would always be more than welcome.

In his spare time he familiarized himself with the blow-out preventer (BOP), a seventy-ton block of steel with several hydraulic-operated valves and different rams to close around or cut drill pipe to control the formation pressure in case of emergency. It was landed on the seabed and used as the last barrier between the well and the semi, protecting its crew against blowouts. It was one of the most important pieces of safety equipment on board.

Above all, one of the most exciting moments on board was when they finally struck oil. Rob would always remember the night when he smelled and caught a sample of the first Shetland oil dripping from the first formation core.

Chapter 8

After two years on the semi, he was promoted to company drilling supervisor. The company transferred him to the Middle East, where he once again worked a four-week on and off schedule.

Twice a year he visited his friend Dieter, and met up with the girl to whom he had lost his virginity. Rob only saw her once in a while, not wishing to make a commitment. The girl didn't seem to mind: she enjoyed his company and the sex they had, but expected no more of him.

During his weeks off he turned into a sexual predator, always on the prowl for an easy lay. He had sex several times a day, each time with a different woman, and in the oddest of places. The women were generally easy and fun loving; they made no demands of him.

His most bizarre sexual adventure was when he made love to an Arab woman on a camel. He met her when he was enjoying the lush surroundings of a wadi, a place where water flows from a well and turns the area into a small paradise in the middle of the desert. He had been taken by surprise when a caravan of Bedouin entered the wadi to rest and stock up on water before moving on, taking with them salt to sell inland and figs and dates to sell along the coast. He felt like Lawrence of Arabia, observing how these men lived and moved across the desert, always carrying a rifle or dagger. It was then that he became acquainted with the woman. Abandoned by her family for having sex before marriage, she had to fend for herself by selling water - and most probably, her body. She taught him how to ride a camel, her lissome body pressed against his back, eager for sexual intimacy, which he was only too happy to provide.

He had women wherever he went: in Holland, in Germany, in the Middle East, while he was travelling, as well as in his hometown area where he was a regular at several discos.

In between his sexual adventures he would visit his uncle, and often spend time with Agnes' children, of whom he had grown fond. Life was good. He had everything he could possibly wish for.

Until the day he visited the bank in Ootmarsum to settle outstanding bank issues. While waiting in line he noticed a girl assisting clients at the second counter. She was attractive in a typical Dutch way, and reminded him of Frau Antje, the girl who often appeared on German television to promote Dutch cheese. But there was something different about her that he couldn't quite place, and he found that unsettling, but intriguing nevertheless.

He changed queues several times as he observed her, in the hope of ending up at her counter. She appeared kind and helpful, and the sun seemed to shine whenever she laughed. But when it was his turn, she was quite curt with him, treating him in a cool and businesslike manner. When she had finished dealing with him, he lingered.

'This is not usual for me to say, but thank you for your excellent service. Would you care to have dinner with me this evening?'

She blushed a lovely pink and leaned forward so that no one could hear.

'No, sir. I know of your reputation, so I wish you a very good day.'

Completely lost for words, he mumbled a few words and left the bank in a daze.

As he sat in his car it dawned on him. He had just met the most astonishing girl, obviously from a good family, who refused to be treated the way he normally handled women.

He visited the bank every other day, but her service was no more than professional and polite. He finally ran out of reasons to visit the bank, so he asked Agnes to find out who she was and where she lived.

But Agnes was very firm with him. 'I'll tell you her name and where she lives under one condition. You don't mess with her. If you do, you'll get into trouble. Not only with me, but with the whole town.'

She went on to explain that her dad raised her. He did one hell of a job, in spite of the depression he suffered after his wife died of cancer. With the help of his daughter and the local doctor, he had slowly picked up the threads of his life again.

'So I'll only help if you promise to be serious about her.'

Her name was Anne. When Anne did not appear for work at the bank the next day, Rob drove up to her house and knocked. Her father opened the door.

'Good morning Sir. My name is Rob Oolderink. Could I please speak to your daughter?'

Somewhat puzzled, the man nodded and let him inside the house, where he waited in the hall.

When he saw her come down the stairs, his day was made. The sight of her radiant, lovely face made him feel as if Heaven had just opened up for him, but her expression changed when she saw him.

'What do you want?' she asked with a frown.

'Well, I'll be honest,' he said, at a loss by her cool manner. 'Normally I would ask you out for a drink, dinner, or to see a movie, and try to make a pass at you, where after I just disappear. But I'm not planning to do any of that. I would really appreciate if you would spend one evening with me. If you don't enjoy it, I'll disappear, and you never see me again.'

She looked at him intently for a while. 'Wait here,' she said. After a few minutes she came back. 'I've told my dad that we've gone to the café next door.'

Once they had ordered coffee, Rob started to talk about himself but she interrupted him. 'I've heard a lot of stories about you. None of them are any good. Tell me, why did you come to my house?'

Tongue-tied, he explained that he never felt this way before. For the first time in his life, he was actually interested in getting to know a woman. He believed that his childhood experience of his parents' odd marriage and other experiences was likely to be the cause of his attitude towards women. They talked and talked, until asked to leave at eleven as it was closing time, and Rob never even touched his coffee. They spent the last two days of his leave together.

Just before leaving home, the office called. He was to replace the drilling manager, as the man had been seriously injured after driving into a sand dune at night. He was told to leave as soon as he received his visa.

Rob and Anne spent another week together, and when he finally had to leave, she promised that she would write to him.

Slowly he worked himself into his new job as company representative in Saudi Arabia. He was still working for Werner Brandt, with whom he got on well and was now on first-name terms.

He wrote to Anne every single day, always making sure that whoever took the mail actually posted his letters. In their letters, they discussed everything that was important to him. The wish to start a family, religion, values of life, children, his worldwide job commitment, etc.

After three months he was informed that his appointment was extended, whereupon he asked permission to go home and arrange for more of his personal effects required for a longer period.

He left Riyadh the following week, and after landing in Amsterdam took the first available train to Oldenzaal. He had not told Anne anything as he wanted to surprise her, and at the station he took a taxi to Anne's house. As soon as she opened the door he knew. It was strange to feel such peace of mind, to simply know with such certainty, that he had found the woman of his life.

'Can I ask you a question?' he blurted as she opened the door.

She stared at him, flabbergasted at the sight of him. 'I don't know. I really don't know what to say.'

'I have this feeling. A feeling that we're born for one another.'

'I still don't know what to say. You've caught me completely off guard.'

'Do you love me?'

'Oh, Jesus.'

'He won't be able to help you this time.'

'Please give me a second to come back to earth.'

'No I won't. I want to ask you a question.'

'What question?'

'Would you marry me, and follow me wherever my job brings me?'

'Oh, Jesus,' was all she could say.

'He's still not available right now.'

'Yes.'

'What did you just say?'

'I said yes.'

'Then let's get married and move to Saudi Arabia as soon as we can.'

'Oh, Jesus.'

'I'm afraid you'll have to do without him and do this by yourself.'

'Rob, what are you doing here?' she finally asked, exasperated.

'Asking you to marry me.'

'Then why are you not on your knees?'

'Hell. I forgot to buy you a ring. I'll have to do it all over again tomorrow.'

'How are you?' she asked, smiling now.

'Well, right now I'm feeling the happiest man on earth.'

'Would you at least kiss me?'

This exchange had taken so long that Anne's father had come into the hall to inquire what on earth was happening.

Rob turned to him respectfully. 'Sir, I know we don't know each other that well, but meeting your daughter has changed my life. I want to spend every day with her, for the rest of my life. I promise to take good care of her, and ask your permission to marry her as soon as we can, so I can take her with me to Saudi Arabia.'

Anne's father stared at him dumbly, and then turned to his daughter.

'Is this what you really want, Anne?' he asked. 'You've only known Rob for such a short time. If you do this, he will take you far away from home. Do you realize this?'

'Yes, Dad. I know,' she said with a soft voice.

'Then so be it,' her father said with a nod. 'But you'd better take very good care of my girl,' he added, wagging his finger at Rob in warning. 'She is all that I've got left.'

'I promise,' Rob said solemnly.

As they drank coffee, he explained why he had come, telling them that his appointment was for an indefinite period, and that he would have to leave again in two days' time.

He looked at Anne and knew instinctively that she, too, felt that this was how it was meant to be. It surprised him that sex was no longer that important to him, and when she asked to keep it for their wedding night, he agreed. After all, there would be time enough for real love making once they were married, and there were so many other things that he wanted to discover and know about her. For now, he was content to just hold her in his arms and caress her.

He informed Werner that he was planning to get married and that his wife would join him in Saudi Arabia once everything was arranged.

The following day he came home early in the morning to find his mam crying in the kitchen. She confessed to him that her left arm and shoulder had become unbearably painful during the past couple of months. She did apply a special ointment to the affected areas, but it only gave her mild relief.

Concerned, he examined her arm but couldn't see anything, so he advised to see her doctor. 'Mam, there is something I have to tell you,' he began, unable to keep the news from her any longer. 'I've met someone. She's the woman of my dreams. We're getting married.'

She gasped at him in surprise.

'And that's not all. As soon as we're married she will be joining me in Saudi.'

Mam didn't say a word, but her eyes were shining as her face broke into a smile.

'Oh, Rob,' she gushed, all emotional. 'I know we never talked about our marriage problems because I always believed you shouldn't involve your children in these things.' She looked at him shrewdly. 'But I always felt you knew more than anyone else. Am I right?'

Rob returned her look, but said nothing. His silence was enough. 'I've always been afraid that our problem influenced your attitude towards women. That it stopped you from committing yourself to anyone.' He could see her eyes mist over. 'I'm so very happy that you finally found someone. Someone who could capture your heart and soul, someone to replace all the old bitterness with love.'

Rob took her hand in his. 'Mam, I never wanted to get married for all kinds of reasons. But with Anne... all those reasons for not marrying... they're gone. She took those away. I just know that I want to spend the rest of my life with her.'

The following day he left for Saudi Arabia, leaving Anne to make all the necessary wedding arrangements. She preferred to celebrate the wedding in their hometown, and not in Germany. As soon as they set a date they informed both their families, as they would not see each other for a long time.

At work, Rob required all his experience and know-how to keep operations running. Most of his time was spent reading daily reports, supporting the drilling supervisor on the rig with his daily issues and taking care of paperwork.

Fortunately his many years of experience and the sequence sheets that he had kept over the years assisted him. Whenever a new drilling sequence was about to take place, he would ask all the right questions. As he noticed a difference in the way his drilling supervisors worked on planning and control, and because of several incidents that occurred, he visited the rig and introduced his sequence system to ensure safe and consistent drilling operations.

On every single page, the system included timely equipment checks and clearly stated every step necessary to complete one operational sequence, including previous accidents and human mistakes. He wanted to eliminate all risk factors and saw to it that his supervisors prepared and followed every step as indicated.

He issued new tenders, selecting drilling and service contractors to drill additional wells. He was responsible for keeping the wells within the given budget and kept a daily summary of drilling expenses.

His staff consisted of a drilling engineer, material supervisor and a local secretary.

The drilling engineer prepared the different drilling programs, after which Rob reviewed and forwarded them to the head office for final approval.

After a while he felt that his company was well organized and managed by Bernard Heumer, an experienced and capable Managing Director who had run various departments during his career with the company.

The man was greatly respected, as told by his drilling engineer, for his vision and leadership, as he had turned a small company into one of the leading energy companies in Germany.

In fact, all the managers working at the company were highly capable, whether they managed the drilling, production or finance departments. Many of them had worked a long time for the company. Rob experienced that whenever he needed advice from any of them, their response was fast and efficient.

The company had been around for several generations before Wedel Shipping Company purchased the company and created Hattenberg Oil, providing jobs in the Hanover area for years. Employees were generally very loyal to the company, and in return, the company treated them well, organizing annual parties to which even retired employees were invited.

Still, the selection of drilling contractors was only based on daily rates and the contractors' rig technical specifications. No one ever looked at their safety records.

Rob suggested they include safety as one of the selection criteria, by looking at the number of days that a contractor worked a rig without any lost time accidents.

Head Office approved his proposal, and if day rates did not differ that much, the contractor with the least number of lost time accidents per year was awarded the drilling contract.

Rob asked his secretary Layla to look around for apartments. He wanted to find something to have a place of their own when Anne arrived.

He appreciated the luxury and convenience of a phone. He had never called his mam before, as phones were either unavailable or too expensive to use. So far, he had only written letters.

Now he suddenly had a phone connection. He could call Anne or Mam whenever he wanted and no longer had to wait for their letters to arrive. He called Anne every single day to discuss their wedding plans in detail.

He asked Werner Brandt's permission for a short leave in order to get married, proposing that his drilling engineer manage the operations for a week.

Werner had no objections and the wedding invitations were sent.

Rob then called his friend Dieter, telling him he was getting married and that his wife would soon join him in Saudi Arabia. 'Would you like to be my best man,' he asked.

There was a stunned silence on the other side of the connection.

'I never expected you getting married and would be more than honored, Rob.'

'Excellent! And how are things at your end?'

'Doing all right. I just completed my first hitch as production engineer on one of the drilling and production platforms near Aberdeen. I manage the distribution of oil and gas from the wells into a pipeline to shore.'

'Which platform?'

'It's not just a drilling platform; they also handle the oil and gas production. Can't say I'm happy about it. This simultaneous drilling and production operation is dodgy.

I would prefer to work on a rig or platform that just produced the wells.'

He yawned audibly, whereupon Rob laughed.

'Not getting enough sleep?'

'Not really. We're getting a lot of alarm signals, especially at night. We all have to respond and shut down operations whenever the alarms go off. Anyone not on duty has to go to the muster stations and wait there until the alerts are investigated.'

'Are these mostly false alarms?'

'Fortunately, yes. But still, it's nerve-racking, especially at night.'

'Dieter, when I started work on the semi, the first thing I did was to explore the shortest escape routes to the lifeboats or the lowest section of the rig to jump. You should do the same, my friend. Promise me.'

'I will, next time I'm on board. Have to go now. I'd be honored to be your best man, Rob. We'll see each other two days before the wedding.'

After work he looked at some of the apartments that Layla had selected, and sent Anne photos of the ones of his preference. After a great deal of deliberation and many phone calls, they opted for an apartment that was partially furnished.

The following Friday he left Riyadh for Holland, the same day that Anne gave her notice at the bank. The wedding was planned on Monday.

It was local tradition for women to marry from their homes, and Rob was to stay with his parents. On Saturday Rob took his parents shopping to buy clothes appropriate for the wedding, after which he drove to the airport to pick up Dieter, who would be staying with him.

On Sunday morning Rob and Anne looked for locations to take wedding pictures.

The last evening he spent with his parents, Agnes, Klaus and Dieter.

Early Monday morning Rob, Dieter and his parents went to the hairdresser's, packed their suits and wedding dresses and drove up to Ootmarsum.

Rob wasn't allowed to see Anne before she was fully dressed for the wedding ceremony, so they all dressed at her home. He waited in the living room until she came down. He knew she was beautiful, but when she entered she left him breathless. He just stood there, staring, as she walked up to him and kissed him gently on his lips.

'Hey, good-looking. What do you think? Are you satisfied with me as your bride?'

'Satisfied? I... I don't know what to say. You look like a dream come true.'

They looked at each other to find that they both had tears in their eyes.

As Rob wanted to get married using his own car, he did not want it decorated with flowers as was local custom. They drove up to the church where their families and guests were waiting.

Agnes surprised him by having dressed her children, whom he utterly adored, as page and bridesmaid. The children walked ahead of them as they entered the church, scattering rose petals as they went.

The ceremony was an intimate nature, as the pastor knew both families well. His words touched them all, especially when he spoke of the difficult time Anne's father experienced after his wife's death, and remarked how well he had managed raising Anne on his own.

After the church ceremony they walked to the town council, where the marriage was officially registered. Then they all walked to the same café where Rob and Anne had enjoyed their first cup of coffee. This time they did drink the coffee, and ate the homemade apple pie while the guests were seated at long tables.

The couple then left with the photographer to have their pictures taken in the gardens of a small castle in the vicinity and at the local mill, a place that was filled with childhood memories for both of them.

They finished the photo shoot by lunchtime and quickly returned to the café, where they served sandwiches with ham and cheese. The guests presented their wedding gifts, after which members from both Anne's and Rob's family told amusing anecdotes about the newlyweds that had taken place during the course of their lives, much to the hilarity of all present.

While having dinner the music started, and Rob asked Mam for the first dance while Anne asked her dad. It was the most emotional moment of the day for booth.

They knew then that they were saying goodbye: Rob to his mam and Anne to her dad. It struck Rob that he would not be the person he was if it weren't for his parents, especially his mam. She was always there for him, whenever he needed her. When he guided her back to the table, they both had tears in their eyes.

'Thank you, Rob, for giving me the honor of this first dance.'

'You earned it, Mam. You know that I love you.'

When the party was over, they said goodbye to everyone and departed to Germany for their two-day honeymoon. While driving they exchanged thoughts on the day, sharing their impressions and the moments they had cherished the most.

At Rob's suggestion, they stopped at Rhűdesheim, a town near the river Rhine. They had not changed from their wedding attire, so when they entered the hotel they were given the bridal suite.

Rob could hardly hold out any longer, wanting Anne so badly that it hurt.

He had to control his urge in the elevator, but the moment they entered the suite he took her into his arms and nuzzled his face into her neck, enjoying the smell of her perfume. He thought he could never get enough of her.

In spite of his urge, he didn't feel rushed. It was a light and easy sensation that he was unfamiliar with: for the first time in his life he wanted to make love gently, tenderly, sweetly. He took all the time to undress her, and she took all the time to undress him.

They looked at each other enraptured, as if it were the first time they saw a man or woman in the nude. Anne suggested taking a bath and they washed every inch of each other's body. He noticed that she wasn't at all nervous or tense, but open and curious, exploring him to his very core. She was like a book opening up to him, with every new page more beautiful than the last. The love they made was so soft and exquisite that Anne's eyes were filled with tears. There was no need for him to ask why, as he felt the same way.

They stayed in the hotel room for two days making love, watching the Rhine flow past the castle, ordering room service and making love again. On the third day they woke up early and left the hotel right after breakfast, as a lot of things had to be done before leaving for Saudi.

They packed most of their clothes as flight baggage, as winter nights could be cold in the desert. Rob had told Anne that there were no Western stores in Riyadh, so she insisted on taking her sewing machine. All other things were packed in boxes to be shipped.

The next morning they said goodbye to their parents, and Klaus drove them to the airport. They were completely exhausted and slept during the flight.

Upon arrival in Riyadh their luggage was searched thoroughly for any forbidden items such as alcohol, religious books or nude magazines. Once they found none of these, they were cleared through customs. Rob's assistant drove them to the apartment.

When they finally arrived it was past midnight. Without unpacking anything, they showered together, something Rob had never done before with any woman.

After their shower he fixed drinks on the balcony, where it was hot and humid.

The stars in the desert sky seemed brighter than ever before, and they ended up making love on the balcony floor, where no one could watch them.

That first night Anne hardly slept because she was not used to the constant whir of air conditioning. They got up early because Rob wanted to be in the office at seven o'clock to check reports and call his drilling supervisor to discuss the progress and planning. They had their first breakfast in the apartment, and then Rob left, promising Anne that he would come home for lunch.

Left alone, Anne unpacked the suitcases and explored the apartment. She went onto the balcony, experiencing the outdoors like a blazing furnace after leaving the cool climate controlled indoors. From there she watched the people on the street. She saw the women in long black dresses, their faces covered in such a way that you could only see their eyes. The men wore long white dresses with a headdress made of cloth that was held in place with a cord. They all carried daggers, attached to a silver belt. Some even had rifles.

The street was very busy and filled with noise. It seemed to Anne as if every single driver on the road was using his horn non-stop. Camels just walked on the streets unattended. With wonder, she listened to the distorted voice of the muezzin, calling the people to come for prayer from the mosque's minaret in a tongue that was so strange to her. All she could make out was the name of Allah. The heat and humidity, all the new sounds and impressions suddenly made her realize that she had arrived in a completely new world with a lifestyle so very different from her own. It was all rather overwhelming. She went back inside and got dressed, as Rob's secretary would arrive at nine o'clock to show her the shopping area. Dressing with special care, she chose a modest skirt that covered her knees and a long-sleeved shirt.

When Layla arrived, she was dressed in an abbaya, the Arab woman's long black dress. She looked Anne up and down, assessing her attire with a slight frown, but said nothing. They left the apartment for the souk, a covered marketplace where everything from food to furniture was being sold. Young boys asking for money immediately trailed them. Layla shooed them away, but they kept on following.

Layla showed her where to buy groceries, fruit and vegetables, and anything else she might need for the apartment. She explained that prices should always be haggled over, as the asking price was usually thirty percent higher than the price the sellers expected. She taught Anne how to haggle by just walking away until the shop owner chased her to agree on a final price.

After she had finished buying all she needed, the two women went to drink coffee at a raised kiosk that had no walls, windows or door. Not long after they were seated, the boys that followed them kneeled down on the street and turned their faces up to peep under Anne's skirt. She felt terribly embarrassed and they left the place.

'I strongly advise you to wear an abbaya,' Layla said. She took her to a shop specializing in selling the traditional women's garment, where Anne bought her first abbaya, as well as the face-covering niqab so that she could go out without being bothered.

When Rob came home for lunch, she told him what had happened. He listened to her story, amused, but then he frowned.

'I heard today that a Western, blonde woman disappeared only six months ago while she was shopping on her own. No one has seen her since.'

Anne raised an eyebrow, shocked.

'They think that she probably ended up somewhere in the desert, as a member of someone's harem.' He looked at her, concerned. 'I think it would be better if you don't go out there alone. I'll get Layla when you want to go somewhere.'

'Rob, perhaps you could check if there is a Dutch embassy to find out if other Dutch or Europeans are living in this compound.'

'Good idea. I'll get Layla to check this afternoon.'

Less than an hour later Rob called to give her the phone number of the Dutch embassy.

Anne called, and was informed that indeed, there were quite a number of Dutch and German families living in their compound. Most of the men worked in the oil and dredging industry, like her husband, the man added helpfully. He gave her a few telephone numbers, and after trying two numbers she got hold of a Dutch woman who lived in the same apartment building.

'Oh yes,' the woman told her enthusiastically. 'There are quite a few Dutch and German families living here. Tell you what, many of the wives meet every other day for coffee and we also go shopping together. There's a coffee set for tomorrow morning. Would you like to join and I'll introduce you to the other ladies?'

'I'd love that,' Anne said, immensely grateful for the social lifeline she was being handed in a land full of strangers. The woman gave her the address and Anne happily proceeded to organize her kitchen, wardrobe and rearranged the framed photos on the side table.

Anne made a special effort preparing their first dinner at the apartment, expecting Rob home at seven o'clock as he promised. She set the table, checked her hair and makeup, lit candles and put on a gramophone.

At seven, Rob called to say that he would not be home until later because there was a problem at the rig. She listened to him as he tried to explain something to her about a stuck pipe, he would have to get a specialist to the rig to free the drilling string and extract the equipment from the hole, and then they would have to install the hydraulic jars...

He lost her about there. She didn't have the faintest idea what he was talking about. Nor did it interest her. She just felt disappointed.

He finally came home at ten. 'It's all part of the job, darling,' he said apologetically after he kissed her while she reheated his dinner. 'I'm responsible twenty-four hours a day. You'd better get used to it, these things happen sometimes.'

In great detail he told her about the problems that had kept him busy that evening. She tried to understand, but didn't grasp any of it, until he made a small sketch to explain the stuck pipe situation.

Once he finished telling her how his day had been, Anne told him about her phone call with the Dutch woman and her invitation to go for coffee the next day.

When they finished their main course, Anne cleared the table and said, 'I'll get the dessert.'

'I would prefer you for dessert.' He got up from the table, picked her up and carried her into the bedroom. He undressed her and started to kiss her feet, slowly working his way up between her legs, where he lingered until she begged him to take her. He did so until deep into the night.

Just before he nodded off to sleep, Anne whispered in his ear, 'I'm pregnant.'

There was a stunned silence. For a moment he did not know how to respond.

'How do you know?'

'I just feel it, Rob.'

He looked at her in disbelief. 'I know we discussed having children,' he began awkwardly. 'And we did agree not to use birth control on our wedding night, didn't we?'

She nodded.

'I know we want to have children, but... Jesus. This is happening so fast, especially if you're right. It's just... I didn't expect it to happen. This really is a big surprise.'

'We will see if my intuition is right,' she said and turned around to go to sleep.

But Rob couldn't sleep. In the darkness he lay, wondering if it was wise to bring children into a world that was threatened by a nuclear war now that the relations between the Soviet Union and the USA had become so tense.

On the other hand, he loved her and had agreed to children. But if she was right, then he was about to become a dad. For a long time, he had been adamant that he would never get married—talk about a change of plans! After several hours of trying to get some sleep, he got up and served Anne breakfast in bed at five.

At the coffee meeting, Anne met four Dutch and one German woman. The Dutch woman just got married, like herself, and recently moved to Saudi Arabia to join their husbands, who all worked on-off schedules at the oil rigs in the desert or dredging ships.

The German woman had two daughters, aged ten and six, and Anne liked her straight away. Her name was Waltraud, and she was ten years older than Anne. She told her that she felt a bit isolated, as none of the Dutch ladies spoke German, and was delighted to learn that Anne did.

After several weeks of having coffee and shopping together, they set a date for dinner so that their husbands could meet. It was the first dinner of many. Anne would cook a Dutch meal, while Waltraud would prepare something typically German. They played cards and other kinds of games. On special occasions such as birthdays, they would go to one of the two luxury hotels in town. There they would have drinks, dine and dance, something which Anne and Rob loved to do.

On weekends most Western families went to the beach for a barbeque, or they organized trips into the desert to visit the small Arabian villages located near the scattered wadis. Anne and Waltraud always went shopping together. While she was alone she spent most of her time reading, listening to music or searching for fabrics to make her own dresses.

Rob was always very busy, visiting the rig for inspections, receiving visitors from head office or dealing with service companies. Twice, he was approached by local representatives of service contractors, who invited him for lunch, strongly hinting that if he were to extend the contract with them, they would arrange a shopping trip for him and his wife to Dubai, all at their expense. But Rob wasn't interested, and made this quite clear by cancelling their contracts the next day.

Rob didn't care. He believed in doing honest business, following the tender procedure according to the rules and the criteria that were set. He refused to resort to corrupt practices.

Those were good times for Anne and Rob. They did not have much time to get to know each other all that well before the wedding—now they had plenty of time. The more time they spent together, the more convinced they became that their decision to marry was the right one. They were just very happy.

Every weekend they would call their parents, exchanging all the news. When he called Mam one weekend Rob couldn't help to notice that she had gone unusually quiet. He asked her what was wrong.

'It's my arm, dear,' she told him. 'It still hurts a lot, and won't get any better.'

'You should really see a specialist, Mam.'

'I know. I've got an appointment at the hospital in two weeks' time.'

Meanwhile, Rob thought that Anne was becoming more beautiful every day. She was like a flower opening up to the sun, and there was not a day that went by that he didn't say that he loved her, and he made love to her every night.

He did pay special attention to her menstrual cycle, remembering her words that first night in their apartment. When he asked if she had her period yet, she blushed.

'I'm a week overdue,' she told him. 'But that happened before. I'll probably get it sometime this week.'

He looked at her quizzically, but agreed to wait another week before seeing a doctor. But when he was back at the office he asked Layla to find a good Western doctor, and asked Anne to make an appointment after his rig visit.

When he returned from the desert a few days later, he entered the apartment and noticed a huge bouquet of fragrant, fresh gladiola on the table. He was surprised, as imported flowers were frightfully expensive; especially considering they only lasted a few days. Anne only bought flowers for special occasions.

She came from the balcony and just stood there, without saying a word. Her eyes were shining and she looked absolutely radiant.

'Yes,' she said simply, as she saw him glance at the flowers. 'I bought them to celebrate. I'm pregnant, Rob. We'll have to think of a name. For a boy or a girl.'

Rob took a deep breath and stared at her. 'Just give me a minute to absorb this. I thought we agreed to wait for the doctor's visit until I got back.'

Anne walked up and kissed him. 'I've already known this for two weeks. I don't need a doctor to tell me I'm pregnant, darling. I know my body; I could feel the changes that were taking place. I'm sick in the mornings and can't stand the smell of cooking without becoming nauseous and throwing up. You'll have to cook now, and spoil me,' she said with a big smile.

'Cook? I haven't cooked for ages. I probably forgot how. You'll have to teach me, as you'll need to eat.'

He swept her up in his arms. 'But let's talk about something else, my dear doctor Anne. Did you ask yourself if is alright for us to make love when you're in this state?'

She shook her head in disbelief and laughed. 'Is that all you can think of?'

'Yes. I have been away for four nights, you know. I've missed you terribly. So, what does my doctor say?'

Anne gave him a flirtatious look. 'That all depends on how much you'll spoil me.'

The next day they phoned their families and told them the big news. The calls wound up with everyone getting emotional, their parents rejoicing for them but at the same time lamenting that they could not be with them to celebrate.

From then on, Rob prepared dinner when he came home. Anne would stay in the bedroom, unable to stand even the smell of food, only to emerge when she felt that she was ready to eat something.

Waltraud was a great help in that she came by every day with fresh fruit, the only thing Anne could eat without getting sick. She would even prepare meals for them several times a week, so Rob wouldn't have to cook.

Rob was immensely grateful, as his cooking skills were limited. Waltraud, on the other hand, was a great cook, and even Anne managed to eat some and keep it down.

Although Anne told him that her morning sickness was quite normal, Rob was still concerned, so he insisted that they visit the doctor. Patiently, the man explained to him that this often happened during the first trimester of pregnancy, and he told Anne to come back after one month if things didn't improve.

Within a month, Anne was cooking again. She had terrible cravings for Dutch cheese and drop, Dutch licorice, which her dad sent her regularly. Rob spent as much time with Anne as he could to observe the changes that took place in her body.

She told him that she could already feel the baby move.

At work, things were going fairly smoothly. Rob was invited to join the annual conference in Hanover, which required attendance of the drilling managers working in different drilling areas. They would discuss new drilling technologies, various drilling problems that had come up, financial results and any other important issues. Rob asked if Anne wanted to join him on this short trip, but she didn't want to fly while she was pregnant and preferred to stay home.

Rob wanted to combine his trip and visit his parents, as he was worried about his mam. She had been very quiet during recent phone calls, and felt something was wrong.

He traveled to Hanover the following week, surprised to find that a new Human Resources Manager had been appointed. There was even a rumor going around that the company was for sale. When he had a chance to talk to Werner Brandt in private, he brought the matter up.

Werner reacted strangely, momentarily lost for words.

'Well,' he said, with an awkward laugh, 'You know that Wedel Shipping, our mother company, doesn't regard oil as its core business.'

Rob nodded.

'They're primarily business is shipping. Having this company under its wings serves to keep fuel and oil prices low, and on top of that, we're making excellent profits.' Werner wiped the mustard off his lips and took another sip of his beer. 'Wedel Shipping Company isn't doing well, Rob. They need new capital to replace their fleet. They need faster ships and many of their ships are outdated.' He set down his glass and looked Rob in the eye. 'You're right. Our company is up for sale. But the asking price is high, so we'll have to wait and see.

'But Wedel Shipping Company has asked us to take over some of their excess staff to reduce personnel costs. An early retirement package has been presented to our senior management. Some of the managers won't accept until the company is sold and may find out that their services are no longer required. Everyone in this business knows that a new buyer will use his own management team to safe costs. Before a possible sale takes place, I think that a number of our best managers will be replaced with Wedel Shipping Company staff. That's why they already appointed a new Human Resources Manager to do the dirty work.'

'So will you be taking early retirement?'

'No. My expertise is drilling and producing wells. Experienced people like me are always required. I hope that this answers part of your question.'

Rob visited the Human Resources department and asked for the previous HR manager's contact details. He then called him and expressed his gratitude for all that he had done for him over the years and wished him very well.

The new HR manager was John Fuchs, who somehow reminded Rob of Harry. Fuchs came across as a snake, and his intuition told him to be very careful.

Before the meeting took place a new drilling manager from Brazil was introduced, and the Managing Director Bernhard Heumer indicated that the marketing and contract manager finally reached an agreement with the local oil company to drill and produce wells. Rob was introduced as the new drilling manager for the Libyan drilling operations. He was impressed how the meeting was organized and the level of experienced and skills from the head office managers and departmental heads. All presentations were carried out very professionally, whether they concerned drilling technology, financial, production or engineering issues, and he found the following discussions more than useful.

After the conference he left Hanover by train, rented a car and drove home. He was delighted to be there, and happy to see his parents. Mam had even cooked his favorite meal: hachee, a stewed beef with lots of onions, bell peppers and garlic, served with mashed potatoes and freshly made apple sauce on the side. The smell in the kitchen made his mouth water.

In the kitchen he fixed a beer for his father and a glass of wine for his mam, and they sat down at the kitchen table. He showed them the last pictures he had taken of Anne before he had left, and Mam told him about everything that went on in town. Yet he couldn't help noticing that she avoided his look. Not wishing to ruin an enjoyable dinner, he ate to his heart's content until all pots were empty.

They moved into the living room to have coffee, but Rob had to pass on the apple vlaai for dessert, as he felt bloated. He even had to loosen his belt a notch.

'That was excellent, Mam. You never did have time to show Anne how to make all these dishes. If I don't want to gain weight it might be better if you don't!'

His mam looked at him. To his shock, he saw that there were tears in her eyes.

'I hope I still have time to show her, dear. Do you remember I told you that I had made an appointment with the doctor?' Rob nodded, frowning. 'They did some tests and found cancer lumps in my breasts. I'm scheduled for breast removal next week.'

Rob looked at her, stricken. For the first time in his life, he saw panic in her eyes, and fear. And there was nothing he could do to help her.

'It's okay,' she said, reading his thoughts. 'Agnes and Klaus will be there to help me whenever they can.'

For a while, they sat there, talking about what could be done. When it got late they all went to bed. Rob could not sleep and went to the kitchen to find his mam crying.

She grabbed his hand, desperate. 'I'm scared, Rob. If I lose my breast, then... it's part of being a woman. I'm just so afraid your father won't find me attractive anymore.'

'Mam, listen to me,' wrapping his arm around her shoulder. 'Love is not about looks—you know that. It's about the person who you are.' Still, he felt that he was unable to comfort her. He stayed with her and they talked for hours. They talked about his life with Anne, about him becoming a dad.

In spite of the fact that he loved his job, all he wanted to do now was stay at home and support his mam through her ordeal. But he had no choice: this was his job, so he had to return.

The next morning he went to see his sister and her family. They talked about their mam for a long time, and Agnes promised she would do everything to help her.

By the time he kissed her goodbye, he knew that she was as worried as he was.

After boarding the plane, he just felt sad. He had never seen his mam in such a state. The way she had panicked and the look of fear that he noticed in her eyes. He had never known her like this. She had always been so bright, always seeing the positive things in life. For the first time in her life, she needed him. She needed him to support her, and he was not even going to be around. He knew that he may have to make some difficult decisions.

When Rob returned, Anne knew straight away that something was wrong. His eyes were red, and he had worry lines beneath them that she had not noticed before.

She put her arms around his neck and kissed away the tears that he was no longer able to stop. All he could think about was his mam.

'Is something wrong with your mam?'

'Yes,' he sniffed, and he sat down and told her everything.

'Well, if you ask me, there is only one solution. And that is to contact the office and ask them if you can return to Germany so you can be there for her. She needs you, Rob. You owe her that, at least.' She took his hand and kissed it gently. 'On the other hand, I'm here in Saudi because of your work. I must admit that I really miss my dad, and I have this feeling he's not doing that well. I'm the only reason for him to stay alive, Rob. And I'm not even there for him.' She fell quiet, looking somber. 'We both know that they would all be grateful if we returned. Think how happy it would make them to hold their grandchild in seven months' time.'

Emotionally exhausted, they finally went to bed, where he made love to her with a tenderness that he had never thought himself capable of. After they climaxed he just held her tight, moving his hand to her stomach. When he felt the child move, he was filled with wonder, and felt a feeling of utter contentment wash over him. He fell asleep in her arms and stayed there until the alarm went off in the morning.

As soon as his work allowed, Rob called Werner to explain his situation. He asked if it would be possible to return to Germany and work closer to home. Werner said that he would have to make some calls and promised to call back.

When he did call back that afternoon, Werner informed Rob that his colleague was recovering well from his car accident in the desert and ready for work within two months. However, the only option for Rob was to work a four-week on-off schedule as drilling supervisor in the Libyan Desert, where the company was finalizing a contract to start drilling operations in two months' time. He told Rob that this project was very important for the company's future and would be pleased if one of his best supervisors was running the operation. He explained that a geologist who supervised exploration drilling in Lease 103 for another oil company approached his boss Bernhard Heumer. This company purchased a lease in the Libyan dessert and drilled a total of three exploration wells.

Most countries divide land and sea into sections called leases and companies can purchase these leases to search for minerals. If minerals are found, the company can drill or produce, and the government claims a percentage.

This lease was returned to the Libyan government, because each well was dry with no future prospect of finding any oil, according to the geologist report.

At that time the geologist was a key person while drilling exploration wells and correlated the expected geology with the soil samples circulated up from the bottom of the well. After drilling three exploration wells, he reported that no formation was found that contained any oil or gas.

The geologist contacted Bernhard Heumer and indicated that, based on his interpretation of soil data, oil could be found in lease 103 if the company drilled 400' deeper than his previous employer.

The company reviewed the geological data, including well data, and hired the geologist on the basis that if oil sands were found, his share would be equal to one percent of the production rate, so the company obtained lease 103 to drill and produce.

Chapter 9

Rob knew only too well that it would be better for his career to stay on as drilling manager in Saudi Arabia. He had asked to be posted closer to home, but apparently that wasn't possible. The supervisor job in Libya was his best available option—at least he was home during his off time to help his mam. Besides, Anne would be there to assist any time and be able to live close to her hometown, near to her dad.

So he decided to accept the job.

First he called Anne and told her that they would be leaving Saudi Arabia in two months. Then he called his mam. When he told her that they would return to Holland, she cried, saying this was the best news she had received in a long time.

Their remaining time in Saudi Arabia mostly consisted of routine work for Rob, while Anne started packing, planning to ship their goods home as soon as possible.

Rob spoke to his mam every Sunday. She was at home after surgery, recovering slowly, yet somehow he had the feeling that she wasn't telling him everything. Time passed quickly, and before they knew, one month had gone by. Within a few weeks, they would be home.

Waltraud and her family were disappointed at the news that they were leaving, having enjoyed the friendship that they built up over the months. In order to say goodbye, Rob arranged a farewell party at the beach for all their friends.

One week before his departure his colleague returned, having fully recovered from his accident. The handover took place, and their personal belongings were boxed up and collected by the shipping company. Waltraud drove them to the airport, where Anne tearfully said goodbye to her best friend.

Agnes picked them up from Schiphol airport. On the way home, she warned Rob and Anne that mam had lost all her spirit. They had placed her bed in the living room so that she could see her garden and watch the people on the street.

When he entered the room, he hardly recognized her. She had lost a lot of weight, and the twinkle in her eye was gone, as was her never-failing smile. Looking the way she did, he did not need to ask her how she felt. The only thing he could do was to kiss her.

'Don't worry, mam. We'll get you back on your feet again.'

That same afternoon he phoned Werner and asked for another two weeks of leave before departing for Libya.

While he was preparing to visit his mam the next day, Werner Brandt called.

'Turn on your television. You'd better see this,' he said, and hung up.

Puzzled, Rob grabbed the remote control and turned on the television. The screen in front of him showed a scene of a burning platform. He peered at the television closely and turned up the volume with a sense of ill foreboding.

'...have confirmed that the platform where the disaster has taken place is located in the North Sea at about 150 miles North East of Aberdeen...' he heard the broadcaster say. 'To those working in the oil industry this platform is known as a drilling and production platform...'

Frantically he checked the different channels, but they all showed that same recorded scene, over and over again. Horrified, he watched the massive flames emerge from the platform, fanned by the incessant high winds.

'...and provides employment to more than two hundred men. Helicopter rescue operations are hampered by high winds, and the authorities fear that many lives will be lost...'

Could this be the platform Dieter was working on?

He grabbed the phone and called Dieter's home number. Helga, Dieter's wife, answered. She, too, had seen the news. Hardly coherent, Helga kept repeating tearfully that Dieter was on board, and she couldn't reach him.

All kinds of scenarios raced through his head. He knew that any survivors would have to be rescued by boat. The flames were too intense for any helicopter to even come close to the platform. The only hope he had was that his friend had managed to escape. The survivors would be brought to hospitals in Aberdeen, St. Fergus or Inverness.

He was unsure of what to do. Flying to Aberdeen was an option, but where would he stay? And how would he start to find his friend? He decided he had no choice but to wait, at least until the rescue boats and helicopters had returned to shore. He knew that if he or Helga did not hear from him within the next two days, he was probably dead.

He assured Helga that he would make inquiries and find out if Dieter was among the survivors. There was nothing else he could do, except hope that he ended up in a hospital somewhere. If that were the case, someone would surely call her.

He called Werner and told him that his friend was on board and asked if there was any news on survivors to let him know.

All he could do was to wait, and pray that somehow, his friend had managed to escape.

When Anne saw the news flashes, she was horrified.

'Oh my God, Rob. This could also happen to you!' she cried. 'I'm not watching any of this. This is going to give me nightmares. That could have been you out there, Rob. My God!' She disappeared into the kitchen and stayed there while he watched different channels nonstop, desperate to find out if there were any survivors.

In the evening Werner called to tell him that rescue boats and fishing vessels in the area had picked up several survivors.

Rob called Helga and relayed the news to her. Once again, he prayed that Dieter would be among them.

That night he didn't sleep and was glued to the television, simultaneously listening to British radio stations for the latest news on the disaster. He didn't get the call until late the next evening.

Dieter had survived and asked a nurse to call his friend from a hospital in Aberdeen, where he was being treated for smoke inhalation and severe burns to his hands. The nurse would notify Rob as soon as he was fit enough to travel.

Rob felt tremendously relieved and thanked God for protecting his friend. He called Helga straight away, telling her that he was alive and that he would be fine. Utterly exhausted and emotionally drained, he went to bed, whispered into Anne's ear that Dieter was alive and well, and fell asleep straight away.

The hospital called him in the afternoon of the following day, informing him that Dieter was declared fit to travel. Apparently Dieter had asked for Rob to pick him up from the hospital and take him home. Immediately he booked an early morning flight for the following day, as well as a one-way ticket for Dieter, departing on the last flight at four o'clock in the afternoon.

After having packed some spare clothes for Dieter, he went to bed early as he had a six a.m. flight. Upon his arrival in Aberdeen he took a taxi to the hospital, where one of the nurses took him to Dieter's ward.

Tears sprang to Dieter's eyes the moment he came in. Rob approached the bed. 'Dieter, it's so good to see you. How are you doing, my friend?'

Dieter reached out to him with his bandaged hand. 'Thanks, Rob, for saving my life.'

Rob didn't need to ask. 'You used the escape route and jumped?'

'Yes. I was one of the few that made it through that wall of fire.'

There was a painful silence as both men pondered the horror of it all. 'We'll talk about it later,' Rob said. 'Do you have any clothes to take with you?'

'No. The clothes I'm wearing were given to me by the hospital.'

'That's okay. If you want to change, I have clothes for you in my bag. What about your passport?'

'I always kept it in a waterproof pouch, together with some money, just in case.'

He grinned wryly. 'I hung it around my neck before I left my room. It's still legible,' he said as he gestured to the pouch on his bedside table.

'Did the company make arrangements for you to fly home?'

'Yes, they arranged a ticket for me.'

He went to the reception and asked the nurse to order a taxi, eager to take his friend on the next available flight back home. After the nurse had given Dieter instructions on how to treat the burns on his hands, Dieter changed and they quickly got into their cab for the airport and left through the back entrance, while reporters and television crews thronged at the front.

Once the airplane was at cruising altitude, Rob called the steward and ordered two whiskeys. They toasted to life and downed their drinks in one go.

'I need to tell you what happened,' Dieter began. 'You know, I haven't been able to sleep since it all happened. The images of those massive flames, the sound of people screaming. The explosions, everything.' He stared ahead, his eyes glazed by the memory of it.

'Remember when you told me to check out different escape routes?' Rob nodded his look somber. 'I did. I found the shortest possible route. There was this staircase going down from our sleeping quarters to the conductor level. I found fire-fighting suits, life jackets and breathing apparatus, all kinds of stuff stored in case of an emergency.' Dieter took a deep breath, coughing painfully as he exhaled. 'I used the docking side, where the supply boats come alongside. That was the fastest way down to the water level, and I went that route several times in the dark, until I was satisfied that I could always find my way down, whatever the circumstances.

'The morning of the explosion there was a shift-change at six. We pumped the standard amount of oil and gas to shore. Everything appeared to be under control.' He laughed bitterly before he continued. 'After I had a shower I went down for breakfast and returned to my cabin to get some rest. It was the explosion that woke me. It must have been around ten. The whole platform vibrated, Rob. It was huge!

'I jumped into my coverall and put on my boots. When I looked out of my window all I could see was flames. There were flames everywhere!' Dieter's staring eyes took on a frightened look, as if he could still see the flames all around him.

'I grabbed my passport and left my room. The corridor was filled with smoke, and there were men everywhere, running in all directions, panicking. I returned to my room and drenched my towel, which I wrapped around my face to breathe.

'The public address system wasn't working, would you believe that? It was supposed to give us instructions on what to do in such an emergency, and it wasn't even working.' He scowled. 'Only the emergency lights were on. When I opened the outer door I saw that the radio room on the helicopter deck was completely destroyed. Then I ran to the galley, to my muster station. There were men on the floor, gasping for air.

'The Offshore Installation Manager told everyone to stay inside,' he said bitterly. 'But I knew that man would be worthless in any emergency situation and decided to save my own life. Can you imagine it, Rob?' Dieter asked him, his despair obvious. 'It was like a herd of sheep waiting to be guided, but no shepherd.' Rob said nothing, mesmerized as he listened to his friend's terrible tale.

'When I came back outside there were three men. I shouted at them to follow me, which they did. We crawled down the stairs to the place where they kept the emergency stuff. We put on the suits, gloves and took the life jackets. I tore off a section of my towel and gave it to one of the men, the thick smoke made it nearly impossible for him to breathe. The other men pulled their sweaters over their face.

'There was fire everywhere. And so much smoke. We were lucky the wind cleared it from time to time, blowing it in different directions. We crawled down the stairs, level by level, to the production and the conductor deck. There we found the supply hoses and mooring rope station.'

He coughed before he went on, a dry, rasping cough. 'We quickly took off the fire-fighting suits, as they would have been too heavy in the water, and put on the life jackets. The mooring ropes were already burning by then, but there was no other way, because my hair was getting singed. So I grabbed one of the ropes and glided down as fast as I could.

'The other men were right behind me. When I reached the end of the mooring rope, I just jumped into the waves. While jumping I think another explosion took place because there was this enormous wall of fire, heading right towards me. It was then that I hit the water.' He coughed again, and he grabbed for the plastic cup of water on his tray.

'Even while I was below the surface, I could see this big orange light over my head. I just swam. I kept on swimming until I had to come up for air. When I resurfaced the heat was so intense that I had to dive back under, away from that terrible orange light.

'Everywhere around me chunks of steel hit the water. I was lucky I wasn't hit. Then there was another explosion on the helicopter deck. The flames must have been at least four hundred feet high. Never seen anything like it.

'I was lucky, Rob. I saw lights ahead of me. I screamed. Never screamed so loud in my life. Someone lifted me out of the water onto a rescue boat. I told them to look for the other three. Thank God they found them, as well.' He fell silent; shaking his head in disbelief at what had befallen him.

'I never want to go back to the U.K. again, Rob. Bunch of sickos. The government sets the profit they make from the oil and gas above the safety of its workers. You know, the men on the other platforms saw the disaster with their very own eyes! They could hear us on the radio frequency, screaming for help, panicking. Yet no one made the decision to stop the supply of oil and gas to us. And only because they were worried about the financial consequences and the time it would take them to re-start the production again.

'And you know what gets to me the most? There were plans to shut down the platform for major renovations.' He swore angrily under his breath. 'But of course someone found a way to make the platform look safer than it really was, on paper. So that production could continue while the modifications took place.

'The automatic fire-fighting pumps weren't even on. They were set on manual, because of diving operations. The government should never have issued the permits to simultaneously drill, produce and carry out major modifications on this platform. They should have put safety first. This was their fault, Rob. They knew the risks, and still they did nothing to eliminate them. No, production was more important!

'I told you I didn't like the simultaneous drilling and producing of wells, didn't I? There were about twenty wells out there, with no more than ten feet between them.

'I always thought it was too dangerous. They were drilling new wells while they were producing oil. What the hell were they thinking?' He toyed with the bag of smoked almonds on front of his tray.

'I only took this job because the money was more than I would ever make back in Germany. Fool that I was.' He looked through the window and stared at the clouds that seemed to fluff past them. Then he turned back to Rob.

'I don't need to tell you how grateful I am that you came for me. Please take me home, Rob. I want to see Helga.' Rob saw him blink away the tears.

'And I'll definitely need some time to recover from this...this apocalypse.'

They landed in Amsterdam, where Rob called Anne to let her know he was driving Dieter back to Germany. Dieter called Helga to tell her that he was on his way home.

As soon as they were on the highway, Dieter fell fast asleep. Even refueling at the gas station didn't wake him up.

He was still asleep when they arrived at his house near Frankfurt four hours later.

He didn't need to ring the doorbell—Helga saw them coming.

'You'd better wake him yourself,' he said with a smile, and waited in the house while she did.

As Rob drove back home, he listened to the news on the radio and realized how lucky Dieter had been.

He didn't know what to tell Anne, because his work involved drilling wells, which wasn't quite as dangerous as the simultaneous drilling and production that took place on Dieter's drilling and producing platform. With just drilling operations the danger of explosions was far smaller. Still, he knew that she would harangue him about it.

When he got home late at night, Anne had already prepared him a hot bath and they went to bed.

'We'll talk about it tomorrow,' was all she said to him before he fell asleep.

The next day he tried to explain to her the difference of drilling a single well or drilling a well and producing these wells at the same time from a drilling and production platform. With a small situation sketch, he showed her what happened at the platform and how Dieter had escaped.

'So he made you a promise, and it saved his life.'

'Yes.'

Flowers arrived in the morning bearing a small card that said: 'Thank you for saving my Dieter and bringing him home.'

During the remaining time, he spent every minute with his mam, showing her the films and pictures that he had taken in Saudi. Anne spoiled her, preparing the dishes that she enjoyed the most. However, he did notice that his father wasn't happy that Anne had taken over the household. He could sense more than just a little friction between the two.

Rob left for Libya, where he boarded a DC3 charter in Tripoli together with drilling contractor and other service personnel. It turned out the plane was chartered by the company on a permanent basis, constantly flying in and out of the desert, and was kept on standby in case of emergency. After landing in the desert, a Land Rover took them to the campsite.

After a brief explanation of the hand-over notes, his colleague left and boarded the same Land Rover and plane. It took Rob that whole night to review the drilling program to get a clear picture of the upcoming drilling operations. The new rig just started rigging up the drilling equipment and derrick to start the first well. As he was going through the reports, he found that there had already been a number of accidents.

In the morning he called the tool pusher and the driller on duty into his office to question them about the accidents. They told him that these accidents took place because of the large number of new hires. Some of them had hardly any experience, they said.

For Rob, this simply wasn't satisfactory. He showed them his sequence sheets for assembling the rig and asked the tool pusher to update the sheets and to include all recent failures and accidents. He did the same with the nightshift driller when he reported for work. In no uncertain terms, he told each driller that they were in charge of the rig up operations. They had to involve all personnel in the planning of every single rig up sequence.

The next few days he spent most of his time observing the work, constantly checking if it was planned and carried out according to the sequence sheets.

His efforts paid off as for the remainder of that week there were no incidents.

But things in Libya were different from what he was accustomed to. Of course he knew from experience that not every person was willing to spend that much time and effort to get optimum results. He worked with supervisors who believed they could manage their work without leaving their office chairs, leaving actual supervision to the contractors.

The problem was that it was the supervisor's responsibility to make sure drilling operations were carried out in a safe and cost-efficient way, while the contractor's main concern was the day rate. Leaving the daily supervision to contractors was asking for trouble.

Rob soon found out that the local drilling contractor never reported incidents or mistakes that took place. He found the Libyan crews lazy, arrogant and dishonest. Equipment and tools went missing, so he decided to store these in locked containers.

He discovered that the Libyans regarded all non-Muslims with hostility, in sharp contrast to the locals in Saudi Arabia, who were always eager to learn and pleasant to work with. There was no phone connection, and hardly any time to write home, because he was fully occupied with his work. He found those first four weeks grueling, and was only too happy flying back home.

Chapter 10

When Anne picked him up from Schiphol airport, her face looked grim. 'Your mother is in hospital,' she told him with a frown. 'She's broken her hip for no apparent reason. The doctor informed us that she has bone cancer, and your father told her, just like that, without even thinking what it would do to her. She's absolutely terrified.' She fell quiet and threw him a glance. 'You've no idea what it's been like while you were away, Rob,' she went on. 'Your father is being so difficult about me doing things around the house. I can't seem doing anything right. I don't even think he wants me there. I honestly don't know how much longer I'll be able to stand this.'

Somewhat bewildered by her words, he assured her things would be all right, after which they drove to the hospital in silence. His entrance into his mother's room seemed to open her emotional floodgate. She started crying the minute he came in, and he could hardly understand a word of what she was saying until she calmed down.

'I thought I was going to be all right, Rob,' she said. 'I believed after the breast removal that they had the cancer under control. But now…now that I've been diagnosed with bone cancer, oh God! There's no hope.' She covered her face with her hands. 'I just want to go home, Rob,' she said between sobs. 'But your father wants me to stay in hospital—he says that I'd be better off here so that I'll get optimal treatment.'

Unsettled by this turn of events, Rob asked to see the doctor and inquired if it would even be possible for her to go home.

'I'm sorry, but there really isn't much more that we can do for her here,' the doctor said. 'If she can get proper care at home, there is no reason to keep her here.'

Rob drove to Agnes' house, where they discussed the situation and agreed that the best solution was to take her home. But when he returned home, he found that his father was insistent that she stay in the hospital.

'No. Mam wants to come home,' he said. 'Even her doctor agrees it's for the best. Anne and Agnes can take care of her here.'

'No!' his father said. 'This is my responsibility. I will take care of her myself. This is something between your mother and me. Stay out of this! You, Agnes and Anne!'

'No, I won't stay out of this!

'That's just not what she wants!' he shouted, frustrated that his emotions had caused him to lose his temper. It was the first big argument between them, ever.

'Can't you just do this for her? She's dying, don't you see? God, you're being so bloody selfish! Mam really wants to come home. For God's sake, can't you do this for her?' he shouted angrily.

'How dare you...'

'Oh shut up. I'm not a child anymore. Christ. I had really hoped that we would be able to work this out. That we would be able to live together, just like we used to. But this...this is no good. This isn't right for Anne or the baby. We'll just have to find some other place to live!' And with that he slammed the door.

In the bedroom he found Anne crying because she had heard most of the argument.

After talking it through, they found that there was only one solution. Anne called her dad and asked if it would be alright for them to come over. He said that he be delighted if they did, and coffee would be ready for them. They left the house without a word to Rob's father, and when they arrived, they explained the problem.

'You're both welcome anytime, and you can stay as long as you want.'

The next morning they moved in with Anne's dad.

When they went grocery shopping later that week, they ran into Marie, a very good friend of Rob's mam in front of the bakery. Rob greeted her warmly and introduced her to Anne.

'Very nice to meet you, dear,' she said. She seemed uncomfortable, hesitant. 'Rob, can I please talk to you in private?'

'Of course,' he said, somewhat surprised. He looked at Anne, who immediately walked into the supermarket.

'This is very difficult for me to say, Rob,' she said with a frown, 'but I really think you should know. I like to visit your mother in hospital, but... oh dear, this is really embarrassing. Rob, I've seen your father with another woman, at this hotel. I don't know her, she's obviously from out of town, but... it was rather obvious. Your mam knows me too well and she'll know immediately something is wrong the minute she sees me. I've never been able to keep secrets from your mum. I feel awful about it.'

So that was the reason his father wanted Mam to stay in hospital, Rob thought angrily. He thanked Marie and promised not to say anything about it to his mam.

Instead of going to the hospital that morning, they went to see Agnes, who wasn't exactly surprised at the news. 'I'll visit her tonight,' he told her. 'We'll meet again tomorrow.'

His mam knew something was wrong the moment he entered.

'You didn't visit this morning,' she stated matter-of-factly. 'You had an argument with your father about me, didn't you?'

He couldn't lie to her. 'Yes,' he said. 'We've moved out, Mam. We're staying with Anne's dad.'

She took his hands 'Oh no,' she said, shaking her head stubbornly. 'I don't want to be the reason that something goes wrong with Anne and the baby. I'll stay in the hospital.'

He felt a surge of resentment towards his father for being the cause of their predicament. Right now, he wanted to do all he could to make the remaining days of her life as pleasant and comfortable as she deserved.

'Mam, I know we've had our ups and downs and I find it hard to say this. I don't like to stand between you and father, but if you don't want to stay in the hospital then we'll get you out. You can stay with Agnes if that's what you want, but if you do we'll have a problem with father. He will never accept that. But you should also realize that the hospital might not be able to keep you here, that they need the room for other patients. And then you'll have to go home anyway.'

He saw the despair and helplessness in her eyes, and he felt sorry for her, but the decision had to be hers.

She took his hands in her own. 'Rob, you're my son. You've always supported me whenever you could. But you've got your own family now. I don't want to interfere in your lives. I love my home. I enjoy looking at the garden, to see people passing by on the street waving at me. I want my grandchildren to come and visit me as often as they can. They bring so much joy in my life!' Her eyes lit up for a fleeting moment as she spoke of them. 'Please ask the doctor to tell your father there is no reason for me to stay here. He'll just have to take me home and care for me.'

Of course the doctor respected her wishes: he was of the firm opinion that it was important that she should stay in an environment that she felt most comfortable in. The doctor called his father to inform him that she would be coming home the next day. But when he went back to his mother to tell her the news, her reaction was one of indifference.

'Before you go, Rob,' she said. 'Gertie is here. In the room next to mine.'

He looked at her, startled. 'Gertie?'

His mother nodded. 'Just go and say hello.'

He kissed her goodbye and stood in the door opening of the next room, wondering if Gertie would recognize him. With her eyes shut, she seemed asleep and he observed her for a while. Just when he wanted to leave she opened her eyes.

'Rob! My God.' Softly she began to cry.

'Gertie, are you alright?'

'Yes, Just a routine procedure, nothing more. I heard your mother was staying here, so I went to see her.' She looked at him and bit her quivering lip. 'Oh Rob. I'm so, so sorry,' she said between sobs. 'You know, I've never forgotten you. I made a mistake back then. I should never have listened to my parents. God, what a fool I was, but I have to live with that decision every single day.'

Rob didn't know what to say. He shook her hand, holding on to it just a little bit longer out of sympathy.

'Goodbye Gertie, I wish you all the best.'

Rob drove home to pick up Anne, and together they went to see Agnes to tell her about Mam's decision. They were now faced with a dilemma: it was her wish to go home, yet they knew that father didn't want her there. Still, they made a schedule for the children to visit during the week and agreed that Rob and Anne would come to see her in the evenings. They all agreed it would be best if Agnes helped with the household chores, especially considering the friction between father and Anne.

They ordered a special hospital bed to be delivered the next morning, which was to be placed in the living room so she would be able to raise the backrest herself, enjoy the garden and watch the people passing in the street.

The following morning Rob and Anne arrived on the doorstep with flowers, because Agnes had told them that she preferred to come by bicycle.

Rob tried his key, but for some reason he wasn't able to unlock the door. Puzzled, he had to give up and rang the doorbell.

'Hi,' he greeted his father. 'Something wrong with the lock? Can't seem to get the key in.'

'That's because I changed it,' his father told him bluntly. 'I'd prefer that no one comes into the house without my permission.'

Rob stared at him, speechless. He couldn't believe it. This was, after all, his house.

He didn't know what to say, but did not want to make an issue at that moment.

Not now, just before his mam was about to arrive.

The hospital bed was delivered and placed before the window. When his mam arrived by ambulance half an hour later, everyone tried to act normal, as if nothing had happened. But in reality they were all tense. Rob knew that his father was furious for overruling him by arranging for his mam to come home. And Rob was still furious that his father had changed the lock.

In spite of the tension between them, they had lunch and discussed the visit schedule they had made. His mam urged Agnes to send the children to come and visit her as often as was possible. They left, promising to come back that same evening.

In the car Rob exhaled audibly, releasing the pent-up anger he had felt in the house.

'I want to look for a place to live, Anne. For you, the baby and me.'

While having coffee they told Anne's dad what had happened. While Anne was preparing dinner in the kitchen, Rob asked him if he knew of any properties that were for sale in the area, as Anne might prefer to live in her hometown. After all, he worked at the local council's finance department and might know if something was available.

But his father-in-law was a cautious man, and he warned him to do nothing rash, considering the economic turndown that Europe was going through.

He was right. The Arab states had decreased their oil production, which had led to sharp increases in oil and gas prices. The government had even proclaimed a number of car-free Sundays, allowing no cars on the roads with the exception of emergency vehicles. Drilling prospects in Holland were not good, especially with activists demonstrating against drilling in certain parts of the country. These activists believed that drilling was unsafe and harmful to the environment, and they had set up barricades at various drilling locations.

But after the first car-free Sunday, the barricades were removed and the oil companies were allowed to drill wells in those areas once again.

The housing market was still in a recession; however, Anne's dad did know that there were a number of building plots for sale. 'You want me to arrange a meeting with my colleague?' he asked.

'Yes, that would be great,' Rob said, and an appointment was made for the next day.

Anne's dad was delighted to have his daughter at home. She surprised him with her cooking skills. Cooking was something that he had always done before she had left for Saudi, while she took care of the washing and cleaning of the house.

Now she was preparing meals for him, such as meatballs with potatoes and boiled red cabbage, knowing that it was one of his favorite meals.

Not only did he enjoy her cooking, he watched in admiration how Anne was gradually growing towards motherhood. To him, she looked more and more like his deceased wife, who had meant the world to him. He never told her, but when she had left to start a new life with Rob he had become depressed again. He had no longer seen the point of living anymore.

But when she had called him to say that she was expecting a child everything changed—he was about to become a granddad. He was being given the opportunity to witness the growing up of his daughter's child. It was something he would fly across the world to see. And now she was home again.

Of course he knew that this was only a temporary arrangement. They would want a place for themselves, for sure. However, if he could be of any help in finding them a house in his town, he would be more than happy to. He looked at her, his emotions getting the better of him.

'What's wrong, Dad?' Anne asked, concerned.

'Nothing. I'm just very happy that you're here. I enjoy seeing you both—you know that.'

She came over and kissed him gently on the forehead. 'We will all have to enjoy every minute of being together. Who knows where we will end up in the future? Especially with Rob's job.'

Rob glanced at her. 'So where would you like to live? I can always continue to work abroad as drilling supervisor, because after four weeks I fly home again.'

'I followed you to Saudi. You know that wasn't the happiest time of my life, being away from Dad, friends and family. Thank God for Waltraud, though, she helped me through a difficult patch.' She smiled at him. 'But as you're asking, I'd like to raise our children in this small, homey village. Where everyone knows and helps each other in times of need. I was always happy here, Rob.'

'Well that's clear enough for me. Your dad has made an appointment for us with his colleague at the property office. Tomorrow we'll see if there are any lots available in this village to build a home for our family.'

She looked at them both with open mouth. 'So when did you discuss this? Rob, how can we effort a second home? We won't be able to afford two mortgages. I know you earn well, but that's just too much.'

'Let's just wait and find out what's available, then we'll see and start counting money.'

After dinner they set off to see his mam.

'Try not to get an argument with your father,' Anne warned him. 'It will only make things more difficult for your mam.'

When he rang the doorbell of his own house, he could feel his anger rising, but Anne threw him a warning look, so he tried not to lose his temper.

Agnes opened the door. 'Come in,' she said, smiling. 'Dad's out playing soccer.'

Rob and Anne were both relieved. At last they had a chance to talk to Mam without having to watch their tongues, without having to play-act.

Mam said she was feeling much better now that she was home again.

'It makes me so happy to see the grandchildren. They make me laugh and distract me from the pain. The neighbors came to see me this morning, and guess what? My dear friend Marie is coming to visit me tomorrow, and that's something else I'm looking forward to. And people are calling Agnes to set appointments to come by.'

But then she grew suddenly serious.

'Do either of you know anything about a woman coming to this house?' Everyone was stunned and silent. 'I can tell, you know. I smell a different perfume. And it isn't mine.' She searched their faces, her eyes shrewd. No one said anything. She turned to Rob, and he knew that he wasn't going to tell her anything. This was something between his parents. Telling her what he knew would only make things worse. Frustrated, he left the house for the soccer fields, where he asked around for his father.

'Well, his team is on tonight, but he's not playing,' someone told him.

Enraged, he drove home, and told Anne about his discovery. 'What can I do?'

'You promised Marie you wouldn't say anything. I'll call Agnes and ask her to be there when Marie visits your mam. If Marie decides to tell her, then that's her decision. And if she does, your mam will need all the support she can get.'

'You won't have to, because Agnes told me that she and Marie are visiting her together, so we'll see what happens.'

Chapter 11

The next morning they cycled to the local council for their appointment.

When they entered Rob saw a familiar face behind the reception desk.

The man's face lit up when he saw him. 'Rob! Good lord, it has been a long time,' he said enthusiastically as he shook his hand. 'How are you? Don't you remember me? I'm Piet. We used to live in the same street when we were kids.'

Then Rob remembered. The man in front of him was none other than the boy who had lived a few blocks away from him when he was living in that dark and noisy house, next to the dry cleaner's. Piet had taught him how to read music and sing in the church choir.

By sheer coincidence, it turned out that Anne knew him, as well. They had met at the local council New Year's party, which she sometimes attended with her dad.

Piet didn't waste any time and showed them an overview of the village and building sites with lots for sale.

'Personally, I'd recommend this lot,' he said as he pointed to a marked space on the plan. 'It was purchased two years ago, but it's on sale again because its previous owners couldn't afford to build a house. All additional costs such as taxes have already been paid. It's still available for the initial price, which is 20% less than the asking price for similar lots. The price is 28.500 Dutch guilders for 1200 square meters. It is situated in an established part of town with schools and facilities close by.'

'What type of house could I build there?' asked Rob. 'I know of a German construction company that builds excellent prefabricated houses.'

'Really?' Piet said, his interest piqued. 'We would be pleased to talk about it. It so happens we're looking into such houses right now. They are highly energy-efficient, which is a priority for us for the coming years. I'll try and find out if you would get subsidized for this type of construction and let you know tomorrow.'

Rob looked at the plan on the table. 'Can we get an option on this lot while we check our finances?'

'Sure. We'll keep this lot on hold until you've decided.'

As they cycled home, Anne was even more excited than he was. 'Let's go and see for ourselves where the property is. I know that area and I'd absolutely love to live there.

It's got everything you'd want, Rob. Lovely houses, young families, schools, swimming and sport facilities, and it's close to the forest.'

He laughed out loud. 'Alright, you show me where it is then. And who's getting excited here? Yesterday you're the one who was worried about the finance and now you're practically already living there. But I must admit, I quite like the prefab idea. Dieter also built a house like that and he's very happy with it. I looked with him at prefabricated houses in Germany, and I must say the quality impressed me. I remember we visited a street full of model homes in the Frankfurt area. The floor plans can be changed any way you want. It doesn't take long to build such houses, as all sections are prefabricated. They only have to mount the sections together, and usually you can move in within two months.'

They cycled on, each of them lost in their own train of thoughts. 'Yes, I like the idea,' he mused, not noticing the smile on his wife's lips. 'I always did want a home that doesn't depend on public utilities. I could drill my own water well and purchase a generator so that we'll have power, no matter what happens. These houses are very well-insulated and suited for the German climate. The more I think about it, the more I like it. The only disadvantage is that brick houses probably last longer.

Mind you, Klaus will be too busy these days building standard brick houses to scrape a living. He won't have time to build another house with me, so this is most probably the best option for us.'

Anne grinned at him as they took a corner. 'See, who is already building the house? But what are we going to do about money?'

'Hum, yes. Where to get the money. I did save enough to buy the land, but not enough to build the house. But perhaps I married a rich woman?' he teased. 'Or did you spend all your money? I remember we told each other that money isn't important, as all our expenses were paid for in Saudi, but now I need to know. Rich or poor?'

She blushed a lovely pink, and Rob was reminded why he had fallen in love with her in the first place.

'I'm neither rich nor poor. I did save some money while working at the bank, but that's not enough to build the house. I'll check my savings account tomorrow, smart guy,' she said as she saw his grin. She knew how he loved to see her blush.

They arrived in the street and saw an empty lot of land. They liked the location straightaway, as the sun would shine on the back yard nearly the whole day. Pleased with what they saw, they cycled around the immediate area, where they came past the school, the sports grounds and through the forest on their way back home.

When they got home Anne's dad prepared tosti's, grilled ham and cheese sandwiches, something they hadn't had for a while. 'So how did your appointment go? You were gone a long time.'

'It went well,' Anne said. 'Very well, in fact. There's a lot available at a good location, so we just went by to see it. We like it, Dad. The only thing is the finance. Rob has sufficient money to buy the lot, and I'd have to check my savings account, but I doubt it will cover the construction costs for the house.'

Her dad smiled. 'I wouldn't worry about that. You should have enough money.'

She looked at him, puzzled. 'Me? No way. I did save some money while I worked at the bank, but that won't be near enough.'

'Maybe. But I've been putting money aside for you into a Zilvervloot account ever since you were three. It's a special savings account for children. The bank pays ten percent interest on top of the standard interest rate until you turn eighteen. Now that you're twenty-two, you should have...' He screwed up his face as he did the mental math, 'About 100.000 guilders. I hope that's enough to build your home. I never told you about it, because I'd always meant it for something like this: a home of your own.'

Rob and Anne looked at each other, stunned.

'So you are a rich woman after all!' Rob said. They all burst out laughing.

After their excitement subsided, Rob suggested that Anne take a rest while he went to see his mam. He knew Anne didn't sleep well lately, as she often felt the baby move, keeping her awake at night.

He was in an excellent mood as he drove into Germany, still buoyed by the news that they might have enough money after all. Now they could start planning. He knew that money would be tight for the next couple of years, but if they saved every penny they might be able to build the house.

Agnes opened the door for him, already there with Marie and the kids. In the hallway she whispered to him that Mam knew about the woman their father was seeing.

Marie had told her, but she had taken it rather well. Now that this was out in the open, Marie promised to come and see her as often as she could.

He greeted his mam and told her about the lot of land that they were thinking of buying, and asked his sister, 'Agnes, is Klaus home this evening? I'd love to hear his opinion about a home.'

'Sure, you can come over after dinner if you like.'

His mam was delighted. 'Now I won't have to feel so guilty about you having to leave the house,' she said. 'So if everything goes according to plan, you can move into your new home before the baby is born?'

'I hope so. But it's a lot of work, and Anne and the baby are already getting restless. We have to drive to Frankfurt to check out the model homes to see which type we'd like.'

That evening he went to see Klaus, who was enthusiastic about the plan. He confirmed that the quality of the prefabricated houses he was looking into was very good, and recommended they consider building a basement, as this would provide them with a lot of additional space.

'Do you need work?' Rob asked. 'I hear the construction business is slow these days.'

'Yes, times are a tough. I've had to lay off some of my crew.'

'Would you be interested in building the basement for us?'

'Sure. It would help me get my crew back to work and see me through.'

'How long would it take you to build a basement with these dimensions?' He gestured at the diagrams on the table.

'Four weeks and I'll only charge you for the labor, which would cost you about 35.000 guilders at the most.'

'That sounds good. Okay, let's do this. I like the idea of additional space. We could also use the basement as a shelter. I'd like to divide the basement into compartments so we can live in it, say, with two bedrooms, a kitchen, a bathroom and a living room. Just to be on the safe side, with all this talk about a nuclear war.'

'If you could provide me with a sketch for the basement, I'd appreciate it. It will save me having to get an architect.'

'Sure. The local council shouldn't pose a problem, as I have good contacts with the people there.'

By the time Agnes came in with coffee, the two of them had reached an agreement. She smiled, pleased that they could help each other in these difficult times.

When he discussed the plans with Anne, she was more than happy to leave it all to him and Klaus, as they had built homes before. 'But I do have one wish: I want a bedroom and bathroom downstairs. When we get old and feeble I don't want to climb stairs like your mam did.'

'I thought you said that you'd leave the building decisions to us.'

'Yes, but I do want a say on the layout and the colors.'

'You'll see plenty of layouts and colors when we visit the model homes next week. That reminds me. I have to call Dieter after dinner. '

He caught Dieter just in time before he left for work. Dieter had accepted an operator job in one of the power distribution plants near his hometown because he needed the money. Helga was happy to have him home at last, but he hated the job and was still having nightmares. He didn't sound at all happy to Rob. To change the subject, he told Dieter of his plans to build a new house. Dieter was more than helpful and provided him useful tips on how to build the basement.

Because he only had three more weeks before going back to work, it was important that the building permit was in place and the prefabricated house ordered.

The following morning Anne woke up very early because the baby kept her awake, so they decided to leave for Frankfurt to visit the model homes. Anne made coffee and sandwiches for the journey, while Rob turned down the seat for her so she could get some sleep. Anne slept throughout the trip, until he pulled up in front of the model homes. As they were too early, the office was still closed, so they ate the sandwiches and finished the coffee. Then they walked around, looking at the variety of houses that were on display. And every time they kept returning to the same one: it had everything that they could wish for. Rob had never seen this type of house before.

The exterior was a mix between the Old Dutch and German style farm houses that Rob liked.

'It's beautiful. I can't wait to see the inside.'

'Let's see if the office is open.'

After they had discussed their wish list and been shown around the different houses, they had to make their choice.

'So which house did you like best?' the saleswoman asked them at the end.

Rob looked at Anne, and she just nodded her head.

'I think I can speak for the both of us. We particularly like the last one you showed us.'

'Shall I give you some more time to think about it, or would you like to discuss the price and conditions now?'

'I think we've already made up our mind,' Rob said, as he smiled at Anne.

'We'd like to place the order.'

By the time they had discussed the necessary details, and Rob had signed the purchase order, it was well into the afternoon. Rob was supplied with the necessary paperwork to apply for the building permit and was told to confirm the order within one week. They still had to choose materials, as the house came complete with heating and lighting. The rest of that day they looked at samples of floors, kitchen and bathroom tiles, and they were given catalogues and samples to look at back home.

It was late in the evening when they finally left Frankfurt. The minute they were on the Autobahn, Anne fell asleep utterly exhausted. Two hours later she woke up.

'I dreamt that we were living in the house already. It felt good,' she told him.

'Keep on dreaming, darling. We've made most of decisions now. Now we'll have to find out how rich you are to see if we can actually afford the house with the basement.'

'I'll check tomorrow. I'll also find out if the bank I used to work for can offer me special mortgage rates as a former employee. Just in case we do need another mortgage.'

'This is getting better every day, my dear finance director.'

'I feel very good about what we did today. My dream seemed quite real, you know.

'Rob?' She gave him a flirtatious look. 'I've never made love in a car before.'

'Are you serious? At one o'clock at night?'

'I had a good rest this morning, and I just slept in the car. Just stop the car somewhere private.'

He did as he was told, found a secluded place and put the seats down. Anne felt very excited and surprised herself how much she had changed. She would have never thought of herself doing anything like this. She had come to love all possible variations when making love, and found that she would do anything for Rob.

He had to be careful with her bump, but the thrill of having sex in the car added to their pleasure.

When they finally drove home it was nearly daylight, and Anne fell asleep with her head on his lap.

While Rob studied the technical drawings and information, Anne looked at the samples of wood, tiles and paint colors. Her dad came home for lunch to tell them that they would be granted a subsidy of five thousand guilders as an incentive to build the first energy-efficient, prefabricated house.

While Anne visited the bank, Rob went to see his mam to show her the catalogues and house plan. She told him that she had problems lying on the bed in the same position for long periods of time, so Anne had given her the lambskin that her mother had used when she was ill to prevent bedsores. The doctor was scheduled to come the next day and they would discuss the matter with him.

On his way back he dropped in to see Piet at the council to confirm the purchase of the property. Rob explained that it was important to get the permit in place as soon as possible, as they wanted to move in before the baby was born.

'I'll do whatever I can,' Piet said. 'It's good to see you both move back to your home town again.'

Anne opened the door for him when he got back, eager to show him her savings account and the amount her dad had put aside for her as a child. For fiscal reasons, and because Anne could get special interest rates as a former bank employee, they decided to take an additional mortgage. They agreed that having a house with a basement was worth living frugally for a number of years.

The following day they studied the documents and looked at samples and appliances, choosing what they wanted to the last electrical socket. They decided on oak-style doors and agreed to include awnings on the outside. Rob wanted a fireplace equipped with a piping system so that it could provide hot water for the central heating when in use.

Once Klaus had checked that everything was in good order, Rob and

Anne returned to Frankfurt to finalize the last details. This time they took their time going through the model home of their choice.

'Is this our dream home or can you think of anything else?' Rob asked.

'Let's just do this.'

Once everything was finalized, they set a construction date because the house had to be finished one month before the expected birth of their first child.

The Marketing Manager opened a bottle of champagne, and together with everyone else that had been involved in the purchasing process, they toasted to their new home.

On their way back to Holland they stopped to have dinner in a small town next to the Autobahn. Rob had not tasted sauerkraut for a long time and knew a restaurant that was famous for it. After their meal they walked back to the car. He looked at her questioningly. 'The same procedure as last year my dear?' He was referring to a German comedy show that was on television every New Year's Eve. It was about a grand lady and her butler, drinking too much alcohol on New Year's Eve. After dinner her butler would ask: 'The same procedure as last year, my dear?' to which her answer would be 'Yes' and he would carry her upstairs and make love to her.

Anne smiled at him. 'Yes, my dear. The same procedure as last year.'

He drove to the same secluded parking lot as last time, where they made love once more.

Chapter 12

During his last week home, Rob made sure that Piet obtained the building permit so Klaus could start on the basement. With Anne he went through the finances one more time, and with that complete, everything seemed to be under control.

Mam's health did worry him, though. Her morphine dosage was increased to ease the pain, so she was only aware of what happened around her part of the time. Now that his departure for Libya drew nearer, it was important that he speak to her while she was still lucid, so he asked the doctor what he could do. He did not like what the man had to say.

The doctor told him, in no uncertain terms, that his mam had no more than six months to live. The only thing they could do for her was to relieve the pain and make the remaining time that was left to her as comfortable as possible.

Devastated, Rob left the doctor's practice and walked to church, where he lit a candle for her and prayed to the holy Mother Mary, to whom his mam was devoted.

He asked her to let his mam live as long as possible. Seeing the statuette of Mary, he was reminded of Lourdes, the town in France where Mary had made herself visible to a girl named Bernadette, which drew thousands of sick people looking for a miraculous cure. It was then that he decided that his mam should go there.

When he suggested his idea to Agnes later that day, she agreed that their mam deserved this change, and she took it upon herself to arrange the trip.

Mam's eyes lit up with joy when they told her that she would go to Lourdes.

That alone made their efforts worthwhile. They had given her hope again: she was a devout Catholic and a firm believer in the powers of the holy waters of Lourdes.

She would be taken in an ambulance on a three-day-trip in the company of other Catholics who were also sick, accompanied by nurses and supplied with all the medical equipment they might need.

When the time came to leave for Libya, Rob found it more difficult than ever to say goodbye to his mam, remembering what the doctor had told him. He was only comforted by the fact that she was in good hands with Agnes, Klaus and Anne. He could do nothing else except pray.

As Anne drove him to the airport, she knew how he was feeling about leaving his mam behind like this. 'We'll take care of her, I promise.'

'You also need to take care of yourself. This whole situation is also affecting you, Anne. If you were to lose the baby…I'd never forgive myself.'

'I know that, Rob,' Anne assured him. 'Dad said the same. He applied for early retirement, and the decision will be made next week. If approved he'll be able to help me out a bit more.'

Rob nodded. 'That would be good. Same procedure as last year, then?'

'No, sir! All you're getting now is a kiss. We'll save that procedure for when you get back in four weeks' time. Please take care of yourself. Stay focused on your work, darling. I want you back in one piece. That's all that's important to me.'

He grabbed his bag from the backseat and kissed her once more before leaving the car. He turned around one last time, waved and entered the airport.

He could not sleep on the flight. Too much had happened the last few weeks, and he needed time to digest it all.

When he arrived in Tripoli he was subjected to a very humiliating body search.

His luggage was searched minutely, and once again he had the feeling of being unwelcome. All around him, he could sense the hostility of the locals towards Westerns.

Back in the desert, he was once again in charge of drilling operations, and it struck him how very differently the work had been carried out during his absence. Most of the drilling supervisors he'd met took their job and responsibility seriously and regarded their work as a challenge. But his relief had left the control in the hands of the contracted tool pusher, whose main concern, as he expected, was payment of the day rate.

The reports showed that no repairs took place during the last four weeks with no time used for the minimal amount of maintenance. From the moment he was back in charge, the time required to carry out standard operations had changed. More repairs and additional maintenance was required. He didn't want to interfere, because that was the job of the drilling manager in Tripoli. If he read these reports, he was bound to notice the difference and had to take corrective action.

Then someone discreetly told him that his relief played cards the whole day with the mud engineer. That at least explained why there was no supervision while drilling.

The six-pen recorder was frequently out of order, so he had to carry out on the spot checks at varying times to observe the operations and asked for the recorder to be replaced. He vowed that if ever he were to become a drilling manager again, he would only select and recruit motivated drilling supervisors.

The only way he could talk to Anne was through the radio, so anyone listening in on the same frequency could follow their conversations. They kept their calls to a minimum and only discussed what was important. The main thing that mattered was that Anne and the baby were doing alright.

In the meantime his mam had visited Lourdes, but there had been no miracle cure. The doctor increased her morphine dosage again. Klaus had started work on the basement, which should be finished by the time he came home. If all went well the building permit would be approved as well.

During all his working years, he found it quite easy to separate work and his private life, having grown accustomed to switching off the minute he stepped on the plane to go home, and vice versa.

It was his mam whom he depended on to take care of things at home while he was at work, until Anne came into his life. Now he depended on Anne. Somehow he wanted to put life at home on hold until his return, so that he wouldn't miss out on anything. Yet he also found his work situation comfortable the way it was: living with Anne for a period of time, knowing that he could leave again for a number of weeks, because she accepted this as part of their life. It worked well for them. They had discussed this in their letters and during the first months of their marriage in Saudi. He found it important, as many of his colleagues' wives didn't like being alone for weeks. That affected the men's focus at work, and usually such marriages ended up either in divorce or they had to look for work at home to do a job that they probably didn't like.

Whenever there were home issues that bothered him, he would take a long walk into the desert and search for rare pieces of petrified wood or geodes, egg-shaped stones that were lined on the inside with crystals.

Three weeks of drilling went by without any problems. The drilling manager informed him that his previous relief would not return to Libya, and they had appointed someone else. The replacement was scheduled to start work immediately so that he would have a week overlap before Rob went home.

When his relief arrived, Rob took him through the daily routines, and after a few days he had a good feeling that operations were about to change for the better.

Anne was waiting for him at Amsterdam Schiphol. On their way home she filled him in on everything that had taken place in his absence, talking nonstop for two hours until they stopped in front of their new property.

The basement was finished and preparations had taken place to install the concrete floor on top.

Rob talked to Klaus briefly, and they agreed to see each other that same evening.

He hardly recognized his mam when he came in. Seeing his expression at the sight of her, she became very emotional.

'It's good to know that you're still happy to see me when I come home,' he joked.

'My dear, I pray every day to our holy Mother Mary for your safe return. I'm always grateful whenever I see you walk through that door.'

'I've got a whole four weeks to spend with you, Mam.'

'And I'll need every single day.'

After lunch he went home. While helping Anne do the dishes he brushed against her hip, suddenly feeling a strong desire for her. They made love on the kitchen table, and he marveled at the passion that he felt.

'I missed you terribly,' he said as he caressed her shoulder. 'Every single night I long for you, but if this is the reward I get for having to miss you for so long, then it's worth it.'

'It's good to have you back. It felt as if I just shed all my pent-up feelings with you. As if I was in heaven.'

'Then let's try and take that route again.' So they went upstairs and did, until they fell asleep in each other's arms.

Early in the morning they had breakfast together, after which Rob changed into his work gear and cycled to the building site were Klaus and his crew were already at work. Rob apologized to him for not coming to see him the night before, but Klaus understood and took him downstairs into the basement, where he showed him every room.

'Wow. You did an excellent job. It's exactly as I imagined it would be. How much time will you need to finish the concrete floor? I'll need to inform the prefab company so they can come and do the measurements for the wall latches.'

'I'll probably need another week.'

'Good. Then I can help you finish the concrete floor.'

'Even better. I'll need every pair of hands I can get.'

Within a week they finished the concrete floor, and the prefab company came to the site to indicate the locations for the house's anchoring points. In the evening he showed Mam pictures of the progress they were making. She was in a lot of pain and kept on a maximum amount of morphine. Sometimes she was quite lucid and followed the discussions without any problems, but more often her mind would wander, and she would seem far away in some fantasy world where she could not be reached.

One evening she told him that she wanted so desperately to be loved and desired, but that his father refused to even touch her. This grieved her so much that it nearly broke her heart. Selfishly, he wished that she hadn't told him that. He had already long time ago taken a strong dislike to his father, but now he resented him even more.

It took a few weeks for the concrete foundation to harden, so he had to accept that the house would be installed a week after his next arrival. As most of his furniture was still in his house in Germany, they would have to buy certain essentials. In Saudi Anne had already shown that she had a good eye and the ability to make a home attractive and comfortable with a tight budget, so he left it to her to make the necessary purchases, which were to be delivered once the house was in place.

When Rob returned to Libya he found that there had been major mud loss problems and much time had been lost in trying to solve these. In the four weeks that he had been away, only small sections of the shale formation had been drilled, as it was too porous, resulting in mud losses. Every section they drilled had to be sealed off with cement, but this required time and caused costly delays.

Rob made a suggestion to the geologist that they drill the remaining shale sections with water instead of mud, which would allow them to seal the complete shale section with casing and cement. They sent the proposal to the Tripoli office and obtained approval to proceed accordingly.

By the time Rob left the rig to go on leave, they were ready to drill the last hole section. Everyone was holding his breath, in the hope that they could confirm the geologist's predictions and discover the oil sands. Over the years, Rob's experience was that the most problematic wells usually produced the biggest amounts of oil. It was as if Mother Earth tried to hide her reservoirs from being discovered.

Anne picked him up from the airport. He could not take his eyes off her because she was a very beautiful pregnant woman. She was in the full bloom of womanhood, and he couldn't resist stroking her breast.

'Watch the road, will you!' she admonished him.

When they came home he wanted all of that to hold in his hands, and they made love with all the tenderness they good give each other.

It seemed that every time he came home, they discovered each other once again as if they had just met and made love for the first time. He told her that, and she agreed, but also mentioned that she missed him terribly when he was gone, and seeing and touching each other again after four weeks was wonderful.

Anne explained that things worsened with Mam and daily visits of friends and neighbors were cancelled because she required more morphine and, therefore, slept most of the day.

When they arrived at his parents' house, he was grateful to find her in a clear state of mind.

Mam held his hand in her own, unwilling to let go. 'The doctors are giving me more medication to relieve the pain. I just hope that I will be given the chance to see your child before I leave this world.'

'You know I've always been honest with you. All I can say is that every day that we can be together is a gift. I hope that you'll be able to hold our child when it's born.'

It saddened him to think that his mam, who loved children so much, would never get to know this grandchild.

Anne made soup for dinner, as it was the easiest food for his mam to consume.

They sat around her bed together in silence, enjoying the precious intimacy of the moment.

They left the minute his father came home, and left for Agnes' house.

When Agnes let them in she took him aside. 'Rob, Mam wants to know the day that you come home again, because she wants to be lucid when you're here.'

'I didn't know, but every day is a gift for us, and she's a fighter, Agnes. Let's hope that she'll last long enough to see and hold our child.'

He talked to Klaus, who told him everything was going according to schedule, and everything was ready for the house to arrive the next day.

'In that case we'd better get a good night's sleep. Did Anne transfer the money to you yet?'

'Yes, thank you. I can really use it right now.'

'You're welcome. You and the guys did a great job.'

On their way home they stopped at the building site for a last inspection. Rob helped Anne down the ladder to see the basement rooms, and she, too, was happy with the result.

'So tomorrow is the big day,' he said to Anne. 'I probably won't be able to sleep tonight. We've waited so long. I never really expected to have a home like this.'

They drove into Germany to buy beer, a variety of cold meats and brötchen, hard-crusted bread rolls, to surprise the builders the following day.

'We'll leave it in the car and store the beer in the basement tomorrow.'

Once they retired to bed, neither of them could sleep, so Anne cuddled up against him. 'Have you thought of a name yet for your son?' she asked suddenly.

'Jesus. You've got some timing. I was actually hoping to get some sleep.'

'I know that you can't sleep. So let's talk about it now.'

'I thought about it during the flight. If we have a son, I'd like to name him Jan, after your dad. He deserves it for raising a daughter like you on his own.' He could see the glint of her tears in the darkness.

'Thank you,' she whispered against his neck. 'Thank you so much. I love you.'

'You are most welcome, my love. But what if we have a daughter?'

'The way you feel about my dad, I feel about your mam. We could call her Jess.'

'I'd like that very much. I do hope she'll be able to hold our child before she leaves us.' There was a silence. 'By the way, I know a good remedy for not being able to sleep.'

She giggled. 'No, I don't want any of that right now. But if you can rub my back gently I'll be asleep in no time.'

That's what he did and within minutes he could hear her breathe rhythmically in her sleep. But sleep evaded him. He tossed and turned the whole night, his mind working overtime, constantly going over everything for the next day.

They were at the building site very early the next morning to await the arrival of the trucks and crane to assemble the house. Klaus was talking to someone, who Rob recognized with some amazement.

'My God! Dieter!'

His German friend grinned at him. 'I checked with the prefab company to find out the date they'd be assembling your home. I wanted to be here with you on such an important day.' Dieter went to his car to return with glasses and a bottle of wine.

'I've been saving this bottle since we finished college, waiting for a special occasion. I think this is as special as they come. I'd like to drink to a healthy baby, that you may live a happy life in this home and, of course, to our friendship. So to all of you, prosit!'

They had just emptied their glasses when the trucks and crane arrived. Rob had arranged for some comfortable chairs to watch at a safe distance the assembling of the house.

The foreman introduced himself and asked Rob if he had provided enough beer for his crew, as German laborers practically lived on beer.

'I think so,' Rob said with a smile.

'Good. Let's see if this Dutch beer is any good. We'll start this job with a beer to drink to your new home.'

Rob went to his car and came back with the German beer and brötchen.

The foreman was impressed. 'Now that's what I call a breakfast. You even arranged for German beer!' He called his men over, and they all sat down to enjoy a good breakfast together. Afterwards the crane was rigged up, and the other trucks with materials arrived in a logistical order. Within one hour the first section of the house was latched onto the concrete foundation, and by lunch time the first floor of the house was in place.

While Rob, Klaus and Dieter watched with interest how each section was assembled, Anne took photographs of every phase. Later in the afternoon Anne's dad and Agnes arrived with the kids to watch the show. The street was filled with neighbors, villagers and passersby who watched in awed fascination how the house was being assembled in just one single day.

The construction workers worked precisely and efficiently, and before dusk all the sections were successfully installed. When they finished Rob ordered Chinese food for twenty persons, and the builders brought in a table and chairs so that they could have their first dinner in their new home. After dinner the crew put a plastic covering over the roof to seal the house and left for a local hotel for a good night's rest.

Anne and Rob thanked Dieter for coming over, and then went to see Mam for a brief visit to show her pictures of their new home. But she was not feeling well, so they let her rest.

Over the next few days the crew worked according to a detailed plan, staying well within schedule. The men made excellent progress, while Rob took care of the beer supply. His task was to finish the drainage system and link the fireplace to the hot-water system.

He visited Mam as often as he could, as the moments that she could talk to him became shorter by the day. When she was unable to speak, he would just sit there and hold her hand. That was usually enough to calm her. He tried to avoid his father at all cost, as there was nothing left to say between them.

Every evening he took Anne and her dad to the house to show them the progress, taking careful note of their remarks and suggestions. Anne was becoming quite heavy now and rested frequently when she wasn't keeping his mam company.

One afternoon Mam told Anne that she had kept Rob's cradle and most of his baby clothing, and said that she could use whatever she wanted. When Anne sorted out Rob's old baby clothes, she was greatly moved. She decided to leave the color on the cradle—it was cornflower blue.

Three days before Rob's departure, the final inspection of the house took place. Everything was perfect. Rob signed the acceptance document, and a bottle of wine was opened to toast to their new home.

'To whom do I give the keys?' the foreman asked, and Rob gestured to Anne.

Beaming happily, she accepted the keys.

'Alright, everyone out now!' the foreman ordered. Once outside, Rob lifted Anne in his arms and they walked inside the house under loud cheering from the men, who had worked on the house for three full weeks for at least twelve hours a day.

To celebrate, Rob reserved a table in a Dutch pancake restaurant. While having dessert, Klaus whispered to Rob that Agnes and Anne's dad had secretly arranged for their bed and toiletries to be brought to their new bedroom so they could spend the night in their new home. Rob looked at Agnes and Klaus as they both grinned at him, moved by what they had done.

'What was that about?' Anne asked, her curiosity piqued.

'Oh nothing, I was just thanking Klaus for everything.'

After everyone had left, Rob paid the bill and got into the car.

'Why are we driving to the house?' Anne asked as she noticed the route they were taking. 'I'm really tired, Rob. Let's just go home, please.'

'I just want to check if all doors are locked. And I want to have one more look inside our castle.'

It took some coaxing to get her out of the car and inside the house, but when they got to the bedroom, Anne gasped. The bed was beautifully made up, there were towels in the bathroom, and she noticed that even all her toiletries and cosmetics had been neatly arranged by the sink. 'Oh my God, this is great! I was thinking how lovely it would be to have our first night in our new home. Your sister and Klaus arranged this, didn't they? Now I know why they were grinning that way.'

'They did it together with your dad. Now we can actually stay in our castle.'

'Perhaps my lord could carry me to the bed and slowly undress me?'

'Certainly my dear. Same procedure as last year?'

'Yes my lord. But be careful. I don't wish to go to the hospital tonight.'

The next day most of the furniture arrived, and for three long days Rob busied himself doing different jobs to complete the rooms. He managed to finish the baby room, their bedroom, the kitchen and the living room. The rest would have to wait until he got back.

In the evenings he visited his mam to show her photos they took of the rooms as they were decorated. She seemed happy and relieved that the house was finished on time for the birth of the baby, and that their having to move out of Rob's parental home was no longer an issue.

The next day Anne drove him to the airport.

'Make sure you take plenty of rest,' he told her. 'I know you want everything to be perfect before the baby comes, but take care of yourself. You're already doing too much.'

'Don't worry, I will,' she said with a smile. They kissed each other goodbye, both of them realizing that Rob might miss the birth of their child if it came too early.

But that was a consequence of the life that he chose to live.

Chapter 13

Rob was exhausted and slept throughout the flight. After arriving in the desert, he found the rig was about to start drilling into a hard sand formation where they hoped to strike oil. Each time the penetration rate increased, they stopped drilling to check for oil or gas samples. While supervising standard drilling operations, Rob stayed at the campsite; however, during the more difficult operations, he slept on the drilling site in a mobile office equipped with a bedroom and drilling recorders.

He consulted the geologist whenever there was a formation change to ensure everything was in line with his predictions. The company had invested a great deal in the well, having based their investment entirely on the geologist's interpretations of the expected formation they had obtained. It was nerve-racking for everyone.

Each morning Rob reported their progress to his drilling manager in Tripoli, and any major change was reported to Werner Brandt, his Operations Manager, immediately. They continued to drill for another two weeks without formation changes.

Then, a drilling break took place: the penetration rate increased drastically. The flow indicator showed additional flow, whereupon the blowout preventer was closed. The well pressure increased immediately.

All indications told him that they had found oil or gas, so he called Tripolis and Werner to tell them the good news.

They decided to pull out the drilling bit and lower the coring assembly to extract a cross-section of the well, so that they could measure the thickness of the oil and gas bearing sand formation.

Extracting the formation core from the well was a risky operation. Throughout the procedure they had to keep the hole filled with mud in order to prevent a vacuum and blow out risk.

Throughout the entire operation, Rob stayed at the site, only calling home once a week. Anne was convinced that she could delay the birth of their first child until he was home. There was no change in his mam's situation—she had good days, but also very bad ones. The family had arranged a schedule so there was always someone with her.

Rob left the rig while they were still coring, confident that he would be in time to witness birth of his child.

After landing in Zurich, he called home and was caught off guard when Anne's dad answered the phone. Instinctively, he knew he was too late. Anne had given birth to a boy that night.

Anne's dad assured him that mother and son were both doing fine, and he would come and pick him up from the airport.

After Rob boarded the plane, you could have knocked him down with a feather—he was completely overwhelmed by the news. He had become the dad of a son. He could barely control his emotions. He knew he didn't have the mentality for a nine-to-five job, unlike so many others from his hometown. He loved the work that he did. Travelling around the world was part of his job, but this came at a cost. Now he realized how high this cost could be. He had missed the birth of his son and was unable to be at his mother's side while she was dying.

Just after landing he made a dash for customs. At the luggage carousel he felt the urge to leave without his luggage. It seemed like an eternity before the system finally spat out his suitcase.

In the arrival lobby he found his father-in-law, whom he practically dragged to the parking lot. He urged him to speed, eager to see his wife and son.

As he practically fell into their bedroom, he was stopped in his tracks at the most incredible sight: Anne was breastfeeding his child, his son. He felt as if his heart had skipped a beat. He had never witnessed anything more intimate, more sacred than this.

She looked up at him and smiled. 'Would you like to hold your son?'

For a moment he felt utterly lost, like a child. 'Yes. Yes, I want to hold my son. If you show me how.'

'Just let him rest in your hands. They're large enough.'

He took the infant from her and held him with both hands, and stared at the child in wonder. Jan, his Jan. That was the name they had agreed on. He kissed him very gently on the forehead.

'He has your eyes and my black hair,' he said, his voice filled with awe. 'Tell me. Was it difficult without me?'

'Yes, Rob. It was. Your sister offered to help me, but I told her I wanted to deliver our baby by myself.'

'Anne, I am so sorry that I could not be here, at your side,' he said with tears in his eyes.

'We already discussed this, Rob,' she said as a matter of fact. 'We discussed and knew it could happen like this, with your job.'

He sniffed. 'Whoa. I do believe my son is trying to tell me something. I smell something. I think he needs a new diaper.'

Anne grinned. 'I'll tell you what to do. This will be one of your tasks for the coming years. Move the changing table a little closer to the sink so I can watch what you are doing. Lay him down on the pillow. Now remove the pins from the diaper, carefully! Keep the diaper closed while you put the dirty diaper in the bucket, over there,' she pointed. 'Okay, now clean his bottom with warm water and soap – it's in that plastic box on the shelf.'

He did exactly what he was told, but with his big hands, he felt awfully clumsy dealing with such a small and fragile baby. Jan, his Jan.

'Well done! The new diapers are in the drawer. Now lift him up -

carefully - and place his bottom on the new diaper. Other way round!' She giggled as she watched him struggle, panicked. 'Before you close the diaper you put some talcum powder on his buttocks - there, on the shelf. Then you close the diaper with the same pins you just removed. There you are! All ready and clean again.'

Rob exhaled, relieved that he had survived the challenge of challenges. 'We never did talk about these special duties, did we? But I can manage this one,' he said, suddenly quite proud. 'So let me know when I have to do it again. You'll be breastfeeding him?'

'The midwife told me to give it a try. I will if I produce enough milk. Otherwise we'll have to feed him baby formula.'

'Do you have to heat that up?'

'Yes, to body temperature. Don't worry, the midwife will show you how. That will be another one of your duties.'

'I hope your beautiful milk factory will produce enough milk so that we can get some rest at nights.'

She scoffed at him. 'Well you can forget about that for now. Your son needs milk every four hours.'

'What the...you never told me that before.'

'Did you ever stop to think about any of this when we made love?'

'No. But don't worry, I'm a proud dad. I'll get up any time to change his diapers or if he needs feeding. So when are you allowed out of bed?'

'It was a pretty tough delivery. The nurse advised me to take it easy for at least a week. Then she's going to review the situation.'

'I'm just wondering, in case you need extra help after I'm gone.'

'We'll see when the time comes. We can always arrange something if I still need it.'

'Family and friends will want to come and see you both. What would be the best time for you, considering you have to rest?'

'I'd prefer them to come in the afternoon, after my nap. I still need to get into the rhythm of feeding and washing him. It takes up most of my mornings. But first I want to call Waltraud. I promised I'd let her know as soon as the baby arrived.'

She made the call, which lasted a good forty minutes, which would normally not be enough for them, but Jan's cries cut the call short.

Rob only got a few hours' sleep each night during that first week. As it turned out, Anne was not able to breastfeed, as she wasn't lactating enough and he tried to help her as much as he could.

As soon as Anne was allowed to get up, they went to show Jan to his mam.

She appeared to be doing alright, and, much to their delight, she could not get enough of her grandson and could hardly take her eyes off him.

They let Jan sleep at her side so that she could watch and talk to him to her heart's content. When they asked her if she wanted to give him the bottle, she was all smiles. They propped her up so she could hold him, and watched her while she bottle-fed him. She simply glowed with happiness.

When Rob and Anne drove home that night, they felt relieved and strangely at peace, happy that she had at least been able to see and hold their grandson.

Rob had just fallen asleep when the phone rang. It was his father, asking if he could come over as quickly as he could, as his mother had taken a turn for the worse. He dressed and jumped into the car, driving as fast as he could. It was then that he realized that he was driving on a car-free Sunday—no cars were allowed on the roads because of the oil crisis. Still he kept going, and thankfully there was no police to pull him over.

Agnes opened the door, looking very pale. It was clear that she had just been crying. 'It's over, Rob,' she managed to say before she broke into sobs. 'She's gone. She died right after Dad called you.'

He walked into the living room in a dream-like trance, and stared at the lifeless body on the bed. His mam was lying there as if asleep, her eyes closed, a benign smile on her face.

Agnes stepped up behind him and held his arm. 'She told me, Rob. She kept saying that all she wanted was to live long enough to see and hold your baby.'

He took his sister in his arms and held her tight as they cried together. Their mam would never be able to see her grandchildren grow up. She would no longer be a grandmother to them, their oma, something that she had become with utter dedication and had so lovingly embraced.

When his father came in with the family doctor, they left and took Agnes home, where he called one of his aunts in Maastricht to notify the family of his mam's death.

On his way home he felt empty and bereft. It had always been his mam who had kept the family together. Now Agnes and her family were all that was left. He had no expectations from his father. He knew that he would pose a problem, certain that he would want that woman of his to move in with him. Rob would never accept that. His mam had been the only reason he agreed to his parents living in his house. He began to resent his father from the moment he learned he was seeing someone else. And it got worse when his father made it clear that he wanted his mam to stay at the hospital, so he could have his freedom. He had truly come to hate him when he not only didn't appreciate Anne's help, but also wanted her out of the house. When he changed the locks on the door, Rob couldn't bring himself to be near him anymore.

He intended to make an appointment with the notary to discuss the matter after the funeral.

Because his mam didn't want to be buried in Germany, the funeral took place in his hometown. As had been her wish, her body remained until the very last minute, on her favorite spot in the living room with the curtains open.

To Rob's surprise, the church was so packed that it couldn't accommodate everyone. He had not known that his mam was still so loved in her old hometown.

He and Agnes spoke in church, looking back at the events that had shaped her life. Rob and Klaus helped carry the coffin outside the church, where it was placed on a horse-drawn carriage and taken to the local cemetery. It seemed to Rob that the whole town had come to see his mam to her grave. Every man and woman dropped a flower on top of her coffin, tossed a handful of sand, and said their farewells.

After the ceremony everyone gathered in the same small café, where Rob and Anne had their first cup of coffee. They stood side by side, next to Agnes and Klaus to accept the offered condolences. His father stood at the other end. Rob refused to see or talk to him anymore.

Within the briefest possible time, he had experienced the most emotional days of his life. One magical moment he had watched Anne breastfeeding his newborn son, and the next he had to say goodbye to his mam. It made him realize how life and death are irrevocably linked.

With his head still in emotional turmoil and with Jan crying every couple of hours demanding to be fed, he hardly slept the nights that followed. When Agnes informed him that a woman had moved in with this father, he made an appointment with the notary.

Anne joined him with Jan in the pram, as they didn't expect to take up much time.

After being served coffee, Rob explained the situation to the notary, and that he paid for the mortgage, services and taxes, while his father lived in his house with a woman they didn't even know.

The notary advised them that by refusing to allow Rob and his family to live in the house with him, his father was in breach of the agreement. But he asked if there was any other solution.

'Well, my father could move into the quarters that I built for myself, or we can add a separate section to the house.'

'I'll contact your father,' the notary said. 'I'll propose these possibilities and see what he says. However, if he doesn't agree, then the only alternative would be that you stop paying the mortgage fees. That could result in a public sale, and if the house is sold, your father would be forced to leave the house.' The man frowned as he considered this. 'Mind you, with the oil crisis the housing market is at its lowest point. If you wait another year, the market might recover. On the other hand, you will save on mortgage fees and taxes.'

They agreed that the notary should contact Rob's father to discuss the options. If he didn't agree to any of them, they decided that the notary would put the house up for public sale within two months. The notary promised to notify the Mortgage Company to ensure that their own credit history or future loans would not be affected.

On their way home they dropped in at Agnes and Klaus' house to discuss the advice they had been given. Agnes was glad that a solution might be available. She and Klaus were adamant that they had not built the house for his father and girlfriend, but for Rob's family. In that spirit of determination and togetherness, Klaus opened a bottle of wine to toast to their future.

Rob went to the cemetery every day, where he talked to his mam and put fresh flowers on her grave. Not a day went by when he did not leave with tears in his eyes.

The notary gave him weekly updates on the house situation. His father refused to accept any of the solutions, so the public sale was scheduled for the second week after his return from Libya. Apparently his father had been livid, saying that he would hire a lawyer, but the notary did not expect any problems.

Before he knew it, it was time to leave again. This time, it was harder than ever before—he had to say goodbye to Anne and his son.

Chapter 14

He tried to sleep during the flight, but too many images and emotions from the previous weeks kept him wide-awake. Holding his son, seeing the smile on his mam's face at the sight of Jan, the grief he felt at losing her, the funeral, and finally the problem with the house.

But in a few hours he would be back in the desert. He would have to concentrate on the job, switching back to work mode. Before he left home he had called Werner who told him that the difficult coring operation was finished.

Werner asked him if he had completed the sequence pages for the well to ensure that the next well would be drilled without making any mistakes.

Rob ensured him he would finish the missing sections as soon as possible.

By the time he arrived in the camp his mind was fully back to work mode. After the handover from his relief, he drove to the rig to discuss the testing program with various contractor companies specialized in well testing operations.

The well testing took two weeks and required his constant supervision. During the first week he only got a couple of hours of sleep each night, but after the production testing was finished, he was able to complete the missing sequence pages and deal with other outstanding issues. The day before he was due to fly home, all testing operations were completed, and the well was closed up to prepare for pipeline hook-up to the nearest production facility.

That last night something woke him. For a brief moment he lay there, listening. Then he was sure. Someone was trying to open the door of his caravan. He always locked the door at night, as he didn't trust the locals living near the campsite, or the Libyans that were hired to work at the rig.

Cautiously, he peered outside through the gap of the blinds. There were at least ten locals out there, surrounding his caravan. And they were all armed with steel pipes and knives. He silently slid the additional latch on the door and grabbed a gun from the safe, and then, as quietly as he could, he radioed through to the office in Tripoli.

The drilling manager came on the line straight away. 'Rob, you won't believe this,' he gushed excitedly. 'There has been a military coup. The army has taken control and disposed of King Idris. They've declared that Libya is no longer a kingdom, but a republic!'

Stunned, Rob quickly told him of the predicament he found himself in at the campsite. 'We need help over here. Urgently.'

'Yes, we've already sent the charter plane your way. It's got fully armed

Indian guards on board. Once it gets there, all non-Libyan employees have to board the plane and leave. Is that understood?'

'Yes. Over and out.' The door rattled, the whole caravan rocked. The men outside were now making a serious effort at opening the door. His heart thumping, he fired a shot at the door. Sudden silence. Something smashed against the window at the other end of the caravan. In a reflex, he fired next to the window, the force of the bullet leaving a perfect hole. He stared at it in shock, suddenly acutely aware of the danger he was in. He stayed down low in his caravan. All he could do was wait, and hope.

Then sound of gunfire, somewhere in the distance, he couldn't quite place from which direction, and that unsettled him. Then he heard the unmistakable roar of a Land Rover's engine. He peered outside past the blinds, where he saw, much to his relief, the familiar Indian watchmen piling out of the 4X4. He quickly threw his most important belongings, the drilling reports and the gun into a backpack and unlocked the door.

The guards expertly inspected all the caravans on the campsite. One man was found badly beaten, right outside Rob's caravan. All non-Libyan personnel were hurriedly escorted to the waiting DC3, where Rob ensured all his personnel boarded the plane.

When all men were accounted for, the plane took off for Cairo, leaving the Indian guards at the campsite to protect the rig and equipment. Once they were in Cairo, Rob called Anne and briefly told her that he would be home that evening. The earliest flight was through London, after which they got a connection to Amsterdam. By the time he finally got home, it was eleven p.m.

Anne had stayed up for him, and seeing the taxi pull up outside her door, she rushed out. They just stood there, staring at each other for a while before he finally took her into his arms and kissed her. She clung to him tightly.

He stroked her hair reassuringly. 'It's okay. I'm back.' She pulled away from him, willing him to look her in the eye.

'I know,' he said softly. 'I know. I was lucky, Anne. But these risks are also part of my job. These oil-rich countries are often unstable. War and rebellions are never far away. It's something you'll have to accept.'

He took her to the bedroom where he undressed her and made love to her as if it were the very first time.

He woke up very early the next morning by the sound of Jan crying. He got up quietly and went to the baby room, which was permeated by a smell that told him it was most definitely diaper changing time. After he had wrapped his son's bottom in yet another clean diaper he held him close, breathing in the fresh scent of his child mingled with the talcum powder. He stood there for a long time, relishing the quiet moment with his son until he slept against his chest. He kissed him gently on his forehead and put him back to bed. Jan never even stirred. It was good to be home. It was good to be a dad.

Unable to go back to sleep, and with his mind still in overdrive after all that had happened the previous day, he got up and turned on the news. Watching the latest updates on CNN, he thanked God that the drilling manager didn't waste any time sending the charter to fly them out. From Cairo, the correspondent reported on what had taken place in Libya, giving detailed information on incidents involving Westerners at several drilling sites, hotels and expatriate housing compounds.

He called Werner Brandt and filled him in on everything that had happened. They both agreed that the drilling manager made the correct decision by sending the plane to retrieve them from the desert. And they both knew that it would probably be a while before the Libyan operations could be started up again, if at all.

Werner asked if Rob would be interested in working on a drill ship. The ship he had in mind was presently in a Singapore shipyard undergoing modifications. He wanted Rob to become an all-rounder, with experience of new drilling equipment and methods to drill all types of wells across the world.

It was something that definitely appealed to Rob. He had always wanted to work with different types of equipment, to apply new technologies. Besides, a drill ship was something completely new for him.

'Well yes,' he said, 'I'd certainly like to discuss this in more detail to find out more about the job.'

They agreed to meet that following week.

While Rob and Anne were busy decorating the house, the notary called to inform Rob that his father was still unwilling to accept any of the options offered to him. The public auction was scheduled in five days. The furniture had been removed, the house keys were already in his possession, and if Rob wanted to come and take any of his own belongings he was more than welcome to do so.

The following evening Klaus assisted him in loading the remaining furniture on his trailer. The bed he intended to use for the guestroom, and the rest he planned to store in the basement.

'Do you want to take a last look inside?' Klaus asked.

Rob shook his head. 'No. I prefer to remember this house as it was in happier times.' When Klaus drove away he didn't even look back.

'Long-term planning, Rob, that's what our strategy is all about,' Werner said after they sat down in his office. 'As you know we're always exploring new territories and acquiring the latest equipment for that very purpose.

The company has recently purchased two large container ships from Wedel Shipping. Our plan is to modify one of these ships into a drill ship and drill wells in deep waters. The second ship we intend to use as a floating production facility.

'And we've just finalized a deal with our preferred drilling contractor. They will provide all the drilling personnel to drill these wells.' Across the table he slid a rudimentary engineer's sketch of a container ship, annotated with suggested changes, towards Rob.

'Have a look for yourself. The modifications are almost done and supervised by our project-engineering department. I want you to go and see the ship, Rob. See if it's capable of drilling in deep water. You've worked on a semi for years; it's pretty much the same concept.'

Rob sat back casually and looked at Werner. 'I'll do it,' he said. 'The only thing is that I need another ten days at home. My house is being auctioned off, and I want to be there to finalize things.'

'That shouldn't be a problem. You'll be reporting to me. You can arrange all matters regarding personnel, services and materials through head office, until we've set up a local base in the operating area. Then we'll take it from there. Any questions?'

'I think I get the picture. Thanks, Werner,' he said, getting up and shaking hands. 'I'll be in touch before I leave.'

Driving home Rob marveled at how things had turned out. He was quite happy not to return to Libya and felt more than ready for new challenges and to broaden his experience, just as Werner proposed.

When he arrived home he offered Anne his services for diaper changing and home improvement for another two weeks.

Rob noticed that Anne looked at him, challenging him. She knew him so well. 'Yes you would, wouldn't you? You'd like to keep me home, love me to death and see our son grow up every day, wouldn't you? Nah. I'd only get bored and you'd be frustrated.'

'Maybe when I'm sixty and saved enough money, then we'll talk about it.'

She came up to him, put her arms around his neck and kissed him.

Rob loved every minute of their family life. He enjoyed being with Jan, going shopping with Anne or just going for a walk in the woods. They often visited his sister, and he enjoyed how Agnes' children played with Jan. Anne's dad came by every day for a cup of coffee and to play with his grandson. It was obvious that he loved watching the way his daughter had become a young mother, and his visits to their house visibly buoyed his spirits.

Rob often went to his mam's grave to talk to her in silence. It felt good to have some normalcy in his life again, a daily routine after mourning his loss.

He decided not to go to the auction; Klaus would go in his place. He had put so much energy and time into the house, and it still saddened him that it was being sold simply because his father refused to be part of the family.

When Klaus came back and informed him of the outcome, he was disappointed with the amount at which the house had been sold. Only a few potential buyers had shown up, and when the starting price was announced, only one person offered a bid. There had been no other bids.

Anne was optimistic, as ever. 'Listen, none of us would be happy to live in that house anymore, with all that's happened. We've sold it. That's the main thing. So let's forget about the money and be glad that we can finally close this chapter and start again.'

Rob and Klaus both looked at her. She was right, of course. 'Let's drink to that.'

Chapter 15

The nearer the date of his departure, the more he wanted to be alone with his wife and son. Agnes and Klaus understood this, and left them to themselves. Anne always drove him to Schiphol airport, but recently a shuttle service had started between Enschede and Amsterdam, which took him only twenty minutes to get to the airport.

This time he could not look back at Anne, as he had always done. He knew that the picture of her standing there, with Jan in her arms, would be too hard for him to bear, and too unfamiliar—it was something he would have to get used to.

It was the first time that he would fly 'with God' to the Far East. The thought of his mam made him smile. He found the food and friendly service of Singapore Airlines excellent during the flight, which was the longest he had ever flown.

After his meal tray was removed, he went through the modification list of the drill ship and the drilling program of the first well that Werner had asked him to review. He fell asleep while making changes in the equipment list, and woke up when he was told to fasten his seat belt for landing. Heavy rains and lightning made for a rough first landing in Singapore.

At the airport he met the agent handling all company affairs, who drove him to the shipyard.

Once on board he was somewhat surprised to be welcomed by the captain, who accompanied him to meet the drilling superintendent.

He explained that the captain was in charge when sailing, while the drilling superintendent had overall responsibility for the safety of the ship and crew while drilling. He was a man with many years of drilling experience and acted as advisor to the tool pusher in case of emergencies

The ship's crew consisted of engineering, maritime and drilling crews that worked together while sailing or drilling.

The captain showed him his cabin, where he changed into work clothes and returned to the drilling contractor's office. There the captain provided him with comprehensive instructions in case of emergencies, showed him where his muster station was located and the life jackets were stored. He was then shown to his own office, which had a clear view of the rig floor and was fully-equipped with recorders and panels installed around his desk.

Here he was introduced to the project manager, Jurgen.

'Nice to meet you, Rob,' Jurgen said. 'I understand you have worked on a semi? I was involved in the upgrading of that semi and I've also supervised modifications on land rigs.'

Rob was impressed. 'They've asked me to look around from a drilling point of view. Perhaps we could talk to discuss the modification program?'

'Absolutely. There's a meeting set for tomorrow morning between shipyard and contractor supervisors to discuss the planning and status of the different projects.'

Briefly, Jurgen explained the ongoing projects and status of the various modifications that were in progress. Then he gave Rob a complete tour around the ship and showed him the work in progress.

At the end of the tour, he was exhausted. The jet lag and the flight had begun to take effect. He retired and agreed with Jurgen to meet him the next day.

Early in the morning the radio operator knocked on his door telling him that Werner Brandt was on the phone.

'There's been a change of plans,' Werner told him. 'You can expect visitors within the hour. They're coming on board to inspect the ship and discuss what modifications can be done. Other modifications than we previously discussed,' he added with a sense of mystery. 'This is top secret, Rob. They've intercepted distress signals from the first Russian nuclear powered submarine, somewhere in the Indian Ocean. And nothing had been heard from the submarine since. They've been trying to locate it, and two U.S. Navy ships and one of their submarines are out there now. No sign of the submarine so far. You know what this means, don't you?' He continued without waiting for a reply. 'The U.S. Navy intends doing all it can to find the submarine and get their hands on the latest Russian technologies. The Russian government denies that one of their submarines is missing. They know nothing of a distress signal coming from that area. The people that are on the way to you are planning to use our drill ship as a salvage vessel. They want to know if it's possible to install a satellite station keeping system and deep-water diving equipment. They also want to build a lifting frame that's capable of holding the weight of the submarine including underwater camera equipment.'

Rob's mind was spinning. Not even a day had gone by, and things were already different from what he expected. Werner told him that the whole operation was kept top secret, with no one else to know until the drill ship was officially contracted by the U.S. Navy to carry out the salvage operation.

Werner made it quite clear to him that this operation would benefit the company.

If they were given the contract, the Navy would install the newest satellite station keeping system on the ship, which would upgrade it to become the first drill ship capable of drilling in extreme water depths without anchors.

And of course, this would improve the relations between the company and U.S. government officials. They could also use this salvage operation as a test case to check if all systems performed as expected.

They just finished the phone call, when Rob heard the whirring blades of a helicopter. Seconds later it came within view and landed on deck. He watched four men get out of the helicopter. They showed their identification to the startled captain and were taken to the bridge, where they asked to meet with the shipyard and rig supervisors.

'I think I know what this is all about, Captain.' Rob said. 'I just spoke to my boss.'

He quickly briefed him on the situation, upon which the captain went to find and order Jurgen, the drilling and shipyard supervisor, into Rob's office.

After everyone was present, a spokesman introduced himself as the Navy's representative. 'First of all, it's important that no one discloses anything of what will be discussed at this table to anyone.' He extracted a document from his briefcase and handed it to the drilling supervisor. 'And therefore you need to sign this confidentiality agreement.'

After everyone had read and signed the document, the Navy rep explained why they visited the drill ship. 'We've done a worldwide search and know that this is the only drill ship in the shipyard with sufficient horsepower to deliver power to the rig floor for hoisting purpose and to a Dynamic Position system at the same time.'

The Navy rep told them that the newest Navy ships were all equipped with a Dynamic Position system (DP), this shipyard had already installed DP systems on some of their vessels, and the Navy was planning to deliver and install such a DP system on this ship. It was also convenient that the ship was in dry-dock because several holes had to be cut into the hull to install thrusters on port and starboard sides.

This DP system would keep the ship on location, making use of the main propulsion, and with the additional thrusters to be installed on port and starboard, would allow the DP operator to move the ship in any direction with a remote control joystick. The system was linked to a satellite navigation system, calculating any deviation from the preset location coordinates received from the beacon and transponder signals at the sea bottom, and would keep the ship on station keeping mode on any preset coordinates. The beacons and transponders could be dropped or lowered on wire line to the bottom of the ocean. The DP system was one of the most advanced and important pieces of equipment to find the location and keep station above the submarine, but several function tests would need to be carried out to check and recheck the correct function of the primary and secondary satellite systems including the beacons, transponders and all other related equipment.

The shipyard supervisor was asked to provide a time estimate to install the DP system. After a quick calculation he estimated that it would take about two weeks to finalize installation, and most of the manpower would be needed to install the electrical cabling and instrumentation panels. Therefore, they would require eight teams to work around the clock.

The shipyard was instructed to stop all other projects and start work immediately on proposals for the necessary modifications, and hire additional men if necessary.

In addition, the Navy wanted to install a deep-water diving system and build a lifting frame that's was capable of holding the weight of the submarine. The Navy rep asked Rob and Jurgen to check drawings and come up with ideas how to lift the submarine. The shipyard supervisor indicated that a lifting frame was available, because the yard used this frame to transport heavy loads. The Navy rep asked Rob to review the available drawings and forward a proposal.

He asked if they could make a meeting room available for internal discussions and to make phone calls. Rob said they could remain in his office.

Two hours later Rob was called in and the Navy rep informed him that the ship met most of the requirements to carry out the salvage operations, and from that moment on, it was under contract of the U.S. Navy.

The Navy rep and his men had to remain on board to plan and finalize the installation of equipment and arrange personnel to carry out additional projects.

Rob informed personnel on board that the ship was prepared and modified for salvage operation.

As from that moment, the shipyard and rig crew worked on the installation of diving and DP equipment.

After reviewing all available submarine drawings and looking at the shipyard lifting frame, Rob and Jurgen came up with the idea to center a drill pipe within the frame and to weld at the bottom, middle and top section of the frame heavy reinforced beams from the drill pipe to each corner. This was to avoid collapsing of the frame under the expected load to pull the submarine free from the bottom.

Heavy chain with sufficient length would be welded to the frame at specific places to ensure the chain was pulling at the reinforced areas of the submarine and to avoid its slipping off from the side when lifting force was applied. After retrieval of the submarine to surface, the frame would be connected to four chains hanging down from the rig substructure, where after the drill pipe was disconnected.

The draft drawings of the lifting frame modifications were sent to the shipyard engineers to review the feasibility and calculate the reinforcement necessary to lift the total weight as indicated and add suction factors for their calculations.

The shipyard engineers approved their modifications, and work started immediately. The frame and chains were to be painted white, so they would be clearly visible for the underwater cameras to watch.

The diving equipment that the Navy installed was never seen before, and only specialized Navy personnel worked on the installation. It consisted of manned and unmanned diving vehicles equipped with hydraulic arms to grab, hold and turn anything.

Sufficient drill pipe was stored on board for the expected water depths, and a target date was set for the ship departure.

Rob requested a wire line unit with explosives, in case the submarine could not be lifted, to separate the drill pipe from the lifting frame.

Jurgen was asked to hire a crew of welders and riggers from the shipyard, and gather specialized cutting and welding gear for unforeseen events.

They learned that the U.S. submarine had detected the Russian submarine with sonar. Two Navy vessels guarded the area and dropped beacons to mark its location.

With that knowledge they knew that the Russians would do everything to find and salvage their lost submarine. Now it became a race against time.

Rob asked for plans after retrieval of the submarine and suggested arranging a barge that could be positioned and lowered on the bottom of a harbor site. The ship with submarine would be moved over the barge where after the submarine was lowered onto the barge, the lifting chains then to be disconnected and the ship moved away. The barge would be de-ballasted/raised and towed away to a marine yard for inspection. His suggestion was appreciated, and the shipyard was asked to check the availability of a barge of that size. Within a short time the shipyard reported that this type of barge was indeed available and asked if an option to hire should be arranged.

The Navy rep made the decision to take an option and have the barge available, in case the operation was successful.

The next day Rob asked the Navy rep, captain, superintendent, diving master and tool pusher into his office and showed a draft step-by-step sequence for each operation to be carried out. He indicated that his draft planning was based on the assumption that the hull was still intact and no explosion took place.

They discussed the sequence of location approach by reducing ship speed to see if a reading from the Navy dropped beacons could be received to keep the ship on location. If this was not possible, they could lower the beacon with wire line to the sea bottom and keep the rig on location with the DP system.

Then the sequence of lowering the frame on drill pipe was discussed.

The last sequence was attaching the chains to the submarine, lifting it from the sea bottom and attaching the frame to the substructure. Here the diving master made all his recommendations and indicated the sequences of events that would take place. His biggest concern was to find out how the vessel landed on the seabed and if there was sufficient space below the hull to connect the two chain sections together.

In case this was not possible, a high pressure jetting device was on board to create a small channel for the chain underneath the hull.

Rob noted all suggestions and action items for each sequence.

Thereafter each person in charge explained his sequence again to ensure that every person under his supervision understood the events, when the next sequence would occur and when the responsible person should take over command. The captain discussed the location approach. The DP operator explained the final location approach and station keeping operation. The tool pusher described how to attach the drill pipe to the frame with reduced make up torque for easy disconnect, in case the submarine could not be retrieved including lowering and recovering of the frame. The diving master discussed attaching the chains to the submarine.

Rob asked the superintendent to discuss the sequences with the night and day crews so that everyone was informed concerning the operation that should take place. He then thanked all the individuals for their input and indicated that he would prepare the final sequence sheets.

After three weeks of hard work and one more completion tests on all systems, the ship was towed from dry-dock and maneuvered out of the busy harbor with tugboats. The captain carried out a complete sea trial to ensure that the main propulsion and DP system functioned properly. After all tests had been successfully completed, the ship returned to the harbor side and was loaded with fuel and food supplies for a two-month period, where after the lifting frame was installed below the hull.

It was then that the Navy rep informed all personnel that the reason for this operation was to recover a Navy vessel that had sunk, and that it was of vital importance to salvage the vessel in order to investigate the reason of this tragedy.

Rob did not call Anne during these weeks, but just before all communication lines were disconnected he called home.

'I'll be leaving Singapore tomorrow Anne. I can't tell you anymore and love you both,' he said, feeling rather uncomfortable with keeping anything secret from her.

A stunned silence on the other side of the line. 'Your son is doing just fine. We miss you, Rob,' was all she said.

Without another word, he hung up. It took him a while to recollect himself, aching for home, his wife and his baby son.

He asked Jurgen if he wanted to go home or if he preferred to stay on board to supervise the welders and shipyard crew during some of shipyard projects while sailing. Rob was pleased with his decision to stay on board, as it would give them the opportunity to discuss some ideas.

The ship was pulled out of the harbor by tugboats, and tug lines released shortly before open sea was reached.

The captain calculated that it would take six days to reach the submarine location with maximum speed.

As no one had slept more than a few hours those last days, all personnel not on duty were given a good long rest to catch up on sleep.

Rob walked around the ship, talking to engineers and crew members. Most of this time he spent in the ship control room, where the power was divided from the engines and generators to all consumers. His main questions were how much horsepower was available and the estimated daily consumption.

The chief engineer explained the available max horsepower, daily consumption and spare power available in case the DP system required more power for the main propulsion and thrusters to stay on location during the salvage operations or adverse weather conditions.

The remaining time, he spent with the Navy DP operator and asked him to explain the system as the ship was normally kept on location with anchors. This was the first time he had to work with a DP system to remain on location.

His main question was how many degrees of freedom in the ship's motion were allowed. Rob used the frame as an example and asked the operator, in case the frame was attached to the submarine and severe weather was expected or a power failure took place resulting in a drive off, how many degrees were allowed to avoid severe damage to the ship or equipment.

The operator told him if flexible drill pipe was used for these salvage operations, and the frame was latched to the submarine, a twenty degree range was most probably the maximum to avoid damage.

Rob stayed in the control room until midnight, and the DP operator informed him about the capabilities and drawbacks of the system.

He knew then that only during a period of normal weather conditions the chains could be attached to the submarine, because they only got one chance to work the submarine free, which could take a long time.

The more Rob thought about it, the more he was aware that this kind of salvage operation, which had never been tried before, would be difficult, even in optimal weather conditions.

Each step in the procedure was as important as the next: electrical power, the DP system, the diving system and divers, the drilling crew and finally the weather, which was something they could not control.

With two days sailing time Rob repeated the sequence sessions daily to ensure that everyone understood the sequence of events and his role and responsibility in it.

During the salvage operations the ship public address system was only used for emergency or to stop the ongoing operations for safety reasons. All walkie-talkies were set on one channel, and only the supervisors of each team communicated on this channel. The only exceptions were the diving master and his divers—they communicated through their own system.

While approaching the location, Rob noticed two Navy vessels that contacted the ship by radio to advise the captain that the ideal approach would be to maneuver the ship in between the two vessels to receive the beacon signals.

The cranes lowered the thrusters on each side of the ship, and the DP operator function tested each thruster, where after the captain slowly maneuvered the ship towards the two vessels. Before they reached the vessels, the DP operator had already received the beacon signals.

The steering and power control of the vessel was handed over from the captain to the DP operator. The DP operator used his manual controlled joystick system to maneuver the ship in between the Navy vessels until he was on top of the dropped beacons. Then he changed manual control of the DP system into automatic mode to keep station at the preset coordinates of the location.

The DP operator reported that the ship was in Dynamic Position mode and handed the command over to the tool pusher, who had already attached the first drill pipe to the frame with reduced make-up torque and removed the hang off chains.

A separate cable was attached to the frame for guiding the underwater camera to the submarine at a later time.

Two additional beacons were installed on the frame as back up in case anything happened to the beacons dropped by the Navy vessels.

The drill crew continuously picked up more drill pipe, and the lifting frame with the guide cable for the camera was lowered into the ocean.

The divers prepared the manned and unmanned diving vessels.

First the remote controlled underwater vessel (RUV) was lifted with the crane and followed the lifting frame down into the ocean. The water depth was already established by the Navy vessels and confirmed with the instruments on board. The drill pipe and lifting frame were lowered until twenty feet above the received sonar signals of the submarine.

The diving master maneuvered the RUV around the lifting frame and found the submarine fifty feet away from the location of the lifting frame.

The DP operator moved the ship above the submarine.

The underwater camera was attached to the guide cable and lowered until the camera detected the lifting frame and submarine.

The total operation up to that time had taken thirty hours.

While the lifting frame was lowered to the seabed, Rob did get some rest, but asked Jurgen to wake him up as soon as the RUV found the submarine.

When Jurgen woke him, the weather conditions were favorable for the next three days, so the go-ahead for the salvage operation was given.

The diving master took over control and instructed the manned diving vessel to be lowered into the sea. The communication and camera systems were checked once more. The diving vessel circled around the submarine and reported no damage to the submarine's hull, but did find that the submarine was tilted to one side. The ship needed to turn thirty degrees in order to place the chains on each side of the submarine.

Once the ship was turned, the divers checked the position of the chains, and the driller was instructed to lower the lifting frame. Divers were ordered to descend to the submarine, where they connected the chains to the diving vessel hydraulic lifting arm. Fortunately the front of the submarine's hull was free to move the chains with the help of the hydraulic arms underneath the hull to the other side, and divers connected each side of the chain together. After inspection of the other side, it was clear that only a small part just past the propulsion area was free to move the chain underneath the hull.

The Navy rep checked the drawings of the submarine to verify if the hull was strong enough to lift the vessel in that area. The situation was not ideal; therefore he contacted his office to inform the supervisor that this was the only area available to lift the submarine. Because the vessel landed on hard rock, the jetting solution was impossible. The supervisor agreed with his assessment, and because no other option was available, agreed to continue with the salvage operations.

Getting the chains underneath the propulsion side of the submarine's hull proved a slow and laborious process, in which they had to repeatedly lift the frame to adjust the chains underneath the hull. This sequence of lowering and pulling was repeated many times, and divers had to pull one side of the chain by hand underneath the hull, because the hydraulic arms of the diving vessels could not grab the chain to assist the divers.

It took three trips and four teams of divers to finally connect the two sections of chains together.

At this time the command was transferred to the superintendent in the diving control room. He checked the camera screens and observed that the chains and frame were ready for lifting operations. It had taken them three days before tension could be applied on the chains.

He instructed the tool pusher to apply ten tons of pull, yet only the chain on the propulsion side moved slightly. Twenty tons. The forward side was still not picking up any tension.

Continuous pull was applied until the forward side chain picked up tension as well. Slowly they increased lifting pull to fifty tons and continuously increased the tension in stages.

The superintendent noticed that the forward chain had moved a little towards the middle of the hull, which meant that the load between the chains was distributed more evenly.

For three hours they repeated the painstakingly slow process, carefully observing all the weight indicators and camera screens to watch the behavior of the submarine and the lifting frame.

It took another full day before they reached final lifting capacity of the frame and chains, and there was nothing else they could do but wait.

Twenty-four hours later the weather changed. The wind increased in strength, as did the swell of the waves. They did not know if it was the wind or waves, but after another twenty-six hours, every person on board the ship could feel a sudden movement.

The shudder woke Rob up. He jumped into his jeans and boots and ran to the rig floor. They had done it. The weight indicator showed that they had reached the expected weight of the submarine—they had lifted it free and had finally managed to break the suction underneath the submarine's hull.

Everyone cheered. They all felt relieved that their careful planning and patience had finally paid off. The remote controlled underwater vessel was lowered into the water again so that they could get a visual on the frame and condition of the submarine.

Rob rushed down to the diving control room to see on the screens what the weight indicator had already told him. The submarine had been lifted, and was now hanging below the lifting frame. Its position was nearly horizontal, and there was no damage to the hull.

The ship filled with whoops of triumph, and everyone was excited.

The Navy rep congratulated everyone on a job well done via the public address system.

Rob ordered the tool pusher to start pulling the drill pipe stands and went back to the bridge to call Werner to inform him that they recovered the submarine.

But then he saw something on the horizon that made him cut the call short. 'I'll have to get back to you, Werner,' he said, and hung up. He grabbed the binoculars and scanned the horizon, until he found what he had seen. It looked like a derrick.

'Captain, you'd better have a look at this,' he said, handing over the binoculars.

'It's a drilling derrick all right. Odd. It shouldn't be here according to the charts, not with these water depths. And this isn't a shipping route, so what is it?'

'This is the competition,' the Navy rep said. 'Looks like they're late for the party,' he grinned.

As the unknown ship approached their location, the radio operator tried to make contact but no answer.

The ship came ominously closer, until they could finally ascertain that it was indeed a drill ship. It was the *Valentine Shashin*, and it carried the Russian flag.

The Navy rep immediately radioed instructions to the two U.S. Navy ships to maneuver themselves between the drill ship and themselves and wait.

They watched and saw that the Russian drill ship seemed to comply—it kept its distance from the Navy vessels and waited.

What would the Russians do? Accept their losses or find a way to sabotage their operations? The Navy rep didn't want to take any chances and instructed the U.S. Navy vessels and submarine to keep very close sonar watch out to detect any Russian submarines.

It took the drilling crew twenty-four hours to retract the last drill pipe, where after the lifting frame with submarine was suspended below the derrick substructure.

By the time the ship was ready to depart, the Navy rep informed Rob that they would not be returning to Singapore, but to the U.S. instead.

He had been instructed by his superiors to set course for one of the American naval bases, under the escort of two Navy vessels and the submarine.

The Defense Department seemed convinced that by salvaging the Russian submarine, they had struck gold.

Once the frame was secured, they set sail for the U.S. coast at a slow speed, as the frame with submarine created considerable drag below the waterline.

Jurgen contacted the Singapore shipyard to let them know that the barge would no longer be needed and suggested to the Navy rep to arrange for a similar barge for undocking in the U.S.A.

Rob assumed that the Russians decided to relinquish on their ill-fated salvage plans for the submarine. There had been sonar activity when they left the salvage area, but no signal was detected after that. They must have known that their submarine had been salvaged by the U.S. and that little could be done to reclaim it.

Before giving in to his exhaustion, he contacted Werner to inform him the ship was sailing for the U.S., and their arrival would be delayed due to the reduced speed.

Rob woke up after sleeping a solid fourteen hours. He called Anne to let her know that he would be home in a week. He felt immensely relieved that they had a military escort all the way, and no further incidents took place.

Together with the captain and the Navy rep, he discussed the offloading of the submarine. The captain intended to offload the submarine onto the ballasted barge as pre-planned. The Navy reported that they owned a location with a suitable water depth, where everything had already been set into motion to prepare for the offloading.

As Jurgen and the captain had prior experience in similar offloads, their input was useful, and Rob finalized the offloading sequence.

During informal discussions with the Navy rep, Rob learned a great deal about the operational control on board their submarines. The rep explained to him that they had lost a large number of submarines due to human failures. They had recently switched to a planning and control system that was not all that different from the one Rob had set up with his sequence planning. It had already proven its worth by reducing the failures and loss of submarines.

The system was automated and continuously updated by the people who were most at risk. Rob said that he wished for a system similar to the recently invented car navigation systems, including a voice that instructed a person to go back in the event of a wrong turning. He hoped that technology would soon make it possible to convert his printed sequences into an automated system that controlled every step carried out as indicated.

'I hope so too,' the Navy rep said. 'Such new technologies would help to avoid disasters, and we had already too much of that.'

The remainder of the trip, Rob made himself more familiar with the drill ship, and there was plenty of time to meet and talk with the people on board. He was surprised—and delighted—to find such a wide variety of nationalities. The marine and deck crews came from Spain. The drilling crew consisted of Americans, Australians, and New Zealanders, while the caterers were from Indonesia. It was something he wasn't used to—so far he had worked in different countries with crews bearing the same nationality.

In most countries, crews were only interested in making money. They didn't seem interested in team building.

He remembered his time in Hannover, and that the best team was the crew that worked a long time together and became friends.

On this ship, things were different. This crew had only worked together for a short period of time, yet there was more camaraderie between them than on any other rig he worked on, whether on land or offshore. Maybe it was because these men lived together at close quarters for four weeks or more, and that they therefore felt they should look after each other.

This he found refreshing, but he was concerned about the drilling and marine crews' lack of experience. Most of the men on board had worked on rigs, but hardly any of them had worked on a drill ship before. For many, operations such as racking of the drill pipe stands on deck, instead of a derrick, or running the Blow Out Preventer into deep waters was new and required continuous supervision from drillers and mates on deck to avoid accidents.

He discussed this with the superintendent and captain and told them that no operation was to take place until each person fully understood the sequence and his function during these operations.

He asked Jurgen to take him through the list of outstanding issues while sailing. They exchanged ideas and Jurgen told him to implement some of Rob's suggestions on their way back to Singapore or once they were back at the shipyard. But he pointed out that the shipyard was unable to design a real-time recording system, so the present system with time delays was the only option.

Rob had never used a computer before and asked Jurgen to show him the ropes, in the hope of being able to prepare his sequence sections on the computer. That way it would be far easier to update the changes that took place.

The day before they were due to arrive in San Diego, they were alerted to the imminent arrival of a helicopter carrying high-ranking marine officers. Upon landing on the ship's helipad, the Navy rep introduced the officers and told Rob that they would like to meet all the crewmembers in the meeting room whenever it was convenient.

When the time came for a shift change, all personnel gathered in the meeting room.

'Gentlemen I'd just like to say how very important the salvage of this submarine is to the U.S. Navy,' the officer highest in rank said. 'As a token of our appreciation, everyone on board will receive a personal check as a thank you for a job well done.'

Whoops of delight reverberated through the room at this surprise. They were presented with a personal check, and this was a big surprise because the amount was for most men a whole month's salary. The canteen was filled with shining, happy faces and excited chatter. A loud 'Hurrah for the Navy' was the crew's response.

Laughing, the second officer asked for silence once more, and said that he hoped the money would be well spent. The Navy also wanted to give each person a gift that would always remind them of the job that they had done so well. He held up a waist belt with the Navy seals logo engraved on the silver buckle.

'Navy seals have always been selected to carry out special operations,' he said. 'And we feel that this special operation was particularly well done.'

As company representative, Rob was expected to say something in return.

'I'm speechless,' he said with a grin. 'All I can say is that each and every member of our drilling crew has worked hard, and my company is very proud to have accomplished this challenging operation.' He turned to the Navy's diving master. 'I would like to thank the diving master. I greatly admire him and his men for their skills and sheer determination to do what they did under such severe working conditions. We could never have been able to do what we did without their expertise.'

The Navy rep proceeded with presenting the belts. When it was his turn, Rob shook hands to express his appreciation, knowing that he was behind this gesture.

Once they approached the San Diego harbor they reduced their speed until the ship came to a standstill, after which the harbor pilot took over the command, the towlines were connected to the tugboats and the ship was maneuvered to the off-load location.

While they started the offloading process, Rob took a shower and dressed in a clean shirt and jeans. The familiar fresh, soapy smell of the washing powder Anne always used filled his nostrils. It made him think of her, he was suddenly eager to go home again. He quickly packed his bag and went to the radio room where he called Anne to let her know that he would be in Enschede the next morning.

By the time the submarine was landed on the barge and the ship was secured to the wharf, it was early in the morning. A bridge was installed alongside the ship, and immigration officials came on board to check everyone's passports.

The relief crews were already waiting, and as soon as the ship was cleared by the authorities, they were allowed on board, after which the handovers took place.

Rob went to his office where his relief already waited, and they discussed the status of the modifications to be carried out. He then said farewell to the Navy rep.

'Whenever we're in need of a drill ship again, I'll know where to find one!' the man said appreciatively.

Within an hour, the public address system announced that the bus to the airport was ready to leave, upon which everyone boarded the bus for San Diego Airport.

It was hot and sunny, and Rob enjoyed the warmth, taking in the exotic palm trees and the luscious green parks of the city, the hills covered with white houses.

He was surprised to find that the airport was located at the center, and wondered how the pilots arriving over the hills still managed to land safely on such a short landing strip.

Once they had checked in, the crew had a final beer together and then split up to fly in different directions. Rob took the flight to Houston, where his connection awaited him—the familiar, welcoming KLM blue bird that would take him straight back home.

Rob was too excited to sleep. Sitting back, he went over the events of the past week, realizing that what had happened was something unknown to the outside world.

They had been lucky. The responsible Russian leaders had accepted the loss of their newest technology. They could just as easily have started a series of events resulting in a serious threat to the ship and every person on board.

Chapter 16

He felt dead tired when he got off the city hopper in Enschede, but when he saw Anne holding his son, he felt suddenly wide awake. God how he had missed them! It was so good to be home, even if it was rainy and cold.

While Anne drove, she began to tell him all her news. He marveled as he looked at her, the sparkle in her eyes, her lovely face, the animated way in which she spoke, and realized that he wasn't listening to a word she said. He looked at Jan, strapped down in the back of the car, and knew that he could not wish for anything else. He felt completely blessed.

He asked Anne to stop at the cemetery so he could visit his mam's grave and asked her to stay in the car.

'Miss you and love you, Mam,' he said as he stood over the grave. 'It's good to be home again. It felt as if you were watching over me the last four weeks.'

Tears stung his eyes, as he wished for holes in heaven so she could see his family and watch over them.

Once they got home he asked Anne to give him some time to walk outside in the garden. As he circled the house, he could not believe that this was their home.

When he had left the house was only just finished, now it was furnished and decorated. They had created their very own paradise.

When he went back inside the house Anne was feeding Jan. Entranced, he pulled out a chair to observe the beauty of the moment.

'Anne, I cannot tell you how happy I am. This…this is so very beautiful,' he said, choked up by the emotions that had taken hold of him. 'If it were up to me, I would just close the door for four weeks to spend my time with you and Jan. Let me please feed him the rest of his bottle. I'd like to hold my son very close for a while.'

She handed Jan over to him and as she watched him, she started to cry.

'I've missed you so much that it hurts. Now that I can see how you hold our son, I am the happiest person in the world. Thank you for that,' she said, smiling through her tears.

Neither of them wanted the moment to end. They wanted to prolong it, hold on to it forever, but Jan had finished the milk and had fallen asleep in his arms, the nipple still in his tiny mouth.

'You'll have to wake him up and burp him. Otherwise the air he inhaled will keep him awake and give him cramps.'

Rob gently straightened the infant, holding him against his shoulder until the telltale burping sound told him he was ready for bed. Together they went upstairs, and after covering Jan with tender kisses, Anne tucked him in for his afternoon nap.

As she slowly walked down the stairs before him, Anne removed her clothes piece by piece. By the time she was down she was stark naked, and Rob marveled at her beauty. Without a word, he picked her up and carried her into the bedroom.

They were awakened when the baby monitor came to life with a gurgling sound.

Rob turned to get up, but Anne grabbed his arm and pulled him back to her. She kissed him softly on the lips. 'We're going to have a daughter in nine months' time,' she said.

He stared at her, stunned. She had been right about Jan, and now she was telling him that they have a daughter.

'I hope you're right,' he said. 'If it's true then we'll call her Jess.' He embraced her, feeling emotional. He believed that if a husband and wife shared their lives on a day-to-day basis, their routine could easily slip into automatic mode. But if separated for a while, they would only appreciate each other much more, making them cherish every moment they could spend together.

They both went upstairs in response to Jan's crying. He was the first to enter the baby room, and as he did, he looked right at the beaming face of his son. He lifted him up, kissed him all over his face and changed his diaper.

'You're doing a good job!' Anne said. 'Do you want to feed him as well?'

'Yes please. If you can prepare his bottle than I can hold him close. I missed him.'

Once again Anne experienced the love Rob had for his son as she observed how he fed Jan, marveling at the doting expression on his face. It gave her the same warm glow as if he was making love to her.

The rest of the day they spent alone. Anne was surprised that her dad or Agnes didn't come to visit that day, yet she enjoyed their precious family time together.

For the first time, Rob lit the fireplace to see if the central heating system that he connected was working. Once the fire was roaring, he checked the radiator temperature and was pleased to find that it was warming up.

After Jan had been put to bed for the night, he went upstairs and came back with a very soft sheepskin that he had once purchased in Germany.

'Hey. Where have you been hiding that? I've never seen that before.'

'Well, I planned to save it for falling in love with the one and only, lighting a fire in my own home and surprising her with this sheepskin,' he said with a grin. 'But that's not all. My next plan was to make love to her so she would get pregnant. But as you know a person can make lots of plans.

Our son has already been born. We haven't done this yet simply because I forgot about it. As you had a nice surprise for me this afternoon, I thought I'd try my other plan.' She was about to say something in protest but he held up his hand. 'I know what you going to say. Let's just pretend that this afternoon didn't happen, and that I just arrived home. Indulge me, please. This is one of my dreams.'

Anne burst out laughing and looked at him in disbelief. 'Is this just one of your tricks to make love to me again or is this story really true?'

'Well partly because I want to make love to you again. But I also like to think that our daughter was created on this sheepskin. Same day. We won't know, will we?'

'Well in that case, can we have the same procedure as this morning please?'

'Yes! I am madly in love with you. I'd like to imagine that I'll always remember exactly when our daughter was conceived. Just as you were able to predict that we would have a boy.'

'You have some imagination. I do love you for that, but before you have some other bright ideas, can you please carry me to that soft and inviting sheepskin of yours? I'll pretend that you just walked in the door.'

It was late when Rob finally doused the fire in the hearth and put the sheepskin back into storage. They took a shower together, and Anne noticed that he was getting aroused once more.

She looked at him with a mock frown. 'Three times a day is overkill. Let's keep that one for tomorrow.'

'I can't help it. Just seeing and touching you is too much for me to bear.'

When he came to bed, he just wanted to be close to her. When she turned over onto her sleeping side he sidled up behind her, her buttocks against his groin. He put his arm around her, and that's how they woke up the following morning to Jan's demanding cry.

Anne was still dozing when he put Jan's soft cheek against her own.

She received him drowsily. 'Did you clean and feed him already?'

'Yes, my love. He told me that he wanted a kiss from his mam.'

She covered her infant in kisses and cuddled up in bed until the phone rang. It was Agnes—she asked if she and the children could come round for a coffee. Rob indicated they would need time to dress and that she could come in half an hour.

While making coffee there was a knock on the back door. Jan Sr. entered the kitchen with a big smile on his face.

'I thought I smelled coffee, and decided that I wanted to see my grandson. And you, of course. It's good to see you back home again, Rob.'

'It's good to see you, Dad,' he said as his father-in-law hugged him. It was out before he knew it. It was the first time that he had ever called him

'Dad'. He looked at him sheepishly.

His father-in-law caught his expression and laughed. 'Thank you Rob, for calling me "Dad". You know, I already accepted you as my son from the moment you married my daughter.'

Rob looked at him with appreciation. No further words were necessary, it just felt right.

Anne walked in with Jan. Rob noticed how his son's face lit up when he saw his granddad, how his small arms reached out to him. Anne smiled. 'Yes you can hold him and give him a soft cookie. Otherwise he'll start crying. This is how it goes between those two every day, Rob,' she said, rolling her eyes to the ceiling.

Rob was delighted in the way Jan gave Dad so much joy just by holding and talking to him. It dawned on him that whenever he left home, he would have to relinquish his position as favorite man in the house to him. Jan needed his granddad. Dad was always there when Anne needed him. He had patience and love to bond with his son, and time. A luxury that he didn't have with his work.

Agnes arrived and the house was immediately filled with loud, love and laughter.

The children demanded that he tickle, play and run after them as he always did.

In between the playful bouts, his eyes met his sister's. He knew she was thinking the same: that their mam was out there, somewhere in heaven, looking down on them enjoying these family moments.

Over coffee he learned that his father had moved in with the woman he was seeing, but it hadn't lasted. Apparently she had asked him to leave within a week. He was now living in a small apartment.

Jan's feeding and sleeping schedule gave them a good excuse to keep the rest of the day for themselves. After everyone left Jan was given his bottle and put to bed for his morning nap, and Rob organized brunch in bed. They finally had a chance to discuss other matters.

'We received the money from the sale of the house,' Anne told him. 'It's a substantial amount, even with the mortgage deducted. What are we going to do with it?'

'I think we should use part of it to reduce the mortgage on this house, part to be put in a saving account, and I'd like to use some of it to buy company stock. It's well-managed and has a long term strategy, and my gut feeling tells me that such an investment could prove lucrative.'

Anne peered at him. 'We have a low interest rate on the mortgage payment because of my previous employment at the bank. If you feel the company is worth investing in I suggest you do. I'd like that money to grow. Interest rates on savings are really low at the moment.'

'Thanks for your excellent financial advice. I'll guess that's what we'll do then.'

That afternoon they visited the bank and invested part of their money in the Hattenberg Oil Company. He rather liked the idea that if his company performed well, he would benefit from it financially.

When they got home and put Jan to bed for his afternoon nap, Rob could barely keep his eyes open—the jet-lag hitting him hard.

'Oh dear. I think my body is trying to tell me something about the different time zone I'm in. Maybe I should have some rest.'

'Well, I actually have a long to do list. Once that's done, we'll discuss your time zone problem, alright?' she joked.

Just at that moment the phone rang. It was Werner Brandt. Rob was surprised—he normally never called him at home. Werner wanted him to visit the office the very next day.

'Okay. Will it take long? Can I take my wife and kid? I just got home yesterday.'

'No, shouldn't take long,' Werner told him. 'Take your wife and son, and I'll see you at ten.'

Anne looked at him quizzically. 'You have to go to the office tomorrow? What was that all about?'

'No idea. We'll find out tomorrow.'

The next morning they left once Jan woke up, had his bath and finished his bottle.

When they were about to leave Anne came out lugging a huge baby bag. He looked at it in consternation.

'What?' she asked when she saw his expression. 'You need to take this stuff when you take your baby out, trust me.' To Rob it looked as if she had packed for a two-week journey.

Once they were on the road, it was clear that Jan loved the ride, and they arrived at the office without any problems.

Anne settled in the lobby with her things, as from there she could easily get drinks, heat the bottle in the restaurant, use the ladies toilet for changing Jan's diapers, and there was a quiet, dark corner for his nap.

Rob went to the reception to let Werner know that he arrived and sat down next to Anne. A few minutes later he was surprised to see Werner coming down the stairs. It was usually his secretary who came to pick him up.

Werner extended his hand in greeting, 'Rob!' and greeted Anne warmly. 'Could you please come upstairs? This won't take long.'

This startled Rob. Visitors weren't normally allowed in the office, especially a baby! Confused, he followed Werner and found that they were not being led to his office, but to an adjacent meeting room.

When the door opened he was stunned to see the ship's captain, chief engineer, superintendent and Jurgen. The company's whole management team, including Bernard Heumer, was present as well.

'Take a seat,' Werner told them with a welcoming gesture. 'Coffee? Tea?'

Somewhat bewildered, they both asked for coffee. Anne finally looked at Rob with a frown. 'Who are these men, Rob? Is something wrong?'

'These men manage the company in which we invested yesterday,' he whispered.

'Oh,' was her only reply.

Bernard Heumer came up and introduced himself to Anne. 'Can you please switch on the viewer, Rob?' he asked, gesturing to the slide viewer that was used for presentations.

Rob did as he was asked. The first slide to appear showed the American eagle crest above the words 'The United States Of America'.

'Go ahead,' Heumer said. 'Please read the text of the next slide out loud. So that we can all hear.'

Rob started reading dutifully, but he faltered slightly when it dawned on him what the text said. What he was reading was a letter from the President of the United States, in which he thanked the company for the excellent salvage operations carried out by the staff on board the drill ship under very difficult circumstances. The salvage operations had contributed to the stability between two powerful nations, considerably reducing the risk between them.

Rob never blushed, but this time he couldn't help himself. He could feel his face reddening, and he began to sweat. He looked at Anne helplessly, but she just smiled.

Heumer asked the ship supervisors to step forward. 'I don't think I need to explain how proud we are with the contents of this letter. This means more to the company than anyone in this room can imagine. We have plans to drill in the Gulf of Mexico, and this letter can help us obtain the required permits to drill. The management team would like to thank you all for a job well done. I'd like to present each of you with a framed copy of this letter, because you've earned it.'

He began to hand out the framed copies and invited them all for an early lunch.

He asked Rob to briefly explain what had taken place on board, without too many details, as the operation was still classified.

It was then that Jan started to cry. Slightly embarrassed, Anne hurriedly left the meeting room to spare the men and to tend to her son's needs. Rob gave a brief recap on the events that had taken place from the moment the Navy helicopter landed on deck until their arrival in San Diego.

When he finished, he excused himself, and Werner accompanied him in the elevator to see him off.

'I'm happy that you were on board during the salvage operation, Rob,' he said.

'The Navy rep told me that he was very impressed with the way you planned and handled things. I want you to formalize your sequence planning sheets. I believe this is the way forward, this is the way we should carry out all our drilling operations from now on.

'Oh, and I've hired this young engineer, Joop. I want you to train him to become a drilling engineer. He's booked on the same flight to Singapore you're on.'

After they shook hands, Rob found Anne in the restaurant. He sat down next to her, still overwhelmed by what had just taken place, relieved to be alone with her.

He only had to look at her to know that there were a thousand questions that she wanted to ask. 'This is still classified,' he told her before she could even voice one of them.

'Oh, don't give me that!' she retorted. 'For all I know you were in Singapore to work, and then suddenly I hear that you're on a trip around the world. Then you're told to show up at the office to receive a letter for a job well done from the president of the U.S.A., and all you can tell me is "it's classified"?'

'It really is classified,' he said, unable to keep a straight face. He watched her, enjoying the way her eyes burned like fire, the way her color changed in her anger.

'So. Are you going to tell me something? Yes or no?'

'This is still classified,' he repeated stubbornly. He knew that he could not keep this up for long, so he told her what he had told his personnel on board—that they had salvaged a vessel in order to investigate the cause of the disaster.

'What about the text of the letter?'

'What text?' he asked innocently.

'The text about considerably reducing the risk between two powerful nations.'

'Oh that. That's really classified. Sorry, I can't tell you anymore.'

She threw him a look, frustrated, but she knew him well enough that this was all she would get out of him. He never did talk about his work at home. He had the uncanny ability to switch off from work when he got back.

'Well fine then. But I think you should know that I rather liked the way we were received upstairs. It was good to meet the management team. I think that our money is in good hands.'

'Thank you very much,' he said with mock humility. They finished their lunch in silence, after which Jan woke, and Anne gathered her things for the drive home.

In the car he could feel her observing look. She had that same, aggravated look on her face, just as when he had told her, 'That's classified.' That was all it took for her eyes to take on that burning, angry look, for her skin to redden.

To end this memorable day, he took the last exit off the Autobahn before leaving Germany, stopping in front of a family restaurant. He knew the place well—the food here was excellent. On top of that, Jan had slept throughout the trip, and it was time for his bottle and diaper change.

While the waitress went to heat Jan's bottle, Anne took him to the toilet for a diaper change. Rob bottle-fed his son while giving Anne a chance to study the menu. From experience, he knew that the brown bean soup and liver with baked apples were excellent, while Anne selected onion soup and Hungarian goulash.

After he burped him, Rob put Jan in his pram, covering the top slightly to dim the light. Within minutes he was fast asleep.

They took their time, enjoying the food, the wine and the ambience, knowing that they would remember this special day for a long time to come.

'Thank you Rob. I quite enjoyed myself today,' Anne said. 'It was an excellent idea to stop here.' She reached out for his hand, tilting her head slightly as she looked at him. 'You do know that I would like to know everything, don't you?' He nodded. 'I just hope that you'll tell me all that you can.'

'You know that I would,' he assured her, after which he paid the bill, carried the pram to the car and drove home. Anne selected soft music, resting her head on his lap, feeling happy and secure.

The next weeks Rob managed to assemble a wine shelf, several cupboards and did a number of odd jobs in the basement. He had planned to build a carport, but the weather was wet and cold, so he left it for next time. The final week he just wanted to stay home with his family. He often wished that there were more hours to the days, as he could not get enough of his son and wife.

He would secretly observe Anne, remembering that she had told him she was pregnant. And again, she looked more beautiful every day, like a flower coming into full bloom. When she had been pregnant with Jan, she had needed no doctor to tell her that she was expecting. He had seen the changes himself. Yet he held back, thinking it was too early to ask.

On his last evening at home, she was lying on the couch, her head resting on his lap.

'So why don't you ask?' she asked suddenly.

'What should I ask?'

'If I feel that I'm pregnant.'

'I think it's too early.'

'Well if that's what you think, then we'll leave it.'

'Jesus, Anne. Don't be so cruel. Of course I want to ask. I just wasn't sure if you were feeling any changes in your body.'

'This time you're right. I'm not sure yet.'

'"Not sure yet" is not an answer. Don't you remember that when I came back from the desert in Saudi you already knew? You didn't need a doctor then.'

'Yes I remember that. But it's too early.'

'You'll let me know?'

'No.'

'Why not?'

'Because I want to tell you myself. I want to be able to look into your eyes when I do. See the expression on your face.'

'I'd like to take the sheepskin with me, if that's okay with you.'

'Yes darling, please do.'

Chapter 17

Packing had become a routine. All he took was a toiletry bag, a spare shirt, jeans, socks and flip-flops in case of warm weather. He didn't look back when he boarded the city-hopper in Enschede.

At the check-in gate at Schiphol, he met with Joop, the new engineer. They checked in together so that they could be seated next to each other. After a "with God" takeoff, Joop told him that he graduated from university and just got married. This was the first time he had left home for such a long period of time.

Rob told him about the course of his own career, explaining the various occupations he had before reaching his present position. Then Rob took this opportunity to explain to Joop what his job would involve and at first assist him with the daily planning of the well sequences he wanted to complete during the flight.

He showed Joop the drilling program, explaining the differences between drilling operations on land and on a semi Rob had worked on in the Shetland Islands. He noticed that Joop was exceptionally good at visualizing the sequence of operations, so together they completed the draft sequences. By the time the plane landed in Singapore, Rob had also finished a training schedule for Joop covering the next six months. They agreed that Rob would evaluate his work on a weekly basis and always be available if Joop had any questions.

With stormy weather conditions, including lightening, the descent to Singapore airport was a bumpy one.

The rest of the crew was already waiting at the airport to be taken to the shipyard by bus.

When they got on board he introduced Joop to his colleagues. In his absence, the required modifications had all been completed, and the acceptance tests were to start the following day. The function and pressure tests had already been carried out, and everything seemed to be working fine.

Once the tests had been completed and the green light given by Jurgen, who was responsible for the modifications as project engineer, the ship was to sail for Indonesia to drill its first deep water well. Indonesia had been selected as its first work site for guarantee reasons: it was in the vicinity of the shipyard in Singapore. Should anything not function properly, the shipyard team could be called in to fix the problem. And if that weren't possible, the ship could be returned to the shipyard.

After all hand-over items had been discussed with his relief, the man left to go home, while Rob changed into his light work coveralls. He went on deck to see if all his suggestions had been implemented and if the ship was ready to carry out drilling operations. He found Jurgen on deck preparing the acceptance test sequences with the shipyard supervisors.

One of his main issues was the load test. The ship was allowed to carry a maximum load consisting of fixed and variable loads. Rob wanted to know what his variable load was to load the ship to the maximum with equipment, in case supply boats could not come alongside the ship during severe weather conditions. He therefore wanted most of the equipment on board to avoid waiting on weather.

Rob decided that if he became in charge of drilling operations, he would try to replace some of the steel equipment with lighter materials, such as zinc.

Another important improvement was the replacement of the kelly and rotary, used to drill wells. This was a simple mechanical system powered by an electric motor located on the rig floor. The system was low in maintenance and fairly reliable, but they could only drill a thirty-foot hole section with it. They had now installed a new top drive system, which consisted of electric motor and rotating system mounted below the traveling block. With this new top drive, they could drill up to ninety-foot hole sections, which was a big step forward in the drilling technology.

The only problem was, as with all new sophisticated technologies, there would be teething problems. A system failure required specialist knowledge and, therefore, longer repair times. If the new top drive failed, this would have a great impact on the drilling operations. It could result in stuck pipe, lost time and, in the worst case, putting back the old kelly system.

He was very excited about another new piece of equipment that he had repeatedly asked for and was finally approved. One of the most dangerous manual procedures was men's handling of the rotary tongs to connect and disconnect the pipe, something which he had learned from personal experience. They had now installed a hydraulic and remote-controlled "iron roughneck", to connect and disconnect the pipe. The installation of the iron roughneck would serve to reduce large numbers of accidents and contribute to workers' safety.

He wanted to witness the simulation of a power load test, which determined how much power remained in the event of maximum consumption while drilling to keep the ship on location in DP mode during severe weather conditions.

Over lunch, Jurgen showed Rob and Joop the acceptance procedures they received from the shipyard, and Rob told him which tests he wanted to attend. He assigned Joop to check if all the necessary drilling equipment was on board and to assist Jurgen with the remaining acceptance tests, as this would be an invaluable experience for him.

His relief had assured Rob that everything was on board, but he went through the checklist personally to ensure that this was the case.

Once the scheduled thirty-six hours of acceptance tests were successfully run, the last supplies were loaded, and the captain ordered the harbor pilot on board so they could leave the harbor and depart for Indonesia.

Jurgen wanted to stay on board the ship to complete some minor modifications and finalize the handover upon their arrival in the Java Sea, while Rob spent most of the trip completing and discussing the drilling planning sequences with the drilling and marine crews. Drilling mud was premixed and all drilling equipment and tools inspected and tested.

The ship arrived on location, and beacons were lowered to sea bottom, where after the ship operated in DP mode to remain on location. The 30" conductor with jetting assembly was connected to the guide frame and lowered to sea bottom on drill pipe. The remote-controlled iron roughneck was operated for the first time to connect and make up drill collars with pipe, and the roustabouts appreciated the tool very much.

The guide frame with reflectors was picked up and clearly marked with white paint. Each guide frame post was connected to a winch cable, and all four winches reeled off in the moon pool while the guide frame was lowered on drill pipe to seabed. The camera was lowered on the guide frame cables to inspect the seabed for any debris. The guide frame was lowered and the legs pinned and forced into the seabed with the weight of the drill string until the guide frame base was landed on sea bottom.

The thirty-foot conductor with the jetting tool just one feet outside the conductor was unlatched with a J-slot from the guide frame, and mud pumps started to feed the jetting tool to wash away the formation and at the same time lowering the thirty-foot conductor pipe until the top of the conductor pipe was landed in the guide frame.

Preparations took place to drill a 24-inch hole and run the 16 ¾-inch casing with on top the 16 ¾-inch wellhead

Rob was out on deck to supervise every single operation, and each sequence step was precisely carried out as planned and discussed at their morning meetings.

He observed the crane handling of the deck crew and would interfere if things didn't go to his liking. He did not leave the rig floor until he was satisfied that each person understood his job, making the drillers repeat the sequence again until he was satisfied that the crew carried out the job correctly.

It took them two days to drill the 24-inch hole and run and cement the 16 ¾-inch casing with wellhead.

Rob felt relieved that the start of the well called 'spud in', was completed without any interruptions or accidents. Yet he knew that they would now need to focus on one of the most difficult, simultaneous, important and time-consuming operations: running the Blow Out Preventer (BOP) to seabed and latch it onto the 16 ¾-inch wellhead to create a connection between the ship and the wellhead.

Before the BOP was brought out from its storage area, Rob summoned all personnel in the meeting room, where the subsea engineer explained each separate sequence they had to go through until every person knew exactly what to do. As they now needed to handle heavy equipment and operate winches in the moon pool just above sea level, all personnel working in that area had to wear life jackets at all times.

Rob told Joop that this was the most difficult sequence to explain on paper, as operation took place on the rig floor and in the moon pool, and they all had to be carried simultaneously to avoid accidents or equipment damage. It was hard, even for Joop, to visualize if one had never seen it done before.

While going through each sequence again, Rob explained to Joop that on top of the upper BOP section, the emergency connector was located so that it could be disconnected in case of emergency to separate the BOP from the riser string. Below the emergency connector, the ball joint provided a flexible connection between the rigid riser string and the annular preventer, which was designed to close on different sizes of pipe. The BOP was split up in one upper and lower BOP section connected with one hydraulic connector. On top of the lower BOP section the shear rams were located to shear the pipe in case of emergency. On the bottom of the BOP was another set of pipe rams and the 16 ¾-inch wellhead connector to latch on to the 16 ¾-inch wellhead. That choke and kill line were clamped onto the riser and routed on top of the BOP trough hoses to the choke and kill valves. The hydraulic pump provided volume and pressure to a number of accumulator bottles in the hydraulic control room on the surface and on the upper and lower BOP section.

The pilot pressure to operate each valve was running from the surface control room in hose bundle A and B, attached on each side of the riser pipe to the control pod located on the upper stack, from where control valves were operating each BOP function to open or close as selected on the surface from the operating panels. The second control hose bundle and pod B were used as a backup system. Beacons and transducers were installed on the seabed and the BOP to receive signals from sea level and BOP while lowering.

After Rob's short explanation of such a difficult operation, they went on deck to supervise each step.

The BOP was function tested in the moon pool to ensure that each operating line was connected correctly.

Now they had to carry out one of the most time consuming and dangerous operations—running the BOP with riser joints down to the guide funnel with 16 ¾-inch wellhead on the seabed.

Before the BOP and the first riser joint were lifted, the tool pusher and driller went through the sequence again with the entire crew.

The riser joint was lifted by the crane onto the pipe ramp and moved into the rig floor using the automatic pipe handling system. The lifting sub was installed and the first riser joint connected to the emergency connector. Special locking bolts were made up to lock each connection.

The BOP was lowered to seabed by picking up and connecting a large number of riser pipes with hose bundle A and B connected with clamps to each riser joint.

While lowering the riser joints each choke and kill line was pressure. The process continued for more than twenty hours before they finally reached the guide funnel at seabed.

With only two more riser joints left to run, Rob went up to the rig floor. As he climbed the stairs and glanced towards the sea, his heart stopped. Riveted to the spot, he couldn't quite believe what he was seeing—an enormously high, frothing wave that seemed to stretch the entire horizon was coming right at them.

He made a dash for the intercom system.

'DP operator. This is not a drill! Turn the ship ninety degrees to the port side right now. Cease all operations and sound the alarm. Everyone is to proceed to his muster stations immediately.'

He caught his breath, his eye on the ever approaching, monstrous wave and announced. 'Captain to the bridge. Big wave approaching us at port side.'

He leapt up the stairs to the bridge and DP control room. By the time he got there, the ship had turned fifty degrees. Then the wave hit. The ship listed sharply, some fifteen to twenty degrees. All available engine power was used, and they kept the ship within five degrees from the location center.

Once the wave had passed and the bucking movements of the ship subsided, the captain asked for a report from the engine room and rig floor for damage or accidents.

None were reported, as all operations had ceased the moment the alarm was sounded.

'What the hell was that?' Rob asked the captain and superintendent. 'I've never seen such a big wave.' No one seemed to be able to tell him what it was, but it was vital that they look into ways to reduce the impact on the ship from waves that size.

After evaluating the situation, they agreed to turn the ship always in the direction of the waves and ensure that all engines were always online to have sufficient power to keep the ship on location.

He realized how lucky they were that the BOP and riser were still hanging free, and not yet latched up to the wellhead, otherwise they would have had a serious problem.

He ordered for operations to continue and called Werner Brandt to report the incident, eager to know if anyone at the office could explain this strange phenomenon.

Within twenty minutes someone called him back. He was told that what they had just experienced was a tsunami, triggered by earthquakes or volcanic underwater eruptions. They could occur any time, and vary in size, according to the location and strengths of the eruptions.

Knowing that they were in an area known for its high volcanic activity, Rob suggested to the captain that they arrange for a permanent watch to look out for such waves to give them some warning.

Rob went to the rig floor to witness the installation of the riser slip joint and landing of the BOP. The slip joint consisted of one inner pipe and one heavy wall outer pipe. The weight of BOP and riser pipe was landed on the riser tension support ring that was locked to the heavy wall outer pipe of the slip joint. One pack off seal was installed between the inner and outer pipe to seal off any mud spill into the ocean.

The riser tension ring was connected with steel cables and sheaves to the riser tensioners that function as heave compensators to compensate for the heave movement of the ship.

As soon as the weight of the BOP and riser string was transferred to the riser tensioning system, the heave compensator was activated. The pressure on the riser tensioning system was decreased, and the BOP with riser lowered until the BOP was moved over and landed on the 16 ¾-inch wellhead connector in the guide frame. The hydraulic connector was operated in the closed position, and hydraulic fluid consumption indicated that the connector closed on the 16 ¾-inch wellhead connector.

The riser tensioning air system was increased and over pull applied to check if the BOP was connected to the wellhead connector. The over pull was released and a second ball joint picked up and landed into the mud box. Then the inner pipe of the slip joint was disconnected, raised and connected to the bottom of the ball joint connection. The function of the ball joint was to allow a 10-degree offset from the ship to the wellhead and functioned as a flexible swivel below the rig floor to avoid a rigid set up and possible damage to equipment or moon pool. The connection between the wellhead at seabed and the rig floor was now established and sealed off.

The subsea engineer prepared thereafter the BOP test tool to pressure test the connector between the 16 ¾-inch wellhead and BOP. The test tool was lowered on DP and landed in the wellhead. The BOP and wellhead connection was pressure tested for 15 minutes and no leak was observed.

Rob went to bed, as it had been a long time since having any sleep. In the meantime, the drilling crew started preparing the drilling assembly, consisting of a bit, drill collars, stabilizers and drill pipe. Rob had instructed the tool pusher to take his time with the new crew. It would be the first time for this particular crew to assemble the drilling assembly.

In the past he was always worried that accidents would happen while making up the drill collar connections with the rotary tongs. With the installation of the iron roughnecks, his wish had been fulfilled—the crew could step back, away from the danger zone.

He had asked the tool pusher to wake him up as soon as they started the initial drilling phase, but he woke up after ten hours, feeling rested. He showered, had lunch, and just then the intercom announced that the 16 ¾-inch casing 'shoe depth' was reached and drilled out. He went to the rig floor and instructed the driller to drill about ten feet of new formation and witnessed the formation intake test.

The blow out preventer rams were opened, upon which Rob simulated a rise in tank level to check if the driller reacted to this warning sign that the well was flowing. The driller reacted instantly, closing the rams to check if the pressure in the drill pipe would increase. Pleased, Rob went to the rig floor and complimented the driller on his fast and correct action. The rams were opened, and drilling of the new hole section could begin.

He went to his office and met with the rig superintendent, captain, tool pusher and Joop to go through the next drilling and casing sequences. After all their comments were noted, they were printed and distributed amongst the drillers so that they could be discussed with their crews at the meetings held before they went on shift. One sequence copy was displayed in the changing room.

Then Rob finally managed to catch up on his administration duties. He went through the few remaining outstanding items with Jurgen, as he was about to leave the ship. His work was completed, and Rob signed the handover papers, transferring the responsibility of the drill ship to the operational department, as from the date they arrived at the drilling location. Rob thanked Jurgen, telling him that he sincerely hoped to work with him again.

The next day Jurgen left on the helicopter that brought in fresh crews, and returned to the head office.

By telex Rob ordered the materials that he would require for drilling the next well section. The company had dispatched a material supervisor to Jakarta, whose job it was to hire supply vessels that could bring supplies to the rig and return equipment back to shore.

The supply vessels would, weather permitting, come along the lee side of the ship, where cranes loaded and unloaded equipment, and pump fuel, water and cement into the ship's storage tanks.

The material supervisor also contracted a Sikorsky helicopter for the weekly crew change. One week the marine crew would be exchanged, next the service personnel, followed by the drilling crew. Two crews were on board at all times, working in two shifts, while two other crews were on leave and everyone worked a four-week on and off schedule.

Once drilling was well on its way, he finally had time to think about home again. Yet he did not want to call Anne, as he knew he would not be able to resist asking her if she was pregnant. She had been so insistent that she would only tell him once he was home. Still, he wanted to hear her voice, so he called.

Their phone calls tended to be a bit uncomfortable, and never truly satisfying. They knew the radio operator would be listening in, so they had to limit their conversation to impersonal pleasantries such as 'how are you doing' and 'I'm doing fine.' It was something he hated. There was always so much more he wanted to say. He wanted to tell her how much he loved the weeks at home with her and Jan, and how happy he felt with the life that they lived. Now the big question that he didn't want to ask was left hanging in the air, unasked. On the other side of the line, Anne was telling him that their son was growing every day, that Dad was doing some gardening chores for her, and that he would be able to see all that in a week.

Another week. It struck him how fast the weeks had gone by while he had been working on these time-consuming and challenging operations. He would be home in a week.

As they drilled the next hole section, he had the opportunity to take Joop around the ship to show and explain to him the use of all the equipment on board. Apart from his training scheme, Joop assisted him in preparing the planning sequences and incorporating any changes or suggestions that had been discussed at the daily meetings.

Rob was more than pleased with him. He seemed very comfortable to be around and took everything very seriously, picking up things remarkably quickly during every drilling phase of the well. He was always on the rig floor or on deck whenever a new operation took place, eager to witness equipment inspections or pressure tests before they started drilling. Rob was glad Werner hired him.

After several days of drilling and numerous bit replacements, they ran another BOP test. Rob found that the response time to open and close the BOP functions required more time as when tested on surface.

He wasn't happy about this—BOP functions should close within seconds to avoid additional flow from the formation, which could lead to higher pressure to regain well control again.

He discussed the problem with the superintendent and subsea engineer. They came to the conclusion that the water depth, and therefore the pressure acting on the hydraulic pilot lines at sea bottom, probably caused the response delay. Rob realized that if the ship were to operate in water depths exceeding 5,000 feet, the present hydraulic system could not be used. He contacted the head office engineering department, who shared his concern and agreed to find a solution.

Chapter 18

When the helicopter landed to pick him and the crew up to go home, he wasn't even ready. He hurriedly took a shower, changed and packed, after which he briefly discussed the handover notes with his relief.

The helicopter ride was thrilling, providing them with stunning views over the many islands that passed below them. For the first time, he could see the smoke from the numerous volcanoes, and only then he truly realized how much volcanic activity there was in the area.

But when they came closer to the shore of Java, the pilot informed them that he needed to land, as one of his instruments did not seem to respond as it should. Before they knew what was happening, he landed right in the in the middle of a rice field. The women workers were systematically planting rice seedlings. They stared up at the lowering helicopter in stupefaction, throwing themselves onto their knees, as if Mohammed himself had come to them. It was obvious that they had never seen a helicopter land before.

The pilot got out of the helicopter and checked his beacon receiver used to locate the helicopter port in Yogyakarta. He informed them that he would have to fly at a low attitude and use his charts because his beacon wasn't functioning.

They lifted off, leaving the women on the fields holding onto their cone hats and waving their arms in agitation.

At low altitude they were able to experience Java in its entire splendor, given a spectacular tour of the island's tourist attractions. On their way to Yogyakarta the pilot circled around the Buddhist temple of Borobudur, and Rob was in awe of its architectural glory, a relic from a bygone age. He had always wanted to see one of the World Heritage sites and now he was actually flying over this one and could see it in close up.

The pilot showed them the inside of an active volcano crater and gave them a tour around the beautiful countryside of Java. He peered down in wonder at the watery rice fields, the palm trees, locals looking up at them from their bicycles, the picturesque villages where time had appeared to stand still.

They were taken around once more, this time to an enormous crater that appeared to be filled with water. The pilot explained that it was not lava, but mud eruptions that had covered villages and killed thousands of people.

Upon landing everyone thanked the pilot, secretly delighting in the fact that the board instruments had malfunctioned, giving them the flight of a lifetime.

In Yogyakarta the DC-3 charter plane waited and took them to

Singapore, this time at standard cruising altitude.

After a final drink with the entire crew to toast on their leave, Rob asked Joop to join him, because he wanted to buy something for Anne and Jan. The flight wasn't until that evening, so they had plenty of time.

They hailed a taxi and asked the driver to take them to the closest shopping center. Rob was surprised to find that they had been brought to a three-story luxury mall, the likes of which he had never seen before. Everything was available, and they sold the most expensive brands. A tailor-made suit could be fitted in three hours. Every brand of watch, sound systems, jewelry and leather handbags were sold here.

It took a while to find their way and to get used to the haggling that went on. The asking price for most goods was at least forty percent above the real value.

He decided to buy a watch for Anne and considered buying a toy car for Jan, but he opted for a teddy bear instead, realizing he was still too young to play with cars.

Joop wanted to buy a computer, as the one he used at the university had begun to malfunction. The computers were cheap compared to Holland, and Rob told him to negotiate a price for two. Since Joop knew exactly what brand and type to buy, they got a very good deal.

With all their wheeling and dealing, the time flew by, and they had to return to the airport. Much to their surprise, the same taxi driver was still waiting outside the mall to take them back to the airport.

The check-in went smoothly, and within one hour the plane took off for Frankfurt, Amsterdam and London.

Rob noticed that a lot of oil field workers and sailors boarded the flight. It was obvious that some had already consumed too much alcohol and were downright drunk. It surprised him that they were still allowed to board the plane.

Once they had settled in, most of the men put down their seats and slept even before the plane was at cruising altitude. But not everyone! During takeoff, the Norwegian sailors were already yelling at the flight attendant, demanding more whiskey. They became rowdy and angry when she told them to wait.

Rob knew that alcohol was very expensive in Norway, and Norwegians would often drink too much if it was free. He decided to ignore them and was glad to be seated in a relatively quiet section where people tried to sleep or listen to music.

He asked Joop his opinion on some of the problems they had encountered the last week. They discussed the hydraulic operation pressure and reviewed the diagrams.

After a few hours Rob noticed that some of the Norwegian sailors had become obnoxious, causing annoyance among the other passengers. One of the offenders was forcefully moved to a separate seat, after which the captain announced that he would have to make a non-scheduled landing in Dubai.

Thirty minutes later the plane landed in Dubai, where the airport police removed the drunkard from the plane. Within one hour the plane was back in the air and on its way to Frankfurt. The captain made a short announcement, saying that one of the passengers had to be removed from the plane as he was causing a disturbance. From that moment on, the Norwegians' rowdy behavior ceased and they became as meek as lambs.

Curious to know, he asked the flight attendant what happened.

'He was groping one of my colleagues, sir,' she told him. 'Had his hand right up her skirt. They've arrested him. With charges of indecent assault, he's bound to end up in jail in Dubai.'

Joop was asleep until they landed in Frankfurt.

He told Rob that he had a dream about the BOP hydraulic pilot lines, something over which they had been racking their brains. In his dream, he told the subsea engineer to use the phone system for sending fast messages to the hydraulic pod to carry out its functions. When he woke up, it had suddenly dawned on him that using a phone or multiplex signal, was indeed possible.

Excited, Rob told him to make a brief summary of his idea and forward it to Werner and the Engineering department. The more he thought about it, the more it occurred to him that Joop had the knack of grasping problems and coming up with simple and effective solutions.

Chapter 19

It was early in the morning when they landed at Schiphol. Joop took the train to Amsterdam while Rob boarded his connecting flight to Enschede.

It was a short flight, but the closer he came home, the more edgy he became. It took far too long before the plane landed. The growing impatience that he felt was new to him, but he knew the reason. He was seated in the middle section of the plane, but in his eagerness to get out, he still managed to be the first passenger at the arrival gate.

The moment he saw Anne with Jan in her arms, he knew that she was pregnant. Her eyes were shining and she beamed at him, happy to see him. When he stopped in front of her they just looked at each other—words unnecessary.

He embraced and kissed them many times before he relieved Anne of Jan, who stared up at him with big eyes.

Once they had strapped Jan into his backseat, Anne looked at him. 'This is the reason why I didn't tell you over the phone. I just didn't want to miss that look on your face. I don't even have to tell you. You know. You saw it in my eyes. I'm expecting a girl, Rob.'

'Have you visited the doctor yet?'

'No. I don't have to. I know my body, Rob. I don't need a doctor to tell me I'm pregnant.'

'Jesus. Does this never stop?'

'No. This time I waited so you can join me to the doctor. To make up for the first time. I made an appointment for tomorrow morning and you're more than welcome to confirm what I already know.'

He had difficulty keeping his eyes on the road. Whenever he glanced across at Anne, she flashed him her bright smile.

'Shall we stop at your mother's grave and tell her?' she asked.

'Yes please,' Rob said firmly. 'I'd like that. If your intuition is right and we do get a little girl, she'll be named after her. Let's get her some flowers.'

'Don't have to. Dad takes care of that since you left, and I never did ask him.'

When they approached the grave he saw the lovely bouquet of fresh flowers. He felt immensely grateful to the person who was always there to help others and who required so little for himself.

He felt too choked up to speak. 'Anne. Could you please tell her?'

Anne swallowed, nodding. 'Dear Mam, we've got something to tell you,' she said fondly. 'Our son is about to have a sister. We'll give her the name that is burned into both our hearts. We really do hope that there is a peephole in heaven so you'll be able to watch her grow up in our family.'

The tears were running down their cheeks. 'Thank you, my darling,' he whispered as he turned around. They left the deserted graveyard hand in hand. He felt at peace. Something good was happening that lessened the pain of losing a loved one.

They turned onto their street, and Rob immediately felt that he was coming home.

His first house never did have that effect on him. The events that happened there had turned that house into a place with nothing but bad memories.

But this home was something they created together. The moment he stepped into the house holding Jan, he felt at ease and relaxed. Everything was just right. The large windows that let in the daylight, the oak doors and panels, the fireplace, the comfortable layout of all the rooms and the kitchen with the round table.

Just like the last time he came home, the first thing he did was walk around with Jan in his arms, checking each room to see if anything had changed.

He breathed in that special, unmistakable smell of home, soaking up every inch of it.

After he made his rounds, he said, 'You know, sometimes there is just no time to tell you, or the circumstances won't allow it, but I need to tell you now that I missed you terribly. Usually my job pushes back the pain. But the moment I see you, my heart bursts, and I desperate want to hold and kiss you.'

Silently she put her hand against his cheek, quickly gave Jan his bottle and put him to bed. Then she took his hand and led him to the bedroom. He sat down and watched her undress, appreciating once more how beautiful her figure was. She was perfect for him—her breasts were just the right size. She had legs and a bottom you could actually hold on to.

But it seemed that whenever she was expecting, her body was given an extra dimension. She reminded him of a tulip that needs the sunlight to open, only then allowing you to discover its full beauty. And once again he felt that it was his coming and going that kept their marriage so very interesting and exciting.

'I was just thinking that being apart for so long sometimes makes the desire almost painful.'

She came up to him and kissed him. 'Don't talk about desire. I'm burning inside, and I want you to quench that fire. It may take up all the resources you have.'

'If these changes only take place during pregnancy, I wish you were pregnant all the time.'

Jan returned them back to reality. Rob took him out of his bed and put him in between them, playing with him until he made it quite clear that he was hungry.

They enjoyed the afternoon and evening together, and Rob had the feeling that Jan needed time to get used to him. The frowning way he looked at him would change into a laugh when Rob picked him up or played with him.

As the temperature was still lovely, he helped Anne to set the table outside for their first dinner on the terrace. It was just like they expected it to be—from here they could watch the sun set slowly behind the trees in the distance. It made Rob feel relaxed and very rich.

After a while he went inside and came back with a small box. 'I know that we can't always be together and that I'll have to leave again. I hope that this will always remind you that I love you every minute of the day.'

She opened the box, and by the way her face lit up, he knew that he made the right choice. 'Oh, yes! It's beautiful, I love it. Thank you so much!'

'You are very welcome. Anyway, I think it's getting cold outside. Time to put our son to bed for the night.'

'No way! It's not cold at all! After we put Jan to bed, I'd like a glass of wine outside on the terrace.'

'But...'

'No buts. If you want to start the fireplace on such a sultry evening, we won't be able to enjoy the terrace, and we should do so while we can.'

'This brings back memories.'

'You should always cherish your memories.'

Rob took Jan upstairs and gave him a bath. He played boisterously, splashing water all over the bathroom. He had some difficulty dressing his son, his hands unaccustomed to handling the small buttons and fastenings. Frustrated, he allowed Anne to take over. Rob preferred to feed him, as by the time the bottle was empty, Jan usually fell asleep in his arms.

Carefully, he laid him in his cot and gave him the small teddy bear. The sight of the cuddly toy brought him wide awake again, and he started playing with it.

'I think you just gave him his first buddy,' Anne said. 'It will take a while before he falls asleep now.'

Anne was right. It was a while before the intercom finally fell silent. Quietly, Rob crept up the stairs to check on him. Jan was sound asleep, the teddy bear held in a tight embrace.

They went back outside to enjoy the garden, the setting sun, a glass of wine in their hands and soft music playing in the background. Life couldn't get any better than this.

When it became dark, Anne got up, and when she came back out, she brought his sheepskin, pillows and a burning candle.

'I'm glad that I found your hiding place. And that we have a garden with loads of privacy,' she said as she laid out the sheepskin and pillows on the terrace. 'The temperature reminds me of Saudi.' She looked at him slyly. 'I still have this burning desire in me.'

They cuddled up on the sheepskin, facing the stars. Rob pointed out the various constellations. He spoke about the time he had sat outside on the terrace with his mam at his previous house, and how she had told him which star was her favorite.

'Every night before I go to sleep, I thank the Lord for this day, for all that I have. For the fact that I'm so very blessed to live this life. I always ask the Holy Mary and Mam to watch over you and Jan.' He let the silence envelope them, breathing in the scent of Anne's hair. 'I still talk to this star whenever I have a few minutes alone. That star out there, that's my mam.'

'Then I hope that I'll be part of that conversation in the future, so that I can ask the same star to bring you back home safely.'

They ended up making love, exploring every inch of each other's bodies, finally falling asleep under the open sky until the cold night air woke them up.

Whenever he was home, he usually had the urge to live the full twenty-four hours a day, unwilling to go to bed. Getting home from work always gave him a tremendous buzz. But with Jan's demanding sleeping and feeding schedule, he had to admit that he needed his sleep.

Now he was only too happy when Jan finished his bottle, so that he could go back to sleep for another four hours. And Anne was right—he needed all of his energy to quench the fire of desire that burned inside of her.

After breakfast Dad walked in for a cup of coffee and to see his grandson. He shook Rob's hand warmly. Once again, Rob noticed that Jan's face lit up with smiles the moment his granddad walked in the door.

But he wasn't jealous. He was more than happy that this fine man had found so much happiness in his grandson. As soon as the playful greeting rituals between Jan and his granddad were done, he thanked him for the flowers on his mam's grave.

'Oh, that's nothing,' he said with a dismissive wave of his hand. 'She deserves fresh flowers from time to time.' That was why Rob was so fond of this man. So little words, yet such a big heart.

Anne made fresh coffee and handed her dad a small package. 'Just a little gift for all the work you've done for me in the garden and around the house.'

'I don't want a present for that!' he protested modestly.

'Just take it, Dad, please,' Anne insisted. When he opened it, he unfolded a T-shirt. On it were the words, "I'm going to be a granddad again." He stared at it, his eyes misting over when it dawned on him.

'There was a time that life did not mean that much to me,' he said, his voice quaking as he held Anne's arm. 'But having my daughter and grandson so close to me is an extraordinary gift that has made me very happy. I've come to enjoy every day that is given me.'

To avoid getting too emotional, Anne quickly changed the subject. 'Dad, if I put Jan to bed, could you babysit for half an hour so we can go to the doctor? We've got an appointment.'

'Hasn't he confirmed that you're pregnant yet?'

'No. I just know I am.'

'Well, then you're just like your mam. She didn't need a doctor to tell her she was expecting you, either.'

Together they cycled to the doctor's practice, and within twenty minutes she knew for a fact that she was pregnant. Rob suggested to Anne that they ride past the florist to see if they sold red gladioli. It was a tradition he wanted to keep—they were the first thing he had noticed in their Riyadh apartment when he got back from the desert and when she told him she was pregnant with Jan. They were in luck—gladioli were abundantly available this time of year, so they bought a large bunch.

Happy and exuberant, they cycled home, where Anne beamed at her dad, telling him yes, she was very pregnant, and yes, all was well.

Before Dad left he asked if Rob would like some help with the carport, knowing that he planned to build one.

'That would be great. I could do with some help, especially mounting the roof. I'll let you know when I get started on it. I first have to get over the worst of this jet-lag.'

After he left, Anne looked at him with a sly grin. 'Is it really the jet-lag, or is this just your excuse for running out of energy?'

'This is just typical. First you show someone how and what to do, and then they think they can take over and tell you what to do. You watch it, lady. I'll take you up on your challenge any time of the day. So you'd better think twice before you challenge me again.'

'Yes, boss.'

Rob finished the engineering proposal he had been working on for Werner and cycled to the mailbox to post it. When he returned Jan was awake. Anne had not fed him, as she wanted Rob to do it. She thought that feeding Jan would be the best way for Jan to bond with him, and for Rob to become more popular with his son.

'Did you mind seeing how Jan reacted to my dad this morning?' she asked.

'You mean to ask if I'm jealous? No. I like the fact that Dad gets so much pleasure out of having him around. Jan clearly loves his company. Don't worry; it's just a matter of time. He'll get to know me soon enough.'

He watched as Jan drank thirstily from his bottle, the milk level dropping fast.

'Anne, why don't you invite Agnes and Klaus for dinner tonight? I'd like to tell them and the kids of our surprise.'

'No need. Your sister was the first one to ask if I was pregnant, I don't know if women have some kind of intuition, or that they just recognize the signs faster than men. But I'll ask them to come over tonight, as it's been two weeks since I last saw them.'

Anne made the call, and Agnes told her that they would come over as soon as Klaus arrived home from work.

'Even if Agnes knows you're pregnant, perhaps we can buy a T-shirt for the kids with the text on it, stating that they're about to get a little girl cousin?'

'Done. I already bought them in the same shop where I got the one for Dad.'

'You are good, you know that? What else did you do?'

'Yesterday I checked our company stock. You must have done something right, because we are making money! We could consider selling it.'

'No, I don't want to sell. I'd like to keep the stock and use it for an early retirement.'

'Why don't we buy a boat or something, like other people do, and enjoy it while we can? Live for the moment...that sort of thing?'

'Because my work is my second hobby, which takes up a lot of my time and energy.'

'So what's your first hobby?'

He winked at her. 'I'll tell you tonight. At a certain age in life, I intend to retire and dedicate all my time to you and the kids. Then you will be the most important people in my life and get my undivided attention. With interest.'

'The consultant at the bank advised me to sell the stock as we'd make a good profit, but I'll respect your decision. We'll leave it for your early retirement.'

A knock on the door announced the arrival of Agnes and her family, and the house immediately filled with the three big L's—Loud, Love and Laughter—the two children bursting through the door with boisterous energy, eager to show their uncle Rob their school report cards.

It had become a tradition that Rob paid them if they achieved good grades. So he sat down, made a show of awe at their results, and paid them a guilder for each good grade they had. Jokingly, he tried to renegotiate with them, trying to reduce the rate to fifty cents, but Dagmar and Thomas loudly refuted this, saying that it was 'not negotiable', citing his own words that 'a deal is a deal'. He ended up paying ten guilders to each of them.

'Well, Anne,' he said. 'Looks like we've just spent all our household money. We'll have to live on water and bread for the rest of the week!'

Once their financial reward was paid for and settled, the children's attention went to Jan. They both wanted to give him his bottle, so Anne allowed them to feed him in turns. Once Jan had finished his milk, Rob told them that he needed their assistance with another job, and curiously they joined him to the bathroom. When they discovered that they were to help him change Jan's dirty diaper they quickly returned to the living room, expressing their disgust with pinched noses.

It was good to have dinner together again, and fun to listen to the children's stories. Dagmar and Thomas expressed an interest on how their parents had first met, and at what age they had started smoking.

After dinner Anne give them both a small parcel. They opened them simultaneously—a purple T-shirt for Dagmar and a blue one for Thomas. They said the appropriate thankful words, but they didn't seem to take in the text that had been printed on the shirts.

'Read what it says,' Agnes urged them.

'I'm getting a girl cousin,' Dagmar read aloud. She looked up at Anne quizzically. 'What's a cousin?'

'It means that Aunt Anne will have a baby in about nine months' time.'

'Do you mean like Jan?'

'Yes, but this time Aunt Anne thinks it's going to be a girl.'

When it dawned on the child, she started jumping up and down excitedly, singing 'I'll have a girl cousin to play with. I'll have a girl cousin to play with!'

'Oh calm down,' her brother said. 'It will take ages. Anyway, I think it's going to be a boy.'

Then the question came up on how babies were made, whereupon Agnes tried to change the subject, saying that she would explain that to them some other time.

In the meantime Klaus told Rob that as a contractor, he could get a twenty percent discount if he bought all the materials for the carport, and that he would have them delivered to his house within two days. Rob thanked him, and after a lot of hugs and kisses, they left. The house fell instantly quiet.

Rob looked at Anne with a sigh. 'Boy, that was a lively evening! If that's what's in store for us later... Phew! Is this what you want?'

'You should think of all the consequences before seducing me. Anyway, I'd like the same procedure as last night.'

'Are you trying to wear me out? My schedule is pretty tight with Jan keeping us up at night.'

'I have no mercy. So when are you ready to try out the new bathtub?'

'You mean you want to have a bath together?'

'Yes. We didn't purchase a bath for two only to use it once a year.'

'Can I wash you?'

'You can wash all of me.'

'Can we start now?'

'I thought you had a tight schedule.'

'I can always fit you in.'

'No, I'll wait,' she said with a grin. 'Let me know once you're finished with Jan.'

Rob thought that he'd probably never washed, changed diapers, and fed his son that fast. When he finished, Anne was already in the bath, the bathroom lit with scented candles.

'You really do know how to seduce your husband, my love. And I see you've also created plenty of bubbles to cover up all those beautiful curves of yours.'

'Well, explore and find the treasures.'

So he did, until the water became too cold.

While she wrapped herself in a towel, she looked at him coyly. 'Rob? I never had a massage before. I wonder if I'd like it. Would you mind giving me a massage?'

'We don't have any massage oil.'

'Oh yes we do. I bought a bottle last week.'

Her request came as a surprise to Rob. The oil was deliciously fragrant, and one of the best massage oils he had ever smelled. He had never given a massage to a woman before, so this was new to him. But he took his time and the oil did the job, easily taking his hands to the body parts he preferred.

The next morning his hands were so slick with oil that his shaver slipped out of his hands. He was still smiling when he entered the kitchen.

'What are you smiling about? Anything to do with what we did last night?'

He laughed. 'My hands were still so oily that I dropped my shaver.'

The rest of that day they laughed whenever they looked at each other. They realized this was what life was about. Living apart from time to time was part of it, but building a home together, being blessed with a son and a daughter on the way—that was his dream. It all came down to the basics of life—to care for one another and to enjoy each day they were given.

When Rob received the parts of the carport, he asked Dad to help him out with the concrete foundations for the supporting beams. Together they paved the driveway, and once the concrete was dry, they placed the foundation and overhead beams, including the roof panels.

Dad was very easy to work with, as he was used to doing jobs around the house, and he never needed Rob to explain anything to him. The weather was excellent, so they had coffee, lunch and dinner outside while Jan sat in the playpen, watching the men at work.

Once the carport was finished, Rob had one more week before going back to work. He stayed home, taking walks in the forest, cycling around the village and going to his favorite place—the watermill where they had taken their wedding photos. They loved eating at the old farmhouse that had been turned into a pancake restaurant right next to the mill, where they would sit on the terrace to watch the large waterwheel cup the water and listen to the rhythmic sound of splashing water.

Anne knew that Rob always wanted to spend the last week with just her and Jan. With time running out, he usually didn't want to see anyone else.

On his last evening they walked around the neighborhood until it was Jan's bedtime. Anne took the time to observe how tenderly he handled his son, sensing the love between them. She understood the acuteness of his pain at having to leave them again.

They stayed outside on the terrace until it became too cold, after which they went upstairs to make love until the early hours of the morning. They had breakfast before Jan woke up, and then Anne finally drove him to the local airport. Rob insisted that they say goodbye in the car, as he wanted to say goodbye to his family in private.

He waited outside until she finally drove off.

As if someone were playing a cruel joke on him, the plane flew straight over their house, where he could see Anne getting out of the car, waving up at him. With a cringing heart, he put back his seat, closed his eyes and tried to hold on to the memories of the past four weeks. In all the years that he had worked in the oilfields, he had met many men who really liked their jobs and the money they were paid, but who eventually ended up working onshore. He never did quite understand why, but now he knew.

Chapter 20

At Schiphol he met Joop at the check-in area, and they arranged to be seated together. When they took their seats, Rob couldn't help noticing the pain in Joop's eyes. It was something he now recognized as his own.

Joop closed his eyes without a word, and it took half the flight before he finally got around to asking Rob how his leave had been. Once they began discussing work, Rob informed Joop that the ship had started drilling.

The man sitting on the other side of the aisle leaned over. 'Are you talking about the drill ship that's currently drilling in the Java Sea?'

Rob confirmed that this was the case, whereupon the man told them that he was a driller on his way for his first shift on the same ship. He asked if he could share transport to the hotel, where they would be staying one night before the early morning charter flight to Yogyakarta.

'There's a bus waiting at the airport.' Rob told him.

When they arrived at the hotel, they found that their three rooms were located next to each other. Rob suggested they visit Boogey Street, famous for its excellent food and transvestite shows. They took a taxi to Boogey Street, where they selected an eating place on the street. They were approached by several local beauties, who asked if they could join them for a drink. The driller noted their good looks, finding these women even lovelier than the flight attendants of Singapore Airlines.

'We've only come here for a meal,' Rob told them politely. 'We'll be on our way again once we've finished.'

He loved Chinese food, as there are restaurants in every Dutch town serving spicy dishes such as bami and nasi goreng with chicken or pork. He ordered satays, fried rice and a beer. Joop and the driller ordered bami noodles and satays. The food was exceptionally good, and they ordered another portion of satays. While they waited for the food to come, one of the women who had asked them to join them for a drink earlier returned and started to dance, stripping until she wore nothing but a tiny bikini. Moving on to the next table, she was joined by another girl, who also began to dance and strip.

Somewhat uncomfortable at the impromptu display of female flesh, the men ate their second portion of satays. Trying to ignore the semi-naked women, Rob asked for a dessert and was advised to try spekkoek, a sweet, Indonesian layered cake. Once they had finished, they all ordered another serving and paid the bill. Rob wanted to go back to the hotel as they had to get up early the next morning, and Joop stood up to join him, but the driller decided to stay in Boogey Street for a while longer.

The alarm went off at four a.m., and after a quick shower and a shave,

Rob went down to find Joop at the breakfast table. After they finished eating, the driller still had not come down, so Rob went to check on him.

He knocked on the door. It was opened by one of the women who had danced for them last night. Not only was she stark naked, she also turned out to be a man.

'Wake him up,' he gestured to the driller, who was still fast asleep in bed. 'He's got a flight to catch.' The beautiful creature tried to wake him, but got no response.

Agitated, Rob went into the bathroom, came back with a glass of cold water and threw it into the driller's face. The man woke up, shocked to discover that the beautiful girl he had made love to turned out to be a man. Within minutes he was ready to take the bus to the airport.

During the plane and helicopter flights, everyone tried to get some sleep, as they all had to work a twelve-hour shift once they arrived on board.

Rob went to his office and asked Joop to join the handover meeting. Everything had gone smoothly over the past four weeks, and his relief confirmed the long response time of the BOP functions recorded on the last test. He told him that the engineering department was working on a solution to shorten the time, as the ship was scheduled to drill in the deep Australian waters. Since they had started drilling the smaller, 12 ¼-foot hole section, the geologist had predicted that they may encounter gas bearing formations.

His relief left for home, and Rob visited the drilling contractor's office, where he discussed the planning for the next few days with the superintendent and the tool pusher. The last 'kick' test had taken place a week ago, so he asked the tool pusher to carry out the kick drill straight away, as they expected to find gas in the next formation layers.

He went to the core lab, where the geologist explained the expected type of formations, giving details on the thickness of the sand layers. Armed with this information, Rob returned to the office to update the 12 ¼-foot drilling sequence. He then asked the tool pusher to distribute the sequence sheets to the drillers so that everyone on board knew that they could come across gas formations at these depths.

Joop's training scheme for that week was to join the derrickmen and operate the pipe handling machine, measure all the properties of the mud and add mud chemicals as instructed by the mud engineer. Rob asked him to work the nightshift, instructing him to pay particular attention to the drilling rate. If he noticed a sudden increase in the penetration rate, he was to warn him straight away.

Rob knew that a lot of oil and gas had already been discovered in Indonesia, but this was the first drilling project in deep waters. Sand layers here could be much thicker than on land, and he just had a funny feeling about this location. The last thing he checked before going to sleep was how much barite was on board. Barite is used to increase the mud weight in the event a 'kick' takes place. Once the mud engineer informed him of the amount on board, he ordered another one hundred tons to be shipped ASAP on the next supply boat. He then asked the rig superintendent to check if all the tools required to run the 9 5/8-foot casing were on board.

Drilling continued, and at each sand layer, they circulated to ensure that no gas was present. Rob finalized the next sequence pages and distributed them for further input to the rig superintendent. He was more alert than ever before, testing the degasser daily and instructing the drillers to calibrate all instruments and recorders at the start of each shift. He ordered to make and increase the mud weight in one of the spare mud tanks just in case.

There was little more for him to do than to wait and see what surprises Mother Earth had in store for him this time. And it turned out, that she did. After ten days of careful drilling and just before they reached the next casing depth, Joop woke him up.

A drilling break had taken place, and the well was closed in.

Rob was at the rig floor in minutes, and after looking at the drill pipe pressure and calculating the required mud weight, he instructed the mud engineer to raise the mud weight in the spare tank and to inform him of the weight every ten minutes. In the meantime, the drill pipe pressure increased.

Rob knew what the allowable maximum pressure was. They would have to pump heavy mud as soon as possible to avoid a collapse of the formation. But the mud in the tanks did not have sufficient mud weight yet to kill the well. He could not afford to wait any longer and gave instructions to pump the heavy mud in the spare tank and kill the well according to protocol. The choke line was partly closed to keep constant pressure on the formation to avoid another influx of gas. Quickly Rob left the rig floor to call Werner, asking permission to plug the bottom of the well with cement if it exceeded the maximum allowable pressure. If that happened, then they would no longer be able to control the gas pressure. Werner told him that if possible he would come up with another option and call back.

When he got back to the rig floor, he heard the unmistakable sound of gas expanding at the surface. Immediately, he ordered everyone away from the closed mud box and shaker house and told the rig superintendent to sound the yellow alert. All personnel had to go to their muster stations, ready to board the lifeboats and leave the ship.

The sound of the expanding gas increased in volume, so he ordered for the cement to be mixed and ready to be pumped through the drill pipe in case they had to. He was called back to the radio room, where Werner told him that if the well could not be killed with the mud weight, they had no other option but to cement it.

On his way back to the rig floor, the cover plate of the mud box came partly off because the bolts holding it down had been cut. Rob prayed that there would be nothing to cause an ignition, as the results would be catastrophic.

The mud engineer informed him that the mud tank weight was increased to maximum mud weight and ready to be pumped. Quickly, Rob ordered the driller to pump heavy mud down the hole. They watched the pressure gauge with bated breath. The pressure and time would determine if they could control the well with the maximum mud weight or if they would have to pump the cement plug.

In case the cement plug had to be pumped, he hoped to seal off the gas formation. The only risk was that part of the drill string would be cemented as well. That would result in yet another problem they would have to solve.

By the time the heavy mud reached the drilling bit, the pressure should be zero.

The mud weight should be sufficient to control the gas pressure, and avoid a complete breakdown of the formation. If a breakdown did occur, the gas would find its way up, with disastrous results.

By the time the heavy mud reached the drilling bit, Rob ordered the crew to stop the pump, close the choke and observe the well. The drill pipe pressure gauge remained on 20 bars for 15 minutes, and Rob ordered them to open the choke partly and continue pumping the heavy mud down the well. The expanding gas created gas fumes around the rig floor, making everyone aware of the hazard.

It took two hours before all the gas was circulated out of the well. When the danger was gone, the yellow status was finally changed to green, and the off-duty crewmembers were able to go back to their cabins.

Rob called Werner and recommended they stop drilling and set the 9 5/8-foot casing at the present drilling depth. That way, the 13 3/8-foot shoe pressure would no longer be the weakest link. Werner discussed the option with the engineers and geologists, who all agreed that this was their best option.

Before operations resumed, Rob called everyone to the meeting room and thanked them for a job well done. Now that they knew that gas was awaiting them at the bottom of the well, everyone was aware that the slightest mistake could be disastrous. Rob stressed how important it was to have someone on the flow line to observe the flow of the well at all times, and that it was vital that the drillers pulled the string out of the hole very slowly.

Rob stayed on the rig floor until the bit was pulled into the shoe and returned to bottom again, and the danger had passed. Feeling both drained and utterly relieved that he had managed to control the dangerous situation, he walked to the top of the bridge, searched for his lucky star and thanked his mam for protecting them. Then he went to his cabin for some badly needed sleep.

The next day the drilling assembly was pulled out of the hole, and Rob checked that the casing shoe was functioning tested and connected properly before the first casing joint was lowered into the hole. He knew that after the casing was run, he would not get much sleep for a long time, so he tried to get some rest. But sleep would not come—his thoughts were at home. He went up to the radio room, suddenly in need of hearing Anne's voice.

Once he got through, he found that all was well at home. It was just good to hear her breathe through the phone, to hear her words, even if they told him what he already knew. He went back to his room at peace and finally fell asleep.

The tool pusher woke him up and told him that the casing was run to the bottom and they circulated the mud with minor gas shows. They were ready to cement. Rob went to the rig floor to supervise the cement operations.

The whole operation took ten hours, and everything went like clockwork. Rob could not have wished for anything better after the highly risky well killing operation.

While the drilling crew cleaned the rig floor of tools and equipment, Rob invited the drilling supervisor and tool pusher to discuss the draft drilling sequence for the next 8 ½-inch hole section. They had no reference of any previous wells drilled in this area to go by.

The geologist pointed out the depths at which they could expect drilling problems. Some formations were very abrasive, or the swelling salts could cause the pipe get stuck. All relevant information was highlighted in red. Once again, Rob asked the tool pusher to instruct all the drillers to give their input after their shifts on these sequences.

When Joop went off to finalize the sequences, Rob was left alone with the superintendent.

'Why do you invest so much time and energy into the planning of these sequences?' the superintendent asked. 'Your colleague only provides us with a list of instructions. He leaves it up to us contractors to carry them out.'

'This is a multimillion-dollar project,' Rob said. 'You could compare drilling a well to the protocols on an airplane. No plane can takeoff or land before a list of items is thoroughly checked, whether the pilot has just one or twenty years of experience.

The risk is simply too great. The time that a pilot can fly over his house to let his wife know that he's back are long gone.' He went on to explain that the airline industry invested millions in a control system that could take over in the event of human error.

'I believe they should develop such a system in the oil industry as well.

There is too much at risk to continue drilling operations the way we did just because things have always been done that way. I've witnessed too many accidents because of human failure, with hardly any communication between the parties involved. I'm not saying that we should continually have safety meetings, but that we should review the sequences and always look back at previous incidents to avoid them from happening again.' He smiled. 'You know, I remember someone once told me, "A person does not plan to fail, but he fails to plan." I don't want to be such a person.'

The superintendent nodded in understanding and assured him that he and his crew would give him all their support. 'You're right,' the man said. 'I've seen the way you work. Your approach seems to have its effect. Everything should be done to avoid accidents and mistakes from happening.'

Suddenly the ship lurched to one side, the tsunami alarm sounded. Rob hastily grabbed onto the anchored desk. He dashed for the DP room and told the operator to take manual control, instructing him to apply maximum power to the starboard thrusters to stay within the limits to avoid disconnecting the upper stack.

A call came in from the tool pusher, whose voice shouted through the intercom.

'I'm on the rig floor now, awaiting your instructions to disconnect the upper stack.'

'Wait for my instructions!' Rob told him as he noticed that the ship was four degrees off center.

The starboard thrusters worked at maximum power. The great ship stayed within the four degrees scale for minutes, after which it slowly returned to the center of the well, and the DP operator switched to automatic mode again.

'We're back on center again,' Rob told the tool pusher. 'Any casualties or damage?'

It appeared that one man had hit his head against a beam, sustaining a minor cut on his forehead. Rob was relieved. They now knew that they had sufficient power to control the ship in the event of a tsunami wave.

When the ocean calmed down again, the new drilling assembly was run into the hole and the formation intake test was run. Once the 'kick' drill was done and he was satisfied with the pressure test, he gave instructions to start drilling the 8 ½-foot hole.

With drilling well on its way, Rob had time for his administrative tasks.

Because of the time difference, Rob always preferred to call Werner in the afternoon. The calls were generally short, and mostly to clarify certain operations that required more detail. Rob asked him if any progress had been made on the proposal he had sent in, and he was informed that the technical drawings were completed. They were still awaiting cost estimates from the different suppliers.

Werner felt that the ship should return to Singapore for modifications before going into the deep waters of Australia. The final item Rob discussed with him was his concern about the well kick that they just experienced. He remembered the advice of the deep well geologist in Germany, and asked if the high pressure piping system could be upgraded to 15,000 psi. After all, the formation pressures for deep water wells were practically unknown, and he believed that such an upgrade was necessary. Werner said that he would look into it.

While drilling continued, Rob spent time with Joop, going through his progress and the experience gained since he started on the job. Joop had now been with the company for seven weeks, working in different departments. The coming week he was scheduled to assist the driller. Rob asked him to use his return flight to write down all the questions that he might have for his supervisors or crewmembers, to be used as guide for future trainees' training purposes. He told him to have the list ready when he got to Amsterdam.

It was Rob's last workday before going home. This time he was dressed and ready before his relief arrived on board. Every item of importance was noted in the handover book, and each item was shortly addressed and discussed, especially the well kick incident.

When he and the crew boarded the helicopter, he noticed that the same chief pilot was flying. He greeted him when he recognized Rob. 'What would you prefer, a flight at normal altitude or sightseeing?'

'Sightseeing would be great!' Rob shouted back at him over the noise, and they lifted off. But after about twenty minutes, Rob noticed that something was very wrong. The engine made a strange noise and he could feel the aircraft vibrating strongly beneath him.

The pilot used the intercom. 'Damn. I'll have to set the helicopter on the water and floaters! Don't worry; I've done this a couple of times already. Everyone please stay calm!'

He lowered the helicopter, and just before it reached the water's surface he activated a valve to inflate the floaters mounted on the helicopter legs. But only one of the floaters inflated. The other one failed, causing the helicopter to list badly, turning it upside down in the water.

The full force of the momentum left Rob momentarily stunned. When he recovered he suddenly became acutely aware of the danger they were in. The aircraft was still capsizing, it was hard to know which way was up and which was down. The helicopter stopped moving as it found its equilibrium, but the water was flooding in fast. It was then that he saw the door handle on his left side. He quickly unbuckled his seat belt and glanced across at Joop, whose seatbelt was also unbuckled much to his relief. He grabbed for the door handle, forced the door open and swam to surface.

The pilot and co-pilot had managed to escape through the front. They had clambered onto the helicopter's landing gear, from where they kept track of the passengers as they came to the surface. Spluttering, the others came up, the whites in their eyes betraying their fear. Much to his relief, Joop was hanging on to the helicopter leg, coughing the last water from his lungs. But there was no sign of the three Spanish crewmembers on board. They were still down in the helicopter.

While the co-pilot activated the emergency beacon, the pilot and Rob dove back down into the flooding helicopter cabin. He only had to stick his head in to see that the three men were panicking. Arms flailed about in the remaining air above their heads, their eyes bulging with shock. Having failed to unbuckle their seat belts, they were grabbing each other in a futile attempt to survive.

Rob made his way to one of them through the turmoil of the water, in an attempt to help him open his seat belts while the pilot approached the second person. Desperate, the men grabbed him by his shirt, unwilling to let go. This only hampered him in trying to reach the man's seat belt, and he was quickly running out of air. He tried hard to calm the man down, but he eventually had to use force to free himself out of the man's grasp. He left the cabin and made it back to surface.

'A knife!' he gasped. 'Give me a knife for the seat belts!'

The captain also resurfaced. 'They've lost consciousness!' Armed with cutters, the pilot and co-pilot dove down once more, bringing the men up one by one. There wasn't a moment to lose, and the men took turns to try to resuscitate them, but their attempts were futile.

It took an hour before the supply boat managed to locate them and lift them out of the water. Their rescuers had known something was seriously amiss, as the helicopter had not arrived in Yogyakarta, nor had it reported to the ship after the emergency signal was activated.

The surviving passengers were dropped off in Yogyakarta, where the crew boarded the charter to Singapore. Immensely grateful that he was still alive, Rob said his prayer before takeoff.

Badly shaken by their ordeal and the deaths of the three Spaniards, the men checked in for their various destinations at Singapore airport, and each man went his own way. Each and every one of them had to deal with what had happened. No one wanted to talk about what had befallen them, and they certainly didn't feel like having a beer together.

Rob felt intensely miserable. Every single day in the course of his work he tried everything possible to avoid accidents. And now he had to deal with the worst-case scenario—the death of not just one, but three men.

He was unable to rid himself of that one terrible image, the image of that dying man's face, the sheer panic in his eyes as his lungs had filled with water. The man had been so afraid to die, and there was nothing that he could do to help him. The man's despair had nearly cost him his own life.

This time, they did not visit the mall, but stayed at the airport instead. He bought a stuffed toy dog for Jan and an orchid for Anne. The two of them sought a quiet place in the departure lounge, where Rob began to write down the events as they had taken place. Needing to digest the events on his own terms, Joop sat down several seats away from him. Rob understood. It had been a close call for both of them.

As soon as it was time to check in, Rob asked Joop whether he preferred to sit together or separate. They ended up sitting apart.

Rob experienced the accident over and over again, letting it run through his head like some terrible horror movie. And every time he came to the same conclusion. The only thing that could have saved the lives of these men was training: training to stay calm and what to do if a person ever found himself in a capsized helicopter.

In the not so recent past, crew changes for offshore operations were mostly carried out by boat as the locations were close to shore. But with the focus on deep water, the long distances that they had to cover had made helicopters a necessity. Rob knew what he had to do. He would go to Hanover as soon as he arrived home. Werner would want to have a fully detailed report on what happened.

He knew that practically every Navy in the world used helicopters. Surely there were training programs for helicopter underwater escapes. In any case, he intended to recommend that they find such training facilities for the crews.

He went over to join Joop and asked him to review the draft report and add his own comments.

Sitting back down in his own seat, he wondered what Joop was thinking, how the well killing exercise and the fatal helicopter accident had affected him. Joop was at the start of his career, he would be able to find a job anywhere. Would this affect his decision? Did he like his job enough, or had the dangers he encountered put him off?

After half an hour Joop came over to sit next to him. 'Should I tell my wife about the helicopter accident?'

Rob didn't answer straight away. 'No. Don't tell her about it now. Maybe you can tell her sometime in the future, but if you tell her now she'll only worry while you're gone.'

He considered the question himself. Was he going to tell Anne? Anne had never visited a drilling rig. Her knowledge of the oil industry was based on what she heard and saw on television. None of that put his work in a positive light, and he wanted to keep his work and private life separate. So he told her very little about what he did. Telling her about the accident would only make things worse.

Somehow, he believed that the 'cowboy' days of drilling gushers of oil were a thing of the past. That he was now in a position to change the old way drilling for oil and gas was carried out into something that could be well-planned into a safe and efficient operation.

'I love my job,' Joop said. 'But my wife is very worried about what I do. She prefers to have me home. I'm like you, Rob,' he said, his voice still hoarse with emotion. 'I'm not the type for a regular office job. I want to become a drilling engineer. Hell, I know that I could easily get a job as drilling engineer with other companies. You know what I want? My ambition is to understand every aspect of drilling so that one day, I'll be able to make decisions based on what I've learned from experience. That's why I took on this training job on the drill ship. This ship has the latest technologies, and I can actually learn from the challenges involved in drilling in deep water. Sometime in the future, I want to be able to influence the way drilling wells is planned and carried out. Only experience can get me where I want to be. I do appreciate the training program, Rob. I really do, but what I'd really like now is to work as part of the drilling crew and learn.'

They both sat there for a while in silence. 'So are you going to tell your wife about the accident?' Rob asked him eventually.

Joop shook his head. 'No. I don't think I will. I was planning to at first. I don't want there to be any secrets between us. But now, after talking to you...' He shook his head again, resolutely this time, but Rob sensed a trace of bitterness. 'No.'

Rob leaned back in his chair somewhat saddened, but relieved nonetheless. He was glad they had this conversation. The events that had taken place had affected them both. To bottle up their emotions after the death of the three men wouldn't help either of them.

The risk was part of their job. Yet they traveled far away from home to earn a decent living for their family, who wanted nothing more than for them to return safely.

He made a mental note to himself to find out if drilling contractors provided life insurance coverage for their personnel while traveling. He dreaded the thought of the Spanish families being left without any income now that those men were dead.

'Are you thinking of having children?' he asked Joop.

'Yes, if at all possible.'

'Where would you like to live with your family?'

Joop pondered the question. 'I think I'd like to live near the sea. It's one of the reasons why I applied for this job. The money's good. And I don't have to pay income tax as a Dutchman working in Germany.'

Rob nodded, thoughtful. He had just moved to Holland and it was something he had to consult a tax advisor about.

They landed in Amsterdam and Rob told Joop that he would always be welcome in the east, and coffee would be waiting for him any time.

Joop handed in the questions and remarks that he gathered during his training period, shook his hand and said goodbye.

Chapter 21

When he arrived at Enschede airport he marveled at how he always managed to home in on Anne within seconds. She carried an aura around her that reminded him of the sun. No matter what mood he was in, the sight of her and their fast-growing son would always put a smile on his face. The minute Jan saw him, his little face broke into a wide grin and he held out his arms to him. His heart skipped a beat. This was the reward he received for the time he had taken to play with him while at home. This made it all worthwhile. He practically ran to them, desperate to hold them in a tight embrace.

'My God,' he said as he released her to look her over. 'Why are you already wearing your maternity dress? You're only two months pregnant!'

'Because I'm proud. I want everyone to know that I'm expecting.'

'Did you see that grin on his face, and the way he reached out to me?'

'Yes, I know,' she said, delighted. 'I've been telling him for days that his papa is coming home.'

Jan no longer frowned at him as if he were a stranger, but was all smiles and wrapped his tiny arms around his neck. It felt absolutely brilliant. All he wanted was to kiss and hold his son.

Anne looked at him, mocking a hurt look. 'Hello? I'm here as well, you know. I've been waiting for four long weeks for you to hold and kiss me, but it now seems that you found another love. '

Rob swallowed, his emotions getting the better of him. 'Sorry, darling. It's just so beautiful that he remembers me. I didn't expect him to welcome me like this.'

'Excuses, excuses,' Anne said. 'I'll have to wait my turn. He missed you, that much is obvious. You don't know how happy that makes me to know that.'

'I'll make it up to you when he is asleep. I cannot serve two bosses at the same time.'

Before Jan was born, Anne always had this picture in her mind on how Rob would be with his son. That picture now came close to reality. She looked at how he held Jan in his arms; saw their smiling, happy faces. She wished she could have taken their picture. Next time she must remember to bring her camera.

Anne drove, as Rob wanted to sit in the back with Jan, eager to make up for lost time. It was obvious that he was very happy, not just for being back, but for the way Jan was responding to him. Little did she know what he had gone through twenty-four hours ago. She glanced at him in the mirror, thought she saw a change in his expression when he thought she wasn't watching him. 'You all right? Is there anything wrong?'

'No! No,' he repeated, less vehemently this time. 'I'm just glad to be home. To be with you again.'

He fell silent, for a moment he didn't know what to say. It surprised him that she noticed the subtle change in him, even if he was convinced that he hid his emotions well. It was uncanny how she could read him.

When they arrived home, he told her that he had to make a call to the office. He scheduled an appointment with Werner for early the next morning. Feeling he owed it to her, he asked Anne to join him, but much to his relief, she already had a doctor's appointment. He really preferred to go alone.

He put Jan to bed, went to the bedroom and regarded Anne solemnly, taking in the look on her face, the growing bulge of her stomach.

She gave him a curious look. 'Are you sure nothing is wrong? Normally you pounce on me as soon as we enter the house. Something's different. I've never known you to be this patient.'

'It's nothing. Just a little preoccupied, and I need some time to adjust.'

'Come a little closer,' she urged, beckoning him sensually. 'I'll see if I can reduce the adjustment time a little.'

It was a beautiful autumn day, so he suggested taking a walk to the watermill that afternoon. It wasn't something they normally did, but he was in desperate need of some fresh air. His thoughts were with the three Spanish wives, women who all lived in the same village, waiting for their men to return. He imagined their doorbell ringing, the police or mayor telling them that their husbands would never come home again. Yet he was here, alive and well, together with his wife and son.

They ended up having pancakes for dinner at the restaurant by the watermill. Jan had his first taste of pancake with apple, and insisted on having more. They walked back in the dark way past Jan's bedtime. They gave him a quick bath and put him to bed, Anne singing a song for him.

Preoccupied as he was, he completely forgot all about the presents he had brought. When he wanted to give Jan his, Anne protested. 'No way. He's tired. Tomorrow is another day.' So they kissed him goodnight, and Anne wound up the musical toy that hung above his cot. 'He likes this song. He's always asleep in minutes when it plays.'

He went downstairs to unpack his bag, taking out the boxed orchid he had bought for Anne. When she came down he handed her the box. He was shocked to see how emotional she suddenly became.

'Darling! What's the matter?' he asked, baffled.

'These were my mum's favorite flowers. Every wedding anniversary Dad would buy her one. But they're not easy to get in Holland. They're very expensive.' She kissed him on the lips. 'Thank you for this orchid, my love.

188

Watch how my dad reacts when he sees it tomorrow.'

'I didn't know. I'm glad I followed my instinct. The orchid caught my imagination. It actually reminded me of something else.'

'Oh? And what did it remind you of?'

'Well it reminds me of...'

She put her hand to his mouth. 'Bad boy. You have a one-track mind. Maybe you'd better show me instead.'

He gave in to his lust for her, just wanting to make love, wishing to obliterate all thoughts from his mind.

Later that night, Anne woke him up. 'Rob, wake up. You were screaming your head off in your sleep. You nearly hit me!'

He sat up, the sweat bursting from his pores. 'Sorry. I must have had a bad dream,' he told her, still recovering from the horror of the nightmare that he had just relived. Anne turned around and soon fell asleep, but sleep would not come again for Rob that night.

He left early the following morning for the office, even before Jan was awake. He wanted to beat the peak traffic so that he could be back in the afternoon.

When he arrived in Hanover, the office had only just opened. At the reception desk he asked for Werner Brandt, and within minutes he came down and took him to the meeting room, where most of the management team was waiting for him. Everyone wanted to know about the accident.

He was appreciative of the fact that they made the effort to be there so early in the morning. Werner had already informed them of all the details surrounding the tragedy, up until the moment the three deceased men were delivered to the hospital in Yogyakarta to determine the cause of death.

'These men were employees of our drilling contractor, but their deaths are our responsibility,' Werner told them. 'The accident took place while drilling for the company. Rob Oolderink was one of the passengers on the helicopter. Thank goodness he survived. Rob, could you tell us, firsthand, what happened?'

Rob went through his report, step by step, from the moment he left the ship until they got to Yogyakarta. When he got to the point that he had gone down into the capsized helicopter, he became too emotional to continue. When he finally finished telling his dreadful tale, there was a long silence.

Heumer cleared his throat. 'Do you think we could have prevented the deaths of these three men?'

Rob thought for a moment. 'I think we can learn from this. The company has recently cooperated with the U.S. Navy in a successful salvage operation. We've earned their goodwill, which we could use to our advantage. See if they can contribute somehow in providing their helicopter underwater rescue facilities for training our personnel. Training our crews on what to do in the event of a helicopter ditching in the water could seriously reduce the number of deaths.

Heumer turned to Werner. 'Werner, could you contact the Navy rep, and take this up with him?'

Werner nodded, making a note on his notepad.

'Should we perhaps consider changing helicopter companies?'

'I always check their safety records, and the pilots' flying hours,' Werner said. 'I always do before we contract them. None of the competition ever bothers in that part of the world. But we could become even stricter.'

'Fine,' Heumer said. 'Rob, do you have any other suggestions?'

'Yes. I was wondering if there is any travel insurance for personnel. Is this negotiated in the contract between the company and drilling contractors? I'd like to know. If the HR department could look into this issue, I'd be grateful. This could be very important for the families of these men.'

Bernard Heumer assured Rob that he would personally see to it that the appropriate action was taken, and closed the meeting.

Rob joined Werner in his office, where his secretary served them coffee.

'Did you know any of these men?' Werner asked.

'Yes, I met them. I talked to them on the ship, travelled with them on the helicopter a couple of times.' The memory of that last helicopter flight suddenly washed over him, and he choked up, so emotional he could barely breathe.

Werner looked at him sympathetically 'Did you sleep well last night?'

Rob shook his head, remembering the nightmare he had. 'No. Not really.'

'Rob, I'm going to give you some advice. Don't try to bottle up your emotions. Release them. Shed some tears, talk about it. There is nothing that you could have done for these men. Did you tell your wife what happened?'

Again, a shake of his head. 'You should.' Werner said sternly. 'I'm telling you this, because I experienced something similar. I didn't tell my wife, 'cause I didn't want to burden her. That got me into serious trouble, Rob. Remember your wedding vow? In good times, and in bad. You simply can't carry the weight of bad times on your own, Rob. Excuse me for getting personal, but it was the way you looked when you walked in here this morning that made me take you into my office. I had to ask you these questions. Talking about it helps, Rob.

'And there is another thing. We have twelve rigs operating worldwide with at least twenty-four drilling supervisors in charge of these drilling operations. They run their own little kingdoms. And each and every one of these men thinks that he is the most skilled and capable person to supervise the drilling operation. Some will never be able to accept a different way of planning and control other than their own, simply because their way has always worked fine for him. They're too stuck in their habits.

'I've scheduled a drilling manager meeting next week and I want you to be present. I want you to explain your planning and control system for every single drilling sequence. I know the management team makes the decisions, but I'm part of that team. You're on the right track, Rob, and we have to start somewhere to turn this safety and human mistakes problem around. I've already set in motion that we replace old, dated equipment and controls on the ship with materials that meet a more stringent safety standard.'

Relieved that he had Werner's full support on his quest for greater safety, Rob thanked him for his advice. At the reception he asked for Joop's home number and left.

As he drove home he thought about what Werner had said. He was still unsure if he should tell Anne what had happened—he just didn't want her to worry every time he left home. He toyed with the idea of calling Joop, but decided against it.

When he arrived home Anne had made lunch and invited Dad, as he wanted to see Rob.

Dad joined them, hungry, as he only had some fruit that morning.

Rob watched as Dad squeezed a grape into the mouth of his grandson, so that he just tasted the juice.

He caught Anne peering at him. 'Everything alright at the office?'

He nodded, grunting. 'I have to go back next week. They want me to give a presentation.'

'Anything else?'

'No. Nothing else.' Again he had the uneasy feeling that she knew that something was wrong.

'You've got good taste of flowers,' Dad said. 'Orchids were my wife's favorite.'

'I didn't know that, Dad. I bought them for Anne because of the beautiful colors. And I like the way they're shaped.' He couldn't look at Anne as he said this, knowing that her laughing eyes would give him away.

He quickly changed the subject. 'Have you completed your annual income tax form yet, Anne?'

Dad mumbled something, his mouth full. 'I always did it for her,' Dad said eventually. 'Very straightforward for me to do.'

'Would you mind helping me with mine? I have no idea if I have to pay tax in Holland since I moved here, or whether I should pay tax in Germany.'

'Sure, I'll try to find out. Anything else I can do for you?'

'Well yes, actually,' Anne said cheerfully. 'Could you please babysit Jan on Saturday evening, Dad? I'd love an evening out with Rob for dinner and maybe a dance.'

'Any time. You know I enjoy doing it.'

'Can you come at five? That way you can watch Jan bathe and you can give him his bottle. We will put him to bed before we go, and I'll make sure I have something left over for you for dinner.'

'Excellent. You two can stay out as long as you want. You've got a very comfortable couch.'

Rob's working life was hectic, but at home he liked to get on his bicycle to visit his mam's grave or do the shopping with Anne, Jan strapped into the child's seat that was bolted onto his handlebars. This was such a simple and relaxing life, where nothing else mattered.

Most people in the village knew him by name because they knew Anne. Everyone greeted each other in the streets or in the shops, and people would take time for conversation. They would ask how he was doing, how long he was back home for, and exclaim at how fast Jan was growing. He loved village life. It was the best place for him to unwind from his stressful job.

He finished his presentation for the drilling managers' meeting, and Werner's secretary contacted him to let him know when the meeting was to be held. Rob finally made up his mind not to tell Anne anything about the accident, as his nightmares had stopped and he was sleeping normally again.

The days were getting colder, and the fireplace burned the whole day. Rob and Anne both loved the sound of the crackling firewood, which added to the romantic atmosphere. Rob never stopped trying to convince Anne that the best place to make love was in front of the fireplace.

In the mornings it had become habit for him to give Jan his bottle once he woke up, and play with him until it was his naptime, where after they had a late brunch.

He left early for his meeting in Hanover, having breakfast in the staff restaurant. When he walked into the meeting room he remembered Werner's words, and realized that this wasn't going to be easy. In all the years he had worked on the rigs, his colleagues and supervisors had frequently boycotted his initiatives to try and change things for safety and operational sake. They preferred to keep things as they were, simply because that's how they had always done it.

Werner made the introductions, and was well prepared. He had made a summary of all the accidents and lost time that occurred the past year.

He analyzed each incident and concluded by saying that human failure

or bad planning accounted for ninety percent of all incidents. And that —
he pointed to every one of the drilling managers present—they were
responsible.

'Let me introduce you to Rob Oolderink.' Rob nodded politely, and
Werner carried on, placing a transparent sheet on his overhead projector.
'These are his daily reports, covering a period of four months indicating
human mistakes, incidents and lost time. And here,' he aimed his pointer at
the right side of the sheet, 'are the daily reports from some of his colleagues
working in different parts of the world.'

Rob studied the slide intently, shocked to see the number of human
mistakes, incidents and lost time that had taken place worldwide while there
had been none on his rigs. No wonder Werner wanted things to change.

But his intuition warned him that he wouldn't be making any friends
today. Here he was, a mere drilling supervisor, and a Dutch one to boot,
telling German drilling managers to change the way they managed their
operations. He suddenly remembered Laslo's warning, years back. He
wasn't one of them, and they would not take kindly to this.

There was a coffee break, and the full management team including
Heumer joined the meeting.

Rob began his presentation, taking them step-by-step through the
system of sequence planning that he always used for his drilling operations.
Making use of his transparency sheets, he showed every sequence and
checklist for drilling a well, how he had drawn lessons from past mistakes
and how he addressed safety issues within each sequence.

Rob sensed an uncomfortable tension taking hold of the men, as no one
wanted to be criticized, and Heumer took it from there.

'Thank you, Rob, for you clear presentation. I'd like to welcome
everyone today. I want to begin by saying that this company wants to run
safe and efficient operations, but it is clear that this isn't happening in most
of our work areas. I've already discussed the problem at length with the
management team. We found that there are different options available to
us, but we've decided to select a system that has already proven its value.
This system,' he gestured to Rob's last concluding overhead sheet that still
remained on the screen. 'This sequence planning system that Mr. Oolderink
just presented will be introduced worldwide as from today.'

The way Bernard Heumer handled the issue confirmed that the man had
surrounded himself with a team that all shared the same long term vision on
how to manage and expand the company.

'The operations manager will therefore have a copy for each of you,
giving examples of each sequence of how to plan and drill our wells in the
future. In case required, you will receive all additional support from the
head office to implement this system. However,' and he looked at them
gravely, 'we will not accept any excuse for not implementing this system

within any area. I wish you all a fruitful meeting.'

Once the management team had gone, there was a stunned silence. The faces of the men were somber, frowning. Rob realized that the message that everyone had been given was undeniably clear.

Werner got up to address the men. 'Are there any questions?'

Someone raised a hand. Rob recognized him as the drilling manager he had worked for in Libya.

'I just want to say something,' he said. 'I know that many of us won't be happy at the thought of having to change the way we work, but I happen to know from experience that this system works. I know Rob. He worked for me in Libya, and I saw an obvious difference between the time Rob was on location and when he was on leave. At that time I thought the discrepancy was a lack of experience on the part of his relief, but now I know better. I should have asked him then how he managed his operations. As far as I'm concerned, he's welcome to implement his system within my operation at any time.'

'Excellent!' was Werner's reaction. 'Rob will be available within two months. I will have a visit schedule arranged for each work area. But I cannot stress enough that this is a serious initiative, and should not be taken lightly. If Rob does not get the full cooperation that he needs to implement this system, I want to know. Let it be quite clear that if anyone has difficulty in applying the sequence planning system, and prefers to continue in his old management style, they better start looking for work elsewhere.'

Rob tried not to show his surprise. He had actually intended to stay on his drill ship for longer, planning to mind his own business. He did not really want to get involved in company politics, so he waited for Werner to tell him the next step. As John Fuchs, the HR manager, prepared to present the next item on the agenda, Werner gestured Rob to join him in his office.

'I know this must have come as a surprise to you,' he said apologetically. 'But I've recommended you for this initiative because the alternative would involve rig visits and operational audits, which would require a lot of paperwork. Apart from that, auditors have little knowledge of our business. They would take up too much of the supervisors' time. Besides,' he grinned, 'they can't stand auditors. We thought this option would have the biggest chance of success.'

'I know what you are trying to do here, but you've placed me in the middle of a shooting range. There is a lot of resistance to change out there.'

'Rob, you told me once that one of your ambitions was to standardize the way future wells would be planned, drilled and to improve safety.'

'That's right. It's what I would do the first day I end up in your position. But I don't have any power or authority. There's a difference.'

'You'd still need someone to take on this task. For now, that's you.'

'But I just started to get used to my drill ship. I'd like to complete at least one well.'

'That's all right then. You'll finish drilling the well in the next four weeks. You're to be promoted to Drilling Efficiency Manager and join the management team. You will remain working the on/off schedule but have to join our management meetings from time to time.'

'To whom do I report?'

'To me.'

'Can I at least have a few days to think about it?'

'Okay. I want to know your decision before you return to the ship. One final thing—you will have access to look into each of our operations. By the time you're done, you'll know better than anyone else the strong and weak points of our drilling managers, supervisors and the way drilling operations are carried out.' He looked at Rob conspiringly and lowered his voice. 'My aim is to become Managing Director. And when I do, you must be ready to take my seat.'

Rob was very surprised to hear that. 'You don't have to wait for my decision, because I accept. I'll take this challenge and I'll give it my best shot.'

'I know you will. Make sure you find yourself a replacement on the ship and train him before you leave.' He looked around, as if in search of something. 'So what do we call your system?'

'I thought about the "Look Ahead" system. I think that pretty much covers it.'

Werner nodded, his eyes narrowing in approval. 'I like it.'

'Fine. Then "Look Ahead" it is. Could you send me a copy of your presentation and the monthly area reports from the last two years? That way I can review the past performance before each visit.'

'I'll send copies to your home.'

'Thanks for the opportunity, Werner.'

'You're welcome. By the way, how is Joop performing?'

'He is very good. But he has to deal with the bad experience we had. We'll have to wait and see what he does.'

'Do you think he will leave us?'

'Not if it's up to him. But as you know we've already lost a few good men because their better halves made their decisions for them.'

'Hmm. I hope he stays. He made a good impression. Have a safe trip home and we'll see each other in two months' time.'

While driving home he realized how dynamic the industry he worked in truly was. It certainly required one's flexibility to cope with the changes that were continuously taking place. This morning he was still planning in four-week on/off periods and now, just a few hours later, a complete new path opened up to him. In truth, he would have preferred to stay on the ship for longer and hoped that he would be able to finish the well before leaving the ship, as he considered it valuable experience.

Anne was not at home, so he went outside to do some weeding and mow the lawn.

He got himself a beer and settled into his favorite rocking chair, enjoying the warmth of the autumn sun. He must have dozed off, because he woke up being kissed very gently on the lips.

'You can make all the noise you want, but no more. It's time to wake up and finish your job.'

'I was dreaming that I was on the beach with a gorgeous woman.'

'You are at home. And there's plenty of work to do.'

'No mercy?'

'None at all. Can you take Jan? He's getting heavy. I'll get some fruit for him.'

He took Jan and placed him against his chest. The child fell asleep within minutes.

When Anne came back, they did not wake him, as he wanted to cherish the moment of closeness with his sleeping son.

'Just had a check-up and it all looks good.' she told him

He took her hand. 'I have something to tell you.' He explained what had happened in the office that morning.

'So does that mean you will be working in Hanover, and we have to move to Germany?'

'No. Werner wants to keep me on the on/off schedule and flexible for meetings.

Anne looked at him questioningly. 'Do you like this change?'

'Yes. I think most people prefer to stay in their comfort zones. It's safe because you know the job, and it's more convenient. But I like new challenges. That's probably why they chose me to do the job. If I can motivate my colleagues to adopt the system, and the result is less accidents, drilling problems and major mistakes, then I will get great satisfaction out of that. The job will be difficult, but I'll give it my best shot. It's good for my ego, our future and, last but not least, for our stock and early retirement. On the other hand, I'll have to work on my computer skills, because I purchased one in Singapore. My dear wife takes up so much of my time that I haven't gotten around to working with it yet.'

'I'll give you all the time you need. Maybe you can teach me how to use it.'

'We could get some proper lessons and follow a course in town.'

A cramp in his leg made him adjust, the movement waking up Jan, whose startled eyes looked right into his own. It was then that the garden gate opened—it was Dad. Rob had completely forgotten about their night out.

'So where are we going?' Rob asked once they got into the car.

'Don't know. Any suggestions?'

'Let's drive into Germany. I know this place called Bentheim. There is a restaurant near the castle that I visited before.'

'I've never been there. So surprise me for our first dine and dance night out.'

It was only a short drive to Bentheim. Anne was delighted with the castle on the hill, and Rob parked the car near the Market Square. They wandered around the center, and Rob was surprised to learn that Anne loved to visit each boutique and just looked around.

'I didn't know you liked to shop.'

'Oh, I love to look at these little boutiques. If there's something I like and easy to make, I'd normally make it myself, but I don't have any time left with a husband and child,' she lamented. 'So I have to buy clothes instead.' She grinned at him.

'In that case, I'm glad the shops close within one hour.'

'I already know what I want to buy. Let's go back to the first shop we were in. You can tell me if you like the dress.' So they did, Rob approved her choice, and she bought the dress. Then they walked to a restaurant with stained glass windows and oak paneling on the interior.

'Do you like it?'

'Yes. Now I know why you wanted oak panels in our house.'

They sat down by the window for a good view of the attractively lit castle, and Rob ordered a bottle of wine from Rüdesheim, where they had spent their first night as a married couple. Rob recommended the venison with cranberry relish and mashed potatoes.

Anne enjoyed the wine, but Rob never took more than one glass while driving.

He suggested trying Heisse Liebe: vanilla ice cream with raspberries and cream. She gave him a tipsy smile.

'Is this dessert called Hot Love? And why do I get the feeling that we won't be dancing tonight?'

'Oh, that's not my intention at all,' he said innocently. 'But if you're tired and insist on going home after this lovely meal and wine, then I'll drive you home.'

'Please take me home. I'm feeling very happy right now,' she said, her speech slurring. 'No need to spoil that by looking around for a place to dance.'

'Shall we get a room in the castle or do you prefer to sleep in your own bed?'

'In my own bed, please, and your massage will be greatly appreciated.'

'I'll do my utmost to satisfy your needs.'

Rob drove back, hoping that the old Dutch adage of 'a drunken wife is an angel in bed' would prove true, but then she put her head down in his lap. She was completely knocked out, even before they left Bentheim.

When they arrived at their house, he left her in the car and asked Dad to hold the door open so he could carry her into bed.

Dad looked on, amused. 'So did she dine and dance?'

'No. She only made it to dine and wine.'

'Hah! That's another habit she's most probably inherited from her mother. One glass of wine was enough to knock her out!' He left Rob to it, grinning.

Rob checked on Jan to find him sound asleep and returned to undress Anne, who was snoring lightly on the bed. She looked like Sleeping Beauty. He hoped that one kiss would be enough to wake her up, but he had no such luck—she was too far gone, so he just tucked her in and went to sleep.

During the night he gave Jan his bottle, and by the time it was empty, his son was asleep and Rob had trouble keeping his own eyes open.

The next morning he looked after Jan and played with him. By the time he tucked him in for his nap, Anne emerged from the bedroom, asking for an aspirin to combat her headache. It was nearly noon when she came into the kitchen for a drink.

'Would you like a glass of wine?' Rob teased.

'Oh, don't do that,' and he didn't see her until it was dinner time.

'Why didn't you stop me from having more than one glass of wine?'

'I thought I'd let you enjoy the excellent wine. And besides, I was hoping to find an angel in my bed. You know how the saying goes: A drunken wife is an...'

'And was there an angel waiting for you?'

He laughed. 'I couldn't even wake you. So how did you feel this morning?'

'I don't want to talk about it. How did you manage the whole day without Mama?'

'Barely. I missed you.'

'So what about a dance tonight?'

'I first need to recover from yesterday's dining experiment before we take on a second adventure. I may have to carry you inside again.'

'Coward.'

'Not a coward. My idea was that we would have a romantic night out, get home, have a bath together, give you a massage and then...'

'Oh please stop before I start feeling sorry for you.'

'I love you even now I know you're not perfect.'

She smiled at him. 'I enjoyed myself last night. I'd like to see more of Bentheim.'

'Madam, you have rested the whole day. Now it's time to do your duty. Jan is waiting for his bath and bottle, and then it's my turn to relax and enjoy.'

'Don't you even dare think of that.'

'I know your weak spot, and I intend to make use of that brutally.'

He went to the bedroom, lit some candles in the bathroom and filled the bathtub.

Every time when he was about to make love to her, he felt like a child on Christmas Eve, knowing that a present was awaiting him under the tree without knowing what was in it. That excited him, and it gave him goose bumps.

She did not resist when he undressed her, after which she lowered herself into the warm water. She did not resist when he washed her body, and she did not resist when he massaged her back. She did not resist at all when he turned her around and made love to her.

Rob concentrated on his computer lessons, trying to get the computer to do what he wanted it to do. It was harder than he expected. He was glad that Joop was flying with him, to guide him through the most difficult part of installing each of the drilling sequences onto the computer and show him how to make the necessary changes.

The last day the shutters were closed to be alone with his wife and son. When Anne drove him to the airport, he held Jan's small hand throughout the ride, unwilling to let go. One more kiss at the airport, another glance at the car driving away from him. It was boarding time again.

Chapter 22

'Fly with God,' he muttered to himself as the plane took off. 'My life is in your hands...' The sky was overcast, so there would be no chance to see his house as the city-hopper veered towards Schiphol. Rob wondered what Joop had decided to do, and if he told his wife about the accident.

In Amsterdam they reserved adjacent seats, and once they were at cruising altitude Joop ordered two beers. He turned to Rob with a big smile. 'I'd like to toast on my decision to continue my training period,' he announced. 'After rain comes sunshine, and I sure do hope to get a lot of sunny days. I like my work. My wife and I have decided to buy a piece of land close to the beach, so we'll need the money.'

'I'm very happy to hear that,' Rob said, feeling relieved. 'For you and the company. You can be my drilling engineer any time.'

'Thanks Rob, I appreciate your saying that.'

He told Joop about the unexpected change in his career, and that this was their last hitch together. During the flight Joop helped him out with the installation of the drilling sequences on his computer, and by the time they landed it was all done.

In Singapore they ordered a taxi to Boogey Street, where they had an excellent meal and returned to the hotel early. Everyone slept on the flight to Yogyakarta. When time came to board the helicopter the next day, the whole crew was nervous. Rob could feel his heartrate go up, his mouth dry. He would be the first to admit that he was scared.

'Captain!' he shouted at the pilot. 'Hang on a minute.' He turned to the others. 'I'm scared, too. But this is part of our job, guys. And it's a lot safer than driving a car. Let's pray to the man above to give us a safe landing on board. And there after we'll have four weeks before we see this thing again. We'll be fine.'

The helicopter took off and landed them safely on the helicopter deck of the ship.

Rob had asked Joop to join the handover discussions, and his relief told them that the 9 5/8-foot casing was set and they were ready to drill the last section of the well.

As from the following week, all personnel had to arrive in Singapore one day before crew change to attend a helicopter underwater rescue training program at the U.S. Navy-training center. The drill ship was scheduled to return to Singapore for modifications, and the rest of the crew had to attend this course also. They received theoretical training instructions for the entire crew in different languages so everyone would be able to prepare themselves in case of emergencies.

The new Look Ahead sequence planning and control system had become company policy and was already being used, and he suggested a few minor changes in the handover book. His relief boarded the helicopter to go home. Rob was in charge once again.

He scheduled Joop to work one week with the tool pusher, superintendent, and the last two weeks with himself. He asked him to work during night shift and join him during the morning meeting and the radio report to head office, after which Rob could focus on his administration. When all was done, Rob went to see the rig superintendent.

The man beamed at him when he entered his office 'My congratulations,' he said as he shook his hand enthusiastically.

'What for?' Rob asked.

'For getting all noses at headquarters in the same direction. For the fact that we drilling contractors don't have to adjust every time another drilling supervisor steps on board, with different ideas on how to do the job. I thank you for that.'

Grinning happily, the superintendent went through the Look Ahead planning sheets with Rob, determining their status and deciding what needed to be done next. Everything was ready to carry out the BOP test before drilling the last and most important section of the well.

'This is my last hitch on the ship,' Rob told him. 'Someone else is scheduled to come on board in three weeks' time, to work one week with me and another week with my relief.'

It occurred to him that if his system were implemented on all rigs, the work would be easier for everyone, with the exception of those who preferred not to share their knowledge and experience, but wanted total control for themselves.

With the geologist he discussed the sections where drilling breaks could take place, and he included the geologist's soil information in the next drilling sequence. They found that some of the formation layers were too hard for the normal steel bits, and decided that they would need diamond bits to drill these hard formations.

He inspected the rig and had a coffee with the engineer on duty in the engine room, after which he got some rest, knowing that the upcoming BOP tests somehow always ended up during the night. He wanted to witness the test, as even a small leak could be disastrous.

He was right. The phone woke him up in the middle of the night, and the tests took close to six hours. Every closing device, choke and kill lines with valves and high pressure manifolds were tested with 5,000 psi for fifteen minutes each.

Once the tests were completed, drilling of the new well section could start.

With drilling under way, Rob's daily routine resumed. He spent most of his time with Joop, transferring as much of his knowledge during the time that was left, although Rob was well aware that there was no substitute for on-the-job experience.

One morning, after they had held their daily meeting, the rig superintendent asked Rob if it was true that his company was for sale. He had heard rumors on the subject and wondered if Rob knew anything.

Rob raised an eyebrow, somewhat taken aback. 'No, not that I know of,' he said, but when he returned to his office, it did make him think. After all, he knew that the shipping business wasn't doing well. Selling a healthy and money-making sister company would generate money that could be invested in building modern ships at low cost. The world's shipyards could surely use this work right now.

The more he thought about it, the more he was convinced there could be some truth to the rumor. He went online to find any information on Hattenberg Oil. He knew that the people who had managed the company over the years were more than competent. Everyone had worked in different functions and fields within the company throughout their careers, until they were promoted to manage their own specific departments. They were all well qualified, and highly specialized in their fields.

Especially Bernard Heumer was well respected. It had been he who had established the company's energy section. He intended to ask Werner if any of the rumors were true next time he visited the office.

Rob practiced on his computer, glad that Joop had helped him transfer all the handwritten drilling sequence sheets into the Look Ahead system. His computer skills had gradually improved; he was now able to make amendments to the sequence planning sheets and print the pages within minutes. Previously it took him ages to make these changes, so he was happy that he had switched to the computer generation.

Drilling was very slow, as the formation changed constantly from soft to hard and from very hard to abrasive. They tried all different kinds of bits, but even after a short spell of drilling the bit would become dull or plugged. Because of the inconsistency of formations they continuously had to change the bits due to the wear or the bit or teeth clogging up, which slowed down their progress. He often visited the drillers, as they usually had a better feel for what was happening down in Mother Earth. He discussed the continuous formation changes with the geologist and examined the latest soil samples that had been circulated to surface.

Patience was not his strong side, but he knew from experience that letting the bit drill a while longer instead of constantly changing bits was the best option in these circumstances.

The geologist explained that the current situation would continue until they reach a layer of hard sandstone. It took them a frustratingly long time before they finally reached that depth, where they changed to a diamond bit to drill a longer section.

Once the new bit was run, continuous drilling took place at five feet per hour, and again they had to wait for a break that might indicate the presence of oil or gas sands.

Now that drilling was slow, he asked the captain to start the theoretical training sessions for the helicopter rescue course with the crew.

He had been onboard for three weeks when the first drilling break took place.

The well was closed in, the pressure increased until it stabilized. Heavy mud was circulated and drilling continued. Penetration rates were carefully observed at formation depths that were roughly indicated by the geologist as possible oil or gas bearing.

By the time Rob's successor boarded the ship, they had drilled four of the six sand layers that could hold gas or oil.

He introduced his successor to the team, took him around the ship for an inspection tour and explained the Look Ahead system. After four days he transferred all his responsibilities to him.

The last days Rob dedicated all of his time to Joop, reviewing the drilling problems they had encountered while drilling and trying to come up with solutions for future wells.

The night before his departure, he said goodbye to the crews around shift change time, thanking them for their efforts and the time they had worked together. When the helicopter arrived he shook hands with the rig superintendent, captain and chief engineer. 'Thank you for everything,' he said with a lump in his throat. 'I've truly enjoyed working with all of you. I'll carry out drilling operations with all of you any time.'

The helicopter circled the ship in a last salute and set course for the shores of Java.

Some of his fellow passengers were going through the helicopter rescue course material, and it felt good to know that such information had been made available. The men all seemed more relaxed this time, and the flight was quiet and pleasant.

As the charter plane took off from Yogyakarta "with God", he marveled one last time at the beauty of the island.

In Singapore they took a taxi to the mall, where he and Joop both purchased a handbag made of crocodile leather for their ladies and a toy playing music for Jan.

During the flight Joop showed Rob how to make a presentation of the Look Ahead system on his computer, which Rob planned to use as an introduction in the different areas. He showed him how to add, change or delete things until he was completely satisfied. When they arrived at Amsterdam's airport, Rob thanked him for his help.

'Any time. Think of it as a thank you for everything you taught me on board and for investing so much time in me. I've learned a great deal.'

'I'm sure we'll come across each other again, Joop. Hopefully you'll become the drilling engineer in charge of planning our wells in the future.'

They shook hands warmly, and each man went his own way.

On the flight to Enschede an odd feeling came over him. Somehow it was hard to imagine that he had left the ship for the last time, that he was no longer directly involved in the actual drilling. Where would this new path lead him? A completely different job awaited him; a job that he knew would have its hurdles. He would actually have the opportunity to take a close look into the company's various drilling areas. Hopefully he would meet colleagues who appreciated his initiative and who might contribute with their ideas and experience.

He consciously tried to switch off from work mode, watching as the flat, checkered green landscape below greeted him while the plane prepared for landing.

Chapter 23

His heart pounded when he saw them in the arrival hall. How he had longed for this, to see his beloved family after four weeks, to smell Anne's perfume and hold them both. To see his son laugh and reach up to him with his little arms, asking to be lifted. It was like a movie being played too fast. He wished he could play it in slow motion and be able to observe the tiniest detail so that he would not miss a single thing.

In the car he looked at them again and again, if only to make himself that yes, this was real. And yes, he was home again.

Anne was driving, like last time, as he wanted to hold his son close to him and kiss him every mile. She met his eyes in the rearview mirror, smiling. 'Hey! Save some kisses for me!'

'Don't worry. I have plenty for the both of you.'

'What was it like, saying goodbye to your ship?'

'Strange. I had this odd feeling that I wasn't there for the last time.'

'Well, your intuition is mostly correct. We'll wait and see. How was the flight?'

'Busy. Joop and I completed a slide presentation to introduce the new system. I couldn't have done it without him.'

They stopped by Mam's grave, which had become a good tradition. There were fresh flowers on her grave, and once again, he thanked Mam for looking after them.

'Shall we take Jan for a walk to the mill?' he asked. 'He can sleep in the pram on the way.'

'I had other plans, but I suppose they can wait. Why to the mill?'

'Because I've missed home, the woods, having lunch by the mill.'

'But we can do that any other day.'

'So what would you like to do?'

'To give Jan some fruit and put him to bed. To feel you inside of me, and hear you say that you've missed me and make love to me again.'

Rob's loins quickened at her words. 'Okay, you win. Just hearing you say that makes me want you. On the flight I was thinking, could we make love in each room so that we give each room our blessing?'

'Are you telling me that we exchange our perfectly comfortable bed for a cold room or couch?'

'Yes. We still have our special mattress approved for all areas.'

'Well, the terrace, kitchen, bath and living room already have our blessing. So that only leaves the other bedrooms. I'll think about it.'

Once Jan was asleep he carried her up to the guestroom. He looked around the room, as he didn't come there much. This would be the first time that they would sleep in Anne's old bed.

'I like this room,' he said. 'You did a great job decorating it.'

'Yes, it's nice and light because of the large windows.'

'Let's see if your old bed is as comfortable as ours.'

'We'll have to cuddle up close as it's a twin size.' She shivered. 'You'd better hold me close. It's freezing in here.'

'Anything you wish ma'am.'

'Next time please open the radiators in the room you want to bless. It will take a while to get my blood flowing in here. Can you please warm my feet? I don't know if this blessing thing is such a good idea.'

'Give me time. I'll warm you up.' And so he did.

Jan's noise woke him up, and Rob changed his diaper, taking him into the guestroom. He could see his face take in the unfamiliar room in wonder. As Anne seemed to be still asleep, Rob gave him his bottle and enjoyed watching Jan's laughing eyes fixed on him while he drank.

He put Jan in the bed between them. Obviously feeling quite satisfied, the child began to pull at Anne's hair until she was awake and gave him her attention, as well.

They built a tent with the bed sheets and played hide and seek, to which Jan shrieked with delight. It was moments like these that Rob wanted to capture and save forever in his memory. The truth of it was that he preferred to isolate his family from the rest of the world, but life wouldn't let them. There were others, including family members who he could not shut out.

'Do Agnes and the kids come to see you often?' he asked Anne.

'They come here every Wednesday. I usually make them hotdogs and French fries. Klaus joins us when he comes home from work, and we have dinner together.

Dad comes every day. I've never seen him happier than now. He adores being around Jan.

It's a good thing that we built our home here, so that he can be near us. If there is anything that needs fixing, I only need to call, and he is already on his way.'

'I always assumed it was Klaus who would get things done. I suppose he can't always be around, as he's too busy to make a living for his family.'

'Oh, he always asks if there is anything he can do for me, but I'm happy to have my dad around to take care of small things or to babysit if I have to see the doctor.'

'Did the doctor say you're okay? Is your weight what it should be? I'm used to getting more than a handful when you're pregnant, but you haven't gained as much weight as I expected.'

'You know I never feel better when I'm expecting. We could go for a soccer team if you wish.'

He pulled a questionable face. 'I don't think so. I'd be more than grateful if we have another healthy baby, but I'm not sure if I'd want more than two children. Perhaps I should see the doctor to settle that issue. I wouldn't want you to get pregnant by accident.'

'Let's just wait before we make such decisions. If I watch Jan, it's tempting to have another baby.'

'Hmm. Let's change the subject,' he mused. 'Can you call Agnes and invite them to come over? I owe Dagmar and Thomas money for their grades.'

'You'll see them on Wednesday.'

'Good. That will give me some time to practice my negotiation skills.' He was glad that Anne saw his sister's family on a regular basis. That way Jan would get to know his cousins, just as it should be.

The next few days he spent working on his presentation and improving his computer skills. Over dinner Dad told him the good news that now he was living in Holland, Rob would no longer have to pay income taxes, as he was employed by a German company.

Life was good. He thoroughly enjoyed the quiet village life, cycling to the shops, occasionally stopping to chat with people he knew. On Wednesday he helped Anne prepare hot dogs and French fries, and he drove across the border to pick up Agnes and the kids from their home in Germany. There he was ambushed by Dagmar and Thomas, who showed him their report cards. Jokingly, he told them that he would have to lower his reimbursement as he never expected them to get such good grades.

Their protests continued throughout their journey back to Holland, after which they asked Anne for her opinion. She looked at Rob sternly, playing along nicely.

'Rob, didn't you promise to pay them one guilder for each good grade?'

'Yes, I did.'

'Then what's the problem? Why don't you pay them their hard earned money?'

'Well, building the house and having a baby is expensive. So I thought that we might be able to renegotiate our deal.'

'Didn't you also teach the kids that a promise is a promise and a deal is a deal?'

'That's true but...'

'No buts. I will renegotiate a new rate. For each good grade they get, the rate remains one guilder. For every excellent grade: two guiders.'

Rob spluttered dramatically. 'Anne! That's far too much!'

'Kids, show your auntie Anne your grades. From now on I'll review your grades and pay you the money as was agreed. A promise is a promise.'

'Hurrah for auntie Anne!' They showed her their grades, and she paid the money.

That afternoon they took a walk in the forest so that the kids could use up their energy chasing their uncle Rob. Anne hardly had to do anything, as Dagmar heated Jan's milk and then argued with her brother on who could feed Jan the most. Affected by their boundless energy, Jan didn't want to go to sleep. Anne let him stay up so that the kids could spend more time with him. By the time Klaus arrived, Jan was exhausted, so the whole family ended up putting him to bed.

Anne kissed Rob after their relatives left. 'Thank you for allowing me to be the "good" auntie Anne for them,' she said, as he helped her to clear the table.

'You're welcome. You earned that title a long time ago.'

'I love you,' she sighed, happy. 'This was such a wonderful afternoon. You see why I like to spend Wednesday afternoons with them?'

'It's obvious that Jan likes them around. He didn't want to go sleep.'

'Oh, he'll catch up. He loves to play with the kids.'

'I'll call Werner tomorrow. I'd really like to know where I have to start introducing the Look Ahead system.'

'As long as I can have you at home for at least a few weeks.'

'I'll do my best. As you know, I work for a twenty-four hour industry. This job never stops.'

'I know. But every day you're not at home, you miss seeing your son grow up.'

'I always try to be with you and Jan as much as I can. But there are situations where I just can't.'

'I do understand. And I respect that.'

'Can I ask you to follow me into our next baby's room?'

Anne laughed. 'No. I suggest we go into our own bedroom. I still haven't recovered from our freezing exercise this afternoon.'

The next morning Werner agreed to meet with him the following week, and Rob was scheduled to attend his first management team meeting.

At home, Jan had begun to produce noises that could be interpreted as both yes and no. They kept the baby monitor on, listening to his unintelligible speeches with awe, before it finally fell silent.

That afternoon the phone rang. Anne picked up the phone and for a brief moment there was a stunned silence. He watched her change color as she said, 'I don't believe this! Yes, I'd love to see you. We'll pick you up in one hour.'

Rob looked at her expectantly, Anne's face incredulous. 'What was that all about?'

'Waltraud just landed at Schiphol. She wants to come and see us.'

'You're kidding.'

'She's taking the city hopper to Enschede.'

'Is she alone?'

'No, the whole family is with her.'

'Then I'll pick them up.'

'No, if you don't mind I'd like to pick them up. I want to be the one to welcome her in Holland. She's been more than a friend to me in Saudi, when I was so miserable the first month and... Oh, just please let me do it!'

'Sure, you go. I'll take care of Jan and have coffee ready when you get back. I'll make sure he gets some sleep before the kids arrive. Maybe you'd better stop at the bakery, get something special?'

'I'll get some pastries and fresh tulips. I know how she loves them. See you in an hour!'

'Drive carefully. You're pretty excited.'

She giggled nervously. 'Oh, but it is exciting. I'll simply love to see her again.'

'I'm very happy for you, but you'd better go. Otherwise they may have to wait one minute before you get there.'

'Don't tease me. I'll be careful. Don't worry.'

Rob watched her drive off with a sigh. He put Jan to bed, got the coffee ready and checked with the local Chinese restaurant if it was possible to order takeaway.

The fact that Waltraud's whole family was in Holland made him wonder. Normally they visited their family over Christmas or the children's summer holiday, as it could be unbearably hot in Saudi. This could indicate a return to Germany, or that Heinz had accepted a transfer elsewhere. He'd find out soon enough.

When the whole gang arrived Anne seemed terribly excited. Rob greeted them all enthusiastically and served them coffee and lemonade with apple pie.

'Thanks, Rob,' Heinz said. 'You're probably wondering what brings us to Holland this time of the year.' Rob nodded casually, trying not to show how curious he was.

'I've worked for a Dutch dredging company for ten years now. They've now offered me a job at the head office in Dordrecht. It all went very fast. One of the guys was fired, so I have to be at the office next week.' He grinned. 'Waltraud pressured me to take the city hopper to Enschede instead of the train to Dordrecht. That's why she called you from Schiphol—to see if you were home.'

Rob laughed. 'You know how it is. If the ladies want something done, we'd better play along. Anne insisted on picking you up herself. I think our time in Saudi brought our two ladies together.' He looked from Waltraud to Anne. 'So, Waltraud. What is your plan?'

'We'll be busy looking for a school for the kids, and a house,' Waltraud

211

said. 'We'll be staying at a hotel for the time being.' She glanced at Anne. 'We'd love to stay one night, if at all possible. Catch up on things, drink a toast to positive developments? This year we've had to decide whether to stay in Saudi or not. The girls would have had to go to school in Germany. Either that or return to Germany as a family, and Heinz would have to find another job.' She sat back, relaxed and happy. 'Now the girls can attend international school here in Holland, and Heinz gets a promotion, which is also good financially! Do you think we could arrange something for dinner?'

'Do you like Chinese food? We could get takeaway. There's plenty of wine, so I think we're set for the evening. We can catch up from where we left off in Saudi.'

'Great!' Waltraud said, delighted. 'Oh, Anne, can I please see your son. I know you sent me pictures, but I'd love to hold him.'

'Sure. Come upstairs with me and take the girls. He loves other kids.'

As the four of them thumped up the stairs, Rob fixed a beer for Heinz.

'Will it be a problem for a German to work in a Dutch office because of the language?' Rob asked.

'No. I discussed it before I accepted the promotion. My job is to meet clients around the world, with the office as my base. As we are an international company, English is our common language. The staff at the office is a mixture of different nationalities.'

'Congratulations on your promotion, Heinz. Welcome to Holland.'

'Thank you. So what's happened since you left Saudi?'

Rob was about to answer when the girls came downstairs. One of Waltraud's daughters had already claimed Jan for herself, and Jan was being spoiled with all the attention he was given. Rob suggested they all go for a walk to show them their neighborhood.

Both Waltraud and Heinz expressed their delight, saying how much they had missed the rich colors of autumn. It was something they hadn't seen in a long time. When they returned home, Rob ordered Chinese food and the girls took turns nursing Jan. Rob and Heinz then cycled to pick up the food, and although Heinz had to get used to handling Anne's bicycle at first, he soon found his balance.

At the restaurant they had a quick beer while they were waiting for their order, and when they got back home set the table with all the different Indonesian and Chinese dishes. Rob looked after the drinks, and then they ate in silence, enjoying the food. When they finished there were hardly any leftovers.

'That was a delicious meal,' Heinz said. 'It was a really good idea of yours, Anne. I'll remember this evening for a long time to come.'

'You'd better remember. We'll be visiting you in Dordrecht, and there are Chinese restaurants in every town.'

Rob fetched two spare mattresses from the attic and put them in the 'baby room' as Anne called it. The two girls were allowed to watch television until bedtime.

The four adults stayed at the dinner table, enjoying their beer and wine and finishing what was left of the dishes. Heinz and Waltraud updated them on all the changes taking place in Riyadh, where construction was booming and more people found jobs. Heinz said that the young generation protested openly against the king's power and the great wealth inequality. But then the long flight to Amsterdam and the beer paid his toll, so just after midnight Heinz called it a day.

Rob set the alarm clock early the next morning, as Waltraud and Heinz wanted to leave after breakfast. He took care of Jan while Anne prepared scrambled eggs for Waltraud, fried eggs for Heinz and pancakes for the girls, knowing it was their favorite.

After one last cup of coffee, Rob put the suitcases in the car while the two ladies said goodbye. Waltraud and Anne promised each other that it wouldn't be for long this time.

Rob drove them to the railroad station, making sure they got on a non-stop train to Dordrecht. One last kiss and hug, and the family was on its way to a new adventure, this time in Holland. On his way home Rob bought some flowers and stopped at his mam's grave, feeling the need to talk to her now that there was so much to be thankful for: Anne was expecting their second child, their lovely home and the fact that he was living in his home village. He thanked her for looking after them and walked back to his car.

When he realized that he had left his keys at her grave, he thought of the old days, when he was still living at home with his parents and often forgot his car keys. His mam had told him time and time again to get himself a belt clip. As he picked up the keys he said, 'Yes Mam, I know that I should buy a belt clip.' The next thing he did was to buy one.

By the time he returned home, Anne had already taken down the bedcovers and asked Rob to put the mattresses back in the attic.

'I don't think so. This is the only room we haven't blessed yet. I'll keep them there for a while longer.'

'Then you'd better put on the radiator and separate heater in that room.'

'Leave it to me. You'd be surprised.'

Anne sighed happily. 'Oh, Rob, it was great to see Waltraud. She's actually going to be living in Holland! Now I can visit her whenever I want. It's good to have a friend close by. I've never had a friend before.'

'I just went to visit Mam. I thanked her for all the good things that we have and for looking after us.'

'Good thing. Hopefully you thanked her for me as well.'

'Yes, I did. Right. Back to some quality family time. I feel we've been neglecting Jan, so we'll have to spoil him a little.'

'How do you intend to spoil him?'

'I'll take a few grapes and press the juice into his mouth.'

'Are you guys still doing that? So that's the reason I keep having to buy grapes. I thought they were for you.'

'He loves the juice, that's all.'

'I will try that as well, then.'

'I'll take some upstairs tonight for you if you like.' He gave Jan the grape juice, but when he came back into the kitchen to get some more grapes Anne protested.

'No wait. He won't finish his bottle if you give him too many, and he'll only wake up hungry in the middle of the night.'

'Then I won't give him anymore. I need some rest as well.'

'Hah! You always say you need rest, but when we're in bed you're not tired at all.'

He grinned. 'I only have to touch you to feel rejuvenated.'

When Anne did not have any tasks for him to do, he spent most of his time behind the computer. He became more proficient every day, and showed Anne the basics. Sometimes she would sit next to him while he taught her how to type a letter, how to use the filing system and to create an address book with phone numbers. He also wanted to show her how to make a list of her daily expenditures, but in this she was not interested.

While she was doing the dishes one evening, he asked, 'Anne, you know I always like to plan ahead, right? With another baby coming, we'll only have one guestroom. If Waltraud or my sister visits, we won't have any spare room for the girls. I'm thinking of using some of the materials the foreman left us to build a guesthouse. The other reason is that I like my privacy. I asked Dad if he can help me. We can do most of the work ourselves, and I can ask Klaus to send me someone to do the electricity and gas.'

Anne nodded. 'I think it's a good idea if the work is not too much for you. Let's just do it. You always need a project to work on, anyway.'

'Good. Tomorrow I'll ask Piet if I need to apply for a permit before we can start.'

On Wednesday it was Dagmar's birthday. Anne bought her a dress and some glitter jewelry to wear. As Dagmar loved pancakes, she made these instead of hotdogs for lunch, and Klaus joined them for dinner.

Rob always enjoyed having them around. After dinner Klaus told him that the regulations allowed him to build a guesthouse in his garden of up to fifty square meters, as such a construction was already included in their present building permit.

'You only have to visit Piet and provide him with a drawing to indicate where you want to build.'

Rob left early the following morning for his first day at the office, having breakfast at the company restaurant. He was surprised when Werner suddenly joined him.

'I thought I'd find you here. I left home early so we could have breakfast together.'

They discussed the work that Rob would be doing, and Werner gave him his visit schedule, which showed that he was to visit Australia in two weeks' time. The company hired a French drilling contractor for drilling wells in the Darwin area. The drilling manager had asked if Rob would be available to review his operation and implement the Look Ahead system.

'But before you go there, I want you in Russia,' Werner said. 'Heumer was contacted by a Russian oil company that owns drilling permits, drill ships, semis and jackups in the Murmansk area. Because of the weather, the drilling season is relatively short, and the company needs the cash. The Russians are willing to rent out part of their drilling rigs if we modify each rig to worldwide standards. All we have to pay is a daily rental fee for the time these rigs are contracted outside Russia and share the investment costs.

But first we need to know the condition of these rigs. You don't have to carry out a detailed inspection, but I do want to know if these rigs can operate in the North Sea or the Gulf of Mexico. The inspection can take place any time, so it's up to you when you want to go.'

Rob was a little taken aback. This was something else, to fly off to Russia for one week and then off to Australia. Anne was right when she said that he should enjoy his time off. It was as if everything in this job would be urgent, and that Werner could send him anywhere.

Werner noticed his look. 'Don't worry. Implementing the Look Ahead system is priority number one. I promise that you can remain on the on-off schedule, but maybe you can help me out with this one.'

'Alright, I'll go and inspect the rigs. Is there someone there who speaks English, and would it be possible for Jurgen to join me so he could look at the project side of this?'

Werner shook his head. 'I did consider, but he is too busy preparing modifications for the drill ship return to the shipyard. You'll be travelling from Finland into Russia, where we have an agent who speaks Russian. He can help you.'

'All right, let me know when I travel.'

'You'll need a visa, but that will be arranged by the agent and finalized at the border. I'll call tomorrow and let you know the travel details. Anything else?'

'Yes. I'd like a copy of the monthly reports from the last two years of all areas, as we discussed. I'd also like to see someone from the HR department on salary and tax issues, as I moved from Germany to Holland.'

'I'll have a copy of the reports ready before you go and I'll take you to the HR department myself. There's a lunch meeting at twelve, and I'll introduce you to the management team. This meeting will last about an hour.' He gathered his things on his tray and got up. 'By the way, how is your friend Dieter doing?'

'He needs time to recover.'

'Tell him that when he's ready and if he wants a production supervisor job to give me a call. I think we could use him in our production department.'

'Thank you. I'll tell him that.'

Werner took him up to the HR department, where he discussed the change in his personal circumstances that might affect his tax situation. One of the assistants gave him helpful advice and Rob signed his new employment contract.

At twelve Werner introduced him to the members of the management team, explaining his new function. The thorough knowledge, skills and team spirit of most the team members impressed Rob, but his intuition told him to be wary of the sales manager, the contract manager and the new HR manager. Rob sat through the meeting silently, listening as he did.

Within an hour all items on the agenda had been discussed. The secretary would send the minutes to each member and highlight their action items accordingly. Rob was told he would receive a fax machine to facilitate his communication with the office.

While he drove home it occurred to him that if the company were to be sold, his stock might no longer be in the hands of qualified managers. Most probably, it would fall in the hands of others with completely different ideas on how to run the company. It was a disturbing thought. But as Werner said, he would have to wait and see, especially now that he was a member of the management team. That could be to his advantage.

It was dark when he got home, and just in time to watch Jan getting his bath and soaking the entire bathroom. All creamed and powdered, Anne handed him a fresh smelling boy to feed. While Anne mopped the bathroom, Rob tucked him into bed and tried to sing the same song Anne always did before kissing him goodnight.

When he came downstairs Anne was waiting for him in the living room with a glass of wine. She laughed at him.

'My God. I listened to the baby monitor. That sounded terrible. I'll really have to teach you how to sing that song. I'm surprised Jan fell asleep.'

'Well! I have other qualities. It only takes my presence and voice for him to fall asleep in moments.'

'Yeah, sure. Speaking of qualities, how was your management meeting today?'

'Very interesting. It gave me a very good insight on the company's daily management issues.'

'So did you learn something today?'

'Yes, to not say anything and just listen.'

'Can we apply that in this house as well?'

'I don't think so. Someone has to take the lead, otherwise nothing happens.' He looked at her appreciatively. 'You look beautiful, by the way.'

'Let's finish our wine. Then you can have me any way you want.'

'Any way I want?'

'Yes, that's what I said.'

'Please finish your glass as soon as possible.'

He took his time making love to her, taking in the proportions of his wife's growing tummy. When he lay next to her, satisfied, he was glad that she asked no more questions. He closed his eyes, thinking that tomorrow would be another day.

It turned out that tomorrow came a little fast. During breakfast Werner called to let him know that his travel arrangements were all set: he was to leave the next day for Helsinki where he would meet the agent at the airport and travel to Murmansk by car to meet the company representative for the inspection.

When he returned to the kitchen Anne gave him an accusing look. 'So I assume you forgot to tell me something last night?'

'That was on purpose. I didn't want to spoil our romantic evening.'

'Hmm,' she grunted, not happy. 'Perhaps you were right. If you had told me that you would be leaving tomorrow, you might have had some explaining to do.'

He told her what Werner had asked of him, and said that this was a one-off situation. He wanted to help out Werner, and it was only for one week.

'It's your decision. Just be careful that you don't end up flying across the world and miss watching your son grow up.'

'I will be careful. I do want to watch him grow up.'

'So when do you leave?'

'Early tomorrow morning.'

'Is traveling to Russia safe? I hear all these stories about crime and corruption.'

'They're just stories, Anne. I have an agent to accompany me. I'll have to see if any of these stories are true.'

'I don't have to tell you that I rather see you travelling to Saudi Arabia than Russia.'

'Like I said, I'll be careful. I'll ask Dad to take me to the airport. The flight is at six, so I'll need to leave the house at four.'

'I'll ask if it's okay to have lunch at his house. Jan loves to sit in the stroller. He seems to be taking a great interest in cats, dogs, birds and everything else we come across.'

Once again, it struck Rob how strong the bond was between his son and Dad. They had a simple lunch, after which Jan was put to bed in Anne's old bedroom, which Dad had converted into a baby room, providing Anne with everything she needed.

Dad agreed to take Rob to the airport straight away. 'Any time. I don't like Anne to be out on the road that early in the morning, so whenever you have to travel let me know. I'm always up early anyhow.'

They walked back home when Jan woke up, and as it was a beautiful autumn day, they decided to go to the mill and have an early dinner. They found a table on the terrace in the sun, shielded from the wind. Feeling restless because of the sound of splashing water, Jan refused to stay in his stroller, so Rob took him out. They walked along the waterside, watched the turning wheel cup the water, and listened to the sound of the sawmill cutting the trees into planks. Rob relished the moment, knowing it was special, and tried to capture the memory for the times to come. As the sun disappeared behind the trees, they went inside; the air becoming too cold for Jan. Anne didn't have to ask him if he wanted dinner at home. She knew that he loved the apple pancakes that they served.

They both ordered the apple pancakes and Rob irritated Anne by letting Jan have a taste. 'He's old enough to try,' he told Anne.

'No, Rob, he is not ready for that kind of food yet. It will only give him an upset stomach.'

As they walked back, Jan fell asleep. At home they wanted to give him his bottle, but he wouldn't wake up. In the end they decided to let him sleep, hoping that he would sleep through the night.

Sure enough, at three in the morning, Jan woke them up, hungry and howling. It was Rob who had to get up and give him his bottle.

Rob made sure to pack his thermal work gear, as the temperature in Murmansk was already well below freezing. While he and Dad drove to the airport, they discussed the guesthouse that he planned to have in the garden, saying that he intended to build it himself, but that he would welcome an extra pair of hands. Dad happily agreed to help him build it. Due to his sudden departure Rob did not talk to Piet, so Dad said he would do it.

'Thank you again,' Rob said, immensely grateful.

Chapter 24

When he arrived at Schiphol he had to run to catch his flight for Helsinki. He slept during the short trip, and at the airport in Helsinki he met Viktor, the company's agent, who had arranged his visa and accompanied him to Murmansk.

Together they boarded an inland flight and after two hours landed close to the Russian border. From there Viktor rented a car and after a two-hour drive they reached the border. At passport control, a number of cars waited ahead of them. Viktor left the car to arrange the visa, and when he returned, the car in front of them had been passed through. Still, the gate remained closed as the officials disappeared into an office building. For thirty minutes they waited, but no one returned. Viktor went out to inquire after their status, but came back with the message: 'It's lunchtime. They'll resume duties in two hours.'

This was his first impression of Russia, and it wasn't good. They had no choice but to wait, yet there was no place for coffee or to use a rest room.

After another two hours the officials returned, whereupon Viktor showed them their passport and visa.

'You want to pay for immediate entry or wait another hour?'

Viktor opted to pay, and they were finally passed through.

'This is the first time that I've crossed the border during lunchtime,' Viktor said. 'and now I know that you have to pay to reduce waiting time. We're not done yet, you know. We will be stopped at several army checkpoints. Have to pay money and cigarettes there, as well; otherwise they keep us until we pay.'

Sure enough, they were stopped several times, and Viktor had to bribe them with cash or cigarettes to let them through. The inspections they had to undergo were identical as the ones carried out in Libya, only this time he found himself looking into the barrel of a machine gun. Feeling far from safe, it occurred to Rob that life had little value here.

When they reached Murmansk they drove to the shipyard, where the company office was located. They passed numerous rigs, and when he saw the first drill ship, he gasped. He found himself staring at the *Valentine Shashin*, the very same ship that he saw in the Indian Ocean after they salvaged the Russian submarine. The coincidence made him realize how small the drilling industry really was. He had never thought he would come across this ship again, let alone inspect it.

At the reception he was told that cameras were not allowed. He had to hand his in, because the shipyard was modifying submarines. Fifteen minutes later they were picked up by the Finnish shipyard manager, who, much to his relief, spoke fluent English and German.

The man explained that a Finnish shipyard he worked for had been dealing with the Russians for years to build all kinds of drilling vessels and submarines. He assigned one of his project engineers to assist them with the rig inspection and told Rob that he could start immediately.

A total of twelve rigs were stacked in the shipyard, as the extreme arctic winter conditions made it impossible to drill. With daytime temperatures dropping to minus twenty degrees Celsius, Rob quickly changed into his insulated work gear. The engineer brought him aboard the *Valentine Shashin*, which Rob inspected thoroughly, from the bridge, drill floor, engine and control room, to the derrick and crown, the highest place of the derrick.

The Eastern wind was so utterly cold that by the time they reached the derrick crown, Rob felt that his body had frozen, in spite of his thermals and polar coveralls. He had never felt so cold before, and after a short inspection, he climbed down as fast as he could, desperate to reach the heated office to regain the feeling in his hands and feet. He glanced at his star in the black sky high above and asked his mam to return him home safely.

He then inspected two empty ballast tanks, checking the storage facilities, the pump room, mud chemical storage area and cement silos. Finally he inspected the BOP and control systems, risers and riser tension system. By the time his watch said it was three o'clock at night, he knew the condition of the ship. In the office he found Viktor fast asleep in his chair, his head on the desk.

Entering the hotel driveway, he couldn't help but stare. It was as if he had ended up at one of Hollywood's decadent hotels. The parking lot was filled by the most expensive and luxurious cars he had ever seen. Cynically, he thought that this was probably where all stolen cars of Europe ended up.

They took their baggage from the car, but found that they couldn't get into the hotel as a Cadillac had parked right in front of the hotel entrance, blocking their way. They watched as the driver struggled to get a man, drunk as a newt, into the back of his car. Two high-heeled young women swaddled in mink coats accompanied the man.

Once the car drove off, they finally entered the hotel lobby, where their senses were immediately, violently assaulted. Live music played incredibly loud, the lobby was awash with drunken, drugged couples making out on the dance floor. The women were so scandalously clad; it looked like one big orgy. Rob told the agent to try and get them rooms on the highest floor, as he needed sleep and wanted to have breakfast at six.

He might as well not have bothered. He didn't get any sleep at all. Drunken guests constantly made their way through the corridors, talking, laughing or singing raucously. It sounded as if the room next to his was used by different couples, in shifts. The racket was almost deafening.

Rob called the reception twice to ask if anything could be done about it, but to no avail. When Rob entered the breakfast room in the morning, he found that the party had simply moved there. People were still drinking, dancing and making out heavily.

To his dismay he saw how the guests overloaded their plates with food, eating only small amounts, the rest of it discarded and gone to waste. Around him, people vomited, and no one seemed to come and clear up the mess. The odor was sickening.

Utterly disgusted, they left the hotel and asked the engineer if there was another place for coffee and sandwiches. They stopped in front of a coffee shop, but here, too, everyone appeared to be drunk or stoned. They ordered regular coffees with sandwiches to take to the shipyard, but it turned out they could only get coffee. To make matters worse, the black liquid in the cups tasted like cold tar. No, this was not a good start of the day.

At the shipyard Rob asked the agent to find a hotel that could guarantee him a quiet room. Either that or he intended to sleep in a chair at the office. Alcohol fumes pervaded the changing room; the men were either hungover or still drunk. It appeared to him that this was a generation with no self-esteem in a country where the government controlled everything and allowed no initiative. To him, the people acted like zombies, using alcohol or drugs to escape the reality of their world. *Jesus, what a place to live*, he thought, and felt instantly homesick.

Pulling himself together, he discussed the rig designs with the engineer, soon coming to the conclusion that each rig was identical to the next. Apparently they had designed one drill ship of which they built four exact copies. The same applied to the jackups and semis. At least the Russians had followed the principle of standardization and consistency, which saved them on costs, not only on spare parts, but also on staff training. An added benefit was that their standardization reduced his workload considerably. He would only have to inspect a semi and a jackup, and then all that remained were the rigs' maintenance checks.

He asked the engineer for each rig's equipment list and the design drawings so that he could compare these to the actual status, as well as a list of the wells that had been drilled by each rig. He also wanted to see the crew lists of the rigs.

The staff appeared to be well educated, the Russian education system closely resembling the German. The electrical, mechanical and drilling engineers on board had all completed their master's degrees.

To ensure that he could leave in five days, Rob asked Viktor to make the necessary travel arrangements and to stay informed of the border's opening and closing times.

In the days that remained, it seemed as if he climbed at least a thousand stairs to inspect the drilling equipment, machinery, living quarters and everything else on each semi and jack-up.

Fortunately Viktor found a hotel that closed the bar at ten, so they could get a good night's rest. They had their meals at the shipyard, which was pea soup one day, and alternated with potato soup the next day. Basic office essentials such as paper and pencils were barely available, the more expensive goods stowed in locked cabinets to prevent the office staff from stealing.

At night Rob completed the inspection reports to avoid extra work at home, glad that he had bought a computer and knew how to use it.

The next day Ivan, the oil company's Managing Director and his secretary, who spoke fluent English, invited them for lunch. They asked Rob's opinion on the design and condition of the rigs.

Rob told them that he was surprised by the identical rig design and the reasonable maintenance status of the rigs, and that he would report the inspection results to his operations manager.

Ivan handed him his business card, and said that he was welcome any time. He would discuss the use of his rigs in the Western drilling industry with Bernhard Heumer.

In his eagerness to leave the country as soon as he could, Rob completed the inspection at eleven in the evening instead of staying another night in what he thought was a country in hell. They thanked the shipyard manager and engineer for their hospitality and left the shipyard.

With the snow coming down steadily, Rob was happy that the car was equipped with snow tires. The car's heating system was on full blast, but because of the bitter cold east wind, he was still freezing.

On the way back they experienced the same problems at every checkpoint, but this time the soldiers demanded even more money before allowing them through. Rob told Viktor to pay money up front at the border to avoid having to wait more endless hours, desperate to get out of Russia.

When they finally passed through the border gate, he settled down and tried to get some sleep, but he simply couldn't. He found it impossible to get the images of the past few days out of his mind. Over the years he had learned never to say never, but if it were up to him, he hoped never to return to Russia again.

Viktor drove him to the airport, where they boarded the first flight to Helsinki. When he checked in at the airport hotel, he inquired when the next available flight left for Amsterdam.

'That would be at eight o'clock tomorrow morning,' a Dutch voice said behind him.

Rob turned around to see the familiar, comforting sight of the bright blue uniform of the KLM crew.

'Thank you so much,' he said, relieved and happy. 'I'm sure I'll see you then.'

The first thing he did was to have a hot shower, feeling disgustingly filthy, a sensation that was intensified by everything he had experienced in the past week.

In sharp contrast to the run-down, depressing place where he stayed in Murmansk, this hotel room was tastefully decorated and luxurious. The instant coffee that came with the in-room facilities tasted delicious compared to the awful dredge that he had been drinking in Russia.

That night, he dreamt that he was drilling wells with the *Valentine Shashin*.

The following morning he boarded the KLM flight to Amsterdam. As he reviewed the technical drawings and his inspection report, he came to the conclusion that the Russian jackups and drill ships could be easily modified for drilling operations in the North Sea and Gulf of Mexico. The designs and layouts were generally good, and the equipment purchased from U.S. and German manufacturers were of excellent quality.

He indicated the most suitable rigs, based on their present maintenance status. The semis were too small and their load capacity was too limited, so they would not be capable of drilling in any of the target areas.

At Schiphol he had to wait two hours for his connecting flight. He called Anne to let her know his arrival time. 'Could you please pick me up?'

'Of course! No need to say "please"!'

'It's only because I'm so happy to be back. I'll tell you all about it later.'

'Okay, I'll see you in a few hours. Love you!'

Then he called Dieter, who told him that he still had that same nightmare, over and over again. He dreamt that he was hanging onto the rope, high above the waves and too scared to jump. Then he would wake up, bathed in sweat.

Rob suggested finding a job that he liked. 'There's an opening in our production department that might well suit you. You should talk to my boss about it. A new job would be the best medicine, Dieter. You really need to pick up your life again.'

There was a brief silence on the other side. 'I'll think about it and let you know.'

Chapter 25

Every time he took the inland flight, he tried to get a window seat, as he enjoyed looking down at the towns and cities below. After his grueling trip to Russia he realized how lucky he was that he was born here, and it felt good to be back.

Whenever he came home he was astonished by the enormous leaps in Jan's development. He had only been away for one week, and yet Anne had to struggle to hold him, excited as Jan was to see him. He hugged them in an almost desperate embrace, and reveled sitting next to him on the backseat, his son beaming up at him happily.

Anne glanced at him in the rearview mirror. 'Looks as if you really are happy to be back.'

He laughed. 'You can say that again. Russia is not a country where you want to stay for long. It's going to take at least two generations to solve the alcohol and drug problems. If ever they do solve it. They've got no respect for human life and the corruption is terrible. Worst place I've ever been, I tell you.'

'I'm glad that you're home safe. Agnes showed me how to make hachee. I made it last night, together with applesauce and apple pie for dessert, just to let you know how much I love you. You know the Dutch saying: *the love of a man can be won through his stomach.*'

'Anne, my love for you goes through a lot of channels, but definitely not through my stomach. We'll find out when we get home what those channels are.'

'I just wanted to let you know how much I love you.'

'Still, I wouldn't mind investigating that channel issue a bit further.'

Anne laughed. 'Nor would I. But first we have to visit the doctor. You weren't there when Jan was born, but this time you'll have to learn how to support me to give birth to our daughter.'

He pulled a face. 'That's not one of my strong suits. I might faint or throw up if I see you in pain.'

'That's exactly why you have to join these sessions.'

'I don't think that's such a good idea.'

'You survived Russia. So this should be a piece of cake.'

They stopped at Mam's grave to thank her for bringing him home, and when he got home he faxed his inspection report to Werner. That afternoon they visited the doctor, who told them that Anne was on schedule, although he advised her to follow a salt-free diet. That afternoon Rob attended his first birthing class.

Cracking jokes and hardly paying any attention, the lecturing nurse sternly told him to get his act together. She finally showed a video of a birth to illustrate how important the breathing exercises are. Riveted by the graphic images on the screen, Rob suddenly started paying attention.

'Did you really have to go through all that when you had Jan?' he asked incredulously as they left the clinic.

'Yes. And far more, when I think of it.'

'Jesus. I apologize for my awful behavior in there. I had no idea. I always thought it was easy.'

'I never did tell you, but with Jan they had to stitch me up as Jan was too big.'

He looked at her, aghast. 'Why didn't you tell me? That's terrible.'

'You'd only be worried. I thought you wouldn't want to make love to me as we always do. You're not always that gentle on me.'

He pondered on that. 'That's true,' he said, nodding. 'I would probably have waited longer if I'd known. Perhaps I should examine your stitches to see if everything is okay.'

Anne sighed, exasperated. 'There we go again. Just when I thought we were having a serious conversation.'

'This is serious. I need to know if I have to be careful.'

'You do have to be careful.'

The last week of his leave, the door to the outside world remained shut, their family time closely guarded. They only saw Agnes and her family on Wednesday.

Just like the last time, Jan refused to settle down for his afternoon nap once the kids walked in, so Anne let him stay up late so they could play with him.

Dad joined them for dinner and showed Rob the design drawing that Klaus had made of the intended guesthouse. Together with Klaus, he studied the drawings, and apart from a few minor alterations that could be taken care of later, Rob approved the design. Klaus said he would order the materials and let him know the delivery time.

That evening the fax came in with the details for his next trip. His next area was Darwin, Australia. Rob checked the dates, and saw to his relief that he would be home for Christmas. As a bachelor he had spent nearly every Christmas on board, and he was happy that he could be with his family this time.

Rob called Werner to ask him if he had received his report with sufficient information.

'Yes, it's very well documented,' Werner told him. 'But it's going to take some time to organize the finances. The drilling manager will meet you at the airport in Perth. You'll have to stay in Darwin for a day before you can board the ship. Safe journey, and I'll talk to you when you get back.'

An exuberant Dieter called the following day to tell him that he had accepted a very attractive job offer with the production department, and he thanked Rob for his help.

Chapter 26

Rob believed that all things happen for a reason. Once again, his plane flew right over his house, and he watched Anne look up and wave. In Amsterdam he had to wait one hour before boarding, so he called Anne to hear her voice one last time. This time he would be flying 'with God' on Qantas. The service and food on board were good, but it wasn't until the captain announced the total flight time that he realized he was flying to the other side of the world.

He started reviewing the Australian wells already drilled, and selected the same sequence set-up that had been used for the first well in Indonesia. He made some changes and included the accidents and minor incidents that occurred.

He worked the entire trip to Singapore. Shortly before landing he saw the sky streak with lightning. From experience he knew this was fairly normal and nothing to worry about, but he was concerned when lightning flashed right past them. The plane dropped, causing his stomach to lurch sickeningly. The sudden loss of altitude caused the oxygen masks to drop down. Hurriedly he grasped for it and strapped it on, his heart beating wildly. As the airplane shook and rattled violently, the silence inside the cabin was eerie, the tension palpable. Quite a number of passengers were praying.

The captain assured the passengers that everything was all right, and that they were about to descend to Singapore airport. But Rob noticed that their descent was sharper than usual. When he looked down at the tarmac he could see fire trucks lining up at one of the landing strips. He could feel the plane's sharp turn before landing, the fire trucks on either side. The captain announced that the aircraft had been struck by lightning, and would therefore require close inspection. The departure time of their onward flight to Perth was rescheduled.

After one tiresome hour of waiting in the transit hall, the passengers were asked to board a bus to the hotel. On the way they were informed that the plane required a new engine, which had to be flown in from Hong Kong. Installing the engine would take up most of the night, so they would have to stay in the hotel.

Dead tired, Rob crashed out in his room and slept. The next morning he had breakfast in his room and continued to work on the Look Ahead system, hoping to have it finished before he got to Perth. He intended to show the draft to the drilling manager so that he might be able to include his comments or suggestions.

Just before lunchtime Rob got a call from reception that all passengers had to be packed and ready for the airport transfer. Boarding went smoothly, and as they took off one hour later, Rob muttered a heart-felt prayer of thanks. They were hardly at cruising altitude when lightning seemed to surround them on all sides. That first hour of the flight was unusually quiet, until they finally left the turbulent region behind them. Rob continued with his work and was nearly finished when they landed in Perth.

Upon his arrival the first thing he noticed was the easy Australian accent, which he loved straight away. He was cheerily greeted at immigration, passed through customs without any problems, and was then welcomed by the Chris, the drilling manager, who said he had known about the delay, but the engine problem was new to him.

The next morning Rob was booked on the crew change charter to Darwin, where he would be taken by helicopter to the rig. 'Do you want to go to your hotel?' Chris asked.

'Would it be all right to go to the office? I'd like to show you how the system works. You might have some suggestions before I introduce the system to the staff.'

'Yeah, that'd be just fine,' Chris said.

'You are responsible for the drilling operations,' Rob told him. 'The only reason for my visit is to help you any way I can.'

At the office Rob learned that the drill ship near Darwin had been contracted against a high day rate. If the contractor carried out any repairs on the machinery or equipment, the rate was reduced by twenty percent, so the contractor tried to carry out repairs whenever convenient to avoid such a reduction or delays. He thought that the Look Ahead system might be helpful to achieve this.

Rob gave Chris a brief summary of his system, taking him through each drilling sequence as they went along. Here and there Chris made a comment or gave some suggestions, but said that he would support him all the way and left. Chris had arranged his schedule so that he could work with each drilling supervisor for two weeks.

At six, the crew change bus arrived to take him to the airport. By the time he got to the hotel in Darwin it was 2 a.m. Even though he was exhausted, he still included Chris' suggestions and remarks in his presentation. He finally went to bed, tired but satisfied. With Chris backing him, he could carry out his task. Yet he knew there still would be some difficult hurdles to take.

It was a short night. Rob found himself unable to sleep because of the time difference, his jet lag worsened by staying up so late. He was the first to arrive in the breakfast hall, where he watched the crew come in, one by one.

Most of the crew was Canadian, with a few from New Zealand. The catering staff consisted of various nationalities. Rob was surprised how hot and humid it was, even though it was still early in the morning.

The bus took them to the airport, where a charter flight awaited them. The helicopter flight to the drill ship was longer than he expected, and he was relieved when the aircraft finally touched down on the helicopter deck.

As he disembarked he was greeted by the drilling supervisor, who welcomed him and accompanied him to his office. 'I'm Tim,' he said warmly as they shook hands.

Tim introduced him to the rig superintendent and tool pusher. He was taken to the bridge, where Tim introduced him to the captain and the first mate. After he was shown to his cabin, he quickly changed into his work gear so that he could return to the bridge for alarm and safety instructions. The interaction was pleasant and relaxed.

'Chris told me that you'd be arriving this morning,' said Tim. 'He's instructed me to give you my full support to introduce your system. I understand it could help me with my job.'

'I definitely hope so!' Rob said with a smile. 'Last month I was drilling supervisor on the drill ship in the South Java Sea. I've now been assigned to introduce this system that I created. It's worked well for me during the years. My boss wants to standardize the drilling sequences for all our rigs so that they are more accessible to every person on board. If you have time I'll take you through it.'

'That'd be great, but we're about to retract and change the bit, so I want to be on the rig floor until the new bit is run in the hole. Should take about an hour. I'll be available then. That okay for you?'

'Fine. I'll ask the captain to show me around the ship.'

'Great. See you in one hour.'

Rob discovered that the layout of the Australian ship was nearly identical to 'his' ship in the Java Sea. The captain introduced him to a multitude of people on board, ranging from the chief engineer, mechanics and electricians to the crane operator and the cook. When they got back to the bridge, Tim was waiting for him.

'So what do you think of our ship?'

'Too soon to say, but it's very similar to the ship I worked on.'

Over coffee Rob explained that the Look Ahead was divided into sequences in line with the drilling program, visualized into simple schematics so that everyone was able to understand the different steps and operations to be carried out within each sequence. He explained that he included every incident, accident or human failure that took place during each sequence to avoid a repeat, and a check list to ensure that equipment required for each sequence was on board. He showed him the presentation sheets, while Tim took it all in without saying a word. Then he opened a notebook in front of him.

'I've kept track of all operations carried out by my own crew,' Tim said. 'Always took down accidents and errors made, just like you just showed me. You might want to have a look at it, and we could present this to the drilling team together, so we can start using it straight away.'

'Tim, may I suggest something? Give me your notebook and I'll include your comments and notes. If you don't mind, I'll work the night shifts and supervise, if it's okay with you, and will call you in case its necessary.'

'Yeah, no worries. That will work fine for me. Then I can get some rest, and we can go through the sequences in the morning and discuss the items you cannot read. 'Good. I'll see you around six tonight.' Rob went back to his cabin and he was asleep within seconds.

While the crew lowered a new bit into the hole to start drilling, Rob met with Tim to discuss his notes and comments. He spent most of that night including these into his sequences. He completed the present drilling section and worked out the various sequences, in case of stuck pipe, mud losses and cement operations.

Tim reviewed the altered sequence sheets and suggested a few changes.

He introduced Rob to the captain, superintendent and tool pusher in the morning meeting and explained the reason of his visit.

Rob showed the sequences and asked them to voice any suggestions.

He received some valuable feedback on safety issues, and it took him a couple of nights before he and Tim were completely satisfied with the result. He suggested that Tim would introduce the system to the drilling crews, and after a couple of rehearsals, the Look Ahead presentation was finally held and enthusiastically received by all.

A lively discussion followed, and while presenting the casing checklist, they realized that one vital tool on the list was not on board. The discovery was made in time to remedy the situation; otherwise they would have lost valuable time.

They talked about the accidents that occurred the last time they ran casing and the cement job, whereupon the tool pusher was instructed to ensure that his drillers and mates on deck informed each person of all accidents to make sure they wouldn't happen again.

From then on, Tim assisted Rob in every way possible. As the crews had been given a tool to come up with suggestions and voice concern, teamwork improved, which led to a continuous and efficient operation without human mistakes. The rig superintendent could plan in his maintenance scheduled during non-essential operations.

The next ten days they drilled, and everything seemed to be going according to plan. Until one night the shrill sound of the alarm sounded. The public address system crackled to life. 'All personnel to report to their muster stations immediately. This is not a drill. I repeat: all personal to the lifeboats. This is an emergency.'

The adrenaline rushing through his veins, Rob ran up to the bridge. A sickening feeling of déjà vu came over him as he saw what was happening. His heart practically stopped. A monstrously large vessel, probably a tanker, was coming right at them. The first mate was anxiously trying to make contact with the ship to get it to change its course, but there was no response.

'Flares! Shoot flares in their direction!' he shouted at the mate. The ship still did not change its course. They frantically continued to try and make contact. Flares shot op into the sky to explode brightly above their heads. The tanker kept coming straight at them, its speed unaltered. There was not enough time to lower the boats. Rob silently prayed that the tanker would miss the ship.

The captain shouted into the radio again. 'DP operator, full power ahead immediately!'

The empty tanker came scarily close. They all braced for impact as they saw the huge vessel bear down upon them. The lights passed, and nothing happened. Rob closed his eyes and barely breathed. Nothing. He opened his eyes again and saw to his immense relief that the danger had passed. All they heard was a loud, scraping noise, and then they felt the sudden, violent lilt of the ship as the huge tanker moved away. After several rolls, the ship returned back to drilling position.

With several others, Rob walked to the aft deck to check where the awful scraping noise had come from. They found that the steel netting around the helicopter deck was gone. It had been completely ripped off where it had been attached to the side of the ship. But that was all.

'Thank you, Lord,' Rob whispered, and immediately praised the captain for his action to move the ship forward.

Everyone knew that they just had a very close call, and some men did not sleep that night.

The captain reported the incident, providing the name of the ship to the authorities. The only response they received was that the tanker had seen lights at their location, but assumed that these belonged to small fishing boats. They could only conclude that the tanker had been travelling on automatic pilot, and the mate had probably been asleep.

The next day the steel netting on the helicopter deck netting was repaired and the incident of the previous night left behind them. Rob finally had the time to look around the ship and meet some of the staff. He saw how the sharks circled the vessel, waiting for the food scraps that were shredded and discharged into the sea on a daily basis. It was frightening to watch how a group of sharks turned on each other aggressively, killing one of their own in their fight for food.

One day before his crew change took place, Tim asked him 'Did someone tell you about my relief?'

Rob looked at him, perplexed. 'No? Is there something I should know?'

Tim grimaced. 'Well, the communication between me and him... Let's just say it's not exactly great. It's all in writing, nothing verbal. The handover is done entirely through written instructions that he leaves for me.'

Rob thought about this. 'Is Chris aware of this?'

Tim looked skeptical. 'I never told him.'

'We'll see how it goes. Maybe the introduction of Look Ahead will do something to improve the situation. Do you mind if I join the handover discussions tomorrow?'

'Not at all,' Tim said, obviously relieved. 'I'd appreciate it if you were there.'

The helicopter landed and the drilling supervisor entered the office. He was a rather grim-looking man, who nodded to him curtly.

'Please tell me, are we drilling?' he inquired.

Tim told him that they were.

'Very good. Are all the important issues noted in the handover book?'

Tim handed him the book. 'Yes. It's all in here.'

'Good. That is all I want to know.'

Tim shook hands with Rob, quickly grabbed his bag and boarded the helicopter.

'Allow me to introduce myself,' the man said in a decidedly German accent. 'I am Herr Lindner.'

Rob winced inwardly. He had worked in Germany long enough to know that if German men formally referred to themselves as 'Herr' (Sir), this was to create distance. It usually meant that you would never even come close to knowing his first name. It was a situation that often existed between managers and people on the work floor. They rarely became close, and had to address the person with 'Sie' during discussions instead of the more informal 'du' for saying 'you'.

After Rob introduced himself, Herr Lindner told him that he was a former drilling manager, and just retired. 'A very good friend at head office has recommended me to the drilling manager. I have completed two hitches on this ship. I have managed one of the most difficult well control operations in Germany.' He went on to tell Rob in excruciating detail on how he accomplished this, and told him of all the excellent drilling operations he had run, as well as the many improvements he had initiated in the German oil industry. His stories went on for a full two hours, using up much of their precious time.

Apart from the fact that the man obviously thought highly of himself, Rob had the impression that he must have been a former drill sergeant in the German army. He probably believed that he could run the ship the same way.

'I was informed by the drilling manager of your presence on board,' Lindner said. 'Quite late, in fact. However, he instructed me to provide all the assistance you may require.'

'Thank you,' Rob said, 'I'd appreciate that.' He then explained the reason for his visit to the ship and wanted to show him one of the sequence examples on his computer.

'Not now,' Lindner told him bluntly. 'I would prefer to review the handover notes first. Maybe we can discuss your new system some time tomorrow,' he added with an insincere smile.

'Well, I actually work the nightshift to prepare the planning sequence for the upcoming daytime operations. So that they can be supervised according to the new system.'

Lindner pressed the tips of his finger together in a manner of rejection. 'No, that will not be necessary. I have written instructions for the nightshift. If the operations require my supervision, the rig superintendent will inform me.'

'I thought you just said that the drilling manager told you to provide me with all the assistance I require?'

'The most important issue is the drilling operation. And I am responsible for that.'

'I understand that. But the operation manager has given me instructions to standardize the drilling operation, and to involve the drilling team in the planning and control of each sequence.'

Lindner crossed his arms defensively. 'And I am following the drilling program, as signed by the drilling, engineering and operation managers. I will issue daily instructions on how to carry out these operations. No one informed me of any changes, Mr. Oolderink. I would very much like to see these in writing and signed by the drilling and operations manager.'

'I think we might need to call the drilling manager. He will explain to you again the reason of my visit.'

'I don't have time for that and will discuss this issue with him tomorrow morning.'

'Then I'd like to be present at that discussion.'

'No. I will inform you of the outcome afterwards.'

'Are you telling me you don't want me there for the morning meeting?'

'That is right.'

Rob looked at him in disbelief, utterly lost for words. Frustrated, he turned on his heel and left the office, closing the door behind him with a bang. This was exactly the type of German Laslo had been referring to years ago, when he said that Germans always wanted to be the best in everything, and this conviction was deeply rooted within their genes. He had warned him that he would be up for a fight as a Dutchman when coming across these types of Germans.

He woke up the next morning to find that drilling had stopped. When he called the rig floor, he was told that they had experienced mud losses.

In spite of himself, he smiled. His mam had always told him everything happens for a reason.

He went into the office and before he could even say good morning Herr Lindner got to him first. 'Do you have a sequence for mud losses?'

'Yes. I have,' Rob said with a sense of satisfaction.

'Can I review it?'

'Of course, and you are welcome to use it. Do you need my help?'

'I first want to review it myself,' Lindner said stiffly. 'I will let you know.'

Rob went to the rig floor and asked the rig superintendent at what depth the losses had occurred and the rate of penetration. Then he visited the core lab and reviewed the last soil samples. From the samples he could conclude that they had entered a different formation, called shale. He knew from experience that mud losses often occurred in shale formations. He checked with the geologist for the total thickness of the shale, which was only eighty feet, where after the formation became stable again.

He had drilled these shales before, with very little to show for it. He returned to the rig floor to find that the Look Ahead sequence for mud losses had been distributed to the driller.

Rob went to the office and asked 'Herr' Lindner what he intended to do.

'I intend to circulate lost material around the hole, and if these losses still occur then I will pump and squeeze a cement plug.'

'Did you discuss this with the drilling manager?'

'No. I think that this is the best solution to cure these losses.'

'I disagree.'

'Excuse me?' Lindner retorted, turning red at Rob's defiance.

Rob tried hard not to lose his temper as he explained how he thought they should solve the problem: continue drilling until they came across a formation change.

Lindner sniffed. 'I will proceed with my plan, and we'll see what happens.'

'In that case I would like to make a call to the drilling manager to inform him of the situation we have here.'

'The radio operator requires my permission to make that call.'

'Then I'll make the call at my expense via satellite.'

'That is your decision.'

Rob strode to the radio room and asked the operator to connect him with the drilling manager, and was connected to Chris in a matter of seconds. Quickly he explained the problem to him, saying that Lindner refused to comply with the Look Ahead system and how he intended to proceed, against protocol, with the mud loss situation. 'The man is impossible,' he added. 'If the situation does not change, I intend to leave the ship by boat or helicopter. I'm wasting my time here.'

'Hang on, Rob. Stay on the line,' Chris told him. 'I need to make a quick call.'

Rob waited and within seconds Chris was back on the line. 'I'll be coming on the first available helicopter tomorrow. You should receive a telex within the next five minutes with instructions to continue drilling with mud losses until a different formation is reached.'

The telex came in even quicker than expected, and Rob handed it to 'Herr' Lindner. He didn't even wait for a reaction, and went straight to his cabin.

Drilling resumed almost straight away.

The following afternoon Chris arrived. He immediately asked Rob to join him to see Lindner. 'Why was I not informed of the mud losses and the steps you intended to take?' he asked him.

'Because I was of the opinion that this was a standard situation and my decision how to handle it.'

'If there is anything that is not standard, such as mud losses, you were told before to report such situations to me straight away. I also instructed you yesterday to provide every possible support for the new planning system Mr. Oolderink is trying to implement. Am I right to understand that you have a problem with that?'

'I like to see these changes approved by the drilling and operations managers.'

'So you're saying my verbal instructions aren't enough?'

'When I was an operations manager, these changes always required my signature.'

'Right. I think that the situation on board has already escalated enough. You're coming off the rig and leaving with me right now. Rob, I'll talk to you tomorrow.'

Within the hour, Rob watched as the helicopter lifted off with 'Herr' Lindner in it.

He was relieved that he could finally turn back to his routine, but he knew that he just made an enemy for life.

He informed the rig superintendent that Lindner had left, and that he would be in charge until further notice. Chris called him the next day to say that another drilling supervisor was scheduled to arrive on the ship in two days. When Lindner's replacement arrived a couple of days later, Rob welcomed him. His name was Peter and it seemed that he was well informed of the reasons why Rob was on board.

Rob went through the Look Ahead system, as he had done with Tim, and used Peter's feedback to improve it further. Peter was very pleasant to work with, and within a week the system was up and running as if it had been doing so for years.

Rob prepared his report for Chris and left the rig with a satisfying feeling that he had accomplished something good. Now that everyone was actively involved in applying the new system, they were clearer on how and what to do. Communications between the men improved, which resulted in teamwork. The performance of the next wells should indicate if the new system of planning sequences worked on this rig.

Rob was convinced that it would result in a reduction of accidents and incidents, but only time would tell.

He was on the last plane that left Darwin for Perth. During the flight Rob decided that he wanted to finish the guesthouse. He knew that he would have no time once the baby was born.

Only hours later the city of Darwin was hit by a tornado, in which sixty-six people lost their lives. By the time the world had learned of the Darwin disaster, Rob landed in Enschede to embrace his very curvaceous wife.

Chapter 27

They celebrated Christmas Eve with the whole family at their home, and Christmas Day was spent at his sister's house. They enjoyed every minute of it.

The following day he and Dad started to work on the guesthouse. Rob wanted to finish as much as possible, before snow and frost made it impossible to continue. They dug a hole two feet down, placed the plumbing and sewage pipes, laid the electrical cabling and central heating pipes, and poured the concrete floor.

Whenever Rob and Dad went outside to work, Jan would howl in protest, so Anne had to put him in a rocking chair in front of the window so he could watch the men at work.

As soon as the concrete was dry, Rob laid a two foot high brick wall, onto which they installed the wooden framework, complete with doors and windows. They then closed all sides with wooden boards and on the very last day before he was due to leave home again, they placed the roof of corrugated iron.

'It seems to me that you are only here at nighttime. Is this all I can expect for the coming months?'

'I wanted to enclose it before winter sets in. I'll finish the house after my return. I expect we'll have our hands full especially if your daughter is anything like you.'

'You should be nice to me in my condition.'

'Well, I'm a bit tired, but I'll do my best.'

'I give up. You're beyond saving.'

'You look beautiful, you know. I wish I could have more time just to tell you that I love you.'

'Yeah, right. Excuses, excuses. The guesthouse is more important to you than the family.'

'I'll make it up to you tonight.'

It started to snow when Dad drove him to the airport the next day.

Chapter 28

The next four weeks, Rob introduced the Look Ahead system in Venezuela, where the company was an investment partner for drilling wells in Lake Maracaibo. The crew change was carried out using high-speed motorboats, and when he was taken across the lake, he saw large quantities of gas and oil erupting at the surface. This was no longer a lake, but a dangerous, volatile mix of water, oil and gas. He would not be surprised if the whole lake would one day ignite to become a raging inferno.

Introducing the system here wasn't easy. Rob had to first introduce the sequence sheets to the drilling supervisors, which would in turn be translated into Spanish by the Mexican drilling engineer and then introduced to the drilling crew. Rob had to train both men to keep the English and Spanish versions up to date.

He was hoping that the *mañana* and the buddy-buddy attitude would change by the implementation of his system, because he felt that the operation was not controlled by the drilling supervisor, but by the local drilling contractor, who was also an investment partner in the drilling project. He felt that it was a waste of time to visit drilling operations not controlled by the head office in Germany.

It was at Caracas airport where he was confronted with men openly carrying shotguns. The police did nothing about it—the men seemed untouchable. He was only too happy to leave Venezuela, which he considered poor, unsafe and rife to be taken over by criminals.

Chapter 29

When he returned home, they installed the electrical cabling and insulated the walls and roof, before putting the plaster boards in place. While brainstorming on how they would like to divide the space, Anne suggested an open kitchen plan. They then set to work on building the walls for the various compartments and finished these just on time, before he had to leave on his next mission, to visit Alaska.

The company had contracted a drill ship to drill wells in the summer period, the only time it was possible to enter the Beaufort sea.

It was a tricky operation, because they encountered drifting icebergs, which could easily interfere with the drilling operations.

Because of the time limit dictated by the season, drilling in this area was expensive and risky. Therefore Werner had asked him to introduce the new system and stay on board for the most critical operations.

The drilling supervisor reported to him because of the importance and the limited time to complete the project. Also, the success of the operation was vital to set an example that drilling in these sensitive areas was possible without causing damage to the environment.

Rob already regarded their drilling rigs as zero polluting units. Sewage and rainwater were treated and discharged as clean water into the ocean. Packaging materials, plastic and metal waste were returned in containers to shore, while food leftovers were shredded and dumped into the sea as nutrients for marine life.

Rob introduced the Look Ahead system, discussing the unique circumstances of the environment that they were working under, and ended up adding sequence pages related to iceberg interference and severe weather conditions. They installed an early warning system on board to warn the crew of icebergs coming in too close. In case icebergs did come in too close, high-powered tugboats would put a chain around the iceberg and tow these into a different direction. Because of the large number of floating icebergs in the area, such towing operations were an almost daily occurrence.

He organized his work schedule in such a way that he would assist during the most critical periods, such as running the BOP and casing strings, and left the drilling sections to his colleague, who proved to be very competent.

After the spud in of the well was completed, and the BOP landed without any incidents, Rob left the rig for his leave period.

Werner called him at home a week later, it turned out that things had not gone that well on the ship. Three days after Rob had left, the drilling supervisor had to return home due to family circumstances and was replaced with a short-term relief arranged by the HR department in Germany.

A few days after the interim supervisor arrived, a hydraulic leak on the BOP had forced them to disconnect and retrieve the BOP from the wellhead to surface for repairs.

At the same time, the weather forecasted hurricane conditions. As a precaution, both the subsea engineer and rig superintendent had advised the German interim drilling supervisor to pull the BOP well above the splash zone, as was the protocol. They knew that it would cost them ten hours of extra labor to lower the BOP once the weather had calmed down, but they didn't want to take any risks.

But the interim drilling supervisor overruled them. He did not want to waste any time and instructed the rig superintendent to leave the BOP in the splash zone so that it would be ready to run as soon as weather conditions improved.

The rig superintendent strongly disagreed, and insisted in writing that the drilling supervisor took all responsibility for any damages to the BOP. Convinced that he was right, the German drilling supervisor signed the letter and the BOP was left in the splash zone.

Everyone on board braced himself for the storm and the crew sea-fastened all equipment on board.

The hurricane hit the drill ship with full force. The sea was so violent that no one was allowed on deck, and there were moments that the captain thought that the ship would not come up into the next mountain of a wave and they were not going to make it.

The storm finally subsided after two days.

When they inspected the BOP, they found that the damage was enormous. Every valve, regulator, hose or pod that was installed onto the structure had simply been ripped off, leaving nothing but bare steel.

There was no spare BOP on board and the only decision they could make was to turn the ship and set course for St Johns.

'We've been set back a whole year, Rob,' he heard Werner say on the other side of the line. 'Goddammit, if only that man had followed the sequence instructions and accepted the advice from the rig superintendent. He should have raised the BOP above the splash zone. Why the hell didn't Lindner call us? It's company policy to call the office in case they deviate from standard instructions.'

'What did you say this guy's name was?' Rob asked, goosebumps suddenly rising from his skin.

'Lindner a German guy. Peter Lindner?'

Rob was momentarily stunned. 'Jesus. You've got to be kidding me.' He briefly told Werner what had taken place at the coast of Australia, that there, too, Lindner had insisted on going against the protocol. 'How on earth is it possible that this man got on board? They knew at head office that he is as stubborn as a mule and refuses to follow the protocols. Dammit!'

There was a stunned silence. 'I'm going to get the bottom of this, Rob. You'll have to excuse me. I'll get back to you.'

Two days later Werner called back. 'I really don't know where to start. It seems that one mistake was made after the other. It appears that when Lindner returned from Australia, Chris had asked the HR manager not to schedule him for work on his ship anymore, but Chris never explained why. He never did report the problem they had on board with Lindner.' Werner swore, and sighed wearily before he continued. 'So when Lindner contacted the HR manager to see if he could be of service again, HR was completely unaware of the problems. All they knew was that they needed an urgent replacement for the short term in Alaska, so they sent him there.'

Werner went on to tell him that there had been personnel changes in the office, mostly due to retirement. 'We've been forced to replace experienced personnel with the excess staff from Wedel Shipping. They're an incompetent lot. Jan Fox, the new HR manager, is a ship engineer, while the new engineering manager has no drilling experiences!' He sounded frustrated and angry. 'I'm going to personally make sure that Herr Lindner will never set foot on one of our rigs again.'

They worked nearly eighteen hours a day and plastered the walls, tiled the floors and installed the toilet and bath. In the meantime Anne selected and ordered a basic kitchen, for which they would have to wait because of the delivery time.

He went into the office for a management meeting, during which he just sat down and listened. The HR and Marketing Manager did inquire after the progress of his assignment, to which he only said that things were well underway.

They finished all electrical and plumbing work in the guesthouse.

Before he knew it, the evening before his departure had arrived.

Anne snuggled up against him on the sofa. 'Do you think that the guesthouse will be ready by the time I deliver?' she asked.

'It might be if the kitchen is delivered on time.'

'Rob, I know that we've had little time for each other this period, but I want you to know that you guys did a great job. Klaus has really taught you a lot.'

'Yes. Without him I would have had to pay a contractor and wait and see how the job was carried out. By the way, Dad is taking me to the airport tomorrow. It will be too early for you.' He stroked her hair absentmindedly.

'I forgot to ask you, but what did the doctor say about your blood pressure?'

She chuckled. 'Well, I actually have to tell you something funny. Remember that the doctor told me to follow a salt-free diet?' Rob nodded. 'Everything tastes bland and awful without salt, so I had this idea. I love sauerkraut, and because I thought that it was just pickled cabbage, I've been eating a lot of it lately. Well, the doctor measured my blood pressure today, and it was far too high. He asked me if I was still on the salt-free diet, and I told him that I had been a good girl. I then mentioned to him that the only thing I enjoyed eating was sauerkraut, as I thought it was healthy and just cabbage.' She sat up and looked him in the face. 'He laughed at me, and you know what? He told me that sauerkraut is made of cabbage that is pickled in large amounts of salt. No wonder I liked it so much. So from now on, sauerkraut is off the menu for me. My blood pressure should go back to normal now.'

His hand trailed down to her breast lazily. 'Would it be alright for me to raise your blood pressure for a short time?'

'Yes. Let's move to the fireplace.'

Chapter 30

His next assignment was Brazil, and he knew from the reports that he read during the flight that this would be trouble. The operations in Brazil were amongst the most mismanaged and costly operations that the company ran. Serious accidents took place regularly, while the budget was exceeded by nearly one hundred percent a year. Drilling times required to complete a well were twice that of similar rigs elsewhere, and some of the equipment seemed to be under constant repair.

When Werner told him about his next assignment, he heard that the drilling manager's wife was Brazilian and they lived in one of the oil cities along the coast. Also, most of the married men who were assigned to this area had gotten divorced and married a Brazilian woman. It seemed to him that Brazilian women knew exactly how to snare these oil men and find themselves a way out of poverty by marrying them.

As he went through the report, Rob asked himself why on earth the drilling manager was still in charge of this operation. He updated the sequences from previous rigs with the Brazil drilling program, including all the incidents and human errors that he derived from the monthly reports.

In Rio de Janeiro a bus took him and the other crewmembers to the heliport, where he expected to be met by the drilling manager. No one was there, so he took a taxi to the office, only to be told that the drilling manager was having his lunch.

Rob waited for one hour, looking around the office building, and as he did he realized there was not a single room that was in order or even clean. He discovered that the company's drilling manager shared an office building with the drilling contractor, and that struck him as odd. Usually these offices were always at different locations to avoid a conflict of interest.

When the drilling manager finally arrived, accompanied by a woman, he apologized for not being at the heliport because he had to attend an urgent meeting.

'My name is Leonardo,' he said, grinning broadly as they shook hands. 'And this is my wife. She works here as my secretary and is in charge of the office staff.'

Rob shook hands and asked, 'I wonder if you could make some time available to go through the planning sequences? I've adjusted them according to your drilling reports of the past two years.'

'Oh no,' Leonardo assured him with an expansive gesture. 'I'm already familiar with the system. Let me take you to the heliport, so you can board your helicopter and we can talk on the way!'

Rob got into his car, but the ride was too short to discuss anything.

Once he boarded the helicopter, he knew already what he was up against.

He wasn't sure what to expect on board, but his first impression of the drilling base and drilling manager was very poor. It was only a short flight to the ship, where he was welcomed and given emergency instructions. They showed him to his cabin, where he changed into his work clothes and then found his way to the drilling supervisor's office.

He introduced himself as Mike, and told Rob that his parents originated from Holland, but they had immigrated to Brazil when he was four years old.

'Does everyone on board speak English?' Rob asked.

'Not everyone. All the safety instructions are in English, as well as in Portuguese.' He informed Rob that all the supervisors were American, but that the roughnecks and roustabouts were mostly Brazilian.

Mike seemed pleasant, but he put off his questions until later, saying that there would be enough time to talk during the coming days. Mike introduced him to the captain and the contractor rig superintendent and agreed to have dinner with him that evening.

While having dinner Rob explained the reason for his visit. Mike listened to him amiably, but he said he wanted to review and discuss the new system before presenting it to the crew.

Pretty much left to himself, he spent the rest of the day looking around the rig.

While observing the men at work, he noticed that each time a new connection was made to add another drill pipe into the drilling string, the mud pumps were taken to maximum speed within seconds. Yet he always instructed his drillers to start the pumps up slowly and increase the volume and pressure gradually to avoid a sudden surge on the formation, which could result in mud losses. He watched the driller lowering the drill string very quickly to resume drilling.

He went to his room and checked the previous drilling reports. He found that there had been mud loss problems in nearly every single well. He then checked the formation intake test and detected weak formation strengths. Presumably, the drillers must have been told not to waste time, make a connection as quickly as possible and return to drilling operations as fast as possible.

Apparently no one had bothered to tell them of the hazards of working at such speed.

As he thought of how best to deal with this information, he returned to the office. As he passed the recreation area, he was greeted by a lot of noise. It sounded like people shouting. Curious, he opened the door, and he couldn't believe what he saw. The entire room was filled with people—the whole crew was there. The supervisors were there, including Mike. And they were all watching a soccer game on a large screen. Absolutely astonished, Rob went on deck, and then to the rig floor. The only person who wasn't watching the soccer was the driller operating the drilling controls. Everyone else was in the recreation room, caught up in the game. Rob thought this too incredible for words, but he couldn't do anything about it.

That evening he presented the new drilling sequences to Mike, who listened to him sullenly and did not pass a single comment during the entire presentation.

'So what do you expect from me?' he said finally when Rob was finished.

'That we review each page and include any comments or suggestions you may have, based on your experience from drilling wells in this area so that past mistakes are not repeated again.'

'We don't make the same mistakes again.'

Rob took a deep breath. 'Do you ever review the monthly reports?'

'Yes, of course.'

'Then you must have seen the amount of repair time, and know the reason for it.'

'Well, yes. Of course I do.'

'Then you should check again. I've been through two years' worth of reports, and I discovered that your drillers and supervisors don't measure everything that goes down the hole. Sometimes the wrong tools are run. You take enormous risks making up the casings joints at extended height, instead of doing this safely at working height. I can give you at least a dozen more of such examples, but it's obvious that watching soccer games is far more important than doing your job.'

The moment he said it Rob knew he had gone too far, but in a way he was glad he did. He was fed up playing games. Still, he knew that he had angered Mike.

'You can present this to the rig superintendent and his crew. See if they'll accept it.'

'No,' Rob said, glowering at him. 'You're the one who has to accept and support me in this, because something has to change. And I suggest that you do, because it's not just me you're working against, it's the company. The company wants this system implemented for daily operations as soon as possible. And I have one very important piece of advice for you: that you change your connection procedure. Increasing the volume and pressure as fast as you do on this ship is the reason why you've had mud losses on each well.'

'I like to make quick connections so that we can return to drilling as fast as we can.'

'I like making a fast connections, but you must bring your volume and pressure up in stages and lower your drill string slowly.'

'I'll think about it.'

'Then you'd better do it soon. Otherwise you'll have another mud loss on your hands before you know it.'

Rob knew that he had reached a dead end with Mike. Without his support, he could never get the drilling contractor on his side. After all, it was Mike who they had to work with each day. He was the one who signed the reports and saw to it that they got paid.

His intuition told him that Mike had talked to Leonardo, and that they decided not to cooperate. Yet Leonardo must know that the decision came from headquarters, from the Managing Director himself. So why was he so reluctant to cooperate? Was this attitude due to arrogance, or was it in their culture to decide that this was the way they work in Brazil, with the head office in Germany being so far away?

The management team must have known what a mess it was out here. Had they sent him up here on purpose to fix this can of worms?

He tried once more to persuade Mike to cooperate, but it was useless. He decided not to call Werner yet, but to wait until the arrival of his relief. Perhaps his reaction would be different from Mike's. In the meantime he didn't present the system to the rig superintendent, knowing it would be a waste of time.

Two days later total mud losses occurred, and it took them seven whole days to stop them. In the end they had to squeeze cement into the formation. Rob found everything that was happening unreal. Of all the things that he had learned in the time of his career on standards and safety, none of it was being applied here. This rig was just waiting for a major disaster to happen.

In the days that followed, he did notice that the pump rate was controlled in stages at each connection. At least Mike had listened to him on that count, even though it had taken another mud loss for him to learn this lesson.

He talked to the drilling and deck crew and found out that they all worked for the same third party that provided the complete crew on board. This was strange. Normally the drilling contractor would train and provide all drilling and deck personnel on board.

Something reminded him of the time in Saudi, when the service companies tried to bribe him and he refused to cooperate. In Brazil, bribes were accepted as a normal part of life. He wondered how the company had obtained the drilling permit in this country that never allowed any foreign oil company to drill a well. It did not require a lot of imagination to figure that out.

The staff on board wasn't at all motivated. The men spent most of their working hours in the coffee shop. One night the recreation room served as a porn theater, the next it would change into a casino, where large sums of money changed hands during poker games.

Mike appeared to be in control, so Rob did not interfere with the drilling operation. He was only a guest on board, so he spent his time taking notes to update the sequence pages.

When it was crew change day, Mike asked him to leave the rig.

'I'd prefer to stay on board.' Rob told him. His intuition told him that something wasn't right, and he intended to find out what it was.

'You need to go. We'll need every room for the casing and cement crew.'

'Sorry. I'm staying on board.' Rob repeated firmly.

Mike glared at him hard and boarded the helicopter without saying goodbye.

The minute the new crew arrived on board, everything changed. The new crew was fresh and motivated. There was fun, laughter and an easy, casual interaction. Struck by the marked difference, Rob wondered how this change was possible within one hour. The answer came walking into his office wearing cowboy boots, a silver belt buckle, jeans, a Texan shirt and a broad-rimmed Stetson hat.

'How're you doin', son?' the man said, extending his hand to Rob. 'What brings you to this rig?'

'Do you have time? Then I'd like to explain.'

'Well, this rig and drilling operations are in the good hands of my rig superintendent, so I'll just get myself a cup of coffee and you can shoot right at me. How's that for ya?'

Rob introduced himself and explained why he was on board. 'Would you be interested in seeing the Look Ahead sequence sheets?'

'My name's Bill Turner, and I'd like to see everything you got. I think we're about to have one in-te-res-ting afternoon.'

Bill made detailed comments on the first page, and suggested deleting certain steps. This was repeated until all pages were completed.

'Looks like you've got yourself a good and workable system here. With this you can control drilling operations from A to Z. But tell me, how did it go the past two weeks?'

Rob pulled a grim face. 'Not good. I didn't get the support I needed.' He described what happened at the shore base and on the rig.

'It's time someone from the office looks in on this operation. This whole business has been frustratin' me for a long time now. Tell you what, though. I will introduce the sequences for casing and cementing tonight to the rig superintendent and his drilling crew. We'll see if these guys can come up with some additional ideas.

'But tell me, son. Where're you from? I sure like your accent.'

'I'm from the Netherlands.'

'Oh, I know where that is. You've got a red light district, smoke pot in the middle o' the street, and you guys have some real nice cheese and chocolate.'

'Well, we also have an efficient distribution and railroad system.'

'I'm not interested in all that, but I sure as hell do like your country!'

Once again, Rob was no more than a visitor on the rig, but with Bill in charge, things could not have been in better hands. He asked Bill if he wanted him to work at night so that he could include his suggestions into the sequences and supervise the operations.

'I'd sure like that, son. That will give my body the rest it deserves. My Brazilian girlfriend is ten years younger than me, and she ain't satisfied easy.' He guffawed at his own humor.

Rob thought what a welcome change it was to have such a man in charge. He was honest, without any hidden agenda, a real oilfield specialist and a true leader to his crew. Men no longer lingered in the canteen, but were eager to work hard and learn in the process. They worked efficiently, filled the days with jokes, and communicated well with the different departments. Once the casing and cement job were completed, they took time for coffee.

'So how do you do it? The change since you've come on board is amazing.'

'Very simple, Rob. I hired my own crew. Me and these men,' he gestured at the men around them, 'we've worked together for a long time. Leonardo and Mike wanted to change all that, but I told them in no uncertain terms that if they did, I'd leave and take my whole damn crew with me. Because good people are in demand and the other crew ain't worth a dime, they had no choice but accept. Of course they wanted a percentage of their salaries, but I told them they would get nada. These guys here are worth every dollar they're paid, and these snakes won't get any of it.'

'You mean to say that they get a percentage of each man's salary?'

'Yep. And from that of each subcontractor.'

'What I don't understand is how the local oil company has granted a foreign company a drilling lease?'

'There's only one answer to that. It's to obtain new technology, and everyone benefits from the money chain. An agent or someone in the local company receives a large sum of money every month. He divides that amongst the people in the chain, depending on how important they are.'

'Could it be that people from our own company play a role in this?'

'Rob, I think the answer to that would be yes. Leonardo and his wife—they receive a salary from your company and are also paid by the local oil company as advisors. Only a few people know this.' He grinned. 'I know, 'cause one of my previous girlfriends was dumped by Leonardo. She told me.'

'Why are you telling me this?'

''Cause I trust that you'll keep this information under your belt until it's the right time to use it. Something's gonna have to change.'

'Thanks. My intuition did tell me something was wrong. Now things are starting to make sense.'

'Mind that you're careful, Rob. These people depend monthly on that money and don't like anything to hold up their supply. They'll resent anyone who might be a threat to their livelihoods. I live in a compound of houses with a twelve-foot high fence, high voltage wiring and trained pit-bulls that prowl around to avoid break-ins. Former commandoes protect the compound twenty-four-seven, and I've got guns. I won't hesitate to shoot anyone who enters my property.'

Rob found it hard to concentrate on his work, not knowing whom to trust anymore. Who else in the office played a part in this operation? Any such person would not want him to take a closer look. He tried to remember if any of the managers in Hanover had been against his appointment, but he couldn't recall anyone. Whoever it was travelled to Brazil regularly, and money transfers would leave a trail. He knew he had to be very careful, and look for answers at head office. It would be easy to look into the travel agenda kept by the HR secretary, as she was the one who took care of all the travel arrangements and hotel bookings.

The more he thought about it, the less he liked it. Someone in the company had the authority to approve the payment of a large sum of money on a monthly basis. But who was it? Only the Managing Director, Bernard Heumer. But then why did he assign him to standardize the drilling process? The management team knew exactly which areas didn't perform. It was more likely that whoever it was never expected that Leonardo would not cooperate. They probably underestimated the fact that Leonardo and Mike considered themselves untouchable. If they had cooperated, all would have been just fine, and the bribes would have continued as before.

What about the flow of money? The company paid the drilling contractor a day rate for the ship and services. The marketing and contract managers negotiated this rate. What if this extra service was included in the rate? Could the drilling contractor be involved? He was, after all, the receiving party each month.

His intuition told him that Heumer was clean. He probably didn't know anything about the bribes. It couldn't be Werner, as he didn't have the authority to approve large sums of money without the signature of the management team.

How was he going to report these findings? Should he keep the implementation of the drilling process separate and keep the other issues to himself until he knew more details? He only had two more days before the helicopter would take him back to shore. He decided to stay at the base for a few days to look around.

On crew change day he had a last cup of coffee with Bill, as he had become friends with him during the short time that they worked together. He thanked him for all his support, and told him that he had appreciated his honesty.

'Take care, son. And if you ever visit Texas, I'll fix you the best steak you ever tasted.'

Rob smiled. 'It's always been my dream to live in Texas. As an oilman, it's my Mecca. I'd love to visit the gusher locations, see the fields full of nodding donkey pumps, smell the oil and walk around in cowboy boots and a Stetson hat, just like you did that first day we met.'

'They'd welcome you with open arms with your work experience. If ever you're serious, send me an email if you need anything.'

'Thanks, Bill. And if you ever visit Holland I'll take you to the red light district.'

'You've got yourself a deal, Rob.' He shook his hand warmly. 'Once again, be very careful, my friend.'

'I will. '

The helicopter circled the ship one more time in a last salute before flying for shore.

Leonardo was waiting for him at the heliport. 'My wife has taken the liberty to check the availability of flights for you,' he said with a fake grin. 'We can drive you to the airport if you want to catch the next flight to Paris and Amsterdam.'

It was obvious that they were eager to get rid of him. 'Thank you, but that won't be necessary,' Rob said courteously. 'Could you drive me to a hotel close to the office? This is my first trip to Brazil, and I'd like to see a bit more before I leave.'

Leonardo's smile froze into a grimace, and Rob noticed how he and his wife exchanged glances. While they drove him to the hotel, it struck him that Leonardo didn't inquire about the introduction of the Look Ahead system.

Rob decided not to raise the subject either. Before leaving him at the hotel they agreed that Rob would give them a call in the morning to be picked up.

He checked in and went to the bar where he ordered a lime soda to quench his thirst.

As if by magic, he was joined by a good-looking, somewhat jaded woman who slid onto the stool next to him. It was something he had grown used to in countries like these—it seemed as if someone pressed a button to produce female company the minute a foreign guest walked in.

'Do you mind if I join you for a drink?' she asked, taking him in with one glance.

'Of course not,' Rob said gallantly, and ordered her a drink.

'Are you in the oil business?' she asked.

'Yes. Just got here. I'll be staying for a few days before I go back to my wife and son,' he told her, hoping to discourage any further soliciting.

'Do you work for Leonardo by any chance?'

Rob was taken aback at the question. 'Why do you ask?'

'Because you have the same accent as the three gentlemen that visit this hotel. They come here often. They work for him.'

'Do you know where they're from?'

'Yes, I know because one man told me that he is from Germany.'

'Do you know their names? Maybe I know them.'

'Yes. Two of them like woman and booked my friend and me several times for three nights.' She told him their first names: they were the contract and marketing managers: Andreas Klein and Ronald Schultz. Rob was shocked, but he tried not to show it.

'And the other guy, do you remember his name?' he asked as casually as possible, while the adrenaline raised his heartbeat to three times the normal rate.

'Oh, yes.' And she mentioned his first name. The third man was none other than Johan Fuchs, the new HR manager.

Before Rob could recover from the surprise, she added, 'But this man is no good.'

'Why not?'

'He does not like woman. He wants special services.'

'What kind of special services?'

She glanced around her and dropped her voice. 'I don't like to speak about it. Is no good.'

'Does he prefer men?'

'No. Something else, like I say, is no good,' she repeated, obviously uncomfortable.

Rob was silent for a moment. If a woman who provided all kinds of special sexual services said that something was 'no good', then it was bound to be something shocking. Immediately he thought back to his time in the Saudi desert.

'Does he like animals?'

'No, no animals. But no good.'

'Boys?'

She shifted in her chair uneasily. 'Smaller.'

Rob could hardly bring himself to say the world. 'Children?'

She looked straight ahead at the colorfully lit bottles behind the bar. Her nod was barely perceptible.

Rob straightened on the bar stool, thinking how unbelievable it all was. He was staying at a hotel selected by Leonardo, had a drink at the bar, which he rarely ever did, and ends up talking to a woman who tells him all he needs to know. Back in Germany, these men appeared to be ideal husbands with children.

But the minute they left Germany, they cheated on their wives. To make matters worse, one of them was a pedophile. The thought alone sickened him. At least he would no longer need to check with the secretary to ask her if these men visited Brazil.

Rob pretended to search his memory, and shook his head. 'No. Don't think I know them. I'm from England myself.'

She put a hand near his groin. 'Do you like to book me for one night?'

Rob took her hand and removed it gently from his leg. 'No. I love my wife and family. But can I buy you another drink? Tell me about this Leonardo? Who is he?'

'Very big boss, he owns company, houses on the beach, this hotel and his whole family is working for the company.'

'What company is that?'

'One ship drilling in the ocean.'

'So you know him?'

'Oh, yes. He likes several women at one time. He booked me sometimes for his sex parties. His wife is the big boss, because her brother is a very important person in our local oil company.'

'Oh really?' Rob asked as he stirred his cocktail stick, trying to feign disinterest. He knew enough for now, and she might become suspicious if he inquired further.

'What did you say your name was? Perhaps we could meet up next time I'm here.'

'It's Luisa.' she said with a warm smile.

'Nice to meet you, Luisa.' He paid for the drinks and went up to his room.

But sleep would not come. The room was hot because the air conditioner wasn't working properly, and his thoughts were causing a storm inside his head. And every time, those thoughts came back to the flow of money from his company to the contractor. Had the drilling contractor been selected based on a tender procedure, or recommended by an agent? Was there an agent involved, and if so, who was it?

The first thing he needed was the drilling contract with all its appendixes.

The contract would state when, where and the nature of the work that had to be carried out. Appendix one consisted of a list of all the equipment on the rig. Appendix two indicated the day rate. The third listed the type of personnel that had to be on board, and the fourth described any additional services or equipment that might be required, plus the day rate for these services, if applicable.

He was eager to check the contract once he got back to the office in Hanover. But he was also curious to know the relationship between Leonardo and the contractors rig manager. The more he thought about it, the more he became convinced that these men were part of the web, and that nothing happened without their approval.

No wonder they shared the same office building.

Large sums of money must be involved if a percentage of the day rate was taken. Even ten percent would amount to approximately $20,000 USD per day. That would be plenty of money to be divided up amongst a few people.

Rob tossed and turned and managed to sleep for just one hour before the phone rang. It was Leonardo's wife, asking when she could send the car. He told her that he'd be ready in an hour. As he waited for the car, he suddenly wanted to leave and go home. He had gotten involved in something that had nothing to do with his job, and like Bill indicated, these people would hate to lose their easy source of big money. It was time he went home, so he decided to take the evening flight after meeting with the contractors rig manager.

He was picked up by a company car with driver, something he had never experienced before and which was a true luxury, as even Werner Brandt and Bernard Heumer drove their own cars. When he entered the office, he heard Leonardo talking on the phone to Bill. Leonardo's wife was there, as well as a man with another woman. They were all listening in on the conversation, which had been put on the speaker. From the sound of it, they were going through the daily operations report, and the tone was very businesslike. There was not one friendly word said between them.

'I don't see why you want to change the casing running procedure and order additional short casing joints.' Leonardo was saying.

'Well, I think we should learn from the Look Ahead system, which recommends using pup joints and working at a safe height to avoid repeating accidents from the past,' came Bill's voice.

When Leonardo saw Rob standing there through the open door, he immediately cut the phone call short and asked Bill to call back. It was obvious that he didn't like Rob listening in on the morning report. He quickly got up and introduced him to Kees, who was the contractor's rig manager.

So this man is Dutch, Rob thought. *And the other woman probably his wife.*
This irked him. It was simply not done to have wives present during daily
report meetings. This was business, after all, and not a social event.

Leonardo was the first to break the uneasy silence. 'It seems you
succeeded in finding at least one person to accept your new system.'

'Now that you've raised the subject, can we discuss it? But I don't know
if we can discuss it with Kees and the ladies present.'

That fake grin again. 'We don't have any secrets if it concerns rig
operations.'

'The issue I want to discuss has nothing to do with rig operations.'

'What do you want to discuss?'

'How I should report the findings of my visit to the management team.'

Leonardo blinked; the grin on his face gone. He asked Kees and the
women to leave. When he turned to face him, Rob knew that this man was
dangerous. His eyes were ice cold.

'What do you intend to report to the management team?' he asked in a
low tone.

'That you went against the MD's instructions and refused to even review
the Look Ahead system to give your input. And secondly, that you did not
instruct Mike to cooperate with me on board to implement the system.'

Rob saw Leonardo's eyes swivel in their sockets, obviously searching for
a way out. It was obvious that he felt cornered.

'I was too busy the day you arrived. And Mike did not like to change to
a system that was completely new to him.'

'I had no problem waiting for another day on shore. There is a flight
going each day. You refused to accept the system, and now you'll have to
face the consequences. You know what they are.'

Leonardo turned red. 'Without me, there is no drilling in this country.'

It was a slip of the tongue, and Leonardo knew that he had made a
mistake. 'I mean that I speak the language and have an excellent
relationship with the local oil company.' He flashed his yellow teeth at him.
'I'm sure that we can solve this problem. It looks like we started off on the
wrong foot. What can I do to set things right?'

Rob thought about it. 'I think we can solve this, if we—and I mean you,
Kees, Mike and myself—visit the rig today and return in the evening.'

Was he asking too much? Or would Leonardo accept this as there was
no other way out? It took a while, but finally Leonardo called in his wife,
who arranged for a helicopter to take them to the rig within an hour. Then
he called Mike and Kees and told them that they were both expected to join
them to the rig.

The car took Rob back to the hotel to pick up his baggage and drove
him straight to the helicopter port to meet the others there. Upon their
arrival on the rig, the helicopter remained on standby.

Rob noticed Bill's poker face when he asked if they wanted to use his office, and if the rig superintendent and captain had to join them.

Rob explained the reason why the company wanted to implement the system and went through each sequence, including all previous accidents and mistakes from which they could learn. 'I'll leave a copy of the system on the office computer for Leonardo, so he can arrange a meeting with Mike and Kees to implement their suggestions,' he said. 'Then you can forward their suggestions to Bill, so he can finalize the sequence pages. I'm happy that we all understand the importance of this change, and Leonardo and Kees were able to visit the rig today to show their commitment to ensure that the Look Ahead will be implemented.'

They had a late lunch, and at six o'clock the party was back in the office, where Rob installed the sequences on the office computer. He showed Leonardo and Mike how to make the changes and asked Leonardo's wife to confirm the evening flight to Paris and Amsterdam. By the time the car took him to the airport, he knew that he made enemies for life.

When Rob whispered, 'with God,' as the plane took off, his eyes filled with tears as he saw 'their' star. It shone brightly, and he had the strong sensation that someone was watching over him. His job was not easy, and he needed these quiet moments to deal with the emotions that he so often pushed away. He wished his mam were here to give him his car keys, and he missed his wife and son.

But he had achieved what he had come for, and completed his report. He decided to present the report during the next management meeting, curious to see the reactions from the marketing and contract managers.

After he arrived at Paris' Charles de Gaulle early the next morning, he called Anne to let her know what time he would arrive in Enschede.

'Your daughter misses the touch of your hands on my tummy,' she told him. 'She's been kicking me ever since the first night after you left.'

He smiled into the phone. 'I'll see you in a few hours.'

He thanked Mother Mary that he would be home this time to help Anne through her labor.

Chapter 31

When he arrived at Enschede airport he saw her through the glass partition. She did not see him. He watched her walk, heavy with child, one of her hands on her belly as if she was continually protecting her child, and it touched him. He stopped, and as he watched her, she turned into his direction, as if she felt that someone was observing her. From across the glass partition, they looked into each other's eyes and stayed there for a while to let their eyes speak for themselves. It was just like the very first time he visited her house, when she had come down the stairs, and it seemed to him that the sun just started to shine. This time that sensation was so much more intense. He would see his son again. And he was to witness the birth of their second child.

He came into the arrival hall and made a smart remark to hide his emotions.

'Looks like you don't need a table. You can hold a plate on your tummy!'

'Is that all you can say to a mother who carries your baby to the airport to see her daddy?'

'When I left Brazil, I saw our star through the plane window.'

'And I looked outside the window last night and prayed to God to bring you home safely. I did not have a good feeling about this trip, Rob.'

'This was a trip like any other. Now I can enjoy being home again. Where's Jan?'

'He's in the car with Dad, who didn't want me to carry him inside, so you'll have to wait a few moments.'

They walked from the airport, his arm around her waist. As she fell in step, he felt the warmth of her leg against his. She noticed that he enjoyed the sensation and deliberately pressed against him as they walked.

He looked at her mischievously. 'Is your dad going to stay for coffee?'

She smiled. 'Okay, I'll take my leg away.'

'No. Just keep on walking like that. It makes me feel that I'm still fully alive and makes me want to make love to you.'

'You'll have to be very careful with me.'

'I'll never be more careful as today.'

'Can you at least wait until we're home?'

'I prefer the Autobahn now.'

'That was a long time ago.'

'But still very romantic and adventurous.'

They got to the car and before he even opened the door, Jan held out his arms to him, eager to be hugged by his dad. Anne told Dad not to start the car until Jan was strapped down properly into his car seat and not on

261

Rob's lab, which took a while.

'Thanks for driving, Dad. And for not allowing Anne to carry Jan around the airport.'

'A fax came in for you,' Anne told him as they left the airport behind them. 'Apparently your Managing Director has resigned. They've already appointed someone new.'

Rob looked at her in surprise. 'Really? What's his name?'

'Fritz Von Ritter.'

Rob sat back, stunned. How could this be possible? Werner had told him he expected to be appointed if Heumer left the company.

'And they've invited you to be there when the new Managing Director is introduced to the management team'.

'You know, Anne, I have a feeling that the company will be sold in the near future. The current MD was always against it. I think he was planning a management buyout from Wedel Shipping. My gut feeling tells me to sell our stock and look for another way to invest our money.'

'I'll do that, but first I have to give birth. I have a feeling the moment is getting close now.'

'You'd better listen to her, Rob,' Dad said. 'That's exactly what her mam told me at that time, and before I knew it, Anne was born.'

'Anne, can you please wait until we're home?'

'Yes, but we'd better start preparing everything.'

Rob knew she was serious, because with Jan she went way past her due date, but that was because she wanted him to be there. Now he was home and she could just let it happen. He knew she wanted to have the baby soon so they could enjoy as much as possible time together. From the look she gave him, he knew that he was right.

When they arrived home Rob saw the hospital bed in the living room. The sight of it saddened him, as his mam had died in a bed just like it, and now his wife was about to give birth to their second child. He felt the need for some fresh air, and Dad joined to show him the guesthouse.

The electrical, water and heating installation were all finished. All that remained was the painting of some of the walls and the installation of the kitchen, which had just been delivered.

'I don't have to tell you how glad I am that you're around,' he said.

'Don't even mention it. You know it's good medicine for me to be around my daughter and grandson. Sometimes Anne leaves Jan with me. It's great fun to hear him talk to me.'

'I'm glad you enjoy it.' He looked around the guesthouse's interior. 'We really did build something good together. I hope that it never will, but if something does happen to me, I want Anne to rent out the guesthouse, so she can stay in the house. The rent of this guesthouse should be enough to pay the mortgage of our home.'

'I'll remember that. Let's just hope we can use it as guesthouse for a long time.'

'Did you ever think about living here, with us?'

'Yes, but I prefer to stay in my own home, with my memories around me.'

'I understand that. But if you ever change your mind, please let us know. You will never be a burden to me, and I know that Anne would love it.'

'Thank you. I'll remember that.'

They went back to the main house. Anne asked, 'What took you so long? I've already tucked Jan into bed because he was tired.'

'Your dad showed me all the work he's done. I asked him if he ever considered living in the guesthouse with us. It would be ideal for him.'

'And what did you tell him, Dad?'

'That I prefer to live in our home because of my memories.'

'We wouldn't want to take your memories away, but if you ever reconsider, please let us know. You took care of me for a long, long time, and I shall always be thankful for that.'

'I know, my child.' And with that, he quickly left the house before they could see the tears stinging his eyes.

'That was kind of you to offer the guesthouse. Thank you very much. I know you like your privacy, and I appreciate that you let him in.'

'I know what he did for you, and he's never been a burden to me. But can I now put my arms around your waist and push my hip against yours?'

'Just tell me that you'd like to make love to me, and I'll say yes.'

With his arm around her waist, the two of them walked to the bedroom.

'Just be very careful with me.'

'I'm very tender, and careful.'

Rob awoke to the sound of Jan's cries, demanding his attention. As soon as he walked into his room, Jan held up his arms to be lifted. He kissed him very softly on his eyes and held him close for a while, enjoying the intimacy of the moment.

Once he had gone through the routine of changing his diaper, he laid him in the bed between them. Jan's eyes moved from one to the other, clearly happy in their togetherness as a family.

He read the fax that had come in and noticed that the meeting was to be held the next day. He hoped that their lovemaking would not trigger anything, and that his daughter could wait until her daddy was home.

He called Werner and told him that he finished the report and was ready to join the meeting tomorrow.

'How was the introduction in Brazil?'

'Very difficult.'

'Did you manage to get everyone on the same page?'

'Yes, eventually.'

'We can discuss it tomorrow. Shall we meet for breakfast at eight? Then we'll have sufficient time to discuss Brazil and any other issues before the ten o'clock meeting.'

'Anne, can you please tell your daughter to sit tight and wait until Daddy is home?' Rob asked her before he left the next day.

'I'll try.'

He was at the office early, but Werner was already waiting.

Rob asked, 'Were you surprised that a different MD was appointed?'

Werner nodded as he swallowed his coffee. 'Yes, I was, because our MD Bernhard Heumer and the management team wanted to buy out the company. The bank was interested and willing to finance part of the purchase price, and we would pay off the remaining sum within five years. Wedel Shipping's MD Karl Miller was willing to accept the proposal. He created this company together with Heumer, his best friend. But the board members and shareholders are not in favor. That's probably the reason Heumer was asked to leave.' He wiped his mouth with his napkin and placed it next to his tray with a sigh. 'I would not be surprised if Karl Miller is also replaced in the near future. The shareholders want to sell and receive an immediate return on their investment.'

'What is the background of the new MD, Fritz von Ritter?'

'His father was a high ranking executive at Wedel Shipping. He sure as hell wasn't hired for his skills or education. He's got his bed laid out for him. He is one of those new generation managers with a very large network of friends and buddies who he can call and organize things for him. He has absolutely no experience in the shipping or oil industry. Over the past two years his primary task was selling off Wedel Shipping's non-core assets. Because he doesn't have a clue, they hired a specialized agent to help him during the different selling processes. I wouldn't be surprised if he gets part of the agent fee. I'm certain that the board of directors, including the shareholders, wanted someone who would cooperate with the sale. That's probably why they appointed this guy as MD.'

'What's Heumer going to do?'

'His wife is from the States, so he's going back there to start his own business. He purchased a turnkey company in Houston that drills wells against a fixed price for oil companies or small independents. These companies purchased leases and permits to drill but don't have the know-how to carry out the drilling operations.

I think he's found himself a niche market and will probably be very successful. People of his caliber and experience are not easy to find.'

'Going to the U.S. was always one of my dreams. But what are you going to do, Werner? I know that this was the job you've been working for.'

'They've promoted me as advisor to Von Ritter. I help him in making decisions.' He laughed cynically. 'So now a one-man job has to be shared. Not really a good thing, is it, Rob? You know what they say about two captains running one ship.' He shook his head, looking suddenly tired.

'And who is taking your place?'

'You are.'

The glass of orange juice in Rob's hand seemed to freeze in space. 'Me?'

'Yes. I've thought about it a lot, and my conclusion is that you are by far the most diverse drilling specialist. That and I trust you.'

It took a moment before it sank in. 'When is Von Ritter going to take over?'

'In one month the handover must be completed.'

'And when do you expect me here at the office?'

'In one month's time. I know you just moved into your newly built home. My suggestion is that you work at the office from Monday to Thursday and spend long weekends at home with your family. You should be able to arrange your own schedule anyway, now that we have fax and Internet. But we may have some difficult times ahead of us. More and more old-timers are leaving the company, and we're getting unqualified staff instead. So there you are. You wanted my job. Here it is—your next challenge.'

Rob just sat there, dumbfounded. It was as if he had just completed one round of the Nürbergring racing circuit in a racecar without driving license.

Was this really happening?

'Think about it,' Werner said with a grin. 'Talk to your wife. It will be quite a challenge to take on a job like this at your age. Your salary raise will be significant, which will also impact your retirement pay. And you get a company car.'

He took another sip of his coffee. 'And now to Brazil, because somehow that operation has always been difficult. It seemed to me that operations always slipped out of my hands. First of all the contract and negotiations were handled by the contract and marketing manager, because of the long-lasting and close relationship between the local oil company and the marketing manager. We value his continuous efforts and input, because we are the only foreign company drilling in Brazil '

'Werner it's still slippery, but the good part is that there is an excellent drilling supervisor whose crew is just a delight to watch. On the other shift, though, they've got the worst crew you can possibly imagine.'

'Can this be solved in the near future?'

'Let's wait and see if common sense can take care of things.'

'I'll leave it in your hands.'

'There is one more bit of information that I need for my report, and I have to review the Brazil contract at lunch time.'

'I'll tell my secretary to have it ready for you.'

'Can you please show me where the contracts are filed?'

'I'll take you up there now. The meeting is about to start anyway.'

Werner took him to his office and showed him where he could find the contracts.

'Thanks. I'll give you the Brazil report after the meeting if that's ok with you.'

'Sure, that's fine. It's now your baby, anyhow.'

When Rob entered the meeting room, most of the management team and supervisors were present. He took a seat in the back where he could observe everything. There was still no sign of Schultz, Klein or Johan Fuchs, the HR manager. First Werner came in with Heumer, soon followed by Fritz Von Ritter his successor, who was accompanied by Schultz, Klein and Fuchs. The three men had been talking amiably as they walked in. Rob lifted an eyebrow as he took note of this. It was obvious that the three men already knew each other from Wedel Shipping.

Bernard Heumer welcomed everyone and spoke briefly about the company's history from the moment that it had been purchased. 'At that time we were the only company that was drilling and producing in Germany,' he said, reminiscing. 'The last nine years the company has been drilling wells and producing oil in eight countries. We've achieved this thanks to the dedication, loyalty and hard work from every employee. I'm leaving this sparkling company with pain in my heart, as I feel there is still so much to do. I would like to thank everyone, and I wish my successor good luck.'

He looked around the room and ended his speech with 'Glück Auf!'

These last German words were greeted with a stunned silence. They were usually said by miners when they were about to be lowered into the dark mineshaft to wish each other good luck in the hope that they would come up again to see daylight. No doubt his words were symbolic. Everyone had heard the rumors on the company being put up for sale. Laud applause was the response as he left the room.

The new Managing Director must have felt the tension in the room. He knew that his predecessor was well-liked and respected within the company, while he was regarded as an intruder.

He introduced himself as Fritz Von Ritter, and said that he had made his career in the shipping industry. He admitted that he knew little about the oil and gas industry; therefore, he had appointed Werner Brandt as his advisor. He hoped and expected everyone's support to continue business as usual.

Rob's first impression was that of an octopus, its long tentacles tightly wrapped around various dealings in different places to keep them under close control. It was a vivid image, and one that stayed on his mind while watching Von Ritter. He appeared to him as a man without charisma or passion, and he was no comparison to Bernard Heumer, but only time would tell.

He left the room, went to pick up the Brazil contract in Werner's office, put it in his briefcase and walked down to the restaurant. He selected a corner table so that he could see anyone entering the restaurant and went to the counter to order a sandwich and coffee.

'Congratulations on your promotion,' a voice behind him said, as he sat down to eat.

Rob turned around and looked right into the cold eyes of Ronald Schultz, the marketing manager. It was the last person he expected to see down here, as he usually had lunch at a nearby a la carte restaurant.

Intuitively Rob visualized Schultz as a scorpion, unpredictable and venomous, moving sideways and striking with its sting when you least expected it. *Yes, a scorpion. That certainly befitted this man*, Rob thought warily.

'Thank you. What brings you down here?'

'Werner told me that you'd just returned from Brazil. How was your trip?'

'It was my first visit to Brazil. I didn't have time for sightseeing.'

'What's your opinion of our operations there?'

'I think there's still a long way to go.'

'What do you mean?'

'Not everyone seems to be on the same page. Accepting change isn't easy for some people.'

'I visit the country often to keep in touch with the local oil company. Maybe we could plan a trip together.'

'That's an excellent idea.'

'Can I buy you a drink?'

'No thanks. I have coffee and a sandwich.'

'Then we'll see each other in the near future.'

'Yes, I'm sure we will.'

Rob felt relieved that the Brazil contract was still in his briefcase. After making sure that Schultz was truly gone, he took it out and studied its contents. Everything seemed to be in order until he checked the appendixes stipulating additional equipment and personnel.

The rental rate for specific equipment would not attract attention to anyone who did not visit the rig, but he was sure that the specified equipment was not on board.

A special maintenance crew, which he knew for a fact was not on board.

He also noticed a separate agent fee of ten percent from the day rate.

Normally the agent fee was only paid if an agent was successful arranging a contract without the tender procedure. But why was this fee listed in the contract between the company and drilling contractor? He would need to see the International Association of Drilling Contractors (IADC) report, because it was the official report signed by both parties and listed all persons on board, as well as the agreed operating and repair hours. This was signed by the rig superintendent on behalf of the drilling contractor, and the drilling supervisor on behalf of the company. The monthly invoice was then submitted and paid after thirty days by the company to the drilling contractor.

He would have to check the IADC reports to see if the maintenance crew was listed. Then he would review the resumes of office personnel to find out which employees came from Wedel Shipping. When he finished he went upstairs and filed the contract in Werner's office.

'Rob!' Werner called as he saw him in the filing room. 'Come in! Let me introduce you to Fritz Von Ritter, our new Managing Director.'

Rob didn't like the weak handshake he was given. It felt like shaking a few tentacles.

They briefly discussed the Brazil operations before he went down. He desperately wanted to go home. This office visit had already taken much longer than he expected. He called Anne to let her know he'd be in later, and she assured him that everything was fine.

'I just need you to hang on a little longer,' he said.

'I'll do my best.'

On his way home it occurred to him that nearly every office visit resulted in a career change. But this one was something else. What if the company was sold? If he had remained in his drilling supervisor function, nothing would change. It was different for office personnel. They often became obsolete, because the new buyer would manage the company with its own staff as first savings. He hadn't met anyone from the production department, but he suspected that they worried as well .

He tried to concentrate on the road, the thick fog requiring all his attention. He swore at some drivers who were still speeding as if it were sunny and clear.

He got home and walked around the house, not having had the chance to look into their home after dark before. Anne had done an excellent decorating job. Especially the choice of lightning made it very cozy. He was surprised to see the fireplace burning, and saw how Anne was playing with Jan. It was as if he was looking into someone else's home.

He never wanted to get married, but he had found someone who had made him forget his negative experiences from his youth and who was now expecting his second child. He stood there and watched for a while to store this picture in his mind, and finally entered the living room.

'You don't have to get your love skin,' Anne told him quickly. 'The fireplace is burning because it was just a little too cold for me. Besides, your son likes to watch the flames.'

'I watched you both from the outside. I loved the intimate picture of mother and son.'

'So you were spying on us?'

'I just wanted to look inside. I felt very happy with what I saw.'

'I already gave Jan some fruit and waited for you to give him his bottle. Then I can prepare his bath.'

'Thanks for waiting. How are you doing?'

'I'm fine now that you're home. I'm very hungry, but I didn't make dinner because I'd like Chinese food tonight.'

'I'll call and order, and pick it up when Jan is asleep.'

Together they gave Jan his bath, and Rob was constantly mopping the floor because his son loved to splash the water as vigorously as possible. He carried Jan to his room and observed the little ritual of Anne taking a picture book, reading the text and pointing at the animals. She sang the Dutch nursery song about a sheep with white feet that would drink his milk, and tucked him in for the night. Then she wound up the music box and kissed him goodnight.

He watched her carefully, making sure he knew the exact routine because in a few days it would be his duty to put Jan to bed, and he didn't want to do anything differently.

While Anne was still listening at Jan's door, Rob cycled to the Chinese restaurant to pick up their order. Anne always preferred nasi goring with satay, while he liked the bami goring with satay. The order was ready, and within minutes he was home again.

Anne set the table and opened a bottle of wine.

'I feel at ease and ready to deliver, because everything is in balance. We have a wonderful home, and the most important thing is that you're here with me. Let's toast and pray that Mother Mary gives us a healthy baby girl.'

'I'll toast and pray for that.'

It had been a while since they had Chinese, and every time they did, Rob thought that he preferred the light and well-seasoned Chinese food to the somewhat heavy European meals.

'Did you meet the new MD?'

'Yes, I did, and to tell you the truth, I'm not impressed. I feel sad about the way his predecessor was forced to leave the company.'

'Why was he forced to leave?'

'He wanted to buy out the company and finance the purchase price in separate steps. But Wedel Shipping Company wouldn't accept. Its management and shareholders insisted on one single payment.'

'Do they have a buyer yet?'

'No, because Karl Miller, who is Managing Director of Wedel Shipping, was in favor of the other solution.'

'So he will be replaced?'

'That's what Werner thinks.'

'And what's his opinion on this…this game of chess?'

'He is right in the middle of it all. He is going to be advisor to the new MD.'

'And who is taking over his job?'

'I am.'

She looked at him oddly. 'Did you just say "I am"?'

'Yes.'

'So when were you planning to tell me this?'

'I wanted to tell you after the baby was born.'

'Do we have to move to Germany?'

'No. We're staying here, and I'll work at the office Mondays until Thursdays with a long weekend at home.'

She frowned, shaking her head slowly. 'I know this isn't going to work. You want to be where the action is. And that's not at home.'

'There are different means of communication. If I don't accept the job, someone else will. Besides, I want to see our kids grow up every week and not just after four weeks.'

'That is a very valid point, and probably the only reason I suggest you try this. You can always return to the rig. Anyway, it's good for your ego to get the promotion you deserve. You worked hard for this.'

'Thanks for understanding.'

'So another toast to your promotion. Just don't think this gives you more authority at home.'

'No, boss.'

'If you don't mind, could you please clear the table? I hardly slept last night, and I'd like to lie down for a while.'

Once Rob had finished doing the dishes he went to the guesthouse to check if everything had been delivered for the kitchen. He unpacked all the items, moved the sections into position, connected the drain and water pipes to the sink, and before he knew it, the kitchen was installed. He didn't go to bed until seven in the morning. Anne was still fast asleep, but Jan had woken up, early as ever.

He unplugged the baby phone and took his time to look after Jan, until he heard a voice behind him.

'Are you having a dad and son day today?'

'Yes. I think he's already saying "Dad".'

'In that case, he already said "Mama" a month ago.'

'No, I'm not kidding. Listen to him.'

They both listened to his babbling. 'You're right,' Anne had to admit. 'That's a clear "Dad". But why didn't you wake me?'

'Because you need your sleep.'

'Thank you,' she said as she came up to him and kissed him. 'I did have a good night's sleep.'

'I now hand my duties over to you. I'll make us some fried eggs and coffee.'

'Is this a preview of what you intend to do the days that you are home?'

They heard a familiar knock on the door. They turned to see Dad walk in, eager for his daily dose of hugs, kisses and coffee.

He looked at Rob with a grin. 'So, Rob. I take it you didn't sleep much last night?'

Anne raised an eyebrow. 'Why do you say that, Dad?'

'Well, I just looked in the guesthouse. It looks as if someone installed the kitchen.' He grinned. Anne threw Rob an accusing look.

Rob shrugged his shoulders. 'Listen. We did agree that the guesthouse would be ready before the baby was born. It can be any moment now. I went to the guesthouse last night to check the kitchen parts, and before I knew, it was done. All we need to do now is to paint a few walls. If you can help me with that, we'll be done today.'

'That's the reason I came over. I just thought we'd have much more to do.'

'Then we can have an early glass of wine once we're finished.'

'Wait!' Anne cried. 'Are you trying to tell me that you left for the office very early yesterday morning, and that you didn't sleep last night?'

'Yes, but don't worry. This is just like my rig schedule. I'll catch up on sleep later.'

'No. Those days are over!' Anne admonished him. She went on to tell Dad that Rob was transferred to work at the office for four days, with a long weekend at home.

'Then let's finish the guesthouse today,' Dad said. 'You never know what happens.'

After breakfast they painted the ceiling, walls and doorposts. At the end of the day only a painting job needed to be done. Anne opened the promised bottle of wine, and they brought out a toast to a job well done.

Once they had put Jan in bed, Rob crashed out on his bed, feeling dead tired. But he woke up in the middle of the night because Anne was tossing and turning and could not sleep. Unable to go back to sleep, he decided to get up. 'Have the contractions started yet?'

'No. I'm just restless because of this pain I've got.'

Anne also got up and did some ironing, while Rob started on the last painting job.

He checked on her every thirty minutes, but all seemed to be all right until seven in the morning, when she was leaning over the ironing board in pain. He called the doctor, asking her to come as soon as possible. The doctor arrived within ten minutes and told Anne that she had come just in time.

Apart from the movie this was the first time Rob witnessed the birth of a baby. He had no idea that it was such a painful and traumatic experience for a woman. He tried his best to support her, but felt utterly helpless as he saw what Anne had to go through.

Once the baby was born the doctor held it up for him. Still awed from what he had just witnessed, he stared at the child and noticed that something seemed to be missing. Than he realized that Anne's intuition had been correct. She had just given birth to a baby girl.

It was at that moment that Rob decided there would be no more labor pains for Anne. Two children were enough. They had been given everything they could possibly wish for; they now had two beautiful children to raise. But no more! He had never realized what it was like for a woman to give birth.

The doctor called the midwife agency to inform them that the baby had been born, and scheduled a midwife to come in for the next two weeks to help Anne take care of little Jess.

Rob looked after Jan, positioning him next to Anne so he could watch his sister being fed. The midwife arrived thirty minutes later, and from that moment on, everyone carried out their own tasks.

During nights Rob was on call and did not get much sleep, because Anne was having difficulties with breastfeeding, and they had to feed Jess with the bottle.

After one week Anne began to move slowly around the house. They tried to sleep in shifts, finding it exhausting to suddenly take care of two children. Rob called Werner to tell him of the birth of their daughter and that he would be at the office in three weeks to start his new career.

Anne made a visiting schedule, reserving the first Wednesday afternoon for Agnes and the children. When they came Agnes brought round Dutch rusks with pink candied aniseeds, traditionally served after the birth of a baby girl. While Agnes prepared dinner Dagmar and Thomas took turns to hold Jess.

Klaus arrived, and after he had uttered the expected words of admiration for Jess, Rob showed him the guesthouse.

'Very well done!' he exclaimed, impressed. 'I didn't think you'd remembered everything I taught you, but you did!'

'You taught me everything on how to build a house. I'll never forget those tips and tricks.'

'Is there anything else that you still need to do?'

'No. I finished the last painting job last night when we couldn't sleep. So it's ready for your first weekend.'

'That will be great, especially for the kids. That way they can sleep over at their aunt's and uncle's.'

Having kept in touch constantly, Waltraud was the second guest to come and admire Jess. Rob left the two alone so that they could catch up on everything.

The neighbors were next, dropping in one by one. Rob became quite skilled in making coffee and tea, and quickly learned which cookies and pastries to buy for their guests.

Now that the midwife had gone, Rob was glad that he had accepted the office job.

It was just the two of them now, and they both had their hands full with two children.

Agnes came to help out once a week, and he was at home during the long weekends. As the time drew closer to start work again, he asked Anne if she wanted someone to help her at home, but she first wanted to try with just Agnes' help.

Chapter 32

Dad drove him to the train station on Monday morning. Rob felt badly leaving Anne alone with a baby and a one-year old boy that was about to take his first steps. He was used to saying goodbye, but leaving her now was harder than ever—it felt as if he deserted her.

Once he boarded the train he tried to switch to work mode. It was arranged for him to work with Werner for a full week so that he could observe his daily routine. From then on he would take over his duties.

It was a pleasant train journey to Hanover, and shorter than he expected. A taxi driver was waiting at the station to take him to a small apartment that had been rented for him.

Rob was surprised. He had expected to stay at a hotel while at the office. The two-bedroom apartment was conveniently located within walking distance from the office, right next to a park. Leaving his baggage, he walked to the office, where he was given a security badge and key.

'Good morning Rob, how was your trip?' Werner asked him as he walked in.

'It's always relaxing to travel through the green hills in this part of Germany.'

'What do you think of the apartment?'

'That was a lovely surprise. Hotels are not my favorite place to stay at.'

'That's what I thought. We've rented a two-bedroom apartment for the family, should they want to visit.'

'Very thoughtful of you, and much appreciated.'

'How is your wife coping alone with two small children?'

'If I think about my mam, I suppose each generation has to go through the same rough period.'

Werner nodded and resumed his work, handing Rob a copy of the daily operating reports from each area. Rob sat down and listened in on the telephone conversations with the different operating areas. After one call was finished, the next was made, and this took at least one hour before the reporting sessions were completed.

Rob decided that it would be useful to organize conference calls so that each area would be able to listen in on the conversations and learn from each other's mistakes.

'How shall we do the handover?' Werner asked. 'We can start with going through the contracts, which are kept in this room.'

'I'd prefer if you carried out your daily routine for a week. In the meantime you can show me where everything is kept and direct me to the different departments.'

'That's fine by me. In five minutes we'll join the morning meeting of department heads and managers. I report on the main operational issues.'

In the meeting room Werner introduced him to all those present. The meeting began with Tom Lehman, the finance manager, who reported on the financial commitments made for each operating area, as well as the monthly results. Werner asked several questions about payments for equipment in Libya and took it from there, reporting on the drilling status from each operating area. No one seemed to have any questions.

Rob made a mental note to start this meeting with safety instead of finance issues.

Gunther Meier, the production manager, briefly went through the daily production rate, spoke of problems in one of the plants, and reported on the repairs of two small company-owned rigs.

Eberhart Bauerle, the drilling engineering manager, reported the status of well programs completed for future wells and asked Werner for review and approval.

He also advised him to change the cementation program of the Libyan well.

Then it was the turn of the engineering and procurement managers, who each reported on what was happening in their line of duty. Rob asked Werner why Von Ritter, the new Managing Director, wasn't there for these meetings, to which he replied that the man was on his first inspection trip to Brazil, accompanied by Klein, Fuchs and Ronald Schultz.

The following week Rob was introduced to key personnel of all departments.

He visited the head of safety, and discussed various safety initiatives. He was not impressed, as all the man had to show was a list of dated statistics and pamphlets containing safety information.

That evening he called Anne, eager to hear how his son and daughter were doing and how she managed without him.

Thereafter, he reviewed the contract status of rigs on hire from different contractors, as well as the contracts of service companies providing materials and services required for drilling wells. He reviewed the resumes of managers and departmental heads, paying particular attention to those of Schultz, Fuchs and Andreas Klein, as well as that of the new Managing Director Fritz von Ritter.

He discovered that these four men had worked together for Wedel Shipping Company as mate, ship's engineer, trainee contract manager and engineer. It seemed as if the recent transfer of employees from Wedel Shipping Company to Hattenberg Oil had taken place without taking education, experience or skills into account.

The following morning he joined the rig reporting session and in the afternoon discussed the status of each drilling operation. Another management team meeting was held and important decisions requiring considerable investments or cost approvals were discussed, and finally decided on by vote.

When Rob asked Werner who would be able to replace him while on holiday or sick leave, he was told that either Eberhart, the engineering manager, or Gunther, the production manager, could take over his tasks. Both men could also take over each other's duties if the situation demanded it.

Rob was introduced to the drilling contractor representatives, and he took the opportunity to stress that safety was his first priority. Continuation of their contracts would greatly depend on their safety records. He said that he would support any initiative to create a safer work place, but he did expect their full commitment.

Thursday the official handover took place, and from then on Rob was officially responsible for Drilling Operations. Jurgen was the first person who came into his office to congratulate him.

Rob's first proposal was to make safety a number one priority, and to start the morning meetings with the safety report.

His rental car was delivered in the afternoon, and he called Anne to let her know he would try to be home for dinner.

While driving home it suddenly dawned on him. He finally had the authority to plan and execute all the safety initiatives and ideas that he had ever come up with. He knew that most of the accidents occurred on the rig floor while working with the rotary tongs to connect and disconnect the drill pipes and collars. The iron roughnecks, the first remote controlled pipe-handling machine, had already been installed on the drill ship in Singapore, and this had contributed considerably to their safety record.

He now wanted to install the iron roughnecks on every company-owned rig.

To speed up the drilling process, he would assign Jurgen to place additional mud pumps in each pump room and to make sure that 6 5/8-inch zinc fabricated drill pipes were made available. He planned to install top drives and make use of the latest drilling technology, in which they could drill ninety feet instead of the usual thirty and reduce the number of connections. That way they could avoid stuck pipe situations, which often caused costly delays that could last for weeks.

He wanted real-time drilling recording systems installed, to better control and react on the drilling parameters. Following up Werner's initiative, he would increase the number of company-owned rigs to avoid the drilling contractor's high day rates. This would also give them faster access to suitable rigs for deep water drilling or horizontal drilling to increase the productivity of the present wells.

With Gunther he wanted to discuss if he would be interested to start a fracking job in the shale formation to increase oil or gas production. For this purpose he would contact the Russian company, proposing that they transfer some of their rigs to the Western market.

As from next week he would request copies of the drilling sequences from each rig to check if planning and control were implemented as agreed.

Rob also wanted young engineers to follow a special training program so that they could develop their managerial potential to the full. Then they could avoid what was happening now—the current generation of managers simply didn't have the skills or experience to carry out their tasks properly.

And he would ensure all drilling supervisors were provided with a laptop supplied with the latest drilling technology database to give them access to additional information required to do their jobs.

Now that he had visited all of the rigs, he knew that the company was blessed with excellent drilling managers and supervisors, so he could sleep at night. With the exception of Leonardo and Mike in Brazil, whom continued to feature in some of his nightmares.

His instincts warned him to be careful with Brazil. This would have to wait until a suitable time. All his energy would now be required to attend to day-to-day matters.

Chapter 33

Driving home gave him a warm feeling realizing that he would see Anne and his children for the next three days. Knowing that he would be home within a few hours was an entirely different sensation than having to face the usual twenty-something hours of flying across the ocean to get home.

Anne awaited him in the hallway as he got out of the car. As she opened the door, Jan cried out to him. 'Papa!' It was the first time he had heard him say it.

Anne beamed at him as she saw his look of amazement. 'I told him that papa would come home. He's been saying "papa" the whole day.'

Rob was in total awe. 'To hear that feels as good as when you tell me you love me.'

She smiled. 'I love you, I love you, I love you!'

'Okay, I know that. But this is… just fantastic. And he's getting so big!'

'Yes. He's no longer a baby. He's turning into a little boy.'

'How are you doing? Are you still glad to see me back, even if it's only been a few days?'

'Oh, it's wonderful to count down four days instead of thirty to see you again.' She followed him into the living room. 'I waited for you so you can feed Jess.'

He took Jess from her and noticed how the child observed him in wonder, as if to say, *Who is this person?* Her look changed to one of easy contentment when she lay in his arms, her tiny lips sucking at the teat of the bottle.

'How was it, taking care of two demanding kids?'

'In the beginning I really had to make a strict schedule. I didn't have a spare moment. Every night I was just glad to put up my feet.'

'Then let me know how I can fit into your schedule.'

'You take care of Jan, and I'll take care of Jess while you're home. We'll see how that works out.'

'Who'll be taking care of you?'

'You, my dear. But first we have to wash these two, sing songs for them, and then I'd like a glass of wine.'

While they prepared the children for bed, Rob felt for the first time that his family was truly complete. He didn't know if this was because every room in the house was occupied or whether it was because of the amount of work involved. He poured Anne a glass of wine. 'I just had a feeling that our family is complete,' he said as he handed the glass to her. 'Even though I know you never feel better than when you're expecting, I think I'll visit the hospital to make sure that we don't have another child.'

'You want a sterilization?' she said, somewhat taken aback.

'Yes. Because we don't like using condoms, and you'll be pregnant again before we know it.'

'I'll think about it.'

'No, you will not just think about it, because I know how that ends. We can afford to have more children, but I don't want another child. If we did, you'd only say that a third child is left out, so you'll want to have a fourth one.'

'I think you're probably right, but I still want to think about it.'

'Don't drive me crazy, otherwise I'll be too scared touching you.'

'I'll make you touch me.' She was right, because the glass of wine was hardly finished when he carried her to the bedroom.

Chapter 34

The long weekend went by in a flash, with only short calls from each operating area. Fortunately there weren't any problems. Before they knew, it was early Monday morning and time to get back to work.

'I enjoyed every minute of this weekend,' Anne said. 'I'm so glad you made the decision to take the office job.'

'Please do me a favor, Anne. Visit the doctor, because I really want to have the procedure done before it's too late.'

'I'll think about it.'

'No, Anne. If you don't, I'll call the doctor and arrange it myself.'

'We'll talk about it when you get back.'

Rob sighed. He knew that he would have to arrange it himself. Anne would love to have another child 'by accident'. Before leaving he slipped into the children's bedrooms to find them still asleep. He stood at their beds, still awed by their very existence and the fact that they were his.

The drive to the office was becoming tedious, and he had to force himself to pay attention, often finding himself driving on automatic pilot.

His daily routine was filled with reading drilling reports, phone calls to the areas and meetings with the department heads. At lunchtime he called the doctor and explained his wish. She asked if Anne approved of him having the procedure, and he told her that she did. She scheduled the procedure for Friday morning, and he thanked her, relieved.

He called Jurgen and agreed to have lunch together. Rob found a table in the corner and ordered soup with sandwiches.

'I've been wanting to ask you,' Jurgen began. 'How did your area visits work out?'

'Some required more attention than others. Should find out more this week, because I requested each area to send me a copy of the planned drilling sequences.'

'How did they react in Brazil?'

Rob looked at him sharply. 'Why do you specifically ask about Brazil?'

'Well, I carried out some engineering work for the installation of additional equipment on board. Never heard from them since.'

'What additional equipment was that? I just inspected the rig and can tell you if the installation took place.'

'A mud cleaning system with new shale shakers, de-sanders and centrifuges to separate the cuttings and solids from the mud.'

Rob didn't know what to say. He noticed the additional equipment in the contract, listed against an exorbitant rental fee, but he didn't see the equipment on board.

He remembered because he paid special attention to the brand name of the shale shakers.

'I did not pay special attention to the shale shaker system on board. Maybe I'll remember it later.'

'Oh come on, Rob. You're a drilling specialist. Don't tell me that you can't remember seeing this new type of mud cleaning equipment.'

'Really, Jurgen, I didn't see the equipment on board. To be honest, there is something very wrong with that operation. I need some time to figure out the facts. And I have to be very careful if I don't want to run into trouble.'

'Can I help in any way?'

'No, thanks. I'll need more time to get my feet on the ground in the office and get to know the people I work with. And most importantly I need to find out whom I can trust. When the time is right I'll focus on Brazil again. But let's change the subject. The reason I asked you for lunch is because I want to install additional equipment on all our rigs.'

'What type of additional equipment?'

'First of all, the iron roughnecks you already installed on the drill ship in Singapore to connect and disconnect the drill pipes and drill collars without the use of these big and risky tongs. At the same time I want to look at the different companies that can deliver top drive systems.'

'Rob, I have visited the different companies to select the top drive for the drill ship and know the available systems. There shouldn't be any problems installing that equipment on our rigs because I've already checked each rig. Most of the work would go into reinforcing the guide system of the traveling block.'

'How can we start the process?'

'You'll have to instruct the procurement department to issue a purchase order. Then I'll get involved because an engineering change request needs to be issued, and I'll check if any engineering work is involved. I'll then get all the documentation that is required and leave it on your desk, so you can take a look. I will complete the purchase order and the engineering request form, if that's okay with you.'

'I would appreciate that.'

'Then Werner Brandt has to give his signature to approve the purchase, because the new Managing Director is not in favor of making any investments. Is there anything else you want installed or changed?'

'Yes. I'd like to install a drilling recording system, but recording in real time. I want one additional mud pump and 6 5/8-inch zinc drill pipe to reduce weight on each rig and drill the top hole sections faster.'

Jurgen scratched behind his ear. 'This should keep me very busy! Right. I'll let you know when I'm finished with the legwork. I'll have to check the size of mud pump rooms and look into the latest available drilling recording systems.'

'And to close my wish list, I'd like to purchase laptops for our drilling supervisors and create a drilling engineering database to provide easy access to the newest drilling technology. I'd also like to hire four fresh drilling engineers from the university to follow the same training schedule as Joop. Speaking of which, what's he doing right now?'

'He is a driller on the ship. Doing just fine, too.'

'That's good to hear, 'cause I think it's time for him to come into the office and assist you with everything on my wish list'.

'I think that's a good idea. He is very interested in new drilling technologies and likes to be involved in changes that impact the way we drill our future wells'.

'I'll check with HR when he's off duty so I can invite him to the office. Let me know when you have most of the information on the equipment, and then we'll review and decide on some of the items.'

'Sure, will do.'

'One last thing. Can you join me to Murmansk next week? I need to make a few calls and check to see if we can meet the man I need to talk to.'

'You want to increase the number of rigs?'

'Yes. We need more rigs, especially rigs to carry out upgrades on the BOP and piping systems to 15,000 psi for future deep water drilling operations.'

'We already have approval to upgrade the drill ship system to 15,000 psi in the ship yard.'

'That's great, but I'm also looking for ways to reduce the day rates that we have to pay Western drilling contractors. Their day rates are continuously increasing. I want to use some of the Russian rigs for horizontal drilling, so I'll need information on whip stocks previously used to bypass obstructions in the hole, as well as the newest turbine and steering technologies available to increase our productivity. It's important that we add the same type of rigs with standard drilling equipment to our fleet, and that we're able to add to the number if required. I noticed that most of the drilling contractors are fusing with others to form large companies. They will be able to dictate future day rates, and we have hardly any competitors left. So we must look for ways to upgrade our rigs with the newest drilling technology, and at the same time avoid an increase in our daily operating cost. I think that we can convince the management team of this plan, but I first have to make some calls. I'll keep you posted.'

Jurgen thought about it. 'I suggest we ask Tom Lehman to come with us to Murmansk. As finance manager he will see the advantages, and he is one of the old timers. He can help us to get the management team's approval for projects like this, because he is highly respected. That and we can trust him.'

'I met him at the drilling manager meeting. He gave an excellent presentation on how to calculate new investments within the required profit margins. I will visit him on the way to my office and ask if he can join us. I'll let you know.'

Rob went to see Tom and explained his plans to use some of the rigs in Murmansk for future operations. 'I was there only a few months ago to inspect the different types of rigs they've got,' he told him. 'They would suit our needs very well.'

Together they discussed how to finance the required modifications, and Tom suggested the possibility of entering into a joint venture with the Russians. Rob thought this was a good idea and include all rigs owned by the Russians. They could move these rigs together with the standard Russian crew to a shipyard in Finland to carry out the necessary upgrades. The modifications would only be minor, as the rigs were well equipped with Western drilling equipment, and they could share the modification cost between the two companies.

'The day rates for rigs in Russia are fifty percent lower than in the Western market because of the difference in labor costs,' Rob explained. 'The rigs would operate on a long-term contract instead of just a few months during the Russian summer. It would generate more income for the Russians. I'd like to propose this to the Russian Managing Director, but I think it would be good for them to join us.'

Tom nodded, obviously interested. 'I agree. I'll go with you, but you have to contact Eberhart Bauerle, our drilling engineering manager, to confirm that his future drilling plans require these Russian rigs.'

Rob called Eberhart and explained his plan to add jackups and drill ships in sequence of his requirements.

He thought about it, and as far as he was concerned, they could go ahead with a joint venture.

Rob contacted the Russian MD, who said that he was still interested in making his rigs available. As he was flying to Finland anyway, they agreed to meet the following Saturday for lunch at the airport hotel in Helsinki. Rob asked his secretary to make all the travel arrangements and to check Joop's work schedule.

The rest of the day he spent negotiating a contract with two drilling contractors that had submitted tender proposals for a jackup to drill the first offshore deep drilling well in Germany. It was the first time he had to deal with Andreas Klein, the contract manager. He felt uneasy about it, but told himself to stay calm.

He carefully reviewed the tender documents and drilling contract, paying special attention to the deviations to the contract, as suggested by the drilling contractor the night before. With a highlighter, he marked the items that were of operational interest.

The rigs that were being offered were almost identical, but there was a price difference—the day rate of one of the contractors was about five percent higher. One contractor had included the company's annual safety records for all of their rigs, and it offered one additional Offshore Installation Manager, responsible for all safety issues on board. Rob appreciated this. As far as he was concerned, his decision was made.

Rob ate some fruit for lunch and reviewed the tender documents one more time before his one o'clock meeting with Klein. As he went through the documents, he thought about the contract situation in Brazil. He promised himself to look into the matter as soon as modifications were approved and one Russian rig was on its way to Finland.

At one o'clock Klein came in with the drilling contractor's drilling and contract manager. They introduced themselves, and Klein started the meeting to discuss the list of deviations to the contract as submitted by the contractor. Most of the items concerned a reduction of contractor liabilities, to which both sides had to make concessions. As long as each party was satisfied with the final wording, Rob was fine with it.

When it came to discussing safety issues, he took over and asked for the rig safety records. The drilling manager blinked. 'I'm sorry, we don't keep such records.'

They then went on to discuss the list of drilling equipment.

'Would you be interested in installing a top drive and iron roughneck against an increase in day rate?' Rob asked the drilling manager.

'No we can't,' the man said. 'My company finds the investment too high to write off during the duration of the contract.'

Rob then briefly discussed the 'person on board' list and left the closing of the meeting to Klein, who said that they would review their bid and send them a letter of intent if awarded the contract.

Not long after the drilling contractor's representatives left, three visitors from the competing contractor arrived. The third person introduced himself as the company's Managing Director and said that he always had an excellent business relation with Werner, and hoped that this relationship would continue.

'My company always offers rigs and personnel against fair rates,' he began. 'I'd like to make a proposal before we start contract negotiations. What I want is a variable day rate and long term contracts.'

He proposed to provide rigs and personnel against the average two-year market rate, but offered a ten percent reduction. He handed them the average day rate chart, and explained that the day rate as offered in the tender documents was the two-year average market rate. They would be given a ten percent reduction for one year if his company was given the contract.

He concluded, 'If the two-year average market rate changes, the day rates will be adjusted for the next year,' and he submitted a concept agreement for him to review.

When Rob took over to discuss the operational side, he thanked them for the day rate proposal and for including the company's two-year safety record. In addition, he indicated that he was impressed by their safety standards.

'Thank you,' the contractor's drilling manager said. 'I'd like to believe that both our training initiatives and the fact that we keep the same crew onboard have contributed to increase safety.'

'Would you be interested in installing a top drive and iron roughneck against an increase in day rate?' Rob asked.

'Absolutely. We were planning to install these in the near future anyway. And we'd greatly appreciate if you reimburse us for part of the investment during the contract period. Of course we hope that you will extend the contract once the well is completed,' the man said with a smile.

'If we reach a deal, I want to be involved in the selection of electrical or hydraulic top drive and iron roughneck manufacturers. By the way, I appreciated your initiative to include the Onshore Installment Manager.'

Once the meeting was over and the contractor's representatives had left, Rob asked Klein which of the two contractors he would select.

'I would select the first company. Their commercial conditions are better.'

'Did you consider what impact it would have if we drill the first deep offshore well in this country and are faced with an accident? What do you suppose will happen if the authorities find out we entered into a contract with a drilling contractor that has a poor safety record?'

Klein hesitated. 'No, I didn't think about that. So I take it that we'll send the second drilling contractor the letter of intent?'

'Yes. And please keep me updated on the selection of top drive and iron roughneck manufacturers, and I will add the contractor's rate proposal to the management meeting agenda.'

'Of course.'

Rob watched as Klein left the meeting room. Once again his intuition told him to be careful. Something just didn't feel right.

That afternoon he discussed various reports and planned sequences with his drilling managers. When he left the office that evening, he decided to take the Brazil contract and IADC drilling reports to his apartment. He spent most of the night reviewing the documents, as well as the 'persons on board' list.

The following morning he had come to the conclusion that certain individuals received a considerable amount of money each month. He was almost certain that they obtained this money through payments from his company to the drilling contractor to reimburse for the additional equipment that wasn't on board, the extra personnel that weren't accounted for and the agent fee. As no financial transactions took place at the local office in Brazil, he was sure that their invoices came from a non-existent company set up by those who divided the money.

He only slept for an hour, when his phone woke him up. One rig in Libya experienced a kick, and the crew was killing the well with heavy mud. Rob advised the drilling manager that if the well indicated zero pressure after the heavy mud was circulated to the surface, make a trip to the casing shoe, and if okay, continue drilling.

After a quick shower he walked to the office. His secretary told him that Von Ritter wanted to see him right away.

Wondering what to expect, Rob walked into Von Ritter's office. 'You wanted to see me?'

'Yes that's right,' Von Ritter said. 'I just reviewed the daily reports and noticed that the rig in Libya is having problems. My question is what are you going to do about it?'

'Sir I was informed about the kick this morning. I spoke to the drilling manager, and I advised him what to do, and we're not expecting any problems.'

'So you'll do nothing?'

'Not until the drilling manager informs me that we have a problem. If there is, I will see to it that he gets additional support.'

Von Ritter thought about it, and nodded. 'Fine. There is one other issue. I was informed that a contract was awarded against a higher day rate, and you agreed to pay an additional rate to install a top drive and iron roughneck.'

'That is correct. I think we should start this first deep offshore well in Germany with the safest and best-equipped rig to ensure smooth operations. I want to avoid ending up in the evening news because of a serious accident.'

'I will discuss this with my advisor, Werner Brandt, and let you know if we need further information. In the meantime, let me know if you decide to install any top drive or iron roughneck system. I recommend that we select a hydraulic system.'

'We will certainly consider, and thanks for your suggestion.'

Rob went back to his office, finding it strange that this hadn't been discussed with Werner prior to his being summoned, or waiting until the morning meeting. Von Ritter didn't even know that the drilling string was turning to the right to drill a well. So how would he know which top drive system to select? He was beginning to get a feeling that Von Ritter might be able to obstruct quite a number of his future projects and plans if he kept on interfering like this.

He called Jurgen and told him about the discussion he had with Von

Ritter on the top drive issue.

'Rob I've just been looking into the different manufacturers of iron roughnecks and top drive systems, including the board of directors of these companies. It appears that our new Managing Director is a member of the board of directors from a company that manufactures the hydraulic version.'

Rob raised an eyebrow at this. Why wasn't he surprised? This was a smart move by the hydraulic manufacturing company, designing and assembling its first prototype. He was sure that Von Ritter would be nicely rewarded if he used his influence to purchase the hydraulic package.

He instructed Jurgen to include the hydraulic design in the selection list and asked him to advise him from an engineering point of view which manufacturer to select based on various criteria. 'Oh, and Jurgen, please check if Von Ritter is a board member of any other company we're dealing with.'

Rob had never expected to be maneuvered into his present position. First he became involved in bribe affairs, and now he discovers the MD's involvement in the decision making process. This was not the reason why he accepted this position.

He accepted the job because of the expertise and experience that was needed to advise the management team regarding operational issues and drilling wells safely and efficiently.

There were two options: play along to, have an easy job and make friends, or he could stick to his basic principles of doing honest and fair business.

Feeling the need to talk to someone, he called Werner and asked if they could have lunch.

None of the issues discussed with Von Ritter that morning were mentioned at the morning meeting. Von Ritter did come up with a proposal to introduce a bonus system for the management team. Each member of the management team was asked to set annual targets for his department, which would be reviewed and approved by him. If all targets were achieved, a bonus that equaled three months' salary was to be paid to each member, while the Managing Director would receive six to twelve months' bonus, depending on the company's results. He indicated that this bonus system was also introduced at Wedel Shipping Company and was proven to be very effective for reaching company goals.

Rob was surprised. Why pay an extra bonus for targets that had already been set at the yearly assessment discussions with all the employees? The company paid excellent salaries, and everyone worked hard to reach his or her targets.

The employees regarded this as a personal challenge and took pride in what they achieved. The success of the company was based on the hard work of loyal individuals who had new and innovative ideas to reach the targets set by their department heads.

Werner had come up with innovative solutions for his department, such as the purchase of company-owned rigs and entering into joint ventures with preferred, drilling contractors. He had expanded the search for oil and gas in risky areas. Heumer and his management team had developed a long-term vision of how to expand the company and became a very efficient, well-managed and internationally-recognized company.

One simple example was that Hattenberg Oil purchased rigs at bottom rates when the market was low to be ready for the future.

Was Von Ritter only interested in filling his own pockets? Was his intention to use the management team as a vehicle to establish a culture of greed? He was beginning to understand why Wedel Shipping Company didn't perform. No doubt that the motivation of employees and their pride to perform had been lost. To Rob this was the most important drive for a company to be successful. It was something that simply can't be bought with money.

Wedel Shipping Company clearly didn't have a management team with a long-term vision. They could have built and replaced their ships at bottom rates when shipyards were desperate for work.

The management was probably only interested in short-term financial results to obtain maximum bonus payments. These persons were not at all interested in the future of the company, but only worked for their own benefit. That kind of attitude was fatal for any company.

No. He had learned a very important lesson from the previous management team—act in low market periods to prepare for the future, just as he was planning to do with the Russian Company.

Yes, he did want to have sufficient rigs and experienced personnel available for the upcoming booming market period. The market was mostly driven by the demand for oil and gas, but sometimes manipulated by major oil companies to suspend drilling for a period in order to reduce contractors' day rates.

Once he got back to his office he went through the résumés of Von Ritter, Fuchs, Schultz, Klein and Tom Lehmann. The first three men had all worked at Wedel Shipping Company for a long period. The only exception was Tom. That meant that he could only count on the support of Werner, Tom, Jurgen and possibly the drilling engineering, production and procurement managers.

When Werner walked in around noon he sat down. Rob thought he looked tired.

'I'd rather not go down and have lunch together, Rob. Certain people might think we're trying to undermine Von Ritter. I understand that you had an interesting discussion with him this morning. I told him to discuss these issues with me before calling anyone into his office, and that such matters should be raised at the morning meetings.'

'Thanks, Werner. The real reason I wanted to have lunch with you is to discuss different issues, such as your idea to start a joint venture with the Russian rigs to reduce our operating costs. I'm meeting the Russian MD next weekend. You've already created a joint venture agreement with the preferred drilling contractor, and I want to propose we extend this agreement with a two-year average day rate.

'I want to install equipment such as top drive, a drilling monitoring system and add a third mud pump to reduce drilling time. I'd like hiring additional trainees like Joop to get on-the-job training before they are assigned to the engineering department. I'd also like to drill horizontal wells to increase the production rates of our wells. We can use some of the savings on operating costs to improve safety and install equipment to improve drilling efficiency. All I need to know is if we have enough management support to proceed as for some managers the financial results could be more important to obtain Von Ritter's newly invented bonus system.'

Werner smiled at him from across the desk. 'You have followed the exact path I expected you would. This is exactly in line with our long-term strategy. Continue with your plans, and I'll make sure I get enough support within the management team. But combine your proposals, as you never know when things will change again.' He sat forward for what he was about to say next. 'I also know that you've been selected as one of the drilling representatives from the German oil industry to advise das Bergambt, which is similar to the department of energy, how to change or modify the existing German mining law.

'In England Lord Cullen has completed the investigation on the Piper Alpha disaster, and now each country has to adjust the safety regulations according to his recommendations. This government body supervises all activities, facilities and equipment associated with the mining industry, and includes the promotion and monitoring of operational safety. I know that you think that a government that issue permits to both drill and produce cannot be a safety watchdog at the same time. On the Piper Alpha the production of oil and gas was not shut down for only one reason: loss of revenue.'

'Werner, I've already got my hands full with the day-to-day business, as well as other projects. I'm really not eager to go through this disaster. Plus, I don't like attending endless meetings with government officials.'

'Sorry, there's no way to get out of this one. Government officials shouldn't make new rules and regulations without the input of operational experts like you. If we don't involve people like you, they will make it so difficult and complicated that we will no longer be able to drill wells. We have to ensure that Lord Cullen's recommendations are carried out. He wants the energy departments to issue only permits to drill and produce. He's right. We need a separate health and safety organization to look after safety interests, so there can be no conflict of interest.'

Rob thought about it, nodding slowly. 'Okay. I guess I have no choice.'

After Werner left, Rob gathered his paperwork that he would need for the long weekend at home and his visit to Helsinki.

He called Anne to tell her that he was leaving the office.

'Alright. Drive carefully. I'll wait with dinner,' was all she said.

Chapter 35

While driving home he was thinking how to tell Anne about the sterilization procedure the following day. He should have told her that he made the appointment. They had discussed this many times—he wanted to live well and provide his children with a decent education. Two children were enough. He wanted to be able to enjoy life and did not want to live through an eternity of diapers. He had hoped that she would agree, but last week he saw that strange look in her eyes. He wouldn't be surprised if she didn't mind becoming pregnant again.

Well, he thought, *the first thing I do when I get home is enjoy the kids and take one problem at the time.*

He did not have to wait long to find out that something was very wrong. He kissed Anne warmly, but received very little response, so he went to hug the kids instead. He cuddled with Jess, fed her and put her to bed, and nothing was said between them. He wondered if she knew that he had to travel in the weekend or if something else was wrong.

They kept Jan up a little longer and he could feel her eyes observing him with a strange, intent look on her face. But she still didn't say a word. Once Jan was settled for the night, he asked her if she would like a glass of wine.

'No,' was her cool reply. 'I'm not in the mood to drink a glass of wine. I visited the doctor two days ago. She told me that you'd made an appointment for the sterilization procedure tomorrow. She was rather embarrassed when she realized that I was entirely unaware. So here's my question. When were you planning to tell me?'

'I was thinking of how to tell you on my way home. We already discussed this, Anne. You know how I feel about this.'

'Then you should have told me.'

'Yes, you're right. I should have told you. I'm sorry, but this has to happen.'

'So I have one more night to seduce you.'

'Yes, one night. I'm leaving on Saturday morning for a meeting in Helsinki.'

She scowled at him, angry. 'That's clever planning.'

'I didn't plan it that way. There was no alternative.'

'I had time to think about this. It so happens that I agree that we should be happy with two healthy kids. But still, you should have told me, Rob! I'll make you a deal,' she said coldly. 'We'll light the fireplace, open a bottle of wine and make love as long as we can. If you are lucky, this will be one of your dream nights, and if I'm lucky we'll conceive another baby.'

'That's not fair, because you agreed.'

'I didn't agree. You should have told me.'

'I was only thinking of what's best for our family.'

'You should be happy with this proposal after a long week from home. Didn't you miss me?'

'I give up. I'll start the fire and bring our special bed downstairs.'

'Can you please fill the bath? I'd like a massage, if that's possible.'

'Everything is possible.'

'Everything?'

'Yes, everything.'

Once again she proved that everything was indeed possible, and she did everything in a woman's power to seduce him again and again until he had no more energy left. Finally, after all the sensual tricks she used on him, he fell fast asleep.

Anne had arranged for Dad to drive him to hospital the following day, and within two hours they returned to have breakfast.

After Dad left, Rob asked Anne if they could have a rest together, as he didn't slept well the night before.

She looked at him with a mischievous glint in her eye. 'Your brain wants to check if you're still able to make love. Your body tells you to get some rest, because I took all the energy you had. But you're worried that the hospital did something wrong with that beautiful instrument of yours,' she teased.

It took all of his charm and persuasive powers to convince her to go to bed with him while the children were having their afternoon naps. They found out that everything was still in good working order, and his faith in his manhood was fully restored.

The rest of the day they enjoyed every minute.

On Saturday he met Tom and Jurgen at Schiphol and went through the main points of the joint venture proposal one more time.

At the hotel their Russian counterparts joined them for lunch in a private meeting room arranged by Ivan Golubev, the Russian Managing Director. He was accompanied by his engineering manager and secretary, who also functioned as interpreter.

Once everyone was seated, Rob thanked Ivan for his hospitality and taking the time to meet them. The basic proposal was that the company wanted to modify every jackup and drill ship to Western standards, share modifications costs and approve that long-term contracts would be agreed upon for each separate unit.

Ivan agreed with the principle, and they made a schedule for the day to discuss engineering, drilling and finance issues. The engineering representatives were the first to start.

Jurgen prepared a list of items such as the certification of the units, because drilling rigs were built and certified according to class rules and regulations. DNV and Lloyds are the major certifying companies that ensure that these units operate according to regulations. Their certifying inspectors carried out yearly inspections to ensure that all machinery is maintained according to their standards and operate within the planned maintenance schedule.

It took some time before Jurgen was finally satisfied. He agreed with his colleague to handle the required paperwork and questions that remained unanswered between them. Basically they agreed that all units were certified and allowed to work anywhere in the world.

Rob and the drilling manager discussed the drilling history of each unit, the personnel on board to operate each unit and the safety and training of personnel.

Safety and incidents formed a murky area, as no records on accidents or incidents were kept. In the case of accidents, employees were simply replaced and lost time was regarded as part of the business.

Rob explained his ideas on how to reduce accidents and mistakes on the rig floor by the installation of equipment to reduce accidents and the sequence planning to ensure that each person was aware of the operations to be carried out.

The drilling manager gave a brief presentation on their excellent education program and training schedule for each function on board.

They agreed to have dinner and to discuss the financial conditions the following morning. Ivan felt it was important to have a drink after dinner and get to know each other personally. He wanted to talk about other things such as family, sport and hobbies to get to know the people he was dealing with, as was tradition in his country.

Rob didn't know if this was truly tradition or that the real reason was to influence clear thinking before the financial discussions.

He poured most of his vodka in a fake plant, because he did not want to get drunk or sick.

The next day Tom and Jurgen had serious headaches, difficulty getting up and unable to eat anything. The party required a large quantity of coffee before all brain functions worked again, and financial discussions began.

Tom proposed that both parties financed the modifications and equipment upgrades, because the equipment would remain on the rig once the contract period expired. He said the company could not afford to increase the daily operating cost, so he indicated a day rate that was much lower than the present Western market rate to write off new investments during the contract period. But pointed out that the proposed day rate was still thirty percent higher than the current market rate in Russia. This rate was not only paid during the summer period in which these units were able to drill, but the whole year round. This would have a considerable impact on their yearly revenues.

But Ivan indicated that he expected to be paid Western day rates, and he had no intention of financing part of the investments, because no cash was available.

Once it became clear that they were not making any progress on the financial issues, Rob pushed his chair back and started to gather his papers. 'Maybe we should all take the time to rethink the proposal and schedule another meeting.'

'Perhaps we can come to some other arrangement,' Ivan said quickly. 'The only other way to finance these investments would be that our company delivers oil to a dedicated port in Germany to compensate for the necessary investments.'

'I have no problem with that,' Tom said, so everyone sat down again, and the discussions continued. Eventually they came to the subject of the total number of rigs to be included in the letter of intent.

Rob suggested they include all the jackups and drill ships in the agreement, and Ivan finally agreed. The only remaining issue was the day rate compensation. After hours of negotiations and repeating each other's position, they finally settled using sixty percent of the average Western rig rate to determine the day rate for each year, including the oil to be delivered for new investments.

And finally they discussed the transfer of the monthly payment. 'I have a bank account in Germany and a company account in Murmansk,' Ivan said. 'I would appreciate splitting the day rate payment between these two accounts.'

Tom agreed readily, obviously relieved there was no request for cash payments.

Rob realized that some people in the room would get filthy rich on this deal. It suddenly occurred to him that this could be the same payment set up in Brazil—that all of the agent fee and additional equipment charges were transferred to a separate account. He would have to ask Tom about it, because his intuition told him that he could be trusted.

It was apparent that Ivan was under the impression that the letter of intent was to be signed that day, as the secretary suddenly placed a bottle of champagne with glasses on the table, as well as the prepared letter of intent. Ivan signed it, looking pleased. Tom signed on behalf of the company.

Ivan pushed his chair back and stood up. 'I would like to propose a toast to a long and good relationship, based on trust between our two companies. I look forward to meeting your Managing Director and the management team in Hanover for the final signing of the joint venture agreement.'

Rob responded in kind, thanking him for his cooperation and saying he was pleased that they established a joint venture. They agreed to meet again in Helsinki in the near future to discuss the necessary investments.

Ivan asked to have a few moments alone with Rob and his drilling manager, and everyone else left the room.

'So you were on the drill ship that salvaged our first nuclear powered submarine, and we came late with the *Valentine Shashin*', he said. 'And I understand you were on the first deep wells drilled in Germany. I've read your paper on selection of bits for drilling into high pressure and temperature wells. Quite impressive.'

Rob was stunned that the man knew all this, and was momentarily lost for words.

'Have you ever heard of the Kola project?' he asked Rob.

'No, I can't say I have.'

'It's a top-secret Russian drilling project. Some years ago we started drilling the deepest well ever; the target depth was set at 15 km. But it is vital that you do not talk about this project with anyone. Do I have your word on this?'

Rob confirmed that he did.

'For years every available technology, know-how and experience within the Russian drilling industry has been used to pass the 12 km mark. But we are unable to make any progress because of difficult formations and drilling problems encountered at this depth. I want to ask you a favor. Would you be able to review the drilling reports? Based on your operational experience, you might be able to come up with suggestions or recommendations.'

Rob told him that he was honored and would assist in any way possible, whereupon the drilling manager handed him a file with the translated drilling reports.

'Contact me within two weeks and let me know if you have any suggestions. If you have any questions, call me any time.'

'What was the most important discovery you made at that depth?'

Ivan shrugged his shoulders. 'No one in the world knows the earth. Somehow I think that Mother Earth is protecting her domain and treasures very carefully!'

They were just in time to board the last flight to Amsterdam. The plane was only half full, so they asked to be seated together.

Rob told Tom and Jurgen that the Russians required some technical advice. Then he told Tom what happened in Brazil, and asked how the monthly payments from the head office were arranged.

My department arranges payments according to the conditions of the contract,' Tom said. 'For the Brazil contract, payments are made to the drilling contractor for the day rate against one invoice and one payment for additional services against a separate invoice. The payments are made into two different bank accounts.'

Rob told him, 'I suspect that the day rate payment is transferred to the drilling contractor's head office account, and the payment for additional services is paid to the contractor's shore base account. Someone probably produced a fake invoice for the additional services at the shore base and arranges payments to the people within the money chain. No one at the rig, contractor or company head office would have any idea, because this was arranged between the contractor and company representatives at the shore base. This was supported by a network of people, including representatives of the local oil company receiving payments and making sure that no questions were asked. Tom, could you please check the two payment routings and let me know?'

'Yes. I'll check the routings myself. I don't know whom to trust anymore. Von Ritter, Fuchs, Klein and Schulz visited Brazil already two times since Von Ritter was appointed. One thing's for sure—their hotel and restaurant bills were ridiculously high. Not to mention other services, but I never questioned it, as Von Ritter approved these expense forms.'

They discussed if the bribery was already planned and arranged before the contract negotiations between Klein, Schultz and Von Ritter, because they worked together at Wedel Shipping Company.

'The U.S. drilling supervisor warned me while I was on the rig. He told me to be very careful, because investigating further could be dangerous to anyone.'

The three men felt uncomfortable. Why take such a high risk to stop this organized corruption in a country that doesn't provide any protection and where the people accept bribes as part of their daily life?

Still, Rob wanted to review the situation and to find a possible solution once the payment routing was confirmed.

He asked Jurgen to complete the engineering documents for the modification of the Russian rig including top drive, iron roughneck, drilling data recording system, laptops and third mud pump installations for all company-owned rigs. He wanted to present the Russian joint venture in such a way that the reduced day rate for the rigs would justify the necessary new investments to obtain management approval.

Jurgen replied that all paperwork and recommendations would be completed in time for next week's presentation to the management team.

After landing Rob called Anne to let her know his arrival time in Enschede and asked if Dad could pick him up.

On one hand he felt satisfied because he was close to finalizing one of his targets, which was very important for the growth of the company. On the other hand he felt angry at not able to change the mess in Brazil or the situation at head office. Powers above him were in control, and this frustrated him.

Chapter 36

In Enschede he switched to home mode to become husband and dad again. While Dad drove he looked at Anne next to him, just wanting to hold and kiss her.

She looked at him, a concerned expression on her face. 'Is everything ok?'

'I'm just tired. The meetings were long, and we had to drink a couple of vodkas.'

'No, that's not what I mean. This is the same worried frown I noticed when you came back from Russia, Venezuela and Brazil.'

'Don't worry. This visit was not to one of these countries.'

'We missed you over the weekend. I just had this strange feeling.'

Rob averted her gaze. Could she really sense what was going on in his head? He told her that the meetings had gone successfully, and he wanted to have a glass of wine to toast that with her later.

They took the kids to their rooms and kissed them goodnight. Jess smiled after his kiss and rolled to one side.

Anne told him that she visited Agnes and Klaus over the weekend. The kids played together, and they had an excellent meal.

Rob opened a bottle of wine, and they stayed by the fireplace until early in the morning, waking just in time to leave for the office.

On his way to Hanover Rob realized that this would be a very important week. Werner would try to obtain sufficient support from the management team to approve the Russian joint venture and investments. The upcoming management meeting would also give an indication of who belonged to Von Ritter's network.

After his arrival he first added his items to the agenda for the management meeting scheduled on Thursday, then reviewed the drilling reports and discussed the ongoing operations with the drilling managers before joining the morning meeting.

Rob informed management and department heads about the drilling operations and meeting with the Russians.

No specific questions were asked concerning the upcoming management meeting, but he was sure this would be different on Thursday.

He called Joop and invited him to evaluate and discuss a possible change in his training program, and he agreed to meet the next day.

His secretary informed him that he was to attend a meeting concerning new mining rules and regulations on Monday morning at the office of das Bergambt, the German Petroleum Directorate in Hamburg.

Tom called to confirm that payment for additional services in Brazil was wire transferred to the contractors shore base account.

Rob decided to take up Ronald Schultz's invitation to join him on his next visit to Brazil to discuss the sequence planning. He walked up to Schultz's office, but Von Ritter and Fuchs were there. He didn't want to interrupt, so he asked Schultz to give him a call later. Schultz called him back that afternoon and they agreed to travel after Christmas to Brazil for an inspection trip.

Jurgen sent him the engineering change request forms and purchase orders for top drives, iron roughnecks, third mud pumps, drilling recording systems and laptops for review. He also included the estimated cost to carry out horizontal drilling operations and investments to upgrade three Russian rigs to Western standards.

Rob added the two-year average day rate proposal of the preferred drilling contractor.

He tried to leave office no later than seven o'clock to call home from his apartment. He wanted to hear Anne's voice before going to sleep. Sometimes he wished to be a bird so he could fly over to see his loved ones for a brief moment, but was very satisfied talking on the phone and listening to what had happened that day.

Once he spoke to Anne he worked on the Russian joint venture and investment proposals in detail. After seeing Von Ritter, Schultz, Klein and Fuchs together that morning, he sensed that they were preparing opposition. He would ask Tom, Jurgen and Werner to sit together and prepare for the management team meeting.

He worked the whole night including all his future plans into one proposal as Werner suggested for the management team's approval to complete his targets.

He summarized the benefits, was satisfied with the financial and technical proposals and left early for the office. He asked his secretary to make copies and deliver them personally to Tom, Jurgen and Werner, and ask them to call him if any changes should be made.

After the morning meeting his secretary informed him that Joop was waiting in the lobby with his wife. He called Jurgen to be present in his office, then went down to welcome them and showed them to his office. They were served coffee, after which Rob's secretary took Joop's wife to show her around the office building.

In the meantime, the three men discussed Joop's training schedule, present status and reviewed his assessment reports. Rob asked if he was interested in assisting Jurgen for a one-year period as project engineer to complete the modifications on company-owned and Russian rigs, and in preparing horizontal drilling operations. He would maintain his on/off schedule, visit different equipment suppliers to check assembling and deliveries, and be present at the shipyards during the installation period.

Joop was interested and told them that he had already trained someone to take his place as driller. He asked if it was possible to change his trainee status to drilling engineer, because he had just bought a house, and this promotion would benefit his financial situation.

They agreed on his promotion and his transfer to headquarters after one last trip to the rig. Rob then invited them for lunch where they discussed the purchase of their new house with Joop's wife. She told Rob that it was very difficult for her to get adjusted to the on/off schedule, but was slowly getting used to the part time life with Joop.

'It's part of the job,' Rob explained to her, not unsympathetic. 'My wife and I also struggled with that for a while.'

After lunch they said their goodbyes, and Jurgen joined Rob in his office to discuss the management proposal. Jurgen explained that apart from the large sum for the new investments, one of the hot items was the selection of a manufacturer for top drives and iron roughnecks.

He received several phone calls and visits from the hydraulic manufacturer sales representative, who advised him to consult with the Managing Director on the matter. But Jurgen recommended top drives and iron roughnecks with an electrically driven motor already proven within the oil industry. He did not opt for the complex prototype hydraulic system.

Rob agreed, because he had worked with these motors on most of the rigs. To install the first hydraulic prototype on their rigs would be a risk.

Jurgen asked him to mention the hiring of trainee engineers with the HR manager, because his request had been cancelled.

'I have included hiring trainee engineers in my proposal to the management team and presentation for the meeting on Thursday. That way we combine the proposals and have a better chance of getting approval.'

Werner's and Tom's suggestions had come in, and he completed the final proposal for distribution to the management team.

A visit to Gunther, the Production Manager, was something that was high on Rob's agenda, as he wanted his input on horizontal drilling. When he called, Gunther invited him to come down immediately.

The production department was located in a separate building, so after a short walk, he met Gunther at the entrance hall.

'Eberhart was in my office at the time you called,' he said. 'Do you mind if he joins us?'

'Not at all. That would be very convenient, actually.'

In Gunther's office he summarized the different plans he wanted to propose at the management meeting. He told them about the importance of the top drive and iron roughneck selection, as well as the third mud pumps that would enable them to drill faster. He explained why it was vital that they hire trainee drilling engineers to obtain operational experience, and explained the added value of measuring while drilling without delay to avoid hole problems. He discussed why it was necessary to purchase laptops for setting up a drilling engineering data system. And finally he gave them details of the horizontal drilling plans with them.

Gunther and Eberhart listened without interrupting, and when Rob finished, Gunther asked, 'Is the technology available to measure while drilling horizontal sections of the well to know exactly where the bit is located in the hole, and can you follow the predicted course to stay in the pay zone formation? Secondly, what about the availability of turbines for sufficient rotating power to drill horizontal sections? The friction in the horizontal section would be too high to rotate with the rotary.'

'The turbines are available,' Rob said. 'But more research is required to select a company to supply us with a system that allows us to measure while drilling horizontally. Would the engineering department be able to assist Jurgen in the selection process, as part of the system is already available to measure high deviated wells?'

'I can do that,' Eberhart said. 'I used to work for Schlumberger. They're specialized in hole deviation services. I can help Jurgen in selecting the best-suited company for these services.' He also agreed to compile drilling engineering data for the drilling supervisor's computers.

Rob thanked them for their time and returned to his office to look at the Kola project drilling reports. Every insert or diamond bit suitable for very hard formations had been tried on this very deep well section. Nothing had worked. What would he do in this situation? His first tool pusher in Germany had taught him a lesson on this a long time ago: "If you don't know what type of formation to expect, run the cheapest long teeth roller bit and drill the formation. Penetration rates and the condition of the bit will tell you what type of formation you have encountered, because only a short section of hole can be drilled with no teeth left on the bit if the formation is too hard.

He called the Russian drilling manager and asked him if they had considered using soft formation bits to drill the formation. Running a soft formation bit was the only advice he could come up with.

The drilling manager told him that everyone expected very hard and abrasive formations at this extreme depth, so no bits for soft formations had been considered. He would pass his suggestion on to Ivan and keep him posted on his decision.

He found he was running out of time and worked until late at night to keep up with his workload, which consisted of daily issues such as assessing the Look Ahead system for different areas, preparing for meetings, selecting new drilling areas and requesting permits, new contracts, reports, logistics. All that, plus the joint venture with the Russians, which had to be given the utmost priority.

He decided that the Look Ahead system should be managed by the drilling managers. It simply took up too much of his time to stay involved. But he wanted to keep the Brazil operations under his control, to see if the sequences were still made and followed. The recent incidents worried him. It was very difficult to get answers to his questions from Leonardo.

He reviewed the Russian joint venture agreement and forwarded this to Eberhart and Jurgen to include their comments.

Anne had warned him to take care of himself, but someone had to do the work.

He forwarded the investment proposal to the management team and summarized all the arguments that could be raised against the proposals, countered with good, solid reasons for approval.

He also arranged a meeting Wednesday afternoon with Werner to go through the proposal one final time.

Werner assured him, 'Rob, you've really done your homework well. Remember, the majority of the management team fortunately still thinks of what's good for the company and not what's in it for them. Have faith in these men. We'll wait and see if we can make an important step into the future of our company.'

Still, Rob did not get much sleep that night as his brain was working overtime.

Von Ritter welcomed the management team and began by inviting all the managers and their spouses to the annual Christmas party, to be held at an expensive five-star hotel. Everyone was surprised, as it was tradition to use the company restaurant for the Christmas party. For Rob and Anne this would be the first time to attend the event, and he was very interested to meet everyone's spouses.

When Von Ritter invited him to present his proposals, Rob stepped forward, feeling very nervous. He searched around the room and found Werner's eyes, who gave him a look of encouragement, which gave him sudden strength to present his proposal.

He went through each separate proposal step-by-step and summarized the benefits for the people on the job, emphasizing why such changes were so important for the company.

When he finished, Schultz asked permission to speak. He argued that the large investments Rob was suggesting would not bring immediate savings in the operating costs. He proposed that they use drilling contractors to carry out drilling operations, so that the company could concentrate on their engineering expertise, and that they should stay away from mixing these two concepts.

Rob answered that if none of the oil companies took the initiative to implement changes, such as demanding safer operations, or take the lead in using new drilling technology, the industry would come to a standstill. Then no new innovations such as top drive or horizontal drilling would be stimulated.

Klein was the next to ask for permission to speak. He said that he preferred standard drilling contracts and wanted to stay away from joint venture agreements with different companies.

Rob had expected more resistance, but with their lack of knowledge, the arguments of Klein and Schultz were hardly significant.

Then it was Fuchs' turn to speak. As HR manager he pointed out that working with Russian crews was difficult. Not only because of the language barrier, but also because of their philosophy on safety.

Rob knew that he had a valid point, so he assured him that the Russian project should be viewed as a long-term relationship, with the opportunity to modify the Russian rigs to company standards. The project would require additional effort, with training of personnel as a priority. English courses would be provided during the shipyard period, and all crewmembers would be required to pass an English test before they were allowed to work on the rig, for which he asked Fuchs to make arrangements.

When there were no more questions, Rob finally asked the management team for approval of his proposals.

Von Ritter cleared his throat before he spoke. 'These investments will require board approval of Wedel Shipping. I will have to submit these investments to the board for their decision.'

'That won't be necessary,' Tom spoke up. 'With your permission, Mr. Von Ritter, I would like to point out that Hattenberg Oil is an independent company. I have reviewed the proposals carefully, and as stipulated in the agreement with Wedel Shipping, it is within the financial limits to be approved by this management team. May I suggest that we vote for approval?'

The voting took place, and just as he had expected, Von Ritter, Klein, Schulz and Fuchs all voted against. To Rob's surprise, so did the procurement manager. But everyone else voted to accept, so his proposals were approved.

The next item was the implementation of the bonus system. The majority voted against.

Von Ritter suddenly excused himself, saying that he had to attend an important meeting. He asked the team to continue with the remaining items on the agenda without him, and left the room.

So it was now clear how the management team was divided, and everyone knew that just one or two management changes would completely change the previous long term planning philosophy of the company.

Rob knew that this was probably the last time a voting round would not result in favor of Von Ritter. He was sure that Von Ritter would make certain arrangements to ensure this. But for the moment he felt relieved that all his operational targets could be realized.

Only now did it occur to him why Schulz and Klein had come up with such weak arguments. They had probably thought it unnecessary to prepare stronger ones. It was more than likely that Von Ritter had convinced them that he would be in a position to avoid the investments. Without Tom's interference, Rob would never have succeeded in getting the approval.

Before he left the office, he called Jurgen to thank him for his advice to involve Tom in the discussions with the Russians. As financial manager, Tom was the only person in the management team who knew of the financial limits on investment approvals. Without him, Von Ritter would have used his network to obstruct his proposals.

'I made some interesting discoveries,' Jurgen told him. 'Von Ritter is a board member of several companies. He and his friends left a trail of companies that have been sold or are up for sale. Many of the same names are listed on these boards. The selection of board members is probably organized with the help of his friends and network. But the most disturbing news is that many of these names are also listed as members on the board of Wedel Shipping. Von Ritter is one of them.'

Rob believed that industrial leaders such as Bernard Heumer were born with special gifts, talents and determination to create something, and that everyone with these talents could reach leading positions within the industry. Universities created a code amongst their students—jobs should be divided within the family. Rob had no problem with this, as long as it resulted in honest and innovative leaders such as Von Ritter's predecessor.

Rob felt that every industry and company in the world was being silently poisoned and systematically taken over by a new type of industrial leaders— the type with quick personal financial gains as their only objective.

The new financial culture of unrealistically high salaries and bonus payouts was being protected from within by unscrupulous men who would do anything to defend it in their greed for money. They would always excuse their excessive salaries, saying that they were in line with the English reward system, which has no limits.

He was convinced that these criminally-minded companies and other wealth-oriented groups wanted to get rich in the shortest possible time and seriously intended to combine forces to protect their lucrative system. Even the Dutch and German governments had not succeeded in enforcing maximum salaries not to exceed that of the prime minister, not even for government-subsidized banks, hospitals or the railroad system. Certain individuals, even members of royalty, gained immense wealth by receiving bribes, such as prince Bernhard of Holland in the Lockheed scandal, or the Indian, South Korean and Romanian politicians, to name a few examples. The same situation existed in Brazil, where people were getting paid as long as everybody protected their interests.

As he reviewed everything that had happened during the past months, his feeling of pride to work for a solid and well-managed oil company such as Hattenberg Oil changed into one of shame. He realized that the new generation of managers, who never built or created anything, were destroying the work and long-term planning of those who preceded them. This was a new generation with a mentality to get rich by selling and destroying everything that was built and created during the years of the company's existence.

He was now convinced that this company was about to be sold. The new board of directors was probably going to replace anyone who might oppose the sale of the company. Undoubtedly the board members would be paid absurd bonuses for this selling process. And all at the cost of people, instead of making use of their skills and expertise that could lead to opportunities for expansion and prosperity for both the company and its employees.

Management should lead by example, just like honest work and business ethics should be used to encourage young managers to follow their principles, as did most members of the previous management team—those he had always regarded as examples of how to lead and manage a company.

If selling peoples' innovation, skills, motivation and effort was justified for leaders of the industry just to create personal wealth, then how do they expect to attract qualified staff to work for these companies?

If this culture was accepted in the industry, then why send anyone to prison for stealing? People with attitude, arrogance and the opinion that they were above the law, those who introduce and control bribery schemes, or anyone with bad business ethics, they were all responsible for how he was feeling right now—irritated and very, very frustrated.

Rob was glad he was driving home for the weekend. It gave him the chance to create some distance, if only for a short period of time. He would ask Anne to sell their company stock as soon as possible.

On Monday he had the meeting with the Petroleum Directorate in Hamburg and required time to prepare. This could surely become a lengthy exercise. The rig inspection visits from their representatives were always difficult and very time consuming. Most of these men came up with issues that weren't relevant or important, and they were only interested in free entertainment and reimbursement of their expenses.

The most important issue for him was to correct what should have been done a long time ago—to make the safety of personnel the number one priority of a yet to be established, separate governmental body, and to leave the issue of mining rules and drilling permits with the Petroleum Directorate.

Discussing and rewriting law paragraphs would be carried out with theoretical and judicially-oriented authorities with little understanding of how to drill a well or produce oil. Hopefully there would be support from the different categories within the oil and gas industry, such as marine, electronics, engineering, legal, safety, production, etc.

Chapter 37

Passing road signs with familiar town names indicated that he was close to home. It gave him a warm, comforting glow to know that he would soon smell the fragrances of home and see Anne and the children. As he left the Autobahn, he had to drive carefully, as he was now driving on narrow, winding country roads that connected the rural villages in the area.

When he entered the driveway he could see Jan, who was standing behind the glass of the front door, waving at him. Rob stopped the car and jumped out. Anne opened the front door, and he watched with amazement as Jan cautiously started walking in his direction.

'Jan! What a surprise!' he cried out. 'You can already walk and welcome your dad yourself!'

He met his son halfway up the driveway, lifting him high in the air and hugging him.

'Anne, this is surprise! Why didn't you tell me?'

'This is so much nicer. I wanted to see your face.'

'When did this happen?'

'He could already walk with me holding his hands since you left, and yesterday he walked from a chair towards me. Now he won't stop walking.'

'This is great!' He took Jan's hand, and together they entered the house.

'Well, it's not that great, because walking is one thing. He also likes to open every drawer and investigate what's in it.'

'So you have your hands full?'

'Completely. I'm happy that you're here to see it for yourself.'

That weekend was Jan's first walk weekend. The whole family was invited to watch him take his first steps, and Dagmar and Thomas took him outside, which was a real adventure for him.

Rob didn't have any time to work that weekend, so he left home very early on Monday to review the paperwork before the meeting at the Petroleum Directorate. There was almost no traffic on the Autobahn, so he arrived in Hamburg at seven o'clock. The security guard was very helpful and allowed him to use the meeting room, taking him up there himself. The man even brought him coffee.

Rob read the items on the meeting's agenda and studied the attached documents. The cover letter informed him that the German government had followed Lord Cullen's recommendation after the Piper Alpha tragedy, and the government decided that they should change their mining regulations accordingly.

One of Cullen's recommendations was that a new Health, Safety and Environment (HSE) division should be established. This organization was to be responsible for minimizing the health and safety risks associated with work in the offshore oil and gas industry in U.K.'s territorial waters. The off-shore oil industry had been instructed to submit a so-called safety case, a document that identifies hazards and risks and shows that all necessary steps had been taken to ensure that those risks are kept to an absolute minimum, just as in the rail transport and the nuclear industry.

The letter continued with the instructions that companies with their own safety departments may choose to develop their own safety case, or choose to employ an external safety case specialist. The safety case had to be a summary of the operations of the offshore installation and should describe systems on board that are considered a risk factor. It should also summarize the safety management system, and it had to describe the risk assessment steps carried out to identify and reduce the frequency and consequences of major hazards. And finally, it had to provide details of the emergency procedures and systems that were in place.

His first thought was that finally a separate division had been established to reduce work-related casualties, injuries and health hazards. But he could not find any initiatives or signs of involvement from the work force.

Safety case specialists had to show people like Rob, the drilling managers and the rig supervisors involved in developing these safety cases to learn and understand the complicated calculations to reduce the risks to a minimum. But what did they mean with 'a minimum'?

Then a lot of other questions came up. The most important was if companies would be allowed to operate while completing and awaiting approval of the safety cases, as this would, after all, take a long time to complete and approve.

The meeting room gradually filled up with people. At nine o'clock sharp the mining director welcomed and asked everyone to introduce himself. Rob noticed that every oil and contracting company was represented. The director announced that the main purpose of the meeting was to discuss and change the present mining rules and regulations, but first he wanted to relay one important message: that no drilling permits would be issued to drill new wells unless the safety case was submitted and approved of by a separate, still to be established health, safety and environment organization. Only on existing wells would drilling, repairs and overhaul operations be allowed!

It was completely silent in the meeting room as the impact of his words hit home. No one had expected this. It meant that the whole industry would be shut down for an unknown period of time. Drilling personnel would be forced to look for new jobs, probably never to return to the drilling industry, as the employment it provided became too unreliable. After the approval of safety cases, a large influx of new personnel would enter the market. The training of new hires would have to start all over again.

The director admitted that he was aware that simultaneous drilling and producing operations could not be compared to single drilling operations with barriers of mud and a BOP in place. But his organization wanted to follow the same guidelines as submitted in the U.K., and establish a new HSE organization that would take time. He told them that a safety case template describing the requirements was available, as well as a list of recommended companies specialized in safety cases.

For future operations a bridging document would be required. This was a document that defined how two or more safety management systems co-exist to allow co-operation and co-ordination on matters of health, safety and environmental protection between different parties, in this case Hattenberg Oil and the drilling contractor or subcontractors.

Such a document cross-references the detailed procedures that are used and defined the responsibilities, accountabilities and work activities of the various parties. The director wanted to arrange meetings with the representatives from the various industries that relied on mining rules and regulations to speed up the process. He circulated a program schedule for today's meeting, dividing drilling, production, engineering and all other parties that would need to review and change the rules and regulations according to Lord Cullen's recommendations.

This morning he wanted to start with drilling-related paragraphs and said that non-drilling experts would be excused from this part of the meeting, or welcome to stay.

When a coffee break was announced, Rob called Werner to inform him of the changes. He heard a deep sigh on the other side of the line.

'This is bad news, Rob. We just started our deep well here in Germany. I'd like to know if we can continue or if we have to stop this drilling operation.'

'The director said that it wouldn't apply to existing drilling operations, but I'll check again and let you know.'

As expected, the rest of the day was very difficult, because every drilling related paragraph was reviewed and discussed with drilling company representatives and drilling inspectors of das Bergambt.

Most of the drilling inspectors lacked key competence and understanding, and failed to see the interaction of people and systems. Rob and his colleagues from other drilling companies explained over and over again that for practical and logical reasons, some of the changes were impossible to implement.

During coffee breaks Rob exchanged contact information with his colleagues, whom he appreciated meeting at this occasion.

The meeting finished late in the evening, with two further sessions planned. Rob checked with the Director to confirm that the changes didn't apply to drilling operations for which a permit was already issued, and was relieved to find that this was the case.

Then he called Anne and asked if it was possible for her and the kids to come and stay with him in Hanover for a few days, as they had spent little time together.

But Anne had no intention of coming over. 'Rob, I'd really like to visit, but travelling with the kids at this age is too much hassle. I'm sorry for you, but I'm better off staying at home.'

'I understand. It just wasn't my day , and I wanted your company.'

'You'll have to wait a couple of days.'

He hung up, feeling somewhat despondent and drove to his apartment.

He went straight to bed, knowing that tomorrow would be a busy day.

The next morning he got to the office early to review the present drilling operations and the wells that had been planned for the future. Only two company-owned land rigs could be used for repair work. The remaining rigs would have to be shut down, and the personnel laid off.

At the morning meeting he wanted to propose using the remaining rigs for horizontal drilling operations and invite subcontractors to support this initiative. At least this would keep their personnel at work, as all other drilling and subcontractor contracts were to be suspended until safety case approval.

What should they do with the drilling operations outside Europe once the present wells were completed? Complete shut-down of drilling operations would create considerable financial implications, but by continuing drilling they would risk a blowout or deadly accidents. That was a decision to be made by the management team.

He contacted Gunther and Eberhart to explain the situation, and suggested that they keep the rigs operational to increase the production rate if they were successful. Then he called Werner and proposed that they hold a morning meeting with both management and the department heads to discuss the legal changes and all their implications. Werner agreed and had his secretary notify all parties concerned, while Rob made copies of the Bergambt letter for distribution at the meeting.

Once everyone had gathered for the meeting, Werner explained the reason why they had included the department heads. 'Rob? Go ahead,' he said, and Rob briefly explained the legal changes that affected the present and future drilling operations.

Von Ritter asked, 'What if we got senior directors from the different oil companies to visit the Petroleum Directorate, and ask them to allow conventional drilling operations? Would that have any effect?'

'No,' Werner said, shaking his head. 'Every European country has to follow Lord Cullen's recommendations. Rob, perhaps you can summarize what the consequences of the safety case would be for the company.'

Rob gave a brief overview of the present drilling operations, giving them the number of rigs that were at risk of being shut-down once their wells had been completed. Gradually the impact of the safety case law began to dawn on everyone.

'Is there any solution to reduce the financial impact?' Von Ritter asked with a frown.

'The only solution to avoid a rig shut-down would be for us to concentrate on horizontal drilling operations,' Rob said, and he quickly explained the concept. 'The drilling engineering and production departments will have to get together to discuss the concept with our subcontractors in order to provide the turbines and measuring systems. Then we have to select the well and complete the drilling program for the pilot well. If we are successful, we can use both company-owned and contracted rigs to carry out horizontal drilling operations on different wells. That way we can keep them operational.'

The drilling engineering manager said that he had already investigated the possibilities of measuring systems. A new concept was ready to be tested the following week.

Rob asked for approval to carry out his proposal, and once they had set a budget and put it to a vote, it was approved. He then asked the management team how to proceed with international drilling operations outside Europe, as any incident could have serious implications. After all, deadly accidents and blowouts could still occur while drilling conventional wells in other parts of the world, and they could not eliminate all risks. He was unable to give an indication of the enormous financial impact if all drilling operations had to be suspended for an unknown period of time.

He therefore asked the management team to decide if drilling operations outside Europe should be continued without a safety case, or to suspend all operations upon completion of the present wells, pending the safety cases for each rig.

An uneasy silence followed, as everyone knew the financial implications involved if serious incidents did occur. Werner suggested that they should vote on the matter. Before they all voted, Von Ritter once again stressed the financial impact if drilling operations would be suspended.

The majority voted to continue international drilling operations without safety cases. Rob voted to stop drilling, because he believed such double standards would badly damage the company's reputation in the event of severe incidents.

Von Ritter asked, 'Can we reduce costs by laying off personnel? The drilling supervisors, for example? Or is there some other action that we can take?'

'I'd recommend keeping the drilling supervisors on contract,' Rob said.

'It's up to the safety manager to decide as soon as possible if his department is capable of completing the safety case for our drilling units, or if we need to hire a specialist.'

The head of safety said he would first need to review the safety case template before making his decision.

During the final round of questions, Rob asked the status of the Russian joint venture agreement. Klein answered that the agreement was ready to be forwarded to the Russian Company for comments or approval.

Rob said, 'I'd prefer to discuss the investment and day rate appendix with the Russians at our next meeting in Helsinki.'

Once the meeting was over, he asked Gunther and Eberhart to arrange a meeting with two subcontractors capable of providing the turbines and measuring devices to carry out horizontal drilling.

He returned to his office and called Ivan to tell him that the agreement was ready for review, agreed to send it by mail and set a date for the signing ceremony in Hanover. He then personally informed Von Ritter and the management team that the Russian delegation was due to arrive the first week of January, as Ivan had expressed his wish to meet with Von Ritter in person.

When he checked his appointment diary he realized that the Christmas party was this coming Friday. Feeling guilty, he grabbed the phone to call Anne.

'I'd like to invite you for a Christmas party on Friday.'

There was a stunned silence, then a sigh. 'Are you trying to tell me we've been invited for the company Christmas party this coming Friday? And you forgot to tell me?'

Rob winced inwardly. 'Yes. I'm sorry. I forgot to tell you.'

'Are you coming home on Thursday so that we can drive up to Hanover on Friday?'

'Yes, I suppose that's what we'll have to do. Please could you call Agnes and ask her to stay with us during the Christmas holidays? That way she can look after the kids for one evening. They can stay in the guesthouse as our first guests.'

'The kids will love that. What's the dress code?'

'I don't know. I'll check the invitation.'

'So monsieur received an invitation and didn't even tell his wife.'

'Sorry,' Rob said as he retrieved the invitation from the envelope with one hand. 'It's informal dress, so you don't have to buy anything.'

'Really? Well, I'm in the mood to buy a very expensive formal dress.'

'I'll call you tonight.'

After hanging up he contacted Schultz, setting a date for the second week in January for their visit to Brazil.

Chapter 38

He emailed his Texan friend Bill, asking if his wife could get in contact with Luisa. He explained that he needed information on Leonardo's wife and brother-in-law, who was a highly placed decision-maker within the local oil company, to find out if any recent meetings had taken place between the three German managers and the local company. He added that any information on Kees, the drilling contractor manager, would also be more than welcome. 'I'll be in Brazil the second week of January,' he ended.

Within minutes he received a response. 'Hey, Holland, congratulations on your promotion. I'll see what we can do. Will meet you on board. Greetings from "Texas".'

A smile came on his face. That was Bill.

The rest of the week he spent with Jurgen to determine the investment cost for the Russian rig and with Tom to finalize the proposal for the day rate.

Many meetings were held with drilling and service contractors to discuss the safety case implications and to ensure that each company would complete the safety case as soon as possible.

Rob prepared a presentation and diagram to show the production and engineering managers how the wells could be drilled horizontally. The next morning they met with their contractors to explain the principle, and their intention to select a well that was already drilled at a 30-degree angle into the production zone.

The contractor's representatives explained that measuring equipment was available to drill at such angles, but this was the first time that they would be drilling a long section horizontally, so they would have to upgrade their measuring equipment and turbines. However, they were eager to keep their crews at work, so their engineers would work during the Christmas holidays to deliver the equipment as soon as possible.

With Christmas holidays around the corner, Rob warned his drilling managers to instruct their supervisors to supervise more closely and frequently, as this was the time of year that most accidents and mistakes took place. The crews would often think of home and not be focused on their job.

He called Anne that he was on his way home and took the time to go through the events of the past week. This time Brazil was on his mind. He knew that he would need a local person to gather some information for him, as his stay would be brief and only allow a visit to the shore base and rig. If he stayed longer he would only be tempted to ask questions, and that might arouse suspicion. He wanted to know who had visited the country on a regular basis from the start of the drilling operations, but he didn't want to ask the secretary who scheduled the travel arrangements. He also wanted to know for what purpose the men visited Brazil. Luisa might be able to provide that kind of information, but he didn't know if she could be trusted. His main question was what to do with the information. Von Ritter could be involved, and Karl Miller, the MD of Wedel Shipping Company, could be replaced any time, so he would be unable to do anything. Most of the board members were only interested in the sale of the company, so that they could earn large bonuses and cash in on their shares, the value of which had increased considerably since rumors of the sale had begun to circulate. The board of directors would not be happy if they learned of his little investigation and might even take him to court for disclosing company information.

What was he to do? Could he live with the knowledge of this serious bribe, and pretend that nothing happened as an unwilling, silent witness? No. He decided to go to Brazil and find out if things were truly as he suspected. After that he would discuss the matter with Werner to figure out how to handle this very delicate issue.

Still, he was eager to meet the wives of the three managers involved at the Christmas party. It would be interesting to observe how these couples acted at this annual company event and find out if there was close contact between them.

The snow was coming down steadily now, and he had to drive carefully. Some cars had already ended up on the side of the road.

Chapter 39

'I'm glad you're home,' Anne said, obviously relieved. 'On the news they were covering accidents that happened on the Autobahn.'

'Yes, the snow surprised many people. They hadn't started sprinkling road salt yet, and some idiots were still speeding.'

'The kids are already asleep. I couldn't keep them up any longer.'

'I just want to give them a kiss, Anne.'

'Don't wake them up, Rob. Jan didn't want to go to sleep, because I told him that papa was on his way home.'

'Don't worry, I won't make any noise.'

'Then I'll reheat dinner.'

Rob went upstairs to Jess's room, where he watched his daughter's face for a few minutes. When he kissed her, a contented smile appeared on her face as if she knew that her dad was home.

Jan was sound asleep, a stuffed koala bear he bought for him in Perth in a tight embrace. He really had to keep himself from waking him and hoped that Jan would just wake up from his presence, but a soft voice behind him said, 'Don't you wake him up. Let him sleep.'

He started guiltily. 'How did you know?'

'I know that you missed him. That's why I followed you up here.'

'Okay, let's have dinner. I'll see them later tonight.'

They had dinner in the kitchen, and Rob gradually felt all the pressure and stress from the past week ebb away from his body. Slowly but surely, he returned to home mode and to family life. As he opened a bottle of wine, Anne chatted away, but while Rob knew that she was eager to tell him everything that had taken place that week, he wasn't really listening. His mind was already undressing her.

Anne stopped talking. 'Why are you looking at me that way?'

'I think that you are beautiful.'

'But I'm talking to you. There's still so much I have to tell you.'

'I think that you are beautiful,' he repeated.

'Rob, please listen. You know what Jan did?'

'I think that you are beautiful.'

'This is not fair. Anyway, I still have to clean up.'

'I'll do that tonight. Anne, could you take me to heaven?'

Anne gave up with a sigh. 'Yes,' she said. 'I can.'

He woke up as soon as he heard Jan and got up. He leisurely took his time changing his diaper and covered him with kisses before he put him down for the rest of the night.

He quietly entered Jess's room to find that she was wide awake. He picked her up, and she beamed her beautiful smile at him. It was as if the sun was shining in her sparkling eyes. She definitely took after her mother.

Once she finished her bottle and he had cleaned her up, he put her to bed, but then she started crying. He picked her up again and sat down in the rocking chair, covering himself with a blanket. He covered her face with kisses and held her very close, rocking the chair to and fro.

'What are you doing in here?' The sound of Anne's voice woke him up the following morning, his daughter still in his arms.

'Sorry. We fell asleep.'

'If you do that again, your daughter will cry every night. She'll then want to sleep in her dad's arms all the time.'

'I did not want to wake you up after our visit to heaven.'

'Don't do it again, Rob. She is very clever and knows exactly how to twist you around her little finger.'

'Well, if that's true, then it's a gift she has inherited from her mother.'

Anne chose to ignore his remark. 'Let's take the kids in our bed for a cuddle before taking them outside for their first experience in the snow.'

'Did we get more snow?'

'At least two feet! It's beautiful outside. The sun is shining, and the sky is bright blue.'

'Then I suggest we don't cuddle in bed, but I go out to buy a sledge for the kids before they're sold out.'

'Alright, I'll make breakfast.'

Rob had a quick shower and walked through the snow to town to buy a sledge. It was the first time he'd seen snow in years, as he often missed it during the years that he was working his on/off schedule.

Anne was right—it was a gorgeous day. The snow crunched under his feet, and the kids looked around in amazement, not understanding why their world had suddenly become completely white. They touched the snow to find that it was cold and wet. Jan enjoyed walking in the snow, but Jess didn't like it and preferred her dad to hold her, warm and safe.

Jan and Jess both sat on the sledge as they walked through the beautiful, white forest, with the sun shining through the trees, making the crystalline snow glisten like diamonds.

When they returned home, the kids didn't want to go inside, so with Jan, Rob made a snowman in the garden, while Anne showed Jess how to create eyes, a nose and a mouth, finally placing a hat on his head.

The kids thought it was tremendous fun and refused to go inside until Anne told them that they would be able to see the snowman from the living room.

'I don't think we even have to try to get them to take a nap before lunch time,' Anne said. 'They're probably too excited to sleep. Agnes and Klaus are coming over before lunch.'

'That's excellent. That means we can leave for Hanover right after lunch. It will be a difficult drive with the snow on the roads.'

'Would you like to see the dress I'm wearing tonight?'

'Yes, please!'

Anne went into the bedroom, and when she came back a few minutes later, he felt the exact same way as when he had entered her room on their wedding day. The blue dress she was wearing consisted of a tightly-fitting bodice which showed off her curves perfectly, while the skirt swirled down freely around her slim waist. Around her shoulders she wore a soft, white shawl. Rob thought she looked perfect for the occasion.

He whistled in admiration. 'Do you want to go to the Christmas party? Or shall we just stay in the Hanover apartment for the evening and night? You look breathtaking.'

'We can change at the apartment, but I don't want to stay there. I'd really like to meet the new Managing Director, as well as the other managers and their wives.'

'Well, everyone seems to be coming, so it will be an interesting night for us. I see some of these men every day, but most of our staff works in different buildings or other floors. Some I've never met before.'

'Didn't you go around to introduce yourself?'

'I only met the department heads and the management team. I'd need at least a week to introduce myself to all of them. Does Agnes know how to take care of Jan and Jess?'

'Yes. She was here on Wednesday, as usual. I've shown her the ropes. She knows what to do. The kids absolutely love her. I can't think of anyone better to look after them.'

'We should arrange something in case anything happens to both of us. So that Agnes and Klaus can take care of our children.'

Anne shivered at the thought of it. 'I don't even want to think about that.'

'I will discuss it with Klaus. We can formalize it, if necessary.'

The door opened and the house immediately came to life. Anne made pancakes for lunch, while Rob looked after Jan and Jess with the help of Klaus.

It was then that he raised the subject. 'Klaus, would you and Agnes be willing to become legal guardians to Jan and Jess if something happened to us?'

'You don't even have to ask. Of course we'd take care of your kids. I know you'd do the same for us.'

'Then I'll check and see if we have to formalize it.'

'You know, Rob, that Dagmar and Thomas didn't sleep last night because they were so excited. They were really looking forward to stay in the guesthouse and spend the Christmas holidays with you.'

'I'm glad that we built it. We still have to buy presents. I suggest we let the ladies take care of that tomorrow, while we chop down a tree and set it up with the kids. I think the party should be finished at ten. Depending on the weather, we'll probably be back home at twelve.'

'I'll stay in the house until you get home. Drive carefully.'

'Thanks, Klaus. If something comes up just give me a call, and we'll drive home as soon as possible.'

'Don't worry. We'll have fun.'

After lunch they hugged and kissed them all goodbye and left. Anne was unusually quiet as they drove on the icy local roads before getting to the Autobahn.

'You're very quiet. Is anything wrong?'

'Rob, we're just half an hour away from home, but I already miss them terribly.'

'Now you know what I feel every Monday.'

'Yes, but you can switch on and off. I can't.'

'We'll be back home in a few hours. Anne, can you please do me a favor tonight?'

'What can I do for you apart from staying at the apartment tonight?'

'I'd really like to know if Von Ritter and some of my colleagues meet each other in private. I get the feeling that these men are pretty close.'

'And how do you want me to find out?'

'I'll introduce you to Fritz Von Ritter, Andreas Klein, John Fuchs and Ronald Schultz. They're the contract, HR and marketing managers.

Maybe you can find some way to talk to their wives, while I do the rounds to introduce myself to some of the other staff members.'

'Why do you want to know?'

'Because some of our managers have been replaced. I want to know if these men and their families know and meet each other in private.'

'Do you have any problems with these men?'

'Not yet, but the company is slowly becoming divided. These four men have very different views concerning the short and long-term company objectives, and I want to know what's behind it.'

'Okay, I'll do my best. But if I don't feel comfortable, I won't do it. I was actually hoping to meet some people tonight and enjoy myself.'

They changed at the apartment, walked to the hotel and followed the welcome signs that directed them to the private ballroom. They were welcomed at the door by Mr. and Mrs. Von Ritter, Fuchs, Klein and Schultz with their wives.

Rob introduced Anne to each of them, explaining to her which functions they held within the company. He then took her to meet the other managers and department heads. Von Ritter invited everyone to sit down at their designated seats for dinner. The sliding doors to the dining section opened and the guests all sauntered along the long line of tables in search of their names on the place cards.

Rob immediately noticed that Von Ritter had surrounded himself with his four supporting managers and their wives, while Werner Brandt and the other managers had been seated at the far side of the table. Anne noticed this as well.

'Is this how the company is divided?' she whispered in his ear. He nodded.

Dinner started, and they both found the food and wine to be excellent, with venison served as a main course.

The woman seated next to Rob explained to him in tedious detail how to prepare venison, while he observed each of the women on the other side of the table. He saw that Mrs. Von Ritter was drinking far too much, her eyes disinterested and cold. Mrs. Fuchs was seated right opposite him. She must have experienced some kind of stroke, as one side of her face seemed affected, but he found her to be the only friendly person on that side of the table. Mrs. Klein and Mrs. Schultz looked and acted like Barbie dolls. They, too, were drinking too much.

After dinner the sliding doors opened again to reveal a band, and the music began to play. Coffee and drinks were served, and everyone mingled, with a distinct separation between men and woman, as was usual in Germany.

Rob introduced himself to a large number of people and finally searched for Anne, whom he found talking to Mrs. Fuchs. He joined the discussion briefly, and then asked Anne if she wanted to go home. She nodded, upon which they thanked Von Ritter and his wife for their hospitality, said goodbye to Werner and his wife and left the hotel.

Anne didn't say a word until she had finished changing into more comfortable clothes at the apartment. 'Rob, let's drive home. I'll tell you what happened on the way.'

It was snowing hard, and Rob needed all his attention to tackle the treacherous roads before they got to the Autobahn. When they did reach it, they found that there was only one lane open to them.

'You know, Rob,' Anne began. 'When I first visited the company and met the management team, I felt welcome, appreciated and proud that you worked for this company. First of all, I thought it strange that only part of the management team was at the door to welcome the guests tonight. Why weren't the other managers part of the welcome party? I tried to talk to some of the women, but they clearly did not appreciate my company, except Mrs. Fuchs. She asked me why we weren't staying at the hotel overnight. Everyone at their side of the table was staying the entire

321

weekend.

And yes, they spend a lot of time together. They even travel to Brazil twice a year together for holiday and business. 'They attend parties thrown by the oil company's representatives, and the women all receive the same expensive gifts. She showed me the jewelry she was given, Rob. Even a Rolex watch!

'It appears that each family owns a sailing boat, on which they spend their weekends and holidays together in the Frisian Islands.' She frowned. 'I don't feel welcome anymore, Rob. I think that these men have nothing to contribute to the company. They only think of themselves. My advice? If you have to work with them every day, be very careful. In my opinion, these men are wolves in sheep's skins.

'God, I was actually hoping to meet some nice people and have fun. Tell you one thing; I won't be attending any of these parties anymore.'

Rob had said nothing during her entire speech. What was there to say? What she had just said was a conclusion of what he already knew. But should he tell her the whole story? No. He first had to visit Brazil and find a way out of this mess.

She looked across at him. 'Why don't you say anything?'

'I have to think about what you just said. That and I need all my attention to drive.'

'Be careful, Rob. What is the company doing in Brazil?'

'We are drilling for oil and gas.'

'I gathered that. But then why should a HR Manager visit that country? Or a marketing manager, for that matter?'

That was also one of his questions, and one to which he had no answer. Not yet.

'I don't know, Anne. But I intend to find out.'

'Leave it alone, Rob. Every time you visit Brazil or some of these other countries, I have this strange feeling. Lives don't seem to have value there.'

She didn't say a word until they got home.

Klaus let them in, announcing that everybody was asleep and that all had gone very well. He went to join his family in the guesthouse, and Rob and Anne looked in on the children.

Rob had the feeling that the evening had badly affected Anne. He felt irritated, blaming himself for getting her involved in company politics. As he lay next to her in the dark, he searched for her hand. The only thing he could say was, 'Sorry, Anne, for asking. I shouldn't have.'

'Rob, I know you don't tell me anything because you want to keep work and family separate. But I'm happy that I could speak to one of these women to get some idea of the difficulties you are facing.'

'Thank you. Goodnight, Anne.'

'Did you like my dress?' her voice came back to him in the dark.

'You know you looked beautiful.'
'Only your eyes told me that.'
'You want me to tell you again?'
'Yes. With your hands and everything else.'

Chapter 40

The next day Rob, Klaus and Dad took the kids to the forest on sledges to cut down a Christmas tree, while the women went shopping for presents.

Klaus had brought Christmas decorations dating back to his childhood, and once the tree was in place, Rob lifted Jan and Jess to hang the colorful items in the tree. After surfing the radio channels, Rob finally found a German channel that played continuous Christmas songs. He started the fireplace and felt that everything was as it should be. The women were still out Christmas shopping, the children and dads were decorating the tree, while Dad observed them contentedly as he enjoyed his glühwein.

Rob told Jan the story of Mary and Joseph's travels on foot to Bethlehem, where Jesus was born. Klaus opened another box, taking out a miniature stable and porcelain figurines that were featured in his story. 'Jesus was born in a stable,' Rob continued, happy with the props that were being offered, 'with an angel showing the three kings and shepherds the way to the new-born king. And if everyone behaves well, the good Santa will visit each house and leave presents under the tree.'

He thoroughly enjoyed the atmosphere of Christmas, and he felt like a dad more than ever before.

After the women returned, the presents were carefully hidden from the kids, and Agnes baked the traditional Weihnachtstollen, a raisin bread filled with almond paste that German families make or buy for Christmas.

Dagmar, Thomas and Jan loved eating the leftover dough and were allowed to clean out the mixing bowl with their fingers. Jess sat at the foot of the Christmas tree, mesmerized by the sparkling lights, the colorful decorations and the miniature stable surrounded by sheep. Nothing else seemed to interest her.

While Klaus set the table, Anne marinated chicken legs and put them in the oven for dinner, filling the house with a delicious fragrance, which made them all become hungry. Jess fell asleep while having dinner, so Rob carried her upstairs and put her to bed. The women sang Christmas songs as they cleared the table, while the men played games with the kids until Jan was too tired to keep his eyes open. Smiling, Rob carried him up to his room.

At eleven o'clock Dad emptied his glass of wine, thanked them all for a wonderful day and went home. Klaus and Agnes took the kids to the guesthouse.

Anne sighed happily as they took the last glasses to the kitchen. 'Rob, this was one of the best times we've ever spent with the family.'

'I agree. I missed a lot of these holidays, because I always switched shifts with my married colleagues at Christmas. Today made up for all of those times.'

'Add some wood to the fire, open another bottle of wine and get our love skin. I want this special evening to last a lot longer.'

'Boy, am I glad I visited the hospital.'

'You'd better be, because this is one of those nights that magic can happen.'

The next day was Christmas Eve. As is German custom, everyone dressed up after lunchtime, and the two families gathered to celebrate, playing games and listening to Christmas music together. When Agnes and Klaus went to church at midnight to attend mass, Anne and Rob stayed home to look after the children. They set the table with all kinds of special, seasonal treats and decorated the presents underneath the Christmas tree.

After mass the kids were surprised to find that Santa had brought them presents, which they opened with a great deal of excitement. They then enjoyed a full Christmas breakfast, which lasted until the early hours of the morning.

Christmas Day was a family day, and they spent their time walking in the forest and playing in the snow. On Boxing Day, known in Holland and Germany as Second Christmas Day, they visited the restaurant where Anne and Rob had celebrated their wedding for a special Christmas dinner. The restaurant was packed with all the village's families, whom had been coming there to have their Second Christmas Day dinners for years.

The restaurant boasted a large Christmas tree in the middle of the room, and it had organized a Santa to give presents to the kids while a choir sang Christmas songs as they ate.

It was the first time that Jan and Jess were taken to a restaurant, and the children's eyes sparkled with delight at the sight of the glowing candles and the Christmas tree. The children were free to play with the other kids making it a perfect evening.

The days counting down to New Year's Eve were very much the same—spent together, spoiling the kids with sweets and enjoying too much food and wine.

Rob and Klaus purchased fireworks, champagne and made dough for oliebollen, a traditional Dutch treat served on New Year's Eve. The dough was a mixture consisting of flour, yeast, raisins, brown ale and milk. Once the dough had risen, they heated three gallons of frying oil and scooped four spoons of the dough into the boiling oil until each of the dough balls came up floating and colored a golden brown. This time they prepared enough dough for a hundred oliebollen, which took the men the whole afternoon and quite a number of beers to fry them all in the carport, as Anne didn't like the fumes of frying oil in the house.

Dinner consisted solely of oliebollen dusted with powdered sugar. In the garden Klaus ignited some of the fireworks every half hour so the kids could watch them from the living room. Jess was asleep by nine, and Jan made it to ten.

At twelve they wished each other a happy New Year, toasting each other with champagne. The men went outside with Dagmar and Thomas to set off the remaining fireworks, while the women sat by the window and watched the village's and neighbors' firework displays.

Dagmar and Thomas went to sleep at one, and Dad cycled home because he had drunk too much glüwein and was unable to drive.

The four of them sat around the fireplace and made a top ten list of things they wanted to change or do in the New Year, which took them until four in the morning.

'I forgot to mention my number one item on my to-do list,' Rob said after Agnes and Klaus had gone to bed.

'I know your number one, but you did not prevent me from drinking this excellent champagne. You know what effect alcohol has on me.'

'I found a cure for that.'

'I wish you good luck with that cure. I'd appreciate it if you could carry me into our bed, because I feel tipsy.'

'Same procedure as last year?'

'No Rob, next year.'

On New Year's Day they watched the New Year's Strauss concert broadcasted from Vienna, after which Dagmar and Thomas thanked their aunt and uncle for a marvelous time, and the four went home.

Anne breathed a sigh of relief. 'Rob, I'm exhausted. I'm so glad that we don't have more than two kids.'

'I knew that one day you'd be grateful for my decision. By the way, I'd like to watch a television show with you on one of the German channels.'

'What kind of show? What's so special about it?'

'I haven't watched it for a long time, and they only show it on New Year's Day. You'll see.'

He found the channel, and they watched it together. Anne wasn't familiar with the show, but she seemed to enjoy it. 'How did you like it?' he asked.

'It's very funny. I especially liked the part where she wanted to have dinner with him next year again.'

'Eh… she did not mean "dinner", Anne.'

'Oh yes, that's what she meant.'

'I'll show you what she meant when the butler asked her if she wanted the same procedure as last year.'

'Please go ahead.'

Chapter 41

Monday morning started very early with Rob looking after Jan and Jess before leaving for work. Conditions on the roads were terrible because of the ice and snow, and it took him an additional hour driving to the office.

He was relieved that the drilling managers reported no accidents or incidents, but the New Year started with an unpleasant surprise at the morning meeting: Von Ritter announced that based on his excellent performance, Tom Lehmann had been promoted to financial controller at Wedel Shipping Company beginning the first of the next month. He was to be replaced by someone who was presently working at Wedel Shipping's financial department.

The first thing that went through Rob's mind was, *yet another obstruction removed.*

After reporting on the status of the drilling operations, he informed the team that a Russian delegation would be visiting the office on Thursday to sign the joint venture agreement. 'Ivan Golubev, the Russian Managing Director, looks forward to meeting you at the signing ceremony, Mr. Von Ritter,' he said.

'Oh, I'm so sorry,' Von Ritter said, looking apologetic. 'I'm afraid I won't be available due to some other urgent business elsewhere. I'm sure Werner will be able to sign the agreement instead.'

Rob couldn't believe his ears. What urgent business could be more important than to be there for the signing of this major joint venture? Golubev had made a special request to meet with Von Ritter some time ago. How could he possibly ignore that? Irritated, Rob tried to focus on his work, interviewing the new trainee candidates and meeting with Tom and Jurgen to establish the investment costs necessary to upgrade the Russian rig. They calculated the day rate for a one-year contract period and forwarded the proposal to the management team for approval.

When they were finished, both Tom and Jurgen lingered. 'I have to tell you, Rob,' Tom said, obviously feeling uncomfortable, 'that this job transfer really surprised me as well. I think Von Ritter intends to remove anyone who gets in his way. I approved your investment proposal, which he was dead against, and I'm the one who has been asking questions concerning his very expensive business trips. I made a point of asking him why he, Klein, Fuchs and Schultz always had to stay at expensive, five-star hotels, instead of the convenient airport hotels where everyone always stays. Their expense declarations of costs made in Brazil were abnormally high and not clearly specified.' Tom closed the door to prevent anyone from eavesdropping.

'But you know why he's really getting rid of me? Von Ritter wants to transfer a large portion of the company pension funds to boost the company's profit figures. It's just not right, Rob. These pension funds belong to company personnel. And he knows I don't agree. And what's more, Von Ritter personally appointed John Fuchs as HR manager to make sure that he would hire his own people to support the sale of the company. Schultz doesn't know a thing about marketing. He doesn't make a single decision without outsourcing his work to expensive marketing consultants. Do you know what he does all day? He takes care of his private business, keeping an eye on the stock market to see how his shares are doing.'

Rob nodded, frowning. None of what Tom had just told him surprised him.

'So how would you go about solving the problem in Brazil?' he asked.

'Listen to me, Rob. Either you go with the flow like some of the others or you can stand for what's right. Transferring money from the staff's pension funds to boost the company results isn't what I call acceptable. Especially if this is done to achieve targets to obtain maximum bonuses. But if you do put up a fight, be prepared for the consequences. This is an internal company affair, and legally they've covered the bases of what they're doing. They've got a whole team of lawyers working the scheme.'

Rob thought about it. Tom's words were an echo of what Anne had said to him—either benefit from the situation, and if he couldn't do that, he should leave the company.

'What if it's reported to the media?'

'You mean like a whistle-blower?' Tom shook his head. 'No. People who report these issues to the media are not protected by law. They'd only get crucified by their employers and become social pariahs. The law needs to change to encourage people to come forward to speak up on such criminal acts.'

'Thanks, Tom. I appreciate the advice. I really hope to see you again, and if I can be of any assistance in the future, don't hesitate to give me a call.'

'Rob, I know we only worked together for a short time, but I like your attitude. Just be careful, whatever you do.'

Rob chuckled without humor. 'I get that advice from a lot of people these days. It's just that I hate injustice.'

'I know. But you're on your own. No one will help you, because they know they could lose their job. That and you have to take care of your family as well.'

'We did accomplish quite a lot together, didn't we? I'm proud that the Russian joint venture will be signed on Thursday and that horizontal drilling technology will be applied to our wells.'

'I'm also proud that I was able to assist in that. I hope we meet again,' Tom said, shaking his hand warmly. When he left he and Jurgen looked at each other.

'You know, Jurgen, let's just finish this now so that we can place all the orders before Von Ritter and his gang try to stop us.'

Jurgen nodded. 'Joop just completed the last purchase orders for upgrades to the company rigs and sent them to the suppliers. We already agreed on the top drive manufacturer with the drilling contractor for the deep German well. The electric top drive can be installed while drilling in three weeks' time.'

'Excellent, work Jurgen. When will the 6 5/8-inch drill pipe be available?'

'Before the next top hole drilling operation.'

'Anything on the recording system?'

'Joop is in Munich right now to witness testing. But what are you going to do about Brazil?'

'I fly there next week. I'll make up my mind after that. When is the drill ship due in the Singapore shipyard for upgrades?'

'Next week. The modification period will take another four weeks.'

It was late when both men left the office, and Rob called Anne after he arrived at his apartment.

'Thanks for taking care of the kids and letting me sleep this morning,' she said appreciatively.

'You're welcome, darling. We didn't get that much sleep while having those busy but marvelous days.'

'Dad did have a marvelous headache this morning.'

Rob laughed. 'Like dad, like daughter?' he teased.

'No. The champagne you bought was excellent, so I'm fine. Your "cure" worked very well.'

'I want you to know that I'm a very happy man. And dad.'

'You don't have to tell me. I know you are.' He could almost see her smile.

'How are the kids?'

She grinned. 'The first thing they wanted to do was go outside and play in the snow. Even Jess is getting used to it now. Did you have time to think about it?'

'About what—the butler?'

'No, you know perfectly well what I mean.'

'No, to be honest I didn't. The roads are pretty bad with these weather conditions, so I had to concentrate.'

'I think that's only partly true, but we'll talk about it when you get home.'

'Please give the kids a big hug and lots of kisses from their papa. Good night, Anne.'

'Be careful, Rob.'

It was the first time that she told him to be careful. It irritated him, and he regretted once more that he had gotten her involved.

That evening he reviewed the investment costs for the Russian joint venture and fell asleep in his chair.

The next day he went to Hamburg to discuss the new regulations. Although he agreed that something needed to be done, he strongly felt that the Bergambt's approach on the safety case was too focused on the method used to determine risks. He was concerned that the safety case documents would be too difficult for the workforce to understand.

On Wednesday he prepared everything for the Russian visit, and his secretary made restaurant reservations for lunch and dinner with the management team.

He also invited Jurgen for the dinner, so he could meet the Russian drilling manager and get to know each other.

On Thursday he booked two taxis and drove to the airport to welcome the Russian delegation and take them to the office. The management team waited in the conference room, where Werner Brandt apologized for Von Ritter's absence, explaining that he had to attend to some urgent business elsewhere.

'It's an honor for me to welcome you to our office for the signing of this joint venture between our two companies,' he said as he shook Ivan Golubev's hand.

'Thank you for your warm welcome,' the Russian said. 'But I must say that I am very disappointed that I will not be meeting your Managing Director on such an important occasion.'

During coffee and brötchen with a selection of cold meat cuts, everyone introduced themselves. The ambiance was relaxed and pleasant, as Golubev seemed genuinely interested, politely asking the managers personal questions to get to know them better.

Just before lunchtime Werner suggested they finalize the details and sign the agreement. Klein raised a few minor issues that had come up, and after some adjustments, they were accepted and integrated into the agreement.

When they mentioned the day rate proposal, the negotiations suddenly tensed, just as Rob had experienced in Helsinki. Once again, Golubev tried every possible argument to increase the day rate, but Tom Lehmann remained calm and explained that the proposal had already been discussed and agreed upon in Helsinki. Rob quickly intervened, saying that these rates were set for one year only, after which they would be reviewed and adjusted depending on the average market rate.

Golubev finally relented, and from then on everything went smoothly. They were soon ready for the signing ceremony, which was accompanied by champagne and speeches in which both Werner Brandt and Ivan Golubev toasted to long-lasting relations between the two companies.

Rob breathed a sigh of relief. At least one of his main targets had been achieved. He touched glasses with Tom, Jurgen and Werner, who complimented them on this major achievement.

As Rob had some phone calls to take care of, he asked Jurgen to accompany the Russians to the restaurant, saying he would see them there for dinner at seven o'clock.

First he returned a call to the representative from the Survey Company, who explained that one additional test was necessary and results available on Monday. Rob thanked him and assured that someone else would call him the following week.

He then called Schultz to ask him what travel arrangements had been made for Brazil, and learned that Schultz was flying on Monday. They agreed to meet in Paris for the direct flight to Rio di Janeiro. Rob's return flight was booked for Thursday, to arrive home on Friday. He quickly contacted Eberhart to make sure that he would call the survey company and set up a meeting for the following Monday.

Just before leaving the office the phone rang. It was Joop, who was in Munich visiting a drilling recording factory for a function test.

'Rob, I heard from Jurgen that Von Ritter said that he wouldn't be able to attend the meeting with the Russians because of urgent business.' Joop sounded excited, like a child.

'Yes, that is what he said.'

'You're not going to believe this. He's here, in Munich, and he's staying right here, in this hotel.' Rob heard him say. 'Together with the HR manager's secretary. Looks to me as if he's not here for business, but for pleasure. They're staying in the same room, Rob.'

'Are you sure?' Rob asked, incredulous.

'One hundred percent. They are here already two days.'

'Thank you, Joop,' he said, and hung up, his mind whirring.

He quickly called Werner. 'Werner, did Von Ritter tell you why he wouldn't be able to make it for the signing of the joint venture?'

'Yes. He told me he had to attend an urgent board meeting at Wedel Shipping.'

'Thanks, Werner,' he said, and slowly hung up. Why would Von Ritter start a relationship with a married woman with two children?

He called Anne to let her know that he was having dinner with the Russians and would be home late. Then he hurried to his apartment, changed and drove to the restaurant.

The dinner was excellent, but the Russians drank too much German schnapps and Rob had to help them into the taxis and make sure that everyone made it on the last flight to Helsinki.

He called Anne and told her not to wait, because he wouldn't be home before midnight and began his long drive home.

What a week! By the end of the month the company would lose its best financial expert, who was one of the key and most respected members of the management team. With Tom Lehmann gone, the voting majority would also be lost when it came to making company decisions.

And there was the sickening, cheap love affair between Von Ritter and one of the secretaries. And all he could do was watch, while he was extremely busy securing drilling units to ensure they would cover the company's future demands. They would have to start the horizontal drilling project as soon as possible to avoid having to lay off personnel.

Chapter 42

When he arrived home, the lights were still on. He found Anne sleeping on the couch, the fireplace still burning. Not wanting to disturb her, he kneeled down by her side to observe her asleep, enjoying her beauty. As if she sensed his presence, she opened her eyes. They looked at each other, the love between them almost tangible.

'I told you to go to bed, because I'd be late.'

'I wanted to wait for you. Looks like I didn't make it.'

'The drive was difficult.'

'Did everything go well with the Russians?'

'Yes, everything went very well. We now go ahead and transport one of the rigs to Finland for modifications and upgrades.'

'We'll drink to that. After all, this took a lot of your time and effort. Can you get the bottle of wine? I'll put more wood on the fire.'

'Aren't you tired?'

'No. I've already had some sleep.'

'Then I'll first go and kiss the children.'

'Just don't take too long, otherwise I'll be asleep again.'

'I thought you said you had your sleep already.'

The ritual with his daughter was similar, as Jess smiled when he kissed her. He hoped that Jan would wake up after his kiss, but had no such luck.

'Isn't it difficult for you not to wake them?'

'Every time. I always want to hold them, talk to them.'

'You can hold and talk to me.'

'Move over so I can sit closer.'

'First a toast to your Russian rig.'

'That they may stay with us for a long, long time.'

'We'll drink to that. Did you have time to think about what I said?'

'Yes, but it will take some more time for me to digest and come up with the right answers.'

'As long as you promise to be careful and watch out for those wolves.'

'We'll drink to that as well.'

'Rob, I'd like to visit Waltraud this weekend, because they bought a house and invited us for the housewarming party tomorrow.'

'That's good timing, lady. It's nearly time to wake up.'

'You once said that this would never be a problem; that you'd be able to catch up on sleep later.'

'And I remember you saying that you wanted no more of that.'

'Okay, but I didn't know that you'd be getting home this late.'

'It's going to get even later.'

'Aren't you tired?'

'Not anymore, not since I sat down close to you.'

They went to Waltraud and Heinz's housewarming party.

The couple had bought a lovely home close to the office, and the women had plenty of time to catch up. Waltraud insisted that they stay overnight, saying that she had cots for the kids, so the whole family slept in one room.

They had an excellent time, and it wasn't until late the next evening before they left. Jan was asleep in the car within minutes.

Rob knew that the time had come for him to tell Anne that he had to leave the next morning for Brazil.

'I have to leave on a business trip tomorrow. I come back on Friday.'

'Are you going to Helsinki?'

'No. This time we're visiting our operations in Brazil.'

She frowned. 'I have a feeling that you waited telling me this on purpose.'

'It's just a business trip, Anne.'

'We discussed Brazil only two days ago. You know how I feel about you going to these countries.'

'I arrive, visit the rig and return to Amsterdam the next day.'

'So who is travelling with you?'

'Schultz. He's the marketing manager.'

'You mean one of the people I warned you about.'

'I have to work with him, Anne.'

'That's different. Now you're actually going to Brazil with that guy.'

'Anne, I have no choice. I have to go. I'll be back in a few days.'

She didn't say another word the rest of the drive, and when they arrived home, Rob lifted the sleeping children out of their seats and carried them straight to bed.

'I really appreciated your joining me to visit Waltraud after that short night.'

'You're welcome. I know how much she means to you.'

'And you don't know how much you mean to me. Sometimes it really hurts that I have to let you go to these countries were lives don't count.'

'Anne, it's part of my job. That will never change.'

'Just promise me you'll be careful.'

'I promise.'

'Can you please just hold me very close?'

Chapter 43

The following morning he got up early, woken by the children. He took the early flight from Enschede to Amsterdam and the first connecting flight to Charles de Gaulle airport in Paris.

Rob met Schultz at the check-in desk and was surprised to find that they were flying first class. Everyone else in the company flew economy class. Bernard Heumer always insisted on the same standards for everyone within the company, with no special privileges for anyone in order to avoid irritations amongst the other employees.

'Why are we flying first class?'

'Von Ritter has approved the change in travel policy,' Schultz said.

Schultz had booked them separate seats, which was fine by Rob, as there was little to discuss between them.

Rob couldn't sleep, realizing that he was on his own. If he made a wrong move, he might even find himself in danger. Now he knew why people like Leonardo felt so secure in this country. It was simply because no one could touch them. No wonder Bill and several other expats hired former army soldiers and lived in the relative safety of gated compounds with their families. Rob would just have to depend on his own observations and wait until Bill had some useful information for him.

After landing in Rio the company driver drove them to the office. This time Leonardo and his wife were there to welcome them.

'So what's your schedule, Rob?' Leonardo asked.

'Well, I'd appreciate it if I could join the meetings with Ronald and the local oil company's representatives. That way I'd get to know them.'

'I really don't think you want to be there, Rob,' Schultz said firmly. 'You'd be wasting your time. We'll only be discussing marketing issues. No need for anyone from Operations to be there.'

'My main purpose is to visit the rig to see if the Look Ahead system has been implemented and that everyone on the rig is involved.'

'There's a crew change scheduled for this afternoon,' Leonardo said. 'You'd be welcome to join that flight.'

That afternoon the captain welcomed Rob on board and showed him to his room.

'Bill is still asleep,' the captain told him. 'We just completed a casing and cement job, so he's been up for quite a while.'

'No problem. Would it be okay if I take a look around?'

'Sure, go ahead.'

Once he had changed, he first went to the shale shaker area and still found the old type shakers installed. Then he visited the control room where he had a cup of coffee with the engineer on duty. He inquired after the engineer's salary scale. He was also curious to know why the engineer was working in Brazil and not in some other country.

'My girlfriend's Brazilian. But I'll be leaving for another company soon.'
'Why is that?'
'Salary reasons,' the man said, and he told Rob the difference in pay.

Rob then looked for the mate on duty and asked to show him around the ship.

'Looks like the ship could do with a new coat of paint,' he remarked upon seeing paint chips curling off the walls of the living quarters and deck.

'Tell me about it. I've asked for additional maintenance workers several times. My crew is fully occupied with other duties. Nothing so far.'

Rob thanked him, went to his room and fell asleep in no time. He didn't know how long he'd slept when he heard a short knock on the door.

'Good morning, Holland! Did you sleep well?'
'Excellent, Bill! How are you doing?' Rob asked, truly happy to see him.
'I'm fine. I just thought I'd bring you a cup of coffee.'
'Thanks a lot, Bill. I'll take a shower and see you in the office.'
'Take your time!'

While showering, he felt somewhat uncomfortable that he had gotten Anne involved in this mess. He should never have done it. And why had he involved Bill in all of this? If Bill could confirm that his suspicions were correct, what should he do? He knew the answer to that. He was determined not to let go. To do so would go against his honest and fair business ethics.

Upon entering Bill's office, the two men shook hands warmly. He quickly closed the door behind him, eager to voice his concerns before Bill could say anything.

'Bill, I know I sent you an email to ask for information. I also asked my wife if she could get some information for me at the Christmas party. I regret that I did that, because I really shouldn't have involved her in company politics. Nor do I want to get you involved in anything that can ruin your career or your private life. It's very easy for me to send an email from my safe office in Holland, but the moment I arrive in Brazil the rules change. I now realize the danger. My friend, my honest advice to you is don't tell me anything. Let's just enjoy the time that we have together while I'm on board.'

Bill took a long time before he answered. Then he frowned, as if offended.

'Now you listen to me, Rob. I was raised on a Texas cattle farm with the principle, "a man is only as good as his word." I left that farm because it had a future for just one of my brothers. Me and my other brothers had to find something else to make a livin'. One of our neighbors was lucky. They discovered oil on his land and he contracted a driller to drill some o' his wells. I asked the driller if he needed a roughneck in his crew, and the man decided to give me a chance. That was at a time when drillers organized their own drillin' and maintenance crew, such as mechanics and electricians. You know, I'm still part of his crew now. And when I'm home we have a beer together, or we organize a barbeque.

'I became part of his drillin' crew overseas, because that way we made more money. We added tool pushers, crane operators, welders or whatever other personnel was required. When I became drillin' supervisor, the crew stayed with me. We're all very close, Rob. Our families live in the same town. My crew works a 28/28 schedule and we fly home every four weeks.

'I never did get married, 'cause I always found a woman wherever my work was. I like Brazil because not everything is regulated as in most countries. And besides,' he grinned at Rob with a wink of an eye, 'the ladies here are warm-blooded and wonderful. I met a few of these ladies in the same hotel you stayed at. I always stayed there whenever I had to fly back to the U.S. My girlfriend Carmen and Luisa know each other well, because they served the same clients. She was a hooker, Rob. But I took her out of the hotel, rented a house and we're still together because she's good for me. Many of these ladies will do anythin' to marry a foreigner, get out of this country and live a life in luxury. But Carmen accepts me for what I am, and we enjoy each other's company.' He drank his coffee and took a bite of his donut.

'But now to come back to your well re-spec-ted advice. When I told you about what was happening here—things that go against everything I believe in—I was well aware that they're happenin' in a country where strangers cannot ask questions without a risk to themselves. It's just that I hate injustice. I hate the mentality of these white-collar criminals. If I can do anything to stop these people, I will. I asked Carmen if she was willin' to contact Luisa to get some additional information. But I also told her about the dangers involved. She hates Leonardo's guts, Rob. It was he who got her addicted to drugs, and he abused her, too. She is still a friend of Luisa's, and they meet each other on a regular basis. They had the same German clients, and they've exchanged client information before. But you should know that every guest room is wired, and everything is recorded on hidden cameras during your stay in that hotel.'

Bill stopped and looked at Rob candidly. 'My question to you is, Rob, did you take Luisa up to your room? 'Cause if you did, then everything you said and did was recorded.'

'No. We had two drinks in the bar, and I went back to my room alone.'

'Okay. In that case I'll need more time to tell you everything she told me. Right now I have to take care of the BOP test.'

'Shall I take the night shift again so that you can get some sleep?'

'You're the boss now!'

'Not on this rig I'm not,' Rob said with a smile. 'Besides, I'd like to return to the job I always loved for just a short while. Where bribes and office politics are not an issue.'

'I'd like that, son. That way we're more flexible with the time we've got.'

Rob took an afternoon nap and joined the Look Ahead meeting before the night shift came on duty. He was surprised to find how the system had been adopted and that the crew had forwarded some very valuable suggestions on safety and operational issues. He complimented Bill, who merely remarked that the system was alive and kicking in all his crewmembers, and that it had enabled every man to do a better job.

Rob made some handover notes and visited the driller who was retrieving the BOP test tool, after which the drilling assembly was made up to drill the new formation. He enjoyed stepping back into his previous role to manage the drilling operations hands-on, to observe and advise people on the job. It was also good to know that this job would always be available if he could no longer get any satisfaction from his present function. Everything went like clockwork—the team was motivated and cheerful.

He checked the IADC reports and saw that there was no record of any maintenance crews. He reviewed the drilling reports and recording charts of the past three months, and found a big difference in the time taken to carry out standard drilling operations between the two drilling supervisors and crews. The other crew had made the same pump start-up mistakes, again resulting in mud losses. He even discovered that there had been an accident that wasn't reported by Mike.

He joined the morning meetings with the contractor rig superintendent, the tool pusher and technical staff to discuss maintenance issues and the Look Ahead system.

He was present at the morning call to the shore base drilling and contract managers, and noticed that only a bare minimum of information was exchanged. There wasn't a single suggestion or remark concerning the Look Ahead sequences or safety issues. Nothing had changed since his last visit—the shore base clearly wasn't interested in the safety or drilling performance of the rig.

Rob and Bill took all the time they had to discuss matters, and on his last day Rob summarized the main points. Carmen had been an invaluable source of information.

It was Leonardo's wife who was in charge at the shore base, as her brother was head of the Exploration Department that issued the license to Hattenberg Oil Company to drill and produce local wells. She was the agent who arranged the contracts with the company, as well as the contracts between the drilling contractor and service companies. And for this, she received a considerable agent fee.

She purchased nearly every building that came up for sale and already owned a large number of properties in the city. It seemed that Leonardo was just a puppet on a string who followed her instructions. Leonardo had previously been employed as drilling supervisor for the local oil company. Apart from his salary, he also received consulting fees to supervise the drilling operations on behalf of the local oil company.

The same situation was applicable for Kees, the drilling contractor manager. Kees had worked for different drilling contractors around the world, but his wife was in charge, and he did what he was told right from the start of their marriage.

Both Leonardo's and Kees' wives lived a very luxurious lifestyle that had already attracted unwelcome attention. There had been several attempts to break into their well-guarded homes, and their children were escorted to school to avoid kidnapping.

The most disturbing information was that Andreas Klein had offered Luisa a job with the company as liaisons representative between his company and the local oil company, and to provide 'special services' in Germany.

At one of the frequent sex parties, Klein was completely drunk, and he had promised to pay for Luisa's apartment, boasting that he had a Swiss bank account. The last months these four German men visited Brazil frequently, inviting guests and arranging parties every day in a five-star hotel at company's expense.

On one occasion John Fuchs was arrested for having sex with children, but he was released after Leonardo bribed the police by paying them a large sum of money. So on top of everything else, it was now clear that a Swiss bank was transferring the money. And there was no way anyone could get any information on transfers or accounts from Swiss banks.

'I need to know what you're gonna do, Rob,' Bill said from across the table, which was scattered with paperwork and empty coffee cups. 'If you open this basket of snakes, we don't want to be in this country anymore. I've been here too long. I don't want to work for Leonardo anymore. So if you're planning to take any action, I need to know. As we're renting, I can leave within one day, and I generally travel light. I don't intend to return here again. I just have to find a way to take Carmen with me to the U.S., but I'm sure I can manage that. I'll most probably end up working in the Gulf of Mexico with my crew. A large number of oil companies are planning to start drilling there, and I'd like to spoil my little girl.'

'Bill, to tell you the truth I don't know what to do. I first have to discuss the available options with someone I can trust. But I understand that you drilled the third well, and up to now there has been no indication of any oil or gas whatsoever. Am I right?'

'Yes. We haven't had any signs of oil or gas, but don't stop drillin' on my account. I want to end this bribery, whatever it takes.'

'I agree. I'll let you know if I find a way. If I start this, people in the payment chain will know there's a leak, and they might come looking in your direction. I wouldn't want that to happen.'

'You know, Rob, I'm glad that I met you. At least somebody has the guts to do something about this,' he said with a look of disgust. 'I no longer recognize the standards of the oil industry in this country as the ones I always worked with. I believe a man should be proud to work for honest and fair companies.'

'We're not there yet, but I will do everything I possibly can.'

'Will you be stayin' on shore for a while longer before flyin' back home?'

'No. I've got what I came for, and I don't want to spend another minute with these people. I just want to get home as soon as possible.'

'Your helicopter will be here in one hour.'

'Thanks Bill, for everything. We'll keep in touch because I'd like to start drilling in the Gulf, so I'll have a job for you.'

'Just let me know, and I'll be there.'

Rob took a shower and changed into his clothes that smelled of home. While he was in the shower, he thought about what Bill had said about still not finding any oil. It suddenly occurred to him that he may not have to open a basket of snakes. He might be able to solve the issues from an operational point of view.

Feeling refreshed and optimistic once more, he went to the office and told Bill that he may have found a way to handle things. If he was successful, he'd let him know.

'Goodbye, my friend.'

'So long, son. And good luck.'

Rob waved to him one more time before boarding the helicopter, and after a short flight he landed on shore, where the limousine was waiting for him.

On his way to the shore base office, he considered his options. It occurred to him that none of the shore base staff was involved in the daily drilling operations. He wanted these people to understand that operations were run from Head Office, and that the Brazilian office was not an independent company with its own rules. Something needed to change. Maybe he had found an elegant way to solve two issues at the same time.

Rob found Schultz in the office. He asked Leonardo to get Kees and to join him in his office.

'Gentlemen, I have been on board now for five days,' he began, addressing the two Brazilian men as Schultz looked on, startled. 'I listened

342

in on the daily morning calls, and my conclusion is that neither of you are in the least bit interested in sharing your drilling experience or managing performance and safety issues. In the two reports from the different drilling supervisors, I noticed big discrepancies in performance for simple standard operations that should have been noticed by you as well. It seems that none of you are willing to act upon the advice that is given. Nor do you appear to learn from lessons learned, such as the pump startups, which repeatedly led to mud losses.

'The issue that disturbs me most is that Mike did not report the accident that took place recently, and I want to know why. Absolutely nothing has changed since my last visit. The men on board are left to work almost unsupervised, and my conclusion is that you are not at all interested in managing or supporting the drilling operations.

'First I will contact the drilling contractor and request a replacement for Kees, because I already warned him last time to improve matters. He hasn't. This is what I call gross negligence from both of you. You are paid to manage and support the drilling operations, and from where I stand, I don't see that you have.

'The second person that will be replaced is Mike. As drilling supervisor he has hardly shown any interest in performance or, far more important, the safety of our personnel.

'I will discuss the shore base situation of not following the MD instructions with the management team and let you know the outcome. If you have anything to say then let's hear it now.'

There was a stunned silence. The three men looked at each other in shock. Rob wondered if it was panic that he saw in their eyes.

Leonardo was the first to speak. 'I can explain the matter of the accident,' he said apologetically. 'The person involved in the accident did return to the rig for work after two days. In our opinion this should not be reported as an accident.'

'In your opinion? The official definition of an accident within our company—not to mention the entire drilling industry—is that a person should return to work within twenty four hours. Otherwise it has to be reported as an accident.'

'It was not our intention to cover up this accident,' Leonardo countered.

'Then you should have reported it. Kees, do you have anything to say about this?'

'No, the only thing I can say is that I'm sorry. I will change and do things better.'

'You had every opportunity after my last visit to do things better. If this is all you have to say, I'd like to go to the airport now. I just need to make a few calls first.'

Not another word was said, and Rob called Werner to arrange a replacement for Mike as soon as possible, so he would be able to work one full week with Bill. He also asked Werner to meet him after his return to discuss a certain matter with him. They agreed to see each other on Thursday at the hotel close to the office.

He then called the drilling contractors' Operations Manager and asked him to replace Kees, briefly explaining the reason why, adding that he would send him a rig visit report with the full summary upon his return.

Once the car was waiting in front of the office, he left the building without a word.

It took a while before Schultz finally joined him. It didn't surprise him. He had probably stunned them by throwing a major wrench in their works and schemes. They were probably still trying to catch their breaths in there.

What next? Von Ritter would undoubtedly call him into his office the minute he got back. But first things first—he knew that Schultz would have to say something about it.

'Are you seriously planning to discuss the situation concerning Leonardo with the management team?'

'Yes, I'm very serious.'

'But you can't do this!'

'Why ever not?'

'Because he was recommended to us by the local oil company. He has been working for this company for a long time.'

'He was hired by our company as drilling manager with certain responsibilities, and it seems that he does not take his job seriously. This is not the first time we discussed this. He did not support the introduction of the Look Ahead system until I warned him that it would be reported to the Managing Director. I warned him that he would be fired if he didn't cooperate.'

'Can't we come up with another solution?'

'What do you suggest?'

'Give him one more chance.'

'Why would we have a problem with the local Oil Company?'

'Because they recommended him for this job.'

'When the company employed him, he accepted the tasks and responsibilities as described in his job description. He simply isn't doing his job.'

'I know. But I'm telling you, we just can't do this. If we fire him we'll have a serious problem with the local Oil Company. It's our local partner, after all.'

'I still don't see the problem. This is an internal company issue, and our partner should be just as interested in safe and efficient drilling operations as we are.'

Schultz's face was grim. 'I'll have to report this to Von Ritter.'

'You already called him, didn't you?' Rob said accusingly. Schultz pressed his lips together in a tight line, but didn't answer. Rob knew enough. They didn't say another word to each other and checked in separately for the Paris flight.

On the plane Rob prepared a detailed rig visit report for the drilling contractor's manager. He also finished a report for the management team, explaining the reasons why he had fired the contractor shore base manager and company-drilling supervisor. He summarized the facts concerning Leonardo and strongly recommended that he, too, should be replaced as soon as possible. He carefully reviewed the report several times to ensure that all details were correct and that he hadn't forgotten anything important. He sincerely hoped that the contractor's Drilling Manager wasn't involved in the bribe setup.

As he put the papers away, he felt tired but satisfied. At last he had taken the first steps to shake the belief of those men and women that they were untouchable. He tried to sleep, but his brain worked overtime to find a way to end the Brazil contract. The only solution he could think of was to remind every member of the management team of honest and fair business ethics, as well as their loyalty to the company. Then he would suggest that the management team should vote to terminate the contract, based on poor drilling results against the large investments that had been made, with no real prospect of finding oil or gas. He would have to tell Werner about the bribery business, so that he could take it up with Eberhart Bauerle, the Drilling Engineering Manager, and stop the drilling.

He was glad that Tom was still employed until the end of the month. That way he could confirm the payment methods and absurd expenses that were being made. This could just work.

The sun came up just as the plane landed in Paris, and Rob had to run to catch his connecting flight to Amsterdam. He didn't see Schultz on the flight, and assumed that he was busy making phone calls.

He called Anne from Amsterdam and told her that he would only be home for a short time, after which he had to drive to the office for a meeting.

'How was your visit?' she asked.

'It was a very fruitful visit.'

'That could mean anything.'

'I'll see you at home. Kiss the kids for me.'

He wanted no more involvement from Anne. She'd get worried and would only make things more complicated, asking questions that would need answering.

Each time he flew closer to home, he would feel the same butterflies in his stomach as he thought of her and the kids.

Chapter 44

When he arrived home he explained that he didn't have much time, and after he faxed the reports to Werner and the drilling contractor's Operations Manager, he left again. He wanted to get to the hotel as soon as possible to discuss his plan with Werner.

There wasn't much traffic on the Autobahn, and when he arrived at the hotel, he found a quiet corner and called Werner to let him know he was there.

Werner came in and looked at him questioningly. 'Hi, Rob,' he said before taking a seat. 'I received your rig visit report. My gut feeling tells me that this is an important meeting.'

'Correct. I need your advice on quite a number of disturbing issues.'

He told him about the poor functioning of Leonardo, Mike and Kees, and why he had to fire them.

Werner shrugged his shoulders 'I wouldn't have handled this problem any differently. A new drilling supervisor will be on board in two days. So what's the issue?'

Then he told him everything about the bribe setup, and that he was certain that Von Ritter, Fuchs, Klein and Schultz were involved. Rob added, 'Equipment and personnel were included in the contract, but not on board. The labor costs quoted were not the rates being paid, the company is paying a ten percent agent fee to the drilling contractor, and money is being transferred using Swiss bank accounts. These managers charged ridiculously high expenses to the company's account for their business trips, and fly first class! And do you know why Von Ritter wasn't there for the signing of the Russian joint venture?' He lowered his voice, making sure no one was listening in. 'He wasn't in a board meeting! He stayed at a hotel in Munich with one of the secretaries!'

He noticed that Werner's face changed color. He seemed to be aging in a matter of minutes.

'Who knows about this?' Werner asked, once he found his voice.

'Tom, Jurgen, Joop and Bill Turner, the American drilling supervisor on board knows part of it.'

'How come Joop knows?'

'Because he was staying at the same hotel in Munich as Von Ritter and his lady friend.'

Werner shook his head slightly as if to refocus. 'Rob, I need some time to recover from this all. But what do you expect from me?'

'Before I went to Brazil last week I didn't know what to do, but if you look at my report, then we may clean up this mess from an operational point of view. Bringing these people to justice is nearly impossible.'

'I agree.'

Rob explained his plan and waited for Werner's reaction.

'Let's have something to eat. I need time to digest this horror story.'

After a few minutes he excused himself and left Rob alone. When he came back, he seemed like a different person. 'I've organized a conference room in the hotel. Von Ritter called a meeting this morning to discuss the financial results of the company. He wants to transfer pension funds to improve the annual results. He left before the meeting was over, and the others are still in the meeting room. Most members of the management team are on their way here. I'll arrange for sandwiches to be brought up.'

After half an hour everyone who had voted for Rob's investment proposal was present.

'I want you all to regard this as a meeting among friends,' Werner began as he handed everyone a copy of Rob's rig visit report. 'But of vital importance to the company nonetheless. The issues in this report are of no real significance, as the operational department has already taken action. Rob, go ahead. Tell them your story, and what you propose to do about it.'

Rob told them what he knew, and once he was finished the room was filled with silence.

Eberhart was the first to speak. 'Since I found out this morning that Von Ritter is planning to transfer part of the company pension funds to boost financial results, nothing will surprise me anymore. I refuse to be involved in any form of bribery, and you can count on me to stop all drilling operations in Brazil. We were already discussing if the next well should be drilled anyhow. We're no longer interested in drilling wells if that means being involved in corruption. But we just had a management meeting. It would be a bit strange if we called for another one.'

It was Tom who spoke next, 'Further investments for the next three proposed wells in Brazil will require approval. But if we cancelled the drilling program in Brazil, we would need to call a separate meeting with the drilling engineering department. We could distribute the well reports and get the geologist to provide valid reasons to discontinue drilling operations in Brazil.'

They scheduled the meeting for the following Tuesday to make sure that Von Ritter couldn't make any unexpected moves and advised Rob to send an official warning letter to Leonardo. In order to separate the issues in Brazil, they planned to propose the termination of the Brazilian contract during the Monday morning meeting, so that the decision would not be linked to Rob.

After everyone left the room, Werner thanked him for his swift action.

'There is no one else I can trust who has the authority to call these men to take action. You are the only well-respected senior manager left in this company.'

They shook hands. 'You know, Rob, after all that's happening, I need some time to rethink matters. My heart left the company already, and I don't know if I want to be part of it anymore.'

Rob called Anne to let her know that he just left the meeting and would be home late.

He had never felt more relieved. A tremendous weight had just been lifted off his shoulders with the knowledge that something that had so affected and disturbed his life was hopefully soon coming to an end.

On the other hand, he had taken Werner's parting words to heart. He was traveling the same road. What should he do if Werner left the company? He could either look for other opportunities, or fight the 'white-collar criminals' as Bill called them.

Would any company be willing to purchase an oil company that was not allowed to drill wells in Europe until safety cases were completed and approved? He tried to put off such thoughts, and decided to enjoy this moment of relief, solve the problems as they come and switched back to home mode.

Chapter 45

When Anne opened the door, he kissed and hugged her longer than he normally did.

'I waited with dinner. I'll be finished in a few minutes.'

'Then I'll go upstairs. Call me when dinner is ready.'

He watched Jess while she slept, trailing his fingers through her baby-fine hair and kissed her gently, enjoying the way her smile lit up the room. Then he went to Jan's room, where he sat down in the chair to listen to the sounds he made in his sleep.

Anne came in and stood beside him. 'He is dreaming lately,' she said softly. 'And making all kinds of noises as he sleeps.'

'Anne, it's just so special to watch them while they're asleep.'

'Dinner is ready.'

They went down for dinner, and he felt that she was observing him.

'So what happened?' she asked.

'Why you ask?'

'Because this afternoon I watched my husband with that worried frown on his face. He had no time for me then. I don't see the frown anymore. There's a different light in his eyes now.'

'It's because of seeing you again. And the children.'

'There was something special about the way you kissed me when you came home.'

'Anne, I was just glad to be home.'

'Rob, just tell me if the urgent meeting you had this afternoon has anything to do with my observations?'

'Anne, I made a mistake. I've decided to leave you out of company politics from now on, because I like to keep work and home separate. I have to deal with my work problems as they come, and I want to enjoy the most valuable time I have with you and the children, at home. To answer your question this time—yes. The meeting had something to do with your—very sharp—observations, and sometimes I wish you couldn't read my face so well.'

'That's why I'm your wife. I don't want to make your life more difficult. I'll leave work out of our home starting today.'

'You shouldn't worry, Anne. These people just aren't worth it. My job takes me to countries where our laws don't apply, but I'm always very careful because I want to return home.

'Can I make love to you?'

'Any time.'

The shutters were kept closed that weekend and no one disturbed their

351

love and family weekend. They spent most of their time in bed, with or without Jan and Jess, who loved to snuggle up between them and play games.

Chapter 46

Monday morning came quickly, and after feeding the kids and getting them dressed, he left for the office early. He wanted to finish all of last week's paperwork, knowing that the meetings would take up all of his time.

Surprisingly, there was no urgent request from Von Ritter's office to come and see him. Apparently Werner had taken care of that.

At the meeting he reported the safety and drilling status from each area, distributed the Brazil rig visit report and informed them of the actions that had been carried out so far. He told them that after seriously considering Ronald Schultz's advice, he had decided not to risk damaging the relationship with their local oil company and withdrew his recommendation to fire Leonardo. Instead, he would send Leonardo an official letter of warning to advise him to improve his attitude and functioning accordingly.

As he said this, he noticed the surprised faces of Von Ritter and the other three men.

It was then that Eberhart requested a management meeting for the next day, with the intention to discuss the Brazil investments, as this had not yet been handled at the last meeting. Because these investment meetings took place regularly, no one questioned it and the time for the meeting was set.

When the management meeting was over, Rob asked Eberhart and Gunther to remain behind to discuss the horizontal drilling status. Eberhart told him that all service companies' tests were completed satisfactorily. One of the company drilling rigs awaiting safety case approval was available to carry out the pilot project.

The drilling program was completed by his department and awaited Rob's signature. The equipment could be loaded once the rig was moved to the location, which was conveniently located close to Hanover. The service contracts for the service companies involved were already signed by him but required Rob's signature.

Rob thanked them for taking care of these important matters while he was gone and said that he would review the drilling programs and contracts within the next few hours. He would instruct the rig move company to transport the rig and equipment as soon as possible and arrange supervisors for the project.

Gunther asked him if it was possible to assign his supervisors, as they managed basic drilling operations, and he knew they were keen to be involved. Rob agreed to interview the supervisors before making a decision and the interview was set for lunchtime.

As he returned to his office, he told his secretary not to disturb him so that he could review the drilling program and the service contracts that

Eberhart had prepared. There was nothing complicated about drilling the well, but the success depended on the turbines to rotate the bit, because rotation of the drilling string with the rotary was not possible. Then onto the complicated measuring system while drilling from a vertical hole to the ninety degree kickoff point and thereafter drilling the horizontal section of three hundred feet into the oil reservoir.

He saved the program on his disk and emailed Eberhart that he didn't have any comments. Then he signed a hard copy and asked his secretary to deliver the documents back to the drilling engineering department.

He called the rig move company and gave instructions to a former colleague—someone who had once trained him his first weeks—moving the rig as soon as possible. The man promised Rob to have the rig ready to drill within one week.

The production supervisors Gunther recommended came into his office, and he invited them for lunch. Both men had worked as drillers on land rigs and followed safety and well control courses. He asked them how they planned the day-to-day work-over and repair operations. Their answers surprised him.

Six months ago, Gunther had instructed them to describe each operational sequence and update them daily if necessary. These sequences were used to plan, discuss and supervise the different operations. The men were both very interested in supervising the horizontal drilling operations, as this project involved the drilling of wells, while it had always been a daily routine for them to carry out repairs on producing wells.

Their initiative appealed to Rob, and he accepted them as his supervisors for the project, saying that they were to report to him. He then asked if they had worked with computers before. They both showed him their laptops, and Rob realized that he was still traveling the world with a case full of fat data books, calculator and slide rules, while the new generation of drilling supervisors traveled the world with just their laptops.

They walked to his office and he explained the basics of the system. He made copies of the sequences used to drill similar wells, including casing and cement operations. Both men copied the drilling program and sequences onto their laptops.

He asked to change the draft sequences prepared by him to reflect the operations as described in the program, and to come back to him once they had finished each sequence. The men set to work in a room that his secretary organized for them.

He called Gunther and thanked him for his suggestion to use his men as drilling supervisors. 'By the way, I was pleasantly surprised to find that they're using the Look Ahead system.'

'I think it's an excellent tool. That's why I introduced it into my organization.'

'Your men are presently preparing the horizontal drilling sequences. They'll probably finish by tomorrow.'

'I would like to review them, if you don't mind. After all, this is a producing well.'

'I'll send you the draft.'

'Thank you.'

Rob felt motivated and energized to start this new project. Yet he knew that the main reason for his mood was that he had come up with a solution for Brazil. He called Jurgen and agreed to have lunch the next day to discuss the project status.

'How was your rig visit?'

'I'll tell you tomorrow.'

'I'm very interested. See you tomorrow.'

The supervisors were very practiced at using the 'copy and paste' method and completed all the sequences in no time. They agreed to meet the next morning.

When he read through the afternoon report from Brazil, he noticed with satisfaction that a second drilling supervisor was already on board.

Once he had completed all his paperwork he called the drilling contractor's operations manager and asked if he received his report. The man told him that, yes, he had, and that he was disappointed at what had happened, but he understood the reasons of his request and would try to find someone to replace Kees.

He stayed late at the office until all previous incidents and accidents had been included into the horizontal sequence draft. It was then that Anne called.

'Do you have already a couch to sleep on in your office yet?'

He sniggered. 'Not yet. But I'm thinking about it.'

'Our son would like to hear your voice before I take him upstairs.'

Rob talked to Jan, telling him what had happened that day. Sometimes he would hear a faint noise on the other side, and always ended his story with 'I love you'.

He promised to call Anne once he got to his apartment, and when he did, he thanked her for all her love during their beautiful family weekend.

He couldn't help feeling nervous. Tomorrow could be 'D-day' if everything went according to plan. Before falling asleep he sent a prayer towards the heavens to 'please support those men who respect certain values in life'.

He was the first one in the office. He began with reviewing the drilling reports and the day started off well, as there were no accident reports. While he was working on the warning letter to Leonardo, Werner walked in.

'This will be my last month here,' he announced simply.

Rob sat back and looked at him. Somehow he knew that this was coming. But it had come sooner than expected. 'You're going to resign? Why, Werner?'

'It's impossible for me to advise Von Ritter on any issue. It's a one-way street. You saw for yourself how things were at the Christmas party. We can never become a team.' He pulled out a chair and sat down across Rob. 'What happened yesterday with the pension funds proposal and the bribe setup—for me that was the absolute limit. I cannot work another day with managers who cannot be trusted and who are not dedicated to the company. I hate dishonesty like this.' He sighed wearily.

'So what are your plans for the future?'

'Bernard Heumer has asked me to join him at his company in the U.S. I'm thinking about it.'

'When will you tell Von Ritter?'

'I still have two weeks' holiday. I intend to use them, and in the last week I'll give him my notice.'

'I don't have to tell you that I owe you everything. You hired me, Werner. You taught me everything. I'm going to miss you.'

'I know, my son. But I refuse to be a puppet on a string.'

'Is everything arranged for the management meeting?'

'Yes. I already discussed the details with Tom and Eberhart yesterday. This is going to end, so I can leave this company with a clear conscience.'

'Thank you.'

'Are operations running as expected? Is the new drilling supervisor on board yet?'

'Yes. No problems were reported, and the man is on board.'

'I'll see you at the meeting,' Werner said, and left Rob alone with his thoughts.

This was the doom scenario he was afraid of. Nearly every week someone who had helped to create this company was leaving, to be replaced by yet another puppet on a string with hardly any experience.

Next he had a brief meeting with the supervisors. Rob showed the draft and asked them to review each sequence and include any comments. They agreed to meet again that afternoon. At the meeting that followed, nothing special was reported, and it seemed a standard day at the office. Until the following management meeting started.

Von Ritter welcomed everyone and handed Tom his investment proposal to drill three more wells in Brazil. Tom gave an estimation of the costs, upon which it was Eberthart's turn. He presented the geology of the drilling areas and depths where hydrocarbons were expected. 'According to our surveys, there is no indication of sands nor any sign of hydrocarbons at these predicted depths.'

The geologist took over from there. 'Based on the geological structure and the drilling results at various depths, our final conclusion is that there are no hydrocarbons present in these blocks. My advice would be not to approve any new investments in these blocks.'

'My recommendation would be the same,' Eberhart said.

Von Ritter and his team jumped up from their chairs in indignation.

'That's impossible!' Von Ritter shouted, red-faced. Andreas Klein looked positively outraged, and Schultz had paled considerably. It was Tom who interrupted their cacophony of protestations.

'The management team makes decisions concerning similar investment on a weekly basis,' he said calmly. 'And the decisions are always based on facts. I suggest we put this matter to a vote, which is, after all, standard procedure. Please, gentlemen, would you be so kind as to write down your votes.'

'Wait!' Von Ritter said; his voice panicky. 'I think we should be given more detailed well information before we vote on this.'

'I think we already have all the detailed reports here on the table,' Werner countered. 'We have all the information necessary to decide whether to approve the investment or not. I agree with Tom. We should put it to a vote now.'

Von Ritter looked furious, but could do nothing. Everyone wrote down their vote on the voting sheet that went round, and when they were done, Tom counted the votes.

'The investments for drilling new wells in Brazil are hereby not approved.' And with that, he filed the votes with the investment proposal.

'I want to see that for myself,' Von Ritter muttered angrily, and he snatched the voting sheet away. As he counted the votes, he turned an even deeper purple.

'Gentlemen,' he said, his voice quavering, 'it looks as if the investments for drilling further wells in Brazil has been disapproved.' And with that, he strode towards the door and left the room.

Rob could have jumped sky high, but he kept his face straight and left the meeting room with his own team, leaving Schultz, Klein and Fuchs behind in a state of shock. They looked as if they didn't know what had just hit them.

Once in his office he called the rig in Brazil and requested to talk to Bill.

Jurgen walked into his office, and Rob gestured to him to take a seat.

'Hi, Holland!' came Bill's familiar Texan drawl.

'Can I speak freely?' Rob asked. 'No one listening in at your end?'

'Go ahead, Rob. The coast is all clear.'

'This will be the last well we're drilling in Brazil.'

A slight delay on the line, and then Bill said, 'That's a very elegant solution, Rob. And good timin', too, 'cause next week we reach our final depth and I'll be leavin' the rig. Carmen and I will arrange everything to leave Brazil within a week. I'll be taking my lady friend to the U.S. and probably end up working in the Gulf.'

'You're not interested in working in Europe?'

'We'll see. To tell you the truth, I think it's too cold for me and my girl.'

'How is the new guy who replaced Mike?'

'He is okay.'

'I hope we'll meet again someday.'

'Don't worry, I'll be visiting you in Holland one day, son.'

'I hope you will. You'll always be welcome in Holland, my friend. And thank you.'

'You're welcome.'

He felt relieved that everything had gone so well, without any risks to anyone. He had won two important battles, but he knew that he could not win them all. He found Jurgen looking at him from across the desk, smiling.

'This is really a perfect way to end this disaster, Rob.'

'Yes, with the support of the more loyal and honest members of our management team.'

'This is great.' Jurgen said. 'I never drink at work, but I'd really like to invite you for a beer and Bratwurst. We cannot celebrate this with just a sandwich.'

'Is Joop in the office?'

'Yes, he is. I will get him to join us.'

They walked to a special place where they primarily served Bratwurst, and Jurgen ordered grilled Bratwurst with mustard on a crusty bread roll with potato salad and three quarter-gallon glasses of beer.

'Tell me why this invitation?' Joop asked, knowing this was a special occasion.

'Because you, too, have contributed to end drilling operations in Brazil.' Rob told him with a grin.

'Was Von Ritter in favor of continuing the drilling?'

'Yes.'

A big smile spread across Joop's 'face. 'Then I'll drink to that. Prosit!'

For Rob it was a long time since his last bratwurst. After the first one, he looked at Jurgen, and they ordered another one, this time flavored with curry.

'Excellent idea, Jurgen. Thanks for the invitation.'

'You earned this one.'

'Mind you, I do have a problem with the large beer.'

'Just keep on drinking until you see the bottom,' Jurgen said, laughing.

But Rob wasn't used to drinking that much beer, so they had to wait quite a while before his glass was empty.

'Jurgen, I don't know if my brain is still functioning properly, but please fill me in on the status of the different projects.'

Jurgen explained that most of the equipment had been delivered to install the top drives, third mud pumps and the 6 5/8-inch drill pipe on their rigs, and that they were now waiting for quotations from various installation companies. The equipment was due to be installed at the German deep well the following week.

The Russian jackup rig had already arrived at the shipyard two weeks ago, and Jurgen stayed on board during the first week. On Monday he would return to witness completion of the project. He estimated it would take approximately ten more days to install all the new equipment, after which the first drill ship would arrive for an upgrade that would take two months.

Joop then gave him an update on his search for a new recording system. He said that he had visited a number of companies that manufactured drilling recorders, but still hadn't found what he was looking for. Rob wanted real-time recording of all operations carried out on board, which required a complete different approach.

All previous systems recorded the operations with a considerable delay, so that corrective-drilling actions could not take place on time. Jurgen did find out that there was a real-time recorder manufacturer in Munich that delivered the systems for space capsules. He had visited the company and was surprised that the system could also be modified to include drilling machinery. So he ordered the system and asked Rob to check the list with machinery.

'Make sure the recorder system can provide real-time information on the air compressors, well control, mud weight and flow from the well,' Rob said.

'It does,' was Jurgen's reply. 'The system allows drilling supervisors to follow the drilling operations on several screens, and it provides any important information you want.'

'I hope that the supervisors won't stay in the office the whole day, and that they'll still visit the rig floor frequently. They have to talk to the drillers, because these guys drill the hole and feel when Mother Earth is talking,' Rob said.

'People do lose contact with the work floor, Rob. That's the only disadvantage of such data systems.'

'Good work, Joop. This is the kind of system I like. It could help us make instant decisions. For example, to stop drilling because the annulus is full of cuttings, or because the pump pressure has dropped due to a leak. Will you be staying on board for the system's installation and function testing?'

'I expect that the system will be delivered on Monday. It requires a week to install. I'll be on board as from Monday to assist Jurgen as well.'

'Thanks for all the work you've done. Unfortunately, I feel that the alcohol is affecting me. I think we should go back to the office.'

When he got back, he checked on his supervisors, who had finished the sequences for the Look Ahead system. He told them to present the draft to Gunther for comments and suggested that they meet early in the morning to include his own comments.

He agreed with Eberhart to arrange a meeting to discuss the horizontal drilling program with the service engineers assigned to the project the next morning at ten.

At the apartment he called Anne and told her that alcohol was the reason for his early bedtime. He chatted to Jan for a while, and fell fast asleep. That night, he dreamt that he was being chased by Brazilian gang members. He only just managed to escape the country in time.

The supervisors came in early to show him the changes that Gunther had made. Rob went through all the sequences again until they thoroughly understood each step. He told them that a meeting with the service companies had been arranged after the morning meeting to review the sequences with the service engineers assigned to the project.

He suggested that one of them should present the sequences, while the other made notes on all the suggestions made, and told them to join the meeting at ten o'clock.

Von Ritter and his staff were not present at the meeting. Rob reported the status of the Russian rig and the horizontal drilling project.

At ten o'clock the supervisors came in and connected a laptop to the big screen.

Then the service engineers arrived, and Rob explained that the new safety case requirements obligated them to postpone the drilling of all new wells for an extended period of time. 'We have to face the fact that we'll have to shut down some of our rigs and lay off personnel. This is why this project is so important. If the horizontal drilling operations are successful, rigs can continue to work.'

He introduced Ernst, one of the supervisors, who presented each sequence, while his colleague took down notes on all the suggestions put forward. The presentation went quickly and smoothly, with each service engineer coming up with valid comments based in his own area of expertise. Detailed discussions were necessary to determine the steps needed to measure while drilling the horizontal section of the well. The sequences were adjusted until the details were clear to everyone involved. Once the sequences were finalized, he had copies made for Eberhart and Gunther and provided the supervisors with a copy of the land rigup sequences. 'The rig is on its way now. You'll have to decide today who gets to supervise the rigup operations. Call me anytime if you need me on location or just need my advice.'

They agreed to visit the location together and arrange an on/off schedule between them. That afternoon he reviewed the operation reports, finally finished his letter to Leonardo and asked his secretary to send the letter by mail. The remainder of that week, he reviewed the service contracts from the various companies involved in the horizontal drilling project and forwarded these to Eberhart for approval.

There was no sign of Von Ritter or his team. They seemed to be out of the office. At least they were quiet, as if in the lull before the storm.

Chapter 47

He drove home early because he wanted to surprise Anne and see the kids before they went to bed. He surprised her by driving right up behind her as she cycled through their neighborhood. At first she didn't see him, but then Jan had spotted him and started pointing and saying 'papa!'

She turned around, and her face lit up as she saw him. She got down from her bike, lifted Jan off the back seat and took him to his car. Rob got out and greeted her and Jess with a kiss. Then he put Jan on his lap behind the steering wheel for his very first car ride, while Anne walked her bike alongside him to the house.

'What are you doing home so early?'

'I wanted to see the kids before they go to sleep. That, and have dinner together.'

'You are just in time to help me unload the groceries.'

Rob glanced at the full saddlebags that hung on both side of her bicycle. 'That's what I call a heavily loaded bike, with Jess in front and Jan in the backseat, plus all those groceries.'

'It was a nice afternoon. Besides, I didn't have enough time to walk to the shops so I took the bicycle. Of course the kids enjoy it more than the slow-walking stroller.'

'You take Jess. I'll take the groceries in the house, and Jan and I will put the bike under the carport.'

'Oh, I really like that we can have dinner together. Would you like a cup of coffee?'

'No thanks, I have turned into an alcoholic. I'd like a glass of wine.'

'No beer?'

'Don't talk to me about beer for a while. That's the reason why I went to bed so early the other day.'

'Did you have something to celebrate?'

He hated these supposedly 'innocent' questions as if she asked, 'How are you doing?'

'No. I just went for a bratwurst and beer with Jurgen, but he ordered me an extra-large beer.'

'So did you have something to celebrate? You never drink at work.'

Oh, Jesus. If she can't read my face she'll always find some other way.

'It was his birthday,' he lied.

'That's a fib, Rob. I can tell from your face that you just made that up.'

'Okay, okay. A meeting went the way I liked. That's why.'

'Why didn't you say so the first time?'

He sighed. 'Can I please have a glass of wine?'

'I have a glass ready for you in the kitchen.'

Jan wanted to help him take the groceries inside, so he give him small, unbreakable items to take inside the house, while he stored the bike in the carport.

When he walked in, Anne handed him his glass of wine, and they toasted to the favorable meeting result.

While Anne cooked, he played with the kids, and gave Jess her bottle and bath. She had the same eyes and smile as her mama and loved to cuddle with him. He read her a bedtime story, sang a song and put her to bed.

Jan stayed up a little longer and had dinner with them.

Anne made meatballs with beetroot and potatoes, mashing some for Jan as it was one of his favorite meals.

It was great to watch his son sitting in his high chair and have the time to enjoy moments like this. Especially because the upcoming horizontal drilling operations were important, and could take up more of his time than he expected.

There was a knock on the door, and Dad came in. 'Hi Rob, I was surprised to see your car and just wanted to kiss the kids goodnight.'

'I wanted to surprise Anne and the kids.'

'How are you doing, Rob? We haven't seen each other for a while.'

'Just busy, Dad. Changes within the company, as well as different regulations we have to comply with.'

'It's always nice to come home and forget work for a few days.'

'The rigs work around the clock, so there is always something to take care of. But I try to switch off when I'm at home. Would you like a beer or some wine?'

'Lovely, a glass of wine, please.'

Anne asked, 'Dad, would you like to have dinner with us? I have enough.'

'Yes, please, especially now that I see that you're having one of my favorites.'

'There are two more men on the table with the same taste, so I prepared for a whole soccer team.'

After dinner Jan played with Dad, and together the men went to his room and watched, as Anne sang a couple of songs and read him bedtime stories, until she finally said, 'No more.' After a lot of goodnight kisses, Jan went to sleep.

'Have another glass of wine with us, Dad.'

'I don't like to intrude when Rob is at home.'

'Come on, Dad! You're always welcome here. I'll get you another glass. Rob, could you please light the fire?'

'Sure.'

They had a cozy, pleasant evening. Rob enjoyed listening to his stories, because Dad knew everyone in town, as he played cards, pool or went bowling every week since he retired. There was always something going on in this small village where everyone knew each other.

'Rob, it was good to see you again. Thanks for a very pleasant evening.'

'Remember, Dad, you never intrude. And if we want our privacy and need some time for ourselves, we'll close the shutters.'

'That's an excellent idea. I'll remember that. Goodnight to the both of you.'

They accompanied him outside and watched his back recede as he cycled home.

'He asked me if it was okay, because he wanted to see you,' Anne apologized as they went inside.

'Anne, I'll always make time for him, because I know that he's always there for us.'

'I know. But our time together is so short. I never want to waste a minute of it.'

'Family, like my sister and your dad, are very important to me. We need to invest in these times we can spend together.' He looked at her. She was happy, relaxed, and very attractive. 'Shall I close the shutters?'

'The evening is still young. I'd like to enjoy the wine and fire.'

'As long as you are very close to me. Because I missed you.'

'I'll be all around you.'

Chapter 48

When the phone rang early on Saturday morning, Rob first didn't understand who was calling him, so he got up and moved into the living room.

'Sorry, who is this?' he asked, still trying to wake up.

The person introduced himself as Alek Frederiksen, a drilling manager with a Norwegian oil company.

'Sorry for this early call, but I was given your number by the reception. My company has carried out a worldwide search to find a jackup rig equipped with a 15,000 psi BOP and well control system. The result showed only one rig. I understand that you are modifying a Russian rig to 15,000 psi at a shipyard in Finland right now. Am I correct?'

'Yes, we are. How can I be of service?'

'One of our rigs was drilling a deep well and encountered unexpected high formation pressures that exceed the well control working pressure of the rig. The authorities and we are very concerned that this pressure could channel to the surface along the different casing strings. We therefore need a rig to drill a relief well as soon as possible.'

'Alek, we'd need another week for modifications, but the rig has no safety case yet. Besides, we've never worked in Norway before.'

'The lack of a safety case isn't a problem. Due to the high risk of an environmental disaster, the Norwegian Petroleum Directorate will allow any 15,000-psi rated drilling rig to drill this relief well. If you need any more people at the shipyard to reduce the modification time, I could arrange for a charter plane to send them in.'

'Alek, give me your phone number, and I'll check if the completion time can be reduced. I'll call you back as soon as I know more.'

He called Jurgen.

'Jurgen, it looks as if history is about to repeat itself. Only now it's different.' He updated him on the urgency and asked if the completion date could be brought forward.

After consulting his project planning chart, Jurgen told him that the rig would be ready for tow-out in five days. They would fly out early in the morning to arrange the changes and increase personnel on the 15,000-psi high pressure piping system.

Rob asked him to call Joop, drive to the airport and call him when they got to Schiphol. A charter plane would be waiting to take them to the shipyard.

He called Alek to inform him that two men would be at Schiphol within two hours for the charter flight, and that the time required could be reduced to five days. They agreed on the day rate, and from that moment on, the rig was on contract.

All shipyard and additional costs to speed up the move-out date was to be reimbursed, including any additional insurance coverage that might be required to carry out such operations.

He instructed Alek to hire two tugs and a rig mover for the rig move, and suggested he organize specialized well control personnel from Houston to assist in the case of an emergency, as well as have his drilling supervisors on board as soon as possible to get acquainted with the rig. Rob asked, 'May I know what caused the mishap?'

'Driller's mistake. He didn't fill up the hole while pulling out.'

Christ, Rob thought cynically. Where have I heard that before? 'Can we assist in any other way?'

'I'll let you know. You've already done a great job helping me by making the rig available to us at such short notice. I'll arrange the charter plane for your men. But there is one more important issue. We really need to keep this operation confidential. We don't want to get the press involved and create a panic. If questions do come up, our statement is that your rig will function as an accommodation and support unit for the drilling operations.'

'Understood. I'll get my crew to sign the confidentiality agreement, as well,' Rob said, and after agreeing to keep in touch on a daily basis, he hung up.

Later that morning he finally had a chance to call Werner and report the events that were taking place.

'Rob, it seems that history is repeating itself with a rig in the shipyard. Only this time the rig is needed to avoid a tremendous environmental disaster.'

'I know you're on holiday, but can you inform Von Ritter?'

'Yes, I'll let him know. Keep me informed, because I still work for the company.'

Rob grinned into the phone. 'Sure. I'll let you know, boss.'

Jurgen called to inform that they had arrived at Schiphol and were ready to board the plane.

Rob told him that he thought about the urgency and decided not to install the top drive with a 6 5/8-inch drill pipe and iron roughneck, as the Russian drilling crew wasn't used to operating such high-tech equipment. And besides, training each drilling crew would require at least another week.

He wanted to leave two service engineers on board after the installation and testing of the BOP to ensure that they would have sufficient experience on the rig. He also wanted to keep Joop on board, not only to represent the company, but to ensure that the data recording system functioned correctly and to have one data specialist on board during the contract period. This operation would be a valuable one-time experience for him.

'Good idea. That will reduce the planning time considerably.'

'Jurgen, I just talked to the Norwegian drilling manager. This operation is again highly confidential. Everyone on board has to sign the confidentiality agreement. If outside people start asking questions, tell them that we are to function as an accommodation and support unit.' He paused, and then added, 'I wish I could be on board that rig to help.'

'I know,' Jurgen said.

At that moment Anne walked into the living room. 'I kept the kids in our bed. This call sounded rather important,' she said, giving him a questioning look.

'It was very important, Anne. Thanks.'

'Is there anything that you can you tell me?'

He told her what had happened and made a small sketch to explain the disaster which could take place.

'We've done all we can for now. Let's enjoy the weekend with the kids. I'd like to take the children cycling after breakfast.'

'Then I'll call your sister and ask if we can have lunch at their house.'

'That is a long bike ride. Investing in family time, are you?'

'They haven't seen you for a while, Rob. I'll take everything we need for the kids.'

They cycled to his sister's house, with Jess strapped onto Anne's front seat and Jan in Rob's backseat. The kids thoroughly enjoyed themselves, and it was good to see and talk to Agnes and Klaus.

The kids pleaded with them to stay longer, so it was late in the afternoon before they finally rode home. That evening they tucked in two very happy, tired children.

Rob asked Anne to join him for an early night, because of his long hours that day, and he didn't know if there might be more surprises in store for him that night.

Early Sunday morning he spoke to Jurgen to discuss the schedule, and called Alek to inform that the shipyard time was reduced to four days. The drilling manager had already arranged for most his personnel to be on the rig, and tugboats were standing by in the shipyard for the rig move.

For the rest of the day they cycled around town, eating sandwiches for lunch and pancakes for dinner at the watermill.

After the kids were in bed, Rob lit the fire, while Anne prepared Glühwein. They were finally able to put up their feet.

'I'm very happy,' Anne sighed. 'I hope we can do this again. It was a wonderful weekend.'

'We'd better take what we can get, because I've got busy times ahead of me with everything that's going on.'

'I understand. But this one was special. I really enjoyed seeing the kids

that happy.'
  'I can live on just seeing you so happy.'
  'I don't think so,' she teased.
  'You're right.'
  'Then come a little closer.'
  'Is this close enough?'
  'Closer.'
  'Enough.'
  'Hmm. Closer.'

It was becoming a routine to let Anne sleep in while he took care of the kids before leaving home, something which he enjoyed doing. He knew he had a busy week ahead of him, with the horizontal drilling operations starting and moving the jackup rig to Norway for the relief well, which could prove to be quite a challenge.

When he arrived at the office, he first called Ivan Golubev in Murmansk to inform him that their rig was on contract to carry out operations in Norway. Ivan was surprised, as he knew how difficult it was to enter the Norwegian waters. The Norwegians protected their market with the most stringent and sometimes ridiculous requirements to ward off any foreign competition. Briefly, they discussed the payment schedule for the upgrades and Ivan told him that the first oil tanker was on its way to Hamburg. Rob told him to transfer day rate payments from that day forward.

'Thank you for your advice, by the way,' Golubev said. 'We used soft rock bits on the super deep drilling project, like you said, and managed to drill another 120 feet.'

Rob prepared a brief recap of the Norwegian sidetrack operations for the morning meeting and contacted Alek. It turned out that a survey vessel carried out a twenty-four hour survey around the drilling location, to find that gas bubbles escaped from the sea bed around the drilling area. This wasn't good. Both men knew that time was of the essence and prayed that Mother Earth was strong enough to keep this roaring monster under her control, protected by the different formation layers.

If these layers collapsed under the unexpectedly high pressure, the rig would be the next to collapse. Explosions would ignite the oil and gas jet stream, with catastrophic results. Without any control of the BOP or mud weight, the oil and gas from the reservoirs would be released into the sea for days or weeks. It would mean a major disaster.

The personnel on the rig was reduced to a skeleton crew, a helicopter was standing by on deck to fly the crew from the rig if necessary. All well control personnel specialized in dealing with such situations arrived on board. Drilling equipment and supplies such as diesel and water had come in from Stavanger.

'Good luck. We'll be in touch,' Rob said, and hung up.

Before the meeting Rob called the supervisor in charge of the horizontal drilling operations, who told him that the rig was ready to drill in two days and changed the Norwegian status report from 'sidetrack' into 'accommodation and support operations'.

When he got to the meeting room, he was surprised to see the complete management team, as well as all the department heads. Had Von Ritter's little regrouping exercise already been completed?

Von Ritter welcomed them all. 'The reason I have asked the management team and department heads to be present is because I have received notice from my advisor that he will end his career with this company. After his holiday, he intends to look for employment elsewhere.'

There was a stunned silence, identical to the one that followed his predecessor's announcement of his departure. He could almost hear the question on everyone else's mind, *who's next?* 'I would like to ask the management team to remain here once this meeting is over,' Von Ritter added.

Still wondering what would come next, Rob started the meeting with his operations report. He distributed the status reports, told them that there had been no accidents and the described the progress made in all operating areas. 'The horizontal drilling operations will start within two days, and I assume that everyone has reviewed the Norwegian recap. He turned to Klein. 'Andreas, could you please establish contact with the Norwegian company to finalize the contract? The rig move is scheduled within three days.'

Fuchs, the HR manager raised a hand. 'Has an English course been organized for the Russian crew on board yet?'

'This contract only just came up over the weekend, John,' Rob explained. 'Please feel free to organize the language course. I'll let you know when to receive the first crew.'

Klein asked further questions regarding the contract conditions, whereupon Rob suggested they meet in the afternoon to discuss the details.

The head of the Marine department asked if tugboats and rig movers had been organized, and Rob confirmed that the Norwegians had already taken care of that.

The head of Safety wanted to know why the rig didn't require a safety case for such operations, to which Rob replied that these support operations didn't require a safety case.

Rob asked: 'What's the safety case status for our own rigs?' and was informed that the safety case template had been received. Once they review the template, they would decide whether or not to hire an external safety case specialist and complete the safety cases as soon as possible.

'I cannot stress enough how important it is to start the process at the earliest opportunity,' Rob said.

After the meeting the department heads left the room. Von Ritter asked Rob to inform the management team of the details of the Norwegian operation. He did, adding that the operations were strictly confidential. He advised the management team to follow the low profile 'accommodation and service' story to all personnel to avoid any questions.

Eberhart asked if information was available on recorded pressures.

'No,' Rob said. 'But most probably it exceeds 5,000 psi, as this is the rating of BOP and control systems on standard rigs.'

Eberhart asked if Rob required any service from his department, to which Rob replied that he made the suggestion to the Norwegian drilling manager, who would let him know.

Gunther shared his experience of a similar event that took place in Indonesia. Due to a driller's fault, the rig drilled into a mud volcano that was still active, emitting 100,000 cubic meters of mud, the flow destroying all villages in the surrounding areas. It had left a tremendous crater with mud gushing from points all round, and there had been a subsidence of up to fifty feet recorded in the area.

Rob thought of his own experiences: the disappearing rig in the desert, the rigging down exercise of derrick sections, his well control problems in the Java Sea area, the helicopter flight above the mud volcano in the same area, and his first blow-out in the desert. And all the result of human errors.

He was sure that everyone in the room realized what a tremendous impact this would have if anything like that would happen in Norway.

Von Ritter asked Rob to keep him up-to-date if there were any developments and closed the meeting.

Rob felt terribly frustrated. Not just because of his own experiences, but because of the fact that the same human failures had done untold damages to the environment, incredible costs and was responsible for loss of lives all over the world. Each oil company was trying to prevent accidents on its own. Still, no initiative had been taken by companies or authorities to combine efforts to avoid them. Data systems could be developed with a Tom-Tom voice saying 'go back' to make drilling operations foolproof and change the public opinion that drilling operations were dangerous. He had made efforts of his own to reach this goal by installing real-time data systems, but that was only the beginning. Enormous investments, time and expertise were necessary to achieve this. Automation was required to minimize the amount of people on the rig floor, but a driller was still required to operate the drilling machinery and drill the well, so the risk of human error remained the same. He decided to bring up the issue during the safety case discussions at the Bergambt meeting scheduled in two weeks' time.

He called Jurgen to discuss the modification status.

'We're making excellent progress now that the welding of the 15,000 psi piping system has been completed,' Jurgen said. 'Pressure testing is taking place right now and will continue throughout the rig move. All drilling equipment, BOP and control systems are functioning and pressure-tested. The tugboats are hooked up, and there are welders on board in case we need to do repairs. All personnel are on board for the sidetrack operations. I'll stay on board until they arrive at the location.'

Rob asked for Joop, because he wanted to know if the data system was functioning as expected.

'A few minor adjustments have been made,' Joop told him. 'But apart from that the system functions very well. One service engineer has been kept on board as instructed.'

'You're our company representative on board, Joop. You'll report to me. I'll arrange someone to relieve you in two weeks.'

'I understand. Thanks for the opportunity for allowing me to witness this delicate project.' There was a pause, and Rob could hear excited voices in the background. 'Have to go. The legs are raised, the rig is moving into the water'.

'Good luck over there,' Rob said, and he sent a prayer upstairs to protect the men involved in this risky operation.

Klein called, and they discussed the Norwegian contract. Rob felt that something had changed between them. Until their visit to Brazil, they had accepted each other as men who had to work together. This had now changed. Their work relationship had become nearly hostile, and it created a very unpleasant atmosphere. 'Is there a problem?' Rob asked him bluntly. But Klein would give him no clear answer, and when the call was finished, he quickly left the room.

His secretary's voice came in through the intercom to say that there was an urgent international call and asked if he would accept. 'Of course,' Rob said, and as he picked up the receiver he immediately recognized Bill's voice. He sounded different from his usual self.

'Rob, something's happened,' Bill said, the concern in his voice obvious. 'Two guys showed up at Luisa's home and showed her your photo. They asked her if she had ever talked to you. She told them that she'd never seen you before, but still got beaten up pretty bad. While one of those rogues left to get some food, she was able to seduce the other guy, and escaped through the bathroom window to call Carmen. We took her, packed everything in the car and left the country as soon as we could. We're in Paraguay right now and will leave for Houston tomorrow. I think that some people have been doin' some investigatin' to find out why there's no more drillin' going on over there. I don't know how this was organized, but it's pretty damn clear to me that some people here think that you are the reason behind their financial disaster.'

Rob could feel his heart beat in his chest. 'Bill, you did well. I wouldn't have done it any other way. I was certain that we'd found a safe solution, but now Luisa has been beaten up and has to leave Brazil. All because of what I started.'

'Don't worry about her, Rob. Luisa's fine. For her this is a once in a lifetime opportunity. It's every Brazilian girl's dream to go to the U.S.'

'Bill, thanks again for taking care of her.' Then a thought occurred to him. 'Bill, would you be interested in working as company rep on a very delicate operation in Norway? Starting in two weeks' time, based on a two-week on/off schedule for the duration of approximately six months?'

A brief pause. 'Define "delicate".'

'High pressure well control problems.'

'I'm available for your project,' Bill said without a moment's hesitation.

'I'll arrange for the change in contract and tickets.'

'Looks like I'll be seein' you much earlier than we both expected. But you be careful.'

'I'll meet you in Holland.'

So now he knew the reason for Klein's behavior towards him. What should he expect from Von Ritter?

He called the HR department and asked to change Bill's drilling supervisor contract from Brazil to Norway. Then he contacted Alek to discuss the reporting system from the rig.

Alek hesitated. 'I would prefer to keep the drilling reports confidential and limited to the rig and my office,' he said.

'I understand that,' Rob said, 'But I must insist that you keep me informed on operations at all times. I really need a daily report so I can advise you whenever I think it's necessary.'

Alek finally agreed that both Rob and Joop were to be copied on the distribution of the daily reports. He advised Rob that the internal blowout probably originated from a high pressure reservoir at approximately 4,000 meters. The gas had found a way through the different layers of formations, escaping at the seabed where gas had already been detected. Because time was of the essence, they prepared two separate 'slim hole' drilling programs. The rig was expected to arrive at their location at nighttime, after which the loading of additional supplies would take place. Then they would establish a connection between the seabed and the rig.

Rob immediately asked the HR department to arrange flights for Bill to arrive in Holland within ten days and sent travel confirmations by email.

Instead of walking to his apartment, he took the car, because he wanted to see the horizontal drilling location and talk to his drilling supervisor. Thirty-five minutes later he arrived at the location, where rigup operations continued around the clock. Ernst looked surprised to see him.

'Is anything wrong?'

'No. I just wanted to see how the operations are going. And I wanted to find out how long it would take for me to get here.'

'Rob, first of all, thanks for the rigup sequences. It has been a long time since I rigged up a land rig. It's really helped us to organize the daily planning. Now we can finish tonight and pump mud to kill the well tomorrow morning.'

'Ernst, could you show me around? It's been a long time ago since I last visited a land rig.'

Ernst showed him around, and after coffee Rob left for his apartment. It was on his way back that he decided to get himself a mobile phone, so he could be contacted at all times.

'I tried to call you,' Anne said. 'Jan wanted to talk to you.'

'I visited a land rig that starts drilling close to Hanover.'

'Will you be home early tomorrow?'

'I don't know. I'll let you know.'

This was the difference between hearing Anne's voice a few times in four weeks while being on board, or hearing her voice close to home. He could detect her silent messages for him not to work too hard and urging him to come home as soon as possible.

The next morning, Werner called to invite him to a farewell lunch at his house.

Then he ordered one of the first bulky, heavy mobile phones that just came on the market.

He carried out his regular work, but felt off-balance. After the weekend, Werner Brandt and Tom Lehmann, two of his closest colleagues, would no longer be there to join the morning meetings.

Werner and Tom had their farewell lunch together, and thanked everyone for coming. All heads of department and most of the management team were present, including Bernard Heumer.

Rob couldn't help feeling annoyed, knowing that the reason these three people had to leave the company was sheer greed. He didn't eat much and was the first person to say goodbye to Werner and Tom, knowing that they would understand his reasons.

When he said goodbye to Bernhard Heumer, the man told him that for him, job satisfaction and pride were the most important factors. 'If ever you feel that these things are lost, call me,' he said conspiringly. 'We can discuss the possibilities of your employment within our company.' Strange how this man could read his mind. Either that, or Werner or Tom had talked to him.

He called Anne to let her know he was on his way home for a badly needed recharge after a turbulent week. But when he got home he received a call from Ernst to say that they were having problems setting the whip stock. He discussed the available options with the service engineer and let him know the results. He had hardly put down the phone when the drilling supervisor from the German deep well reported total mud losses and asked for his advice.

Shortly afterwards Joop called with the news that the weather conditions had changed unexpectedly in the Norwegian waters. The rig was waiting on favorable weather, and they were unable to lower the legs on location.

Calls continued the whole weekend, night and day. He created his own workspace in the basement so he wouldn't disturb Anne and the children at nighttime, and had a place where he could concentrate on his work.

In between phone calls he went upstairs to try and enjoy a few hours of private life. Until now he had been able to handle the operational problems at the office or his apartment, but this weekend several problems were happening at the same time, and he had to deal with them.

'I'm thankful for the time we had together the past weekends,' Anne said graciously.

'It would be more practical to be at the office when these things happen, but I really don't like to miss any minute of you and the children.'

'And I would rather have you here with us for a few hours.'

'I know. And that's why I stayed.'

'Do you have to work tonight or can you sleep next to me?'

'I'll try to sleep next to you.'

The weather conditions in Norway calmed down and the rig lowered its legs on location. Early in the morning the whip stock tool was set successfully, and drilling operations started to cut the hole in the casing on the horizontal well. Lost circulation material cured part of the mud losses and the German well continued drilling.

Chapter 49

As he drove back to the office on Monday morning, he reviewed the events that had taken place over the weekend. Previous experience had taught him to stay calm and handle one issue at the time. He knew that if he rushed things he would become careless, and then the next problem would never be far away.

Before the morning meeting he heard that a management meeting was scheduled in the afternoon to discuss the transfer of funds and bonus system. *Well! They had certainly not wasted any time*, he thought. Everything had been arranged to close off the previous financial year with excellent company results, and a fat cash bonus to boot. Nothing they could do about it, as the majority of votes had been lost.

He felt sick and helpless. After the department heads reported their status, the morning meeting was soon closed and everyone was left to mull over his options. What were his options? Continue or follow Werner's example? No, something told him that he should wait.

He prepared the mining discussions for the next day with das Bergambt until it was time for the management meeting. Von Ritter introduced Franz as the new Finance Manager. All that was needed was a voting formality to steal half of the company's pension funds to beef up Wedel Shipping's financial results and accept the new bonus payout system. Smiles all round. But not on Eberhart's and Gunther's faces. They looked deathly white in their attempts to hide their emotions.

Von Ritter asked Eberhart to reconsider his decision to stop drilling operations in Brazil, as he had received a phone call from the local oil company offering very favorable conditions should oil be discovered.

'The decision was based on sound drilling engineering and geological facts,' Eberhart replied evenly. 'Investments have been transferred to the Gulf of Mexico. We've had some very promising seismic results over there. Rob, when will the Russian drill ship be available to drill the first well there?'

'The ship arrived at the shipyard last week for modification. Should be available in two months' time.'

Von Ritter said, 'Give me the contact number of the Russian Managing Director. I'd like to call him to apologize and explain the reason why I wasn't available for the joint venture signing ceremony.'

Knowing the real reason, Rob had to control his anger and handed him the phone number.

'We might have a possible buyer for the company,' Von Ritter announced. 'They contacted our agent last week. I've already asked our new finance manager, Franz, to complete the audit room and have financial and contractual information available for the buyer's representatives next week.'

Wow! He had organized that one well! Rob thought. So that was one of the reasons they had removed Tom and transferred the pension funds. Was Von Ritter about to resign? With the sale of the company, it would be a wrap-up. He would be done here, only to move on to the next firm to dismantle and destroy.

Dejected, he returned to his office for the afternoon report. The most important update was that the drilling assembly was ready to start drilling the relief well in Norway. On the horizontal well, the hole was cut in the casing and the drilling had begun.

After some setbacks, everything seemed to return back to normal operations.

He prepared for the discussions on mining regulations in Hamburg and called the head of the Safety department. He was disappointed to hear that no decision had yet been made whether or not to hire a third party for the safety case. He disliked the 'wait and see' attitude of the man, whom he thought had taken very little initiative to improve safety standards and was slow to take action on urgent issues.

He explained that it was a matter of urgency and told the man that if he needed advice, he should contact his colleagues from other oil companies or select a company from those recommended by das Bergambt. 'Do this within the next couple of days,' he said, chagrined. 'Otherwise, I'll will do it myself.'

When he arrived in Hamburg early the next morning, the office was already open, and a friendly lady offered him coffee as he prepared for the meeting. This last day would be the most trying, as the Director wanted the various representatives from the drilling industry to advise him on the more difficult issues that had been left unsolved by the different groups.

Once again, this showed that the inspectors lacked key competence, failing to see the interaction of people and systems and that for valid and logical reasons, some of the suggested changes were impossible to put into practice.

The meeting went on until late in the evening, when most of the work had finally been done. When the Director asked if there were any further questions, Rob asked if he would be able to facilitate in developing a data and control systems to eliminate humor error in well control situations.

The Director was silent for a while as he thought it over. 'We have already included the necessary preventive measures and training requirements in the safety case rules and regulations. From what I understand, you suggest that we use a kind of watchdog data system as an additional measure. But this is an issue that has to be initiated and agreed upon between the different oil companies. They should share all their well control experiences and find solutions.'

The Director thanked everyone for their input and closed the meeting.

While driving back, Rob felt that he was back at square one. Up to now, none of the oil companies were willing to disclose its well control failures to the competition. Nor did they wish to go public with such information. It might take another catastrophe to bring the different parties together to combine their available resources, he thought cynically.

For the remainder of the week only a few people visited the morning meetings and operations continued without any problems. Until Viktor called Rob on Thursday morning.

'Your Managing Director called me yesterday,' he said. 'He said that only the drill ship should be modified, as per our joint venture agreement. The agreement for the remaining of the jackups and drill ships is transferred to the shipyard. My company and the shipyard have agreed to modify and sell the remaining vessels to interested parties in the Western drilling market. I just wanted to thank you for the excellent cooperation. I wish you well in the future.'

Rob hung up the phone, unable to believe what he had just heard. So that's why Von Ritter needed Golubev's number! He immediately called Jurgen.

'Can you check to see if Von Ritter is a member of the shipyard's board of directors?'

Within minutes, Jurgen confirmed that yes; Von Ritter had become a member of the board only two weeks ago. The man was probably known in the industry as someone who was for sale, and who would cooperate with any deal as long as he was well rewarded.

He had to breathe in and out a few times to get the fury that boiled within him under control, knowing he had no choice but to continue working as if nothing had happened.

This wasn't a fair fight. He didn't have the right mentality to take on these men. These men were scrupulous and dangerous 'white collar criminals' as Bill called them. The day had just started, and for some reason he expected there were more surprises in store for him.

Von Ritter's secretary invited all managers and department heads to join the morning meeting. As they all took their seats in the meeting room, everyone was probably asking themselves the same question, *What's next?*

Von Ritter came in, accompanied by a man and a woman. He opened the meeting with the safety issues and asked Rob to report on the drilling status. Once they were done, he finally introduced the man at his side as Jack Moreland, the CEO of Buchanan & Ross Oil, an independent oil company in Houston, and the woman as his legal advisor.

'Everyone is invited for dinner to meet the new company owner on Friday evening at the hotel.'

The first thought that came to Rob's mind was, *Very clever planning.* First Von Ritter transferred the pension funds to Wedel Shipping, followed by the shipyard deal, cashed in on the sale bonus and, once he had completed all that, quickly returned to Wedel Shipping Company to plan the sale of that company.

Everyone left the room quietly, asking themselves, What about my job? After all, there would be no reason for an American company to keep a second office with personnel in Europe.

A friendly take-over usually started off with the same story—that all office personnel would keep their jobs. In reality that generally meant that the office would be closed within a year, with most of its staff fired.

He called Anne and told her that a meeting was scheduled for the next day until late in the evening, so he would be home late. Needing time to digest what was happening, he drove to the horizontal drilling location.

When he got out of his car, it was strange to see the drill pipe string hanging in the derrick without rotation. This time it was the pump pressure that turned the turbine to drill the horizontal well.

Ernst showed him the sequence chart indicating the drilling parameters. 'We expect problems at the point where the hole deviates fifty degrees,' he said. Together they visited the core lab where the geologist showed them the chart with different layers, based on the soil samples obtained at various depths. He expected that they would need another ten days of drilling before reaching the oil sands where the horizontal drilling section would take place.

In the next office they found the Deviation Engineer sitting behind his computer, the screen showing the present hole angle and the direction the bit was heading for.

He explained that a new tool had been developed, called the 'measuring while drilling' tool, which was capable of taking directional surveys in real time and that he was responsible for steering the well towards the target zone.

'With these deviation tools that are built into the drilling string, it allows us to change the direction the bit is heading by increasing the weight on the bit.'

Rob was pleased with the progress made, and after drinking coffee with Ernst, he left the location for his apartment.

If everything went according to plan, they would know in two weeks if their initiative was successful.

That night, Brazilian gang members troubled his dreams once again.

Only Gunther and Eberhart were present at the morning meeting, and they took the opportunity to talk about everything that was going on. All three men had wives and children, and their conclusion was that anything would be better than the present situation. But they agreed that the 'wait and see' approach was the best option for now.

Jurgen came into his office before leaving for the shipyard, where he had to supervise the modifications and upgrades of the drill ship. Rob told him everything that had taken place the past week and felt himself getting angry and sick of the whole situation once more.

Jurgen listened to him, and frowned. 'Is there nothing at all we can do about this scandal?'

'Jurgen, I honestly can't think of anything. My last initiative wasn't very successful.' He laughed bitterly.

'Listen to me, Rob. I have a friend working for the most powerful and influential newspaper in Germany. I'll talk to him.'

Rob shook his head. 'You know the risk. If they find out where the story comes from, you'll have to look for another job.'

'I'm not married. And besides, I'll easily find another job.'

'It's your decision. I advise you not to do anything.'

'Keep a close eye on the newspapers this week. You might come across an article covering our Managing Director's scandalous behavior.'

'Jurgen, I can't help you. All eyes are already focused on me.'

'I know. Don't worry about me. I'll leave for the shipyard after I've talked to my journalist friend.'

Dinner at the hotel was nerve wracking. Everyone felt as if they were the twelve apostles seated at their last evening meal, not knowing what to expect next. The new CEO made an effort to break the ice and introduced himself to everyone and tried to engage them in conversation.

It was difficult for all those who had worked hard for years to build up this blue-chip German company, only to accept that they had not only lost the war, but also half of their pension funds. And now, with the sale of the company to this smooth-talking American, they would probably lose their jobs as well.

At this point, Rob just wanted to go home. Once the first people got up to leave, he followed their example and replayed the week's events in slow motion in his mind as he drove home.

Anne was asleep when he arrived home, so he went up to see Jan and Jess and stayed in their room for a while before kissing them goodnight. He did not want to wake Anne, knowing that he would only have to answer her questions. He carefully slipped into bed and fell asleep.

381

Saturday morning he got up quietly to look after the kids. He wanted to slip back into bed, but she woke up and moved into his arms, kissing him softly.

'I wanted to make love to you last night. Why didn't you wake me?'

'You need your sleep. Besides, I fell asleep as soon as I put my arms around you.'

'Can I have the same procedure please?'

'Yes ma'am.'

After making love Anne fell asleep again, but he got up to watch Jess wake up.

For thirty minutes he sat there, watching, before she started to move around. She slowly opened her eyes, looked at him and said, 'Papa!'

Anne must have heard it on the baby monitor, because he had hardly lifted Jess out of bed when she was standing next to him.

'What happened? I heard her say "papa"!'

Rob told her that he had watched Jess wake up, and kissed his daughter on the forehead. 'Yes my love, I'm your papa.'

'Oh, it's so nice to hear your daughter say "papa" when she wakes up.'

'She just made my day, Anne. I'll never forget this moment. Let's see if our son is awake so we can start the day with apple pancakes.'

'How was the meeting?'

'Very difficult. To tell you the truth, it was more like a farewell dinner for the company.'

'Why? What happened?'

'They informed all personnel on Thursday that a meeting was scheduled for Friday morning. Von Ritter introduced the new owner's CEO and invited the management team and department heads for dinner last night.'

'Did you meet the new CEO?'

'Just briefly. But I'll get to talk to him next week.'

'What are you going to do?'

'We agreed to wait and see before we make any decisions.'

'Who are "we"?'

'Some of my colleagues.'

'I leave the decision to you, Rob. You know I could never work with those wolves in sheep's clothes.'

'Let's just close the blinds and enjoy the weekend at home.'

'No, my dear. I'd like to visit the zoo.'

'That's rather a long drive.'

'I have done some homework. We can take the train so that you don't have to drive, and we can spend more time with the kids. They have food on board, and a nursery.'

'Excellent idea.'

Just as she said, Anne had already prepared everything, and they soon arrived at Amsterdam's Artis zoo. It turned out to be a wonderful day, and the kids couldn't get enough of watching the monkeys, lions and elephants, because they had never seen live animals before. They were the last ones to leave the zoo at closing time.

For the first time, Jan and Jess had poffertjes, small pancake-like fritters that were grilled on a hot plate, sprinkled with powdered sugar and topped with molten butter.

During the train ride home, Anne had to show them the zoo catalogue with all the animals they had seen, while Rob produced the sounds of each animal, much to their delight.

It was late in the evening before the house was finally quiet and asleep.

The next day the shutters were closed. It was a day for bath and bed.

Chapter 50

That evening Gunther called. 'Check out the *Bild am Sonntag*,' he said. 'There's a two-page article about "our friend" in the paper today.' Rob immediately took the car to the newsagent's in the village, where he bought a copy of the *Bild Zeitung*, the most read newspaper in Germany.

After quickly reading the article in the car, he knew that this could only mean trouble for Von Ritter. Apparently a team of investigative reporters had been looking into Von Ritter's career past and had closely followed what he had been up to recently. It seemed that he was responsible for the sale and closure of at least six well-established German companies the last four years, and earned a total of twenty two million dollars in sales bonuses. 'The upcoming sale of German Hattenberg Oil to a U.S. firm would award Von Ritter with a staggering amount of eight million dollars as a bonus. Fritz Von Ritter was recently elected to the board of directors of eight different companies that had announced they were for sale or open for takeovers. Von Ritter was always accompanied by at least two close friends when joining any of these boards,' Rob read, and saw that the names of these friends in question had also been published in the article. 'Von Ritter consistently influenced the purchase of equipment and services by accepting bribes from service companies and equipment manufacturers and has earned twenty eight million dollars on the stock market by spreading rumors that the companies were for sale.' The article concluded by saying that Von Ritter was a serious threat to the German industry, and urged the government to interfere and prevent the sale of the renowned German company.

Rob drove home and placed the article on the kitchen table for Anne to read. She looked up when she finished reading and said, 'The shareholders of these different companies probably elected those three men to sell their shares to the highest bidders. Our bank contacted me two days ago to ask if we were interested to sell our company shares at forty percent profit. Because I knew that you wanted to sell, I sold the shares and transferred the money to a savings account until we decide what to do next.'

To put it simply, the shareholders' greed for money had created this financial disaster.

'Do you know who's responsible for this?' she asked, gesturing to the newspaper in front of her. 'It looks as if someone leaked confidential company information to those reporters.'

'I'll have to check.'

'Rob, did you cooperate with this article in any way? 'Cause if you did, this could be used against you.'

'Of course I didn't. I'm not an idiot. I've been attracting enough attention to myself these past couple of weeks.'

'I won't ask you why that is, you probably won't tell me anyway. I know your principles of doing fair and honest business. But tomorrow will not be an easy day for you.'

He nodded, frowning, and went down to the basement to call Jurgen at his hotel.

'Did you talk to that reporter friend of yours?' he asked.

'I did. But he told me that they had already been investigating Von Ritter for several weeks. He said that they were going to publish an article on him in the paper today. I was surprised by some of the stuff they wrote. I didn't even know half of what they wrote. Did you?'

Rob admitted that he knew some of it, but certainly not all. 'So someone else must have talked to the newspaper and provided them with all the details.'

'Rob, it must be someone from within our company. And your name is going to be high on their list of suspects.'

'We'll see what happens. I'll speak to you tomorrow.'

The first person he thought of was Tom Lehmann. Tom knew more details than anyone else. The second was Werner Brandt. After all, Werner had nothing to lose—he already left the company. Another possibility was that Tom had talked to Bernard Heumer. He was a man with a large network and a possible motive.

Upstairs he told Anne that someone else had submitted the details to the press, because his colleague was not involved. He kissed her goodnight and went back downstairs to prepare for 'question day' tomorrow. He had never signed a confidentiality agreement, because Werner didn't think it was necessary. He never made contact with any reporter and was unaware of most of the details mentioned in the paper, should he be questioned. What other questions might they ask him? He wondered if Von Ritter would be at the meeting tomorrow. Had the sale already been finalized, and what would be the reaction of the new owner?

He did not go to bed and left the house to visit the horizontal drilling location and witness the operations. The horizontal section was drilled without any problems and a 5-inch production string of pipe was run to final depth. They would soon be testing the production rate, and within one week they would know if the project was successful or not. If it was, then some of their present rigs could be started up again to drill horizontal sections in existing wells. It gave him a contented feeling to smell the oil in the mud as he walked over the mud tanks.

He stayed on the rig until the six a.m. crew change. After the morning meeting, Ernst asked if he had read the article in the *Bild am Sonntag*, curious to know his opinion. Rob told him that he was unable to say anything.

While driving to the office he realized how satisfying his job could be without the present disturbing issues.

He had hardly come by the reception desk when the receptionist asked him to go up and see Mr. Von Ritter straight away. She accompanied him to his office, where Von Ritter was alone.

'Please sit down,' Von Ritter commanded tersely. 'Because I have a few questions. Did you have any involvement in the cancellation of the Brazil drilling budget?'

The question surprised Rob—it was one question he had not expected.

'I have no authority concerning relocation of drilling budgets. But I did vote against continuation of drilling operations, based on the arguments as presented by the drilling engineering department.'

'Did you read the article in the paper?' Von Ritter appeared to be brimming with anger.

'Yes, I did.'

'Are you in any way involved in this? Did you talk to those reporters?'

'I was unaware of the details in the article, and no, I did not contact or talk to any reporter.'

'You have signed the confidentiality agreement. You must know what the consequences will be if you are in any way involved.'

'Yes, I'm aware of the consequences.' He did not want to mention that he had not signed any such agreement.

'My opinion is that you are involved in the Brazil cancellation, and this article. I promise you I will do everything in my power to obtain proof of that. I suggest you hand me your resignation now, or I will make your life a living hell and personally see to it that no company will ever hire you again!'

Before Rob could even respond, the door opened. Karl Miller, Wedel Shipping's Managing Director and the new CEO walked in, their faces grim.

'May I ask what is being discussed here?' Miller asked in an authoritative tone.

'Mr. Von Ritter thinks that I am personally responsible for the cancellation of the drilling operations in Brazil, and that I'm somehow involved with the article in Sunday's newspaper,' Rob said, very embarrassed. 'He has just demanded that I hand in my resignation.'

'Well? Are you involved in this article business?' he demanded irritably.

'No, sir.'

'That's sufficient for me. Please leave us alone for now. We'll talk to you later.'

Somewhat shaken, Rob went to his office and spoke to the drilling managers until it was time for the morning meeting. When he entered the conference room, he saw that Karl Miller, the new CEO, as well as all the managers and heads of department were there. *Oh, hell. What's next?* He thought as he took a seat.

Once everyone had settled down, Karl Miller opened the meeting.

'Good morning gentlemen, welcome to this special meeting,' he began solemnly.

'I take it that everyone has read the article in this weekend's edition of the *Bild am Sonntag*. As you all know, our shareholders approved the sale of the company last week. This sale cannot be reversed, because documents have been approved and signed by all parties. I have discussed the situation with the new owner, Mr. Jack Moreland, and removed the present Managing Director, Mr. Von Ritter, from his position as of today. The new owner does not want to be linked in any way to Mr. Von Ritter's disturbing practices. We have decided that the management team will manage the company so that the new owner will have time to make his own announcements regarding changes. I would like the management team to remain in this meeting room for further discussions and hope that we can continue our business as usual. I am confident that this very distasteful business should have no negative effect on our performance.'

Rob thought, *That's easier said than done*, but listened as Jack Moreland got up to speak.

The CEO welcomed everyone and assured them once again that Buchanan & Ross Oil was not in any way involved in Von Ritter's foul practices. His company has always done business honestly and fairly, ever since it was established. 'I've made a schedule for myself and Mr. Miller to talk to each and every one of you in private, so that I can get to know all the managers and heads of departments. That way we can better exchange ideas on what's happening.'

It turned out that Rob was first in line, straight after the meeting. He stayed in the meeting room, and Jack Moreland took a seat across him, briefly outlining his own career.

'We've chosen to buy Hattenberg Oil because of the very interesting discoveries they've been making in specific areas of interest, and the fact that you own a small but effective drilling fleet. That, as well as the joint ventures you entered into with a drilling contractor, and the joint venture you recently signed with the Russians.'

Rob was surprised because the Russian joint venture had just been reduced considerably by Von Ritter's actions, and he mentioned this.

'We weren't aware of this latest development,' Moreland said with a frown. 'Karl, you'd better sort this out. I clearly remember that the Russian joint venture agreement as submitted in the sale package included all the Russian rigs.' Miller nodded and made a note of it on his pad.

'Rob,' Moreland said amiably, 'What initiatives would you take if you were in charge of the company?'

'I think my priority would be to avoid human errors. I would make every effort to avoid human error while drilling wells to prevent the loss of lives and environmental disasters such as the Piper Alpha. My second initiative is about to be evaluated—to increase production rates on existing wells by drilling horizontal sections. And my third would be to look into the possibilities of replacing steel with lightweight materials such as zinc or Kevlar. That way we could reduce the weight of drilling equipment and platforms.'

Rob had plenty more ideas, but decided to keep them to himself for now. His time was up. They shook hands, and Rob thanked Karl Miller for stepping in and take action.

'I was glad we could interfere in time.'

While walking back to his office Rob thought about those last words.

In his opinion Karl Miller was first on the list of people to be replaced, because he refused to cooperate with the sale of Hattenberg Oil, preferring the buyout solution and continuing as a separate, independent company. Von Ritter, on the other hand, had succeeded with the help of his friends on the board of directors in selling the company to the Americans. Miller would have a tough time avoiding the sale of Wedel Shipping. Rob was almost sure that this would be the next company to be put up for sale.

But for the time being the management team was in control. It looked like the octopus had lost one of its tentacles.

Every afternoon he discussed the drilling operations with Alek. Rob was embarrassed when his Norwegian colleague asked him what had happened with Hattenberg Oil, having heard the rumors surrounding Von Ritter. Rob didn't feel like explaining and just said that business continued as usual. Alek told him that the drilling operations in Norway were progressing faster than expected because of the small hole size. The well could be at collision depth within one month.

Rob told him that Joop was scheduled to be relieved by another company representative the following week.

The interviews with the CEO lasted the whole week and everyone waited for changes to be announced. In the meantime an I.T. technician was brought in to reprogram all computers to standardize the daily and financial reporting systems.

Chapter 51

On Thursday morning Bill arrived in Amsterdam. Rob welcomed him at Schiphol and took him on a short Holland tour. He showed him Amsterdam's red light district and the famous 'coffee shops' on each street corner. Bill had his first taste of raw herring with chopped onions. They visited the Rijksmuseum and the diamond district, drove past windmills and went to the fisherman's village of Volendam to watch the fishing boats come in to offload their fresh fish. Then they visited the small, traditional fisherman's restaurant, where they had smoked eel for lunch.

After a boat trip around the IJsselmeer they went to a photo studio, to change into traditional Volendam fishermen's costumes and had their obligatory photos taken.

While driving back to the airport, Bill told him what happened since he left Brazil. Rob listened to him in silence.

'We rented an apartment when we got to Houston,' he said. 'Luisa moved out after the first week, because she'd met some guy who asked her to move in with him. She's doin' just fine. We didn't take any chances, as I'd been receivin' some strange phone calls, and left Brazil as soon as we could. We ended up staying at the airport hotel in Paraguay. Looks like we left just in time, 'cause one of my neighbors called to tell me that they had some visitors come by the next day, asking for our whereabouts.' He whistled through his teeth, his relief obvious. 'We went against the flow, Rob. We were lucky that everyone made it through okay, but still it would be wise to be careful. This "octopus" of yours has his tentacles everywhere.'

Bill boarded the flight to Stavanger for his helicopter crew change the following morning, and Rob drove home.

Chapter 52

While driving Eberhart called his mobile phone to tell him the good news that John Fuchs, the Human Resource Manager, was fired because the I.T. technician had found a large volume of child porn on his computer. He was the distributor of a worldwide child porn network. Rob remembered his friendly wife and felt sorry for her.

'Moreland asked me to tell you that we're expected tomorrow morning at ten in the office to talk about management changes.'

'Do you know anything about the changes yet?'

'Not really. He's finished all the interviews. He asked for Gunther, you and me.'

'Fine, I'll see you at ten.'

Anne had waited for him and prepared dinner while he kissed the children goodnight. He told her what happened that week and had to visit the office again the next day.

He just finished dinner when Ernst, the drilling supervisor, called to say that production testing of the horizontal well was scheduled for midnight.

'I'll leave here within the next hour,' Rob said and hung up.

Anne looked at him skeptically. 'Are you back on your rig schedule of minimum sleeping hours?'

'This is too important, Anne. I want to check if everything is carried out as planned.'

'I thought that you had someone on the rig to take care of that.'

'I do, but this is the first time for him and small mistakes could have huge consequences.'

'Will we see you tomorrow?'

'I'll try to be home early.'

'You worry too much,' she admonished him.

'A lot of changes are taking place, and most is out of our control.'

'Concentrate on your driving. And be careful.'

While driving he had time to think. He was happy that the HR manager had been caught with the filth on his computer and was forced to leave the company. But why discuss management changes without the contract, marketing and finance managers?

Once he arrived at the rig he was surprised to see Gunther and Eberhart. 'What are you guys doing here?'

'The same as you. This is too important. We wanted to see the result with our own eyes.'

The mud was displaced with water to reduce the hydrostatic pressure on the formation, and perforating guns shot holes in the 5-inch horizontal tubing section.

Together they watched the pressure increase for an hour, and Rob knew from the previous pressure values that things were going very well. The three men looked at each other, elated, and shook hands. The well was opened and the formation pressure pushed the water up until clean oil was brought to the surface. The well was closed again to observe the pressure for another hour. This was continued until six in the morning to determine the close in and producing pressures.

Gunther was very satisfied and asked Eberhart: 'How many programs did you prepare? This is very good. I want more of these wells.'

'I prepared a total of six drilling programs for the wells you indicated. Drilling is easy and just a matter of keeping the horizontal sections within the producing zone.'

'How many wells do you have waiting to be drilled horizontally?'

'I'll let you know in the afternoon. This was an excellent idea, Rob. This will keep the rigs and crews working. The production on this well alone has increased by three hundred percent. I'm glad we came out here to witness this great result.'

Rob addressed them, 'Gentlemen, let me know the amount of wells you want to drill on our leases. We can use all of our own rigs and the rigs available from our preferred drilling contractor. If we need more rigs we can hire different drilling contractors, as rig rates have never been as low as they are now. This is a one-time opportunity to drill these wells, because we have a head start on every other oil company. But they will soon catch up with us.'

'We'll let you know on Monday,' Gunther said, and after having a quick coffee, the three men returned to the office.

As he drove back, Rob remembered the Hungarian geologist who advised him to drill horizontal wells so many years ago. He was both grateful and pleased that Laslo's recommendations and objectives had worked out so well. They had been very valuable for him.

Back at the office he asked his secretary to find out if the Hungarian geologist was still working at Hattenberg Oil, and if not, to inquire on his whereabouts.

So what's next? he thought. This was something that was out of his hands. He would have to wait until the meeting. Hungry and in need of a change of clothes, he drove to his apartment where he showered and ate breakfast.

Chapter 53

Jack Moreland, Gunther and Eberhart were waiting for him when he walked into the meeting room.

'Gentlemen, thanks for joining me,' Moreland said. 'I'll explain the reason for this meeting. First of all, I have to say that this is the most diversified company we have come across. We know that Hattenberg Oil was originally a drilling contractor and has expanded to become a renowned energy company. That's quite an achievement. The purchase of container ships to drill in deep water, as well as the possibility to modify one of the ships into a floating production vessel, clearly showed the long-term strategy of this company, something which is very important to us.

'Buchanan & Ross Oil has studied the high prospect drilling leases in the Gulf of Mexico. We discovered that your company obtained parts of these leases and has an excellent relation with the U.S. government.

'Your joint venture with a preferred drilling contractor and the Russians is very useful to avoid high day rates. We checked our legal position on the purchase of the Russian joint venture with Wedel Shipping Company, and agreed yesterday that the Russian joint venture will remain part of the sale package.'

Rob nearly jumped out of his seat in his elation, but kept his cool.

'To summarize it all, these factors made it very attractive for us to start discussions with your company. Buchanan & Ross Oil has for years been drilling and producing wells on land in the southern states of the U.S., but we have no well engineering and operational experience to drill offshore wells. I wanted to expand into this area, because our target area is the Gulf of Mexico, and we want to concentrate all our offshore rigs in this area. Those are the main reasons for purchasing Hattenberg Oil.

'I completed the interviews with all managers and heads of departments to get a feel for the people that manage this exemplary company. I also talked to Bernard Heumer, your former MD, as well as the previous Operations Manager, Werner Brandt, to ask for advice on a number of issues we have to decide upon.

'My plan is to transfer those who have experience and skills that we don't have available at Buchanan & Ross Oil to the U.S., and leave a supporting team in Germany. The company will be managed from Houston, so Fritz Von Ritter will not be replaced.

'I agreed with the new Financial Manager that he returns to Wedel Shipping, as most of our financial issues are handled in Houston. That means that only a small supporting team will remain in Hanover. The HR manager won't be replaced because personnel issues are also managed from Houston. We will, however, keep some staff at this office to handle local issues.

'Safety is very high on my agenda, and after talking to the Head of Safety I suggest that we replace him with someone from Buchanan & Ross Oil whom is more motivated to lead this department. I'd like to hear your thoughts on that.'

Rob felt uncomfortable. The counting of staff had already begun—they would now have to decide on who was to stay, and who to leave.

Moreland continued, 'I know that this isn't easy, but I need to know your input on this. I don't want to make the wrong decisions.'

Rob knew that the CEO's evaluation was correct, and that Drilling Operations and Safety were closely related.

'I don't know about my two colleagues,' Rob began carefully, 'but my advice would be to replace the Head of Safety, but keep his assistant as support for the drilling and production departments. We also need to make a decision which third party to contract for the safety cases.'

'Do you have a company in mind?'

'Yes.'

'Then go ahead and arrange the contract. It seems that Von Ritter and some members of the management team were close buddies, including the contract manager, Andreas Klein. My suggestion would be to handle all contractual issues from Houston and transfer Mr. Klein back to the mother company.'

Rob felt that he'd had his say and decided to leave this for Gunther and Eberhart's input.

Eberhart agreed that Klein should be transferred back to Wedel Shipping.

'I would also recommend transferring Schultz, your marketing manager,' Moreland said. 'I found him surprisingly lacking on marketing basics, and he didn't come across as very competent at all. I understand that he has been outsourcing most of his market predictions to costly agencies. That's not we're we pay him for. I want people who are motivated and take initiatives to provide us with realistic market trends. Schulz seems to be lacking in all those areas.'

Rob was the first to agree, so that decision was quickly made.

'We don't know the European suppliers for drilling tools and supplies, so I suggest we keep the situation as is until bulk contracts are negotiated with a selected group of suppliers. We can always review the situation after one year.'

All three men nodded in agreement.

'We want to modify the container ship into a floating production vessel and upgrade all the Russian rigs for the Gulf. We've never modified rigs before, so we want to obtain that expertise. I therefore propose transferring the project manager to our office in Houston where he can set up a project engineering group.'

Again, all men agreed.

'We don't have an engineering department for mechanical, electrical and subsea issues, so we'll need your advice on that, I want to transfer the department to Houston, but I do realize that work is now mostly carried out in Europe. This may change if we go for the option of modifying and operating all rigs in the Gulf. What do you think?'

This was a difficult one for Rob, as the new engineering manager outsourced all the engineering work and had no added value for the company. After explaining this to Moreland, they agreed to transfer him back to Wedel Shipping Company and promote his assistant, who was motivated and capable of supporting the drilling and production departments. They decided to keep the engineering department in Germany for the time being.

Moreland said that he would talk to the people transferred back to Wedel Shipping Company and arrange for the corresponding paperwork with the HR department.

'Rob, perhaps you can notify Jurgen of his upcoming transfer to the U.S. if he is on board.'

'And now to you, gentlemen,' the CEO said with a perfect smile. 'As I explained we have a drilling department specialized in land drilling operations in the U.S., but what we lack is offshore drilling expertise. We can buy this knowledge, but then we don't know what we'll get.

'Rob, you obtained most of your land drilling experience in places like Germany, Libya and Saudi Arabia, but we want all land drilling operations to be transferred to our office in Houston. I want you in Houston, so that you can work together with our staff and share your offshore knowledge and experience with the guys over there. You'll be in charge of the offshore drilling operations. You'll have to join forces with the man in charge of our land drilling operations, so we'll end up with two drilling divisions.'

Oh Jesus, Rob thought. *What's happening now?*

'The same applies to the drilling engineering department. I want you in Houston, Eberhart. I want you to take care of on- and offshore drilling engineering and transfer all your know-how and experience to our staff.

'Gunther, your wells and production facilities are mostly in Europe. For Saudi Arabia and Libya, we pump oil and gas to refineries. Your supervisors are presently in charge of the horizontal drilling operations, so we'll use these men if we drill more of these wells. I therefore want to keep things the way they are. Because of your excellent work relationship with your colleagues here we need someone in charge of this supporting office, as liaison between the Houston and Germany offices, and your title will be Advisor to the CEO.'

He turned to Rob and Eberhart and said, 'Now, before you make any decisions, I'd like to mention that your transfer will be on an expat-basis, with all expenses paid for. And by that I mean: housing, a company car, traveling expenses and utilities, including telephone. Your salaries will be raised to U.S. standards.

'If the company does well, we reward our staff by issuing company shares at the end of each year. I know that you both have families and need time to discuss these changes with your wives. But I do want to know your decisions before the end of next week to prepare salary package proposals for each of you.'

Well there it was, Rob thought. Very short and precise. The cake was now divided into pieces, but how to tell Anne?

'By the way, I understand that the horizontal well testing took place last night. Did we get the report on that yet?'

The three men looked at each other and grinned. 'We all went to the rig last night to witness the testing. The results are great.'

'So you guys have been up all night. Then you'd better get some rest. Thanks for the advice; we'll meet again on Monday morning.'

Rob called Anne to say that he would be home for a late lunch. While driving home his mind was racing. He felt as if a freight train had just rolled over him. This new CEO was very straightforward and quite a smooth talker, but, but… yes why the 'but'? This was, after all, one of his dreams—to live in Texas, Houston of all places! And now it was being handed to him on a silver plate. Had he changed that much? He wanted to see the world, and never intended to live in his hometown for the rest of his life.

Still, now that he was actually living in his hometown, he never felt better. Was this because he had gotten used to this life and because Anne wanted to live close to her dad, or that he loved the village they were living in so much? He was at the beginning of his career. He had come back from the rig once, because of Mam's illness. Was he prepared to do that again?

The drive home did not give him any bright ideas of how to tell Anne. Maybe a good night's sleep would help. When he rounded the corner in his street he noticed Klaus' car. He was relieved that they had visitors; this could buy him some time.

Anne kissed him in the hallway. 'I invited the family for a late brunch because I have to see the children's report cards. Dad will join us in a minute. How did it go at the well?'

'Excellent. Can I take over the grades payment again?'

'You'll have to ask the kids if they agree.'

'No, Uncle Rob,' Dagmar said. 'We have a better deal with Aunt Anne. We're keeping it this way.'

'So be it. Where are our kids?'

'I put them in bed to get some rest before the family arrived, otherwise they won't sleep anymore. You'd better stay here, otherwise they might wake up for some strange reason,' she said with a warning glance.

They had lunch, and Anne inspected the kids' report cards and paid them the promised money, plus a bonus, as their grades were very good this time. Of course 'Uncle Rob' did not agree and complained that this was far too much.

He looked at his family around him and asked himself if he truly wanted to give up these pleasant, cozy family occasions. It was then that Anne caught his eye, so he quickly looked away, turning to Dad, jokingly asking him for his support due to his 'difficult financial' situation, but Dad was on the children's side.

Again Anne looked at him. 'How was the drive home? You didn't get that much sleep last night.'

'I had to concentrate, but it was very quiet on the Autobahn.'

'And how was the meeting?'

'We have to continue on Monday, because Gunther and Eberhart joined me last night on the rig. It got a bit late.'

'So nothing special?'

He ignored her question. 'Anne, did you already tell them that the company has a new owner?'

'No, I waited for you.'

Rob briefly explained that there had been a takeover.

'Can I check if the kids are awake now?' he asked Anne. He was desperate to escape her sharp eye, to avoid her questions. Somehow, she was always able to read his mind.

Dad and the kids joined him to see if Jan and Jess were awake, and with all the noise that they made, this was the case. The kids used the bedrooms as playgrounds, and the house was full of loud, love and laughter once again.

Agnes suggested spending the afternoon at the outdoor playground with slides, merry-go-round and rowboats that she visited frequently with her kids.

Dad sad goodbye and after lots of hugs and kisses he set off to join his bowling friends.

The two families went to the playground were Uncle Rob and Klaus took the kids rowing on the lake, joined them on the slides, climbed ropes, sat on the swings and spun on the merry-go-round until Rob got dizzy and stepped off.

The kids didn't want to stop, turning endless rounds until the sun disappeared, and only the prospect of hotdogs and French fries got them to stop. After kissing everyone goodbye, Klaus managed to get his family in the car and drove home.

Anne took Jan and Jess for two more rounds on the merry-go-round and under loud protest they also went home. Jess fell sound asleep while drinking her bottle, and Jan dozed off before Anne had even finished singing her first song.

'Anne, I managed to keep my eyes open, but you have to excuse me now. I'm exhausted. I really need some sleep.'

'Sure. I'll clean up and join you in a minute.'

He did not have to pretend, because as soon his head hit the pillow he was out like a light.

The whole family slept until nine, and everyone felt like a newborn.

'I saw you observe everyone at lunch yesterday. You were looking at them in a funny kind of way. Why was that?'

This question had been hanging in the air since yesterday afternoon. He knew there was no escaping it any longer.

'At the meeting we discussed how to integrate the two companies and to determine which departments will remain in Germany and which should be integrated into the U.S. office.'

She looked at him intently, turning slightly pale as it dawned on her. 'Please don't tell me that we have to move to the U.S.,' she said with a low voice.

'Yes, that's what I have to ask of you.'

'Oh Jesus,' she muttered, the tears springing to her eyes.

'I feel your pain, Anne, and I wish it were different. But in one of my first letters to you, I did explain that my work is everywhere. And now my job takes me to Texas. I took a career step back for my mam, but do you really want me to go back to work on the rigs again? It would mean that we could only live part of our lives together. The children are now at an age where schooling is no issue. Learning a different language will be excellent for them. You can travel to Holland whenever you want, and Dad can come and visit—or even live with us—at any time.

'We have to make this decision together, Anne. My suggestion is that we give it a chance and see if we like it or not. We can keep the house for visits to Holland.'

He only noticed more pain in her eyes, because she knew that he had already made up his mind. Any other option, such as going back to the on/off schedule and be together only part of the time, was unacceptable for both of them.

Anne sighed, wiping away the tears. 'When do we have to decide?'

'By the end of next week.'

'Please just give me some time to absorb all of this before we tell Dad and Agnes.'

'Take as much time as you want. And if you want me to tell them, let me know.'

Seeing her so despondent made him feel as if the sun had stopped shining and that dark clouds had gathered above the house. 'Let's take the children outside to get some fresh air.'

They walked through the forest and automatically ended up at the watermill were Jan and Jess fed the ducks and birds on the terrace. He listened to the familiar sound of the water splashing below, and it made him feel homesick already.

His mobile phone rang—it was Alek, who told him that a change in the drilling program was necessary to speed up the drilling process. They had recorded a considerable increase of gas escaping around the rig, and decided that after the casing was set and cemented within the next couple of days, the following drilling section would be reduced to a 4 ¾-inch hole size to speed up the drilling time.

'Do you have any other ideas how we can speed up the process? Everyone is very concerned over here.'

'Alek, change from rotary to turbine drilling to create faster rotation. That might increase the drilling rate.' He gave him the contact information of the recommended company.

'By the way, I hear you're drilling horizontal wells,' Alek said. 'How is that going?'

'Quite well. The first well has just been completed.'

'I'd be very interested to learn more about this.'

Rob promised that he would summarize the drilling program and discuss the process with him on Monday.

In the meantime Anne had taken the children inside and found a table near the fireplace. Of course, she had ordered apple pancakes for him and the children and pan-fried fish for herself.

Suddenly he felt the same as the other day, when the whole family had been at their house. Once again, he asked himself if he was really willing to give up these moments of utter contentment.

Anne caught his look, their eyes locking.

'Thanks for taking the children inside so I could answer my call.'

'I was just in time to get this table by the fire place.'

They did not want the evening to end, and Jess fell asleep in his arms while walking home. Once the children were in bed, Rob started the fireplace, while Anne poured two glasses of wine.

'Do you think we might be able to find a small town like this near Houston? You know I don't like living in a big city.'

'I don't know, Anne. But I'll certainly try.'

'What about preschool for Jan and Jess?'

'We'll find out when we get there.'

'I get very sad when I think about leaving Dad and your sister's family behind. I will no longer hear his knock on the door, and he won't be able to see the kids.'

'Anne, he is enjoying his retirement with his friends. Anyway, it's only a nine-hour flight to Houston.'

As his mam always used to say, 'Things always happen for a reason'.

At that very moment there was the familiar knock on the door. It was Dad.

'The shutters are not closed, and I wanted to bring the tax forms.'

'Would you like a beer or wine, Dad?' Rob asked.

'A wine, please,' Dad said, and then looked at his daughter. 'What's wrong, Anne?'

She started crying, so Rob answered for her, telling him about the changes and the decision they had to make.

'My dearest, dearest daughter of mine,' Dad said, sitting down next to her to put an arm around her sobbing frame. 'You've already given me so much joy all these years. You helped me find my way back! Don't worry about me. I like being in the company of people of my own age, the bowling, the cards, playing pool. I did warn you at the time you got married that Rob needs to go wherever his job takes him, and now you'll have to follow him. For sure, I will miss you all terribly, but you also know that I don't like the cold winters in Holland. Maybe I'll ask for a room to stay in the wintertime. Look at this as an adventure! As a new learning experience, and an opportunity to meet people on the other side of the ocean. Take this chance.'

He kissed her forehead. 'I love you more than anything else, but you have to live your life with Rob and these wonderful children.'

'Dad, I appreciate your saying that, but I just feel so sad when I think about leaving you here behind.'

'Someone has to take care of your home,' he said with a wink.

They talked about it until Dad saw that his daughter had calmed down. With a big kiss and hug, he headed home.

'Is it possible that people can actually feel when they are needed?' Anne asked.

'I've always been convinced of that, because I strongly feel that you need me.'

'Don't joke about this. I'm being serious.'

'I'm very serious.'

'Rob, I've made my decision. We'll go to Houston and see what happens.'

'Thank you Anne. I'll try my best to reduce the pain as much as possible.'

'Now that I've made up my mind, I suddenly feel much better. Could you please take me into your arms and make love to me?'

Chapter 54

As soon as he arrived in the office, he called Alek to discuss the horizontal drilling operations. Rob shared his knowledge of how to save time.

Alek thanked him for the information and told him that the decision was made to drill the 4 ¾-inch hole section with a turbine.

Then Bill called in for the morning report. Once they had gone through the operations status, he asked, 'Rob, I heard that Hattenberg Oil has been sold. That's true?'

'Yes, there has been a takeover. We have a new owner, Buchanan & Ross.'

'Yeah, I know the company,' Bill said with a small laugh. 'And I should warn you. You'll find that working for Buchanan & Ross Oil is not like you're used to.'

'Can you elaborate on that?'

'As things are now, we are able to discuss the necessary changes, where after you can make your own decisions and propose these to the management team for approval. This company is completely different; you first have to organize the troops behind you before making any proposal. The CEO is the only decision maker, and his staff all go to the same church and bible lessons. Most of those men are followers and will never go against him, because they want to keep their jobs'.

'Thanks for the advice. I'll remember that.'

'You have to, otherwise you're in trouble.'

Tom Lehmann also called Rob after he heard about his assignment to Houston.

'Rob, make sure to transfer your pension fund from Hattenberg Oil to an insurance company in Holland. Tell the others to do the same. That way you are in control of the money. Before signing the contract for your transfer, make sure that Buchanan & Ross Oil continue to make the same monthly payments into your pension fund while working in the U.S. Otherwise you'll run short when reaching pension age.'

'Thanks. That's good to know. Do you have any other tips or advice?'

'Yes. In case your employment with the company is terminated for whatever reason, agree on a settlement package plus a fixed sum to enable your family and household return to Holland. Also, get a U.S. account to transfer money to cover the first month before you receive salary payment. I'll send a settlement draft for you to review, as well as the forms to transfer the pension fund.'

'Really appreciate this, Tom. It's been good knowing you.'

'We'll keep in touch, Rob.'

After talking to his drilling managers he made notes for the morning meeting.

He then received a call from a colleague working for another Oil Company—an American who lived in Germany he had met during the safety case discussions at das Bergambt's office.

'Is everything alright?' the American inquired.

'Yes, but Hattenberg Oil has been taken over by Buchanan & Ross Oil.'

'I know that. That's not why I'm calling. The thing is our company has received instructions to put you on a blacklist of people not to be hired.'

Rob was stunned into silence, allowing the words to settle. Then he told him about the newspaper article and Von Ritter's threat a week before.

'Ah, that explains it. In that case I'll remove your name from the blacklist right now.'

When he hung up, Rob wondered what he should do. Contacting all the oil companies to personally remedy the situation was hardly feasible. He realized that the octopus had started a campaign against him, and decided that he would wait and see.

It was hard for Rob to see only a few of his colleagues and department Heads at the meeting. He knew that everyone must be nervous and that they all had the question 'who or what's next' on their minds.

Jack Moreland started the meeting and informed them that some of their colleagues would return to work at Wedel Shipping again, as their departments would be managed from Houston. He clearly explained how the different departments would be divided between Houston and Hanover, so that they could all go back to business as usual.

'But I want to make one thing very clear. Buchanan & Ross Oil took the option to purchase Hattenberg Oil at a certain date. This date was before the pension funds were transferred to Wedel Shipping Company. I have made sure that Wedel Shipping Company will return these funds to Hattenberg Oil's pension fund, where the money belongs.'

Jesus! Rob thought. This man made not only his day, but also everyone else's!

'Rob, I'll let you take over from here,' Moreland said, upon which Rob went on to say that there were no accidents to report. He outlined the present status of the drilling operations and announced that they had outsourced the safety cases for all company rigs to a third party. He asked Gunther and Eberhart for the total number of horizontal wells so that he could contract the required number of rigs for the project.

'Over to you, Eberhart.'

After the meeting he called Jurgen to ask him if he was interested in setting up a project department in Houston, which would be under his supervision.

Jurgen was momentarily lost for words. 'Rob, this is one of my dreams.'

'Well then, let's go to Texas, Jurgen.'

'Are you transferred as well?'

'Yes. I'll manage the offshore rigs.'

'Wow. I'd really like that. And thank you, Rob.'

He told Jurgen of Tom's advice, emailed him the appropriate forms and told Eberhart the same. It was then that Jack Moreland walked into his office. 'Have you made your decision yet?'

'Yes, I'm definitely interested. But I do have a few conditions. I want payments into the pension fund to continue during my time in the U.S., and I'd like an advance payment to purchase household effects for when we arrive in Houston. There is one more thing: should my contract with Buchanan & Ross Oil be terminated for any reason, I will require a separation package of one year's salary, the shares that I own, plus a lump sum payment to return my family and our household effects back to Holland.'

Moreland nodded. 'I can agree to that. We'll include these terms in your contract.'

'When do you want me to start in Houston?'

'As soon as possible. The HR department will assist you with your visas, social security cards, driving licenses, bank accounts, housing, and a household moving company. They will also arrange airline tickets for the family.'

'I still need some time to go through some issues with Gunther regarding the horizontal drilling operations. After that I can focus on my departure to Houston.'

'Then we'll meet again in Houston.'

This was like going on a business trip, Rob thought.

For the remainder of that week Rob carried out his routine work and organized phone numbers, fax and email address for the Houston office. He arranged for monthly payments to be made into his pension fund with the HR department and his insurance company. He told the drilling managers to contact him in Houston starting the following week. Then he discussed all outstanding issues with Jurgen.

Gunther and Eberhart agreed on the total number of horizontal wells so that they could discuss the number of required rigs with the contract department in Houston. Rob asked Eberhart if he wanted to fly together.

He went home early and asked Anne to see Agnes and Klaus and tell them the news of going to Houston. The mere mention of it brought tears to her eyes.

It was pouring with rain from the moment they arrived at Agnes' house, the miserable weather reflecting their mood. While having dinner they tried to explain to Dagmar and Thomas why they had to leave. The children simply couldn't understand why sleeping in the weekend house, their hotdog days and payment for good grades would no longer be possible. It was difficult for them to accept, and it hurt terribly to see them cry.

On Sunday the shutters were closed. Anna went through their things to decide what to pack in their suitcases and what to ship. They weren't going to take any furniture, as they wanted to keep their home as is, and planned to buy whatever they needed in Houston.

Rob would first look for a rental home in Houston and then arrange airline tickets for Anna and the kids.

The next morning he hugged Anna and the kids for a long time, and Dad drove him to the airport.

Eberhart was waiting at the check-in desk where they booked seats next to each other, and he took off 'with God' on his favorite blue plane. They had time to talk about the unexpected changes taken place during the past few months. Eberhart told him that his wife loved the prospect of moving to Houston, but both his parents were still alive, and he was very close to his brothers and sisters, so it would be difficult for him.

They agreed to give it their best shot and to wait and see what the land of opportunity would bring them. For a while they went through the items to be discussed in Houston, after which Eberhart fell asleep.

As Rob walked to the restroom, he came across the American colleague he met at the safety case discussions in Hamburg.

'Rob! What a coincidence!' Rob shook hands and sat down next to him. The American told him that he was transferred back to the head office in Houston and be in charge of the drilling department.

'I hear that your rigs are using a look-ahead planning system. And quite successfully, from what I understand. I wonder if you could tell me something about it?'

'Sure,' Rob said pleasantly, and spent the next forty minutes explaining the principles of the system. 'Call me in Houston if you want to discuss things further,' he said, upon which they exchanged phone numbers, said goodbye, and Rob returned to his seat.

He thought about the past years and knew that a completely new start was awaiting him. Most of his first operational goals had been achieved, or were in progress. Rob was used to setting targets for himself during the course of his career.

He was thinking about the fact that they often found oil and gas traces while drilling shale formations in the top-hole section of the well.

No one had paid that much attention to it, because financially it was not lucrative to produce. Therefore they increased the mud weight and set the casing to close of these sections. But the same geologist had told him about the concept of fracking shale layers to increase the production rate. Fracking of deep sand formations to improve production rates had been done ever since the first rotary wells were drilled, and that this could also be applied for shallow shale formations.

The advantage was that these formations could be found at shallow depths, although it did require very careful well planning to apply the technology that close to the surface. But it could be done. After all, when drilling wells at much deeper depths, Rob always had to ensure that casing and cement was tested to the maximum pressure before any fracking took place to avoid channeling.

He decided to make this his number one target to look into while in the U.S.

Part 3: Houston

Chapter 1

When Rob and Eberhart left the Houston airport, they ran into a wall of high humidity and heat, and appreciated that the rental car came with air conditioning.

He had never experienced eight-lane traffic before, but noticed that all cars kept to their own lanes and the American drivers were courteous by keeping their distance, not honking their horns—like in Europe, where aggressive bumper driving was the order of the day—made it a very relaxing drive. On the I-10 highway he took the Dairy Ashford exit and drove to the office, following the directions given on the company brochure.

At the reception desk Rob asked for the Drilling Engineering and Operations Manager. A secretary came down and explained that both men were in a meeting and that they would be returning in one hour. She showed them to their offices, which were located in a large space with at least twenty open cubicles, each measuring no more than ten by ten feet.

They looked at each other in dismay. This was quite a change compared to their German offices, where operations and engineering staff worked in separate rooms.

In the meantime the secretary prepared forms to obtain their working visas, social security cards, driving licenses and bank accounts. 'Will your families be living in a rental or purchased home?' she asked.

'Rental,' Rob answered for the both of them.

'Good,' she said. 'A real estate agent has been arranged to show you homes over the weekend. I've rented two cars for you. If you want another brand, please go to the car rental company and leave the airport car in the parking lot. Will you be shipping any household and personal effects?'

The two men nodded.

'Alright, if you could supply me with the details, I'll arrange for a transport company. Do you want me to book the flights for your family members?'

'No, I think we both prefer to wait until we rent a house.'

'Good. I've booked rooms for you at the hotel next door, you'll find this convenient.'

It was then that the door opened. Two men walked in, one of them black.

'Welcome to Houston!' the black man said in a decidedly African accent. 'How was your flight?'

'Thank you, very well, but we had to get used to the traffic.'

'Hi, my name's Abel. I understand you're from Holland! So we're both visitors to this country. I was born and raised in Mozambique. I'm responsible for the Drilling Operations, and this is my colleague, Brad. He's responsible for the Drilling Engineering department.'

Rob and Eberhart introduced themselves and thanked them for the arrangements already made by the secretary.

'If you're not too tired after the fifteen-hour flight, we'd like to show you around the office and introduce some of our staff members.'

'We'd appreciate that.'

As they walked down the stairs, Abel explained that the Head Office was in downtown Houston, with a subsidiary here at Dairy Ashford taking up four floors.

'Logistics and procurement occupy ground level, production, finance and personnel the second, while our geologists, the drilling engineering, operations and safety departments are on the third floor,' Abel went on. 'The CEO, marketing, finance and contract managers all work on the top floor. That's also where the meeting rooms are.'

They started at ground level, shook a lot of hands, heard a lot of names and were bombarded with a lot of 'Hi, how're you doin'?' and 'Nice to meet you.' They ended up having coffee with the CEO in the meeting room upstairs.

Jack Moreland inquired after the planning status for the Gulf of Mexico wells, to which Eberhart said that the well planning was completed for four wells awaiting approval and signatures.

'Great. Rob, what's the status of the jackups, semis and drill ships?'

'The Shetland semi will be drilling development wells for another year. One ship is still pending the decision to be modified into a floating production or drill ship. The second drill ship is in the Singapore shipyard and ready for Australian waters within one month. The Russian jackup is in Norway right now for sidetrack and well-killing operations. The Russian drill ship is still in the shipyard. It should be ready to drill within two months. We still have to decide which type of Russian rig we want to upgrade next.'

'We shall discuss that Monday morning. Tomorrow is Thanksgiving. I'd like to invite all of you to my house to celebrate this special day with us. I do believe you Europeans don't know the meaning and history of Thanksgiving. In the whole of the U.S. it's the day we give thanks for the blessing of the harvest. But here in Texas we celebrate our pioneers, the first colonists, who thanked the Lord for enabling them to set foot on dry land after a long journey at sea. Right. I'll be expecting you at my home at eleven. You can help us prepare the turkey.' He handed Rob a piece of paper. 'Here are the driving directions to my house. I'll be seein' you both tomorrow.'

Well, this was a nice welcome reception! Rob thought.

As they walked back downstairs, Abel told them that the office would be closed the next day. He handed them both two office keys. 'Here,' he said. 'This way you can still find your way in if you want to look at reports or make phone calls. Because of the different time zones you might want to set up a time schedule to call your Drilling Managers. There's a seven hours' time difference.'

After finding their cars, they drove to the parking lot of the hotel next door, where they had dinner together and agreed that their welcome reception had been very friendly.

Chapter 2

Rob woke up in the middle of the night, unable to sleep anymore. He got up and walked to the office and called his Drilling Managers, with whom he arranged to have their daily calls at 5 o'clock a.m. Houston time.

Then he called Anne and told her about the pleasant welcome they received.

'The CEO invited us for Thanksgiving dinner tomorrow. And we'll be looking for houses in the weekend. I'll take pictures and send them to you.' A brief silence. 'Can't sleep,' he said. 'Someone's missing over here. Love to hear your voice. Will you give our beautiful children a kiss from their dad?'

'We love you,' Anne said before he hung up.

He unpacked his office kit, filed his contracts and reorganized the office the way he wanted. Then he called Alek in Norway, providing him his new phone and fax number, and agreed to call him in the morning Houston time.

Slowly he began to adjust to his new environment. It occurred to him that as long as he had his communication means set up, his office could really be set up anywhere.

He reviewed the drill ship specifications to ensure that drilling the wells at maximum water depths was still within the design criteria, and walked back to the hotel. There he asked the friendly woman at the front desk for a Houston roadmap and advice on where to look for rental homes.

'I suggest you go and have a look at the nearby city of Katy. Especially if your office is located in the Dairy Ashford area. I live there myself to avoid long commuting times. Katy has all the characteristics of a small Western town. You'll find mostly cattle and horse ranches over there. Real pretty, too,' she added.

She gave him driving directions, and since he couldn't sleep anymore, he took the I-10 Highway until he got to Katy, where he drove around town. He loved the old-fashioned train station, the small shops, the banks, the post office, police station and traditional hardware store. He noticed a woman inside a hairdresser shop, parked his car in front and went in.

'Good morning. I wonder if you could cut my hair?'

'Mornin' honey,' she said in his favorite Texan drawl. 'I'm here because I forgot something and not really supposed to be workin', as it's Thanksgiving. I usually only work by appointment, but what the hell. I've got time. You can sit yerself down here.'

It seemed to Rob that he could not have selected a better place to get hometown information, as she told him where to look for houses, where the bank was, what shops to go to, which restaurants were nice and many other things that were of use.

This was so much better than a local newspaper, because she told him the town gossip, her political opinion and before he knew it, she was finished. Pleased with his haircut and equipped with useful information, he thanked her and said goodbye.

He drove to the places she had advised him to visit and noticed that most of the houses were in different housing development sections surrounded by tall pine trees.

He immediately liked Katy. It was quiet, provided country-style living, and it was only a short drive from the office.

Yes, Anna would like this area, as in some ways, it was similar to their hometown. He took several pictures of the city and returned to the hotel, where he thanked the lady at the reception desk for her excellent advice. He asked her which part of the city she would prefer to live in, and she indicated two areas on the map.

He thanked her again and walked to the breakfast room, where Eberhart had just arrived.

While having breakfast, Rob told him about his early excursion.

'Good idea, Rob. That means that we don't have to spend that much time searching in the weekend.'

'My suggestion is that we drive back, so you can see for yourself. We still have time before visiting the CEO's house.'

They finished breakfast, drove back to Katy and looked at the areas the hairdresser and lady at the reception desk suggested.

Rob was surprised that there was no new building there. Nevertheless, all the houses looked well maintained with manicured gardens and most with swimming pools.

While driving through these neighborhoods he noticed many 'for sale' signs. He stopped at a few houses that had 'for rent' signs, retrieving flyers from the box underneath the signs. The flyers gave detailed specifications of the homes, showing photographs of the interior, as well as the rental rate.

After looking at three different rental homes, Rob stopped to study his map. He suggested driving to a different direction, to a town called Pecan Grove. But after a twenty minutes' drive, he stopped the car. 'It's too far. This will take us too much commuting time.'

Chapter 3

Eberhart agreed, and they consulted the roadmap to find their way to Jack Moreland's place. It took them longer than expected, until they finally ended up in front of a long driveway with tall palm trees on either side. What they saw at the end of it was a three-story house they thought resembled one of the Queen's palaces in Holland.

'Unbelievable,' Rob said.

'I agree.'

'Is this the address?'

'Yes, the street and number are correct. So let's visit the Queen.'

As they turned into the driveway they saw large water fountains in front of the house. 'This man is really showing us the big American dream,' Rob said.

'Yes showing off success is no problem in this country. Completely different to Europe where most people don't like to show off their wealth or success.'

Rob parked his car in a separate parking area, and when they got out of the car, they could fully appreciate the actual size of the house. The place was surrounded by beautiful green lawns, flower borders and tall, shadowy trees, just as in Louisiana movies.

They took their time to look around and didn't see Jack Moreland walking towards their car.

'Welcome to our home, gentlemen! And happy Thanksgiving.'

'Happy Thanksgiving to you, too. You have to excuse us, sir, for gaping at your house like this. In Holland only the Queen lives in such a palace.'

'Thank you very much. But let's join the family and other guests.'

They walked around the house and noticed children playing in a large swimming pool. Moreland introduced them to his wife, three sons, both his parents and his parents-in-law, his brothers, sisters and two company executives. Rob counted at least thirty people, some of whom were gathered in the kitchen to assist his wife with preparing the food.

He noticed two huge turkeys with bread rolls in the oven, green beans in a special sauce and other dishes he never seen before, all beautifully laid out on two large dining tables.

Jack Moreland offered them a drink, and they both stepped back to observe the family gathering from a distance. Rob was surprised to see most people dressed casually, in contrast to Europe, where people usually dress up for such celebrations.

Moreland asked everyone to take a seat, saying that name cards could be found at each place setting. Rob was seated between Abel and his wife, while Eberhart sat between Jack and his wife.

Jack took one turkey out of the oven, carved it into thick slices and invited everyone to help themselves to a piece. After everyone was seated he asked for silence, said a prayer to thank the Lord for the food, his family, and the guests that had joined him around the table on this special day.

It was then that Rob realized that being there on that Thanksgiving day was something very special. For a moment he even felt part of the family. The atmosphere was very relaxed, with children coming in for food and playing outdoors while the adults enjoyed the traditional Thanksgiving feast. Rob had never tasted turkey with cranberry sauce and sweet potatoes before, and he loved it.

Abel told him that this was also his first Thanksgiving invitation, which he appreciated very much. 'The company's morning meetings always take place at seven a.m. Most people get to the office around six,' he told Rob. 'I'm real excited that the company has started offshore drilling in the Gulf. I would love to discuss the details with you after the meeting on Monday.' He wiped the cranberry sauce from his lips. 'What's your faith, Rob? Are you religious? Perhaps you'd be interested to join us at church on Sunday. It's more than just the church service. There's also a restaurant, a pool and it's got sports facilities as well. My family usually ends up spending the whole day at church.' He took a swill of his wine. 'I suppose I'd better tell you that our CEO and most of the executives attend bible lessons and church together.'

This surprised Rob. 'Well, actually, I'm a Roman Catholic. I usually try to spend most of my limited spare time with my family. Thank you for the invitation, but I was planning to look for a home over the weekend, so that my wife and children can join me as soon as possible.'

As he had his first taste of carrot cake, he somehow had the feeling that Abel was slowly guiding him through all the company's do's and don'ts. In Holland and Germany, religion, work and spare time were kept completely separate. After five days at the office, everyone wanted to enjoy family time and attending Sunday mass only took one hour. It was obvious that things worked differently at Buchanan & Ross Oil.

After an excellent Thanksgiving dinner, Rob and Eberhart followed the other guests' example and thanked Moreland and his wife for a wonderful day.

'Rob, this was really something else,' Eberhart exclaimed once they drove off. This man must be making real money to be able to afford all this. I've been part of the management team for years, but we never spent special days like this together. We always kept work and private time separate. I don't know if the sale of Hattenberg Oil or our arrival was the reason for inviting us, but I sure appreciated it.'

'I agree. Did Jack ask you about your religion?' Rob asked.

'Yes. I found that rather strange. I told him I was raised without religion.

Why do you ask?'

'Because Abel asked me the same question. I think this is high on the company's agenda. We'd better be careful. I didn't get much sleep last night, so if you don't mind, I'm going to get some rest and see you tomorrow at nine to meet the real estate agent.'

'Fine. I'll see you tomorrow morning, Rob. Goodnight.'

Chapter 4

This time Rob woke up at three, went to the office and called his drilling managers.

The Brazil well was plugged and abandoned, and the rig was on its way to Africa.

Bill reported that they were making good drilling progress and re-enter the problem well within a week. Rob told him that he was looking at houses in Katy. It appeared that Bill wanted to buy a house in that area if he found a job in the Gulf of Mexico.

'Why don't you work for me?'

'Normally I would, Rob. But I used to work for Buchanan & Ross Oil. I was promised the Operations Manager job, but didn't get along with the CEO. The company culture is built on stock price and financial results. Word has it that they tamper with accident records to show their shareholders excellent safety statistics.

'Rob, we have years of experience drillin' wells all over the world. Our decisions are based on long-term planning; we don't go for short-term financial results. I don't like working for a company where one man makes the rules, and necessary changes take forever.

'I'm not much of a follower, Rob. I use my own ideas to avoid accidents and implement changes that benefit the drillin' operations. We should not be hampered, but respected for that. Playin' politics is not my strong side. I already told you to play the game, otherwise you're in trouble. There's only one captain on this ship.

'There is one benefit, and that is that you can manage your own rigs. It will take a while before other "captains" will try to interfere and tell you how and what to do. My advice is to lay low, observe and don't stick your head above the grass. I've already sent my resume to different contractors and oil companies planning to drill in the Gulf. I'm pretty confident that I'll find a job.'

'Thanks for warning me, Bill. I'll keep it in mind.'

Yes, he certainly was planning to. This was already the second warning that Bill had given him. He walked back to the hotel and had breakfast with Eberhart. They went through the flyers of the rental houses and made a priority list of homes to visit.

At nine o'clock the real estate agent arrived, and while having coffee she recommended they visit three areas. She asked for the total number of family members and would show them one and two-story homes. 'Do you have any other preferences?'

Rob told her that short commuting time was high on his list. She explained to them that Katy was closest to their office on Dairy Ashford.

'We already had a look around in Katy,' Rob told her and showed her the flyers. After studying the flyers, she consulted her files and added three more rental homes to their selection. They agreed to use one car and drove to Katy.

It was a nice sunny day, and after taking the Katy exit, they parked the car in the town center, walked around and found all the shops or restaurants they might need or enjoy. Rob was surprised that the people on the streets greeted them. He saw cowboys driving their big trucks, and instantly liked this friendly, easygoing town.

When they left the town center, the agent explained that houses were built in different developments, and each development had a different name. They stopped at the first house, and when the agent opened the door with a special lock, they found no one at home.

'I always call the owner or people that rent before a viewing. Usually they leave the house to go shopping," she explained as they followed her.

They looked at six houses, but after the second one he found his home. The house he chose was a single-story home with three bedrooms and two bathrooms. It was built in a similar way as most houses in the south of Germany, with black wooden beams visible from the outside and surrounded by a nice garden, trees and swimming pool. Rob especially liked the walk-in closets next to the bedrooms. This was so different in Europe, where closets are placed inside the bedrooms. He took pictures from inside and outside, and the home exceeded his American dream by far.

Eberhart chose a two-story house, as he wanted more room for his family and guests.

The agent suggested they visit one more housing area near Cypress, but the traveling distance was greater. Besides, there was only a single lane road with continuous traffic jams. After reviewed their options they decided to rent the houses they chose in Katy.

The agent advised them to hire a home inspection company to ensure everything was in good order, and made the necessary call. Then she showed the market rates for rental houses and asked permission to submit a rental offer to the owners. After negotiating with the homeowners, they finally came to an agreement, pending the home inspection results. They would be able to move into their homes within two weeks. After returning to the hotel, she completed the paperwork, and after lunch they each signed the rental agreement documents. The home inspector would contact the agent and if everything was in order, she would deliver the signed by owner rental agreements to the hotel.

This was a very fruitful morning. They thanked the agent for the excellent service, and Rob quickly walked to the office, where he emailed the pictures and called Anne.

'Rob I can't believe this! Is this the house we will be living in?'

'Yes. Things are happening fast, and I'm sure that you'll like it. You'll love the area.'

'How are your colleagues? What's your office like? And what do you think of Buchanan & Ross Oil?'

He laughed at her questions. 'It's too soon to tell, Anne. We'll have to wait and see.'

'So you want us in Houston as soon as possible?'

'Please.'

'I need one week to pack and close up the house.'

'Fine, I'll book the tickets. Can't wait for you and the kids to come. One of my dreams was always to live in Texas. Looks like my dream is about to come true. The only things missing are the nodding donkey pumps and the smell of crude oil.'

'We love and miss you.'

He returned to the hotel and asked Eberhart if he wanted to join him for a drive and ended up in Katy to have another look at their homes. While driving he told Eberhart that Bill had worked for Buchanan & Ross Oil before, and the reason why he was now looking for work elsewhere. He also told Eberhart about Bill's warnings.

They discussed the importance to support each other, because they ran the risk that their employment was only for the short duration, to pass on their expertise to Buchanan & Ross Oil, after which their staff would take over. This had happened before.

Rob would manage his drilling operations and arrange all rig modifications with Jurgen and the new engineering manager. In principle nothing had changed, but they didn't know if they were allowed to manage their operations as before.

Their first visit on Monday morning would be the contract department to ensure that all contracts for the horizontal drilling rigs and safety case could be finalized.

He wanted to see more of the surrounding area so they drove west on I-10 and took a side road. The land was dotted with oil rigs and nodding donkey pumps pumping oil to the surface and into storage tanks. Some farmers here became rich because oil was discovered on their land, and according to Texas law, the rights to drill and produce belonged to the landowner.

And then something happened that made his perfect picture of Texas complete. As they approached a small town called Luling, he could smell it. The undeniable smell of crude oil. He stopped the car and wound down the window to enjoy the moment.

Eberhart didn't understand what he got all excited about and wanted to return to Houston. For him, this was an unhealthy and unpleasant smell.

Rob laughed and said, 'Your reaction clearly shows the difference between an engineer and a rig man struggling to bring this black gold to surface.'

On their way back they passed a Mexican restaurant, and since they had never tasted Mexican food, they completed their weekend with a very tasty Tex-Mex dinner. The waiter asked if they wanted to take the leftovers in a 'doggy bag'. Rob thought this was an excellent way to avoid wasting food, because in Europe leftovers went into garbage cans.

Chapter 5

Rob's first workday at the office began with early phone calls to his managers and a message from Bill that well-killing operations would take place in two days. If everything went according to plan the rig could be finished within two weeks. Also, Bill was offered a job in the Gulf of Mexico as an engineer for a survey contractor, and he decided to take the job since nothing else was available.

Abel came by his office and asked if he could talk to him after the meeting. Together they went up to the meeting room, where Jack Moreland introduced Rob and Eberhart to the drilling managers.

Each area manager reported the status of his rigs and Rob learned that the company drilled wells in three Southern states, as well as in Mozambique. The reporting started with the budget and actual expenditures of each well, which prompted detailed questions from Abel and Moreland on why certain expenditures were necessary or whether they could be reduced.

After Rob reported the status of his rigs, Moreland asked him how the budget and expenditures were controlled. 'This is included in the morning report, under the different expenditure sections,' Rob answered. 'It's easy to check on a daily basis.'

Moreland asked him to update his staff on the safety case situation. Rob told them about his experience with the German Department of Energy and the huge task the drilling industry was facing in Europe to comply with the new regulations. 'We've already contracted a specialized company to complete the risk analyses according to template guidelines for rigs in the European sector.'

'Do you agree with these steps in Europe, Rob? Do you think this will avoid future disasters?'

'A huge number of risk calculations have to be made. I'm afraid it will generate a lot of paperwork that might be hard to understand by the workforce. Safety and operational departments will face a huge task to explain that in plain and simple language to the people on the rigs. But all the energy, efforts and money spent on this exercise could be undone by one human mistake.'

Moreland asked, 'Why did Hattenberg Oil choose to continue drilling outside Europe without safety case?'

'The management team made that decision. It was a hard call to make.'

'Do you believe that experience, know-how and teamwork are less important than these risk calculations?'

'To me, those three concepts are the most important drivers. I just hope that the safety case will prove to be effective in avoiding disasters like the ones we've seen. The thing that always disturbed me is that I feel that a government issuing permits to drill and produce should never be the safety body to identify and eliminate the risks for people on the job. This is a conflict of interest. I think there should be a separate health, safety and environment department. Is this the case in the U.S.?'

Moreland answered. 'We do not have a separate health, safety and environment department.'

'If I may ask, what are your plans regarding the offshore rigs working in the European sector, and what's the number of rigs to be moved to the Gulf of Mexico?'

'My plan is to move the Russian jackup, the North Sea semi and the two drill ships to the Gulf as soon as possible to drill wells and determine which rigs are best suited for drilling in different water depths. The remaining Russian drill ships and jackups are to be upgraded in sequence and moved to the Gulf. The spare ship will be modified as a mobile production vessel, in case we are successful in finding oil.'

'Do you intend to complete the safety cases for these rigs?'

Moreland shook his head. 'Because this is not a U.S. governmental requirement, we will not complete safety cases for these rigs. We'll only complete the safety cases for the European rigs.'

'So you accept that disasters like the ones in Norway and the Piper Alpha can also take place in the Gulf of Mexico?'

Moreland met his look levelly and responded, 'Yes.'

'In that case I suggest drilling the U.K. wells with contractor rigs.'

'I agree with that.'

Well, this was a short and clear decision. And quite a solitary one, Rob thought.

'Then I'll check with Eberhart to determine what the water depths of the different leases are and make a selection of rigs to drill these wells. I'll let you know the estimated arrival dates of these rigs in the Gulf.'

'Yes, please. And what's the total amount of land rigs required to drill the horizontal wells?'

It was Eberhart who answered. 'Four company-owned rigs could drill fifty wells, and four additional rigs could drill the remaining wells in one year.'

'Very well. Rob, could you organize the drilling contracts with the contract department and let Abel in on these discussions? He will be responsible for these operations. And Eberhart, could you discuss and handover the horizontal drilling programs to Brad for review?'

Well! He did not waste any time to transfer part of their responsibilities to his own men!

And with that, the meeting was closed without even touching upon safety issues.

Rob joined Abel in his office. 'How did the house hunting go?' Abel asked.

'Pretty good. We both found what we're looking for. Can I ask you something? I was wondering why safety issues weren't discussed at the meeting.'

'Oh, safety issues were discussed between the area managers and the rigs before the meeting. These people have worked for the company for quite some time now. The crews are very experienced, and each rig has been accident-free for years.'

'What criteria do you use to determine an accident? Do the men have to return within 24 hours after an incident for it not to be defined an accident?'

Now Abel seemed lost for words, and he began to look irritated. It seemed to Rob that he didn't know the answer, especially when Abel brusquely changed the subject to the horizontal drilling project and summoned the contract manager to his office.

After his arrival Rob explained the scope of work involved in completing the safety case for the European rigs and showed him a copy of the contracts as negotiated with the contractors working on the current horizontal well. He was about to read the most important contract clauses, but Abel interrupted him.

'I want to review the contract before any further discussions take place, and I'll finalize it later in the day.'

Rob thought of what his friend had said, 'Lay low, observe and don't stick your head above the grass.' He told Abel to give him a call if he needed any help and left.

He called the HR secretary to book the flights for his family, to arrive next Friday so that he could spend the weekend with them.

During the week he kept quiet, went with the flow and determined which rigs were capable of drilling the wells in the various leases with Eberhart.

He received a call from his American colleague whom he had met on the flight to Houston. He told Rob that he had suggested the use of his look ahead system to senior management, but they didn't think it was necessary, based on the long-term experience and know-how of their staff.

Then he called the drilling contractor to negotiate the conditions to replace the semi in the North Sea and asked him to email the contract to him.

He was too excited to let small things ruin his mood. His family would be joining him next week! He called Anne every day to hear her voice, but hardly listened to what she had to say. Several times she asked him, 'Are you really listening to me?' But he was fantasizing and thinking about where they could make love for the first time in the U.S. Would this be in the back of a big Texan pickup truck?

'Rob do you listen to me? Because I need to know what clothes to bring.'

'You won't need any.'

'Be serious!'

'I cannot be serious when I hear your voice. I've missed you for too long.'

'I'm hanging up now.'

'That's probably the best idea at this moment.'

'We love you. And be careful!'

The rental agreement was delivered, and the move-in date set for the weekend. So he had ten days to arrange everything before Anne's arrival.

He called the house owner and asked which items would remain in the house.

'You can take anything you like,' she told him. 'The previous tenants returned to the U.K., and I paid them a lump sum for everything they left behind. Just give me a fair price and let me know what you need. You're free to collect the keys and move in anytime.'

Rob collected the keys that evening, drove to the house and found the home just as the day of inspection and completely furnished. The beds were already made, so he decided to stay in the house beginning that day. Outside he listened to the birds, and in the evening he watched their star just appear above the house, and thanked his mam for protecting them.

Chapter 6

The next day Rob talked to Jurgen about the progress of the Russian and Singapore drill ships and about how to move the semi to the Gulf of Mexico. Tugboats could be used for 'wet tow' or the second option was to 'dry tow' the semi on board a transport vessel to avoid weather delays. Jurgen summarized all pros and cons including the cost and forwarded these with his recommendations.

'Do me a favor,' Rob said. 'See if you can find anything on Abel or his family. I have this feeling something isn't right.' Just like I did with Schultz, Rob thought. Just like Schultz, Abel appeared to depend on others to camouflage his limited skills.

He went to the geologist and asked if he could study the well logs.

'Why do you want to know?' the man asked, somewhat suspiciously.

Rob explained that he needed to see them to determine the thickness of the different shale formations in order to decide the casing depths for offshore drilling. When he looked at the logs he knew for sure that gas was present in these formations. He asked Gunther to confirm.

'Why are you looking at those logs?' Gunther asked. 'They are mostly high pressure, low volume formations. They often caused problems for us in the past.'

Rob told him about his idea. 'But keep this to yourself for a while. At least until we're sure that the decision to move here is without risk of losing our jobs once we've passed on everything we know.'

Bill called and reported that the problem well had been plugged at the final depth and they had not detected any gas during the latest inspections. Rob felt hugely relieved that they managed to prevent a major disaster and he congratulated Bill and the crew on a job well done.

He had hardly put down the phone when a very elated Alek Frederiksen called him, happy that the very difficult and risky operation had been so successful. Alek wanted to give the crew a gift to remember this operation and asked him for any suggestions.

'Give them a Rolex. That will last a lifetime.'

'Good idea. I'll do that,' Alek said. 'The rig should be released in approximately two weeks. Really appreciate all you've done, Rob. You've been a tremendous help. If you need a job anytime, just give me a call.'

Rob quickly called the CEO to report the good news and walked to Eberhart's office to invite him for a Mexican dinner with beer and music to celebrate. Now they could move two rigs to the Gulf of Mexico, so he called Jurgen to include the jackup rig in his proposal.

'I have some info for you on Abel,' Jurgen said. 'Turns out that his family is very rich, and he's involved in every lucrative financial deal going on over there. He owns a lot of land and offshore leases where drilling is taking place and appears to have considerable influence within the government.'

'Wow. That explains a great deal. Thanks, Jurgen.'

At lunch he told Eberhart what Jurgen just told him, that Bill had been bypassed as Operations Manager, and Abel was appointed instead. 'It seems that Abel and his family are very important to Buchanan & Ross Oil to open doors in Mozambique. My intuition tells me we have to be very careful. I don't trust this man.'

Just before leaving the office Werner called and told Rob that Karl Miller, the Managing Director of Wedel Shipping, had been replaced by some financial controller from the banking sector. No surprise that no one at Wedel was enthusiastic about the appointment. How could he contribute apart from producing the annual financial report or preparing the company for its sale? 'Anyway. That's my news. How are you doing?'

'Doing great. The good news is that we have the problem well in Norway under control. The well has been safely plugged, and we have managed to avert a major disaster. Feels real good, I can tell you.'

'Thank you, son. That really is good news. Keep me informed. The door is always open if you decide to work for me again.'

Rob and Eberhart went for dinner at the Tex-Mex restaurant and celebrated the evening with too much Mexican beer. Just before going to sleep he called Anne.

'Okay, what's going on? You sound different,' she said.

'Do you remember the good news I had back in Hanover, and me celebrating it with too many beers?'

'Yes, I remember you had a bad hangover the next day.'

'Well, I'll probably have a bad hangover tomorrow. We managed to solve the problem well in Norway, and we celebrated it with Mexican beer,' he grinned drunkenly into the phone.

'I think you'll have a Mexican hangover tomorrow. Can't help you with that.'

'Oh, but you can help me a lot,' he said with a hiccup.

'We can talk about that in a few days.'

'I'd like that. Now if you don't mind I want to rest my head.'

'I love you, Rob.'

'I can't feel that.'

'You will in four days' time.'

Chapter 7

He paid dearly for his beers the following day and promised himself again he would never drink again.

At the morning meeting Moreland informed everyone about the successful well-killing operations in Norway. 'Rob and Eberhart have submitted a detailed plan with recommendations to move two rigs and one drill ship to the Gulf of Mexico. I'll be making my decision about this within a week.'

Rob and Eberhart answered the questions they were asked, but kept a low profile and volunteered little. Both Jack and Abel would come into

Rob's office every day probing for information. Rob gave Abel a very short recap of the problems experienced while drilling the Libyan and Saudi onshore wells and told the onshore drilling managers to report to Abel from that day on.

In spite of the long working hours of everyone, it seemed that many of the staff were spending quite some time on private matters or monitoring the stock market.

Rob went shopping for food and household supplies and nearly forgot to buy car seats for the kids. On the day that Anne and the children were due to arrive, he was at the airport one hour before landing. He went to the roof of the airport building to watch the planes land and take off, eagerly looking out for the familiar, sky-blue plane.

Then he finally saw the big 747 come in and touch down gently on the runway, upon which it taxied towards the gate beneath him. His heart was beating overtime as he ran down to the arrival hall.

First he saw Jan running towards the door, waving happily as he called out to him. He picked him up, felt his small arms around his neck and couldn't stop the tears.

Then he saw Anne walking towards him with Jess, and the next moment he held both his children in his arms.

'Where is your baggage?' he asked, seeing her with only a handbag.

'I hired someone to take care of that,' she said airily. 'He should be here in a minute.'

It was then that he saw Bill, pushing a trolley loaded with suitcases. He stared at him blankly for a moment, completely lost for words.

'What were you doing on this flight? I thought you were planning to leave the rig next week?' he exclaimed.

'We had some inside flight information. Joop volunteered to relieve me so I was able to assist your beautiful lady during the flight.'

'That's good of you, Bill. Thanks a lot.'

'You have to thank Jurgen. He arranged this.'

'Can we drive you home?'

'Thanks, Rob, but my lady is waiting outside in the car.'

Happily they went outside to say hello to Carmen, and agreed to have dinner sometime the following week.

Rob stowed the baggage in the boot of the car and put Jan and Jess in their seats.

'Do you now have time to give me a kiss?' Anne asked teasingly.

'You can have all you want.'

'This is not the Autobahn in Germany, darling. Besides, we now have two pairs of eyes watching us very carefully.'

'It's wonderful to see you all.'

'I was glad that Bill was on board. We were both seated in the middle section with three seats in a row. Jan nearly slept the whole flight on Bill's side and I took Jess.'

'That's great! I'll thank Jurgen for that later.'

'Rob, Bill is a good guy. He told me he's proud to be your friend.'

'I owe him a lot.'

As he was about to leave the airport car park the children pointed at the planes landing and taken off on the tarmac. 'How was it to leave home?'

He saw the tears sprung in her eyes, and she quickly rested her head on his shoulder. When they came to the Katy exit, Anne and the children became alert. Rob drove around town and showed them everything, and he delighted in their reactions as they tried to take it all in.

Anne looked around her in wonder. 'You made a wise decision to choose this city, Rob.'

'Just wait until you see our home, Anne.'

When he stopped the car in front of the house, she just sat there and stared at it, unable to say a word.

'It's... it's lovely, Rob,' she almost gasped. 'Thank you for choosing this house.'

'What do you want to see first? The garden or the inside of the house?'

'The garden, please.'

Rob took the children and opened the garden gate. Anne stepped in first, followed by two very excited children who pointed and shouted with absolute glee once they had spotted the pool. Rob could see from Anne's expression that she loved what she saw.

'Can you please carry me inside, my lord?'

'If you take Jess, then I'll take Jan. We'll do this for the second time.'

They carried them inside the house, and Jan ran from room to room, loudly exclaiming his amazement at everything he saw. Anne walked with Jess around the house in quiet wonder, taking it all in with a broadening smile. She finally came in to the kitchen and sat down at the kitchen table.

'I must admit I had a lot of sleepless nights over this. I shed a lot of tears, Rob. But thank you for this. It's wonderful. We'll create our second home here. I'm glad that you brought me to Katy, Texas.'

He reached over and took her hand in his own. 'Thanks for taking this step with me, Anne. I know it was a difficult one for you to take.'

Rob had prepared spaghetti Bolognese and set the table so that Anna could put the kids in the bath and get them ready for bed.

After dinner he helped Jess into her pajamas. She looked up at him with her big blue eyes.

'Yes, I'm your daddy and I love you very much,' he said, and she gave him a smile so bright that it seemed to light up the entire room. He could not resist kissing her on her belly, which made her giggle so much that he didn't want to stop, feeling delirious at having his little girl near him again. Anne finally told him to stop because she was getting out of breath.

'So,' he said, content at seeing Anne in Jan's room, which had previously been so empty. 'Do you think you could get used to this way of life?'

'I would give part of my life for this.'

'Don't say that. We'll enjoy this every day.'

Rob read Jan a story and tucked him into bed, but Jan wanted another story and more kisses before he was finally ready for sleep.

At last the house fell quiet. Together they wiped down the bathroom and cleaned the kitchen, when Rob accidentally touched Anne's breast. It seemed as if everything inside of him sprung to live.

She, too, felt the sparks between them. 'I assume that you don't have your 'love skin' here. Shall we get some towels and go for a swim?'

'You know that water has little effect on me in that department. But sure, let's go for a swim.'

He switched on the pool light, which caused the pool to shimmer in bright, blue light. The water was warm, and he watched her move through the clear water. 'Please take off your swimsuit,' he said.

'Aren't you coming in?' she said with a provocative smile as she slipped off her top.

'This is cruel. You know that I want to make love to you. You'll only tease me to death.'

'Just come in and catch me.'

He jumped in, and pulled her naked form against his own. Neither of them knew that making love in a swimming pool could be that exciting.

Afterwards they put the towels on the grass and watched their star above them, and made love until the cold forced them to move inside.

'Rob, did I already tell you that I love you?'

'Yes! I felt it in every part of my body.'

'Please come and hold me close to you. I'm dead tired. But wake me if you can't sleep.'

Chapter 8

He was the first to wake up, so he dressed and went to the garage to drive out the car he bought from the lady that belonged to the previous tenants who returned to the U.K. He parked the car in the driveway and went back inside, where he prepared breakfast and listened to the baby monitor, eager for the children to awaken.

He had dozed off when he felt two hands covering his eyes.

'Guess who?'

'I know those hands, because they brought me a great deal of excitement last night.'

'Do you recognize these lips?'

'Yes I also recognize those lips, for the very same reason.'

'Good morning my dear,' Anne said as she luxuriously draped her arms around his neck. 'How long have you been waiting for me?'

'A couple of hours.'

'Liar!'

'I'm waiting for the gardener to come and advise us on which plants to put in the garden.'

'I think he's here now. I noticed a car in the driveway.'

'That's not his car. He drives a big truck for all his tools.'

'Whose car is it then?'

'Yours.'

'Mine?'

'Yes, yours. Because you can't do your shopping and take the kids to preschool on a bike as you did back home.'

She was beaming now, like a little girl. 'Can I please go and see the car?'

'Here are the keys,' he said, dangling them in front of her. 'Go ahead.'

He followed her and watched how she first circled the car, inspecting it from all sides. Then she opened the door and sat down, started the car and drove back and forth on the driveway. Her face was flushed with excitement.

'Is this really mine?' she asked, her voice awed.

'Yes, this is your car.'

'I love everything about it! An automatic! I won't have to switch gears anymore.'

'That's right.'

'Do you have any more surprises in store for me?'

'I think this is enough for one day.'

'Thanks. I'll take really good care of it. But could you please buy me a bicycle? I noticed concrete walkways on the side of the road to the town center. I'd love to cycle here.'

'Anne, you'll be in the local newspaper front page if you do. No one rides bicycles here.'

'I'm Dutch, and I want to ride my bicycle.'

'Okay, we'll check if there are bicycle paths leading into town. It's too dangerous to cycle on the road because drivers don't expect cyclists there.'

It was a thoroughly enjoyable weekend. He told Anne about the deal he had made with the homeowner and that she could choose which items of furniture to keep or return.

They ended up buying bicycles and cycled into town. The kids absolutely loved it, as did the people in town, for whom it was a novelty to watch these crazy Dutch riding their bicycles.

When it was time to get back to work on Monday, he didn't want to leave them alone, but this time he was only minutes away.

The first thing he did was call Jurgen to thank him for putting Bill on the same flight as Anne.

Chapter 9

Eberhart and Rob quickly adjusted to the company's management style. Bill's advice had been very valuable. If there was something they wanted done, they would carefully let it drop as a suggestion during lunch. Within days, the idea would come up in one of the meetings, usually at Brad or Abel's initiative, taking the credit after Jack give it the green light.

Abel wanted to know how Rob managed his operations, so he explained the planning system by showing him examples on his PC. 'Oh, but I don't think we'll need a system like this,' Abel said. 'My drilling supervisors are very good. They've got years of experience.'

'Well, no one is perfect. Anyone can make a mistake. Why don't you put the system to the test, just to try it?'

'No, I don't think so, Rob, but thank you anyway.' Rob left it at that, but he still had the feeling that Abel was interested, but too proud to ask for more details.

Every week they had dinner with either Bill and Carmen or with Eberhart's family, evenings which they very much enjoyed.

Anne loved to visit the mall at Katy Mills and was just amazed at the quantity and variety of the shops, often going there with Jess while Jan was at kindergarten. Jan soon spoke better English than Dutch, as he easily picked up words while at play.

It didn't take long before Rolex watches were delivered with the names and well-killing date for every person involved in the Norwegian project, and he thanked Alek for that.

Rob visited the production manager and asked for the company's gas production rates. 'Why do you want to know?' That same question again, suspicious as always.

'I want to compare them with the rates of wells that I've drilled.' What he really wanted to know is which wells had large shale sections. If the production rates of these wells had decreased, they could try to frack these formations to increase production rates again.

The man provided him with the information, but the next morning Abel asked him why he wanted to know. Rob wondered why everyone was being so difficult about sharing information. Or did they have something to hide? He gave Abel the same answer as he had given the production manager, but Abel didn't seem satisfied.

Rob talked about it to Eberhart, and they decided to bring the idea forward, instead of Abel and Brad getting all the credit. They would complete the engineering and operational work to carry out fracking operations on one well and then propose the project to Jack.

Two weeks later, at a morning meeting, Jack asked Rob why he had asked for the gas production rates. Rob sighed. There was no reason to put it off any longer, so he explained his idea. All their engineering and operational work for a pilot project had nearly been done, and would be ready for his approval. They had carefully selected the deepest shale sections, and ran another string of casing to avoid any channeling to the surface or into drinking water formations.

Moreland looked astonished. 'Has this process been used before?'

'Yes,' Rob confirmed. 'This technology has been used for years to stimulate production rates of existing wells. The only difference is that these wells mostly produce from deep sand formations. The fracking pressures used at these depths can't be applied at shallow depths.'

'Has this been discussed with the other members of staff yet?'

'Not yet. We first wanted to complete the engineering work and check the availability of equipment before we put the idea forward. We wanted to avoid disappointment in case the project couldn't be executed.'

He noticed the looks on their faces. He knew for a fact that they would have liked to have gotten credit for this idea.

'So when will the proposal be ready? And how long will it take to carry out the pilot project?'

'The pilot project should take approximately one month to set and cement the casing,' Eberhart said. 'Fracking and injecting large volumes of fluid will take up most of the time.'

'Can't the fracking be done without running and cementing an additional casing string?'

Rob answered, 'Risk to the environment would be too high if we did the fracking without, because these top-hole sections are only protected by one casing string. I'd like to be put in charge of the project, as I already have considerable experience in this field.'

Everyone was excited. An increase in gas production with the present gas prices would result in additional cash flow and with that the company's stock price.

Moreland asked Abel and Brad to give them their full assistance, as he wanted the proposal on his desk as soon as possible.

'Do you want to "dry tow" or "wet tow" the vessels?' Rob asked. 'Personally, I'd recommend dry towing.'

'Then dry towing it is,' Moreland said. 'You can go ahead and finalize the contract with your Dutch towage company; they're specialized in this kind of work.'

Rob had already finished everything on the operational side for the fracking project, so he dedicated most of his time finalizing the contract with the towing company to load the jackup within two weeks.

The semi would complete the well within three months, so he would need another vessel to transport the rig. They intended to use the same principle as with the salvaged submarine, where the ship is ballasted with water and submerged, the rig pulled in place after which the ship is de-ballasted and raised to start dry towing the rig to the Gulf of Mexico.

He checked the drilling program for the Gulf wells, made some adjustments and left his office to take them to Eberhart. When he returned he found Abel at his desk looking at and printing some of the planning sequences of the wells.

Abel looked up, embarrassed at being caught red-handed. 'I hope you don't mind that I printed these sequences. I was just waiting for you to have a look at the drilling programs for the offshore wells.' He flashed a smile at him, but Rob knew that it wasn't sincere.

'First of all, I don't like it when someone comes snooping in to look at my papers, computer and starts printing copies of stuff when I'm not there,' Rob said, annoyed. 'Ask me next time. I did show you the system and offered you to use it. And if you want any information concerning the drilling programs, Eberhart has got it. He has to make some adjustments.'

'Thank you. I will ask him for a copy.'

So it had already begun. He was right—this man couldn't be trusted. It was obvious that Abel wanted to be in charge of the complete drilling division.

The next thing he did was to remove the planning system and all of his personal information from the company computer.

Chapter 10

The fracking project was approved by the CEO and began within a week. The operations went like clockwork, and within two months they had yielded a large volume of gas from the shale formations. Moreland decided to transfer the responsibilities for the next wells to Abel, as the operations were to be carried out with his land rigs.

The jackup and the semi rigs were moved to the Gulf of Mexico, soon followed by the drill ship. Rob was kept busy starting up the wells, ordering equipment, negotiating the contracts and hiring personnel. Before each rig startup he went on board to introduce the planning system until everyone knew and understood his role during the different drilling sequences. He always had the sequences of each operation on his desk before the next sequence took place to make sure nothing was left out.

They estimated that it would take up to four months to drill one well, and hoped to carry out the well-testing afterwards.

Jurgen moved to the U.S. and traveled between Houston and the shipyards, while Joop remained in Holland. Rob, Eberhart, Jurgen, Joop and Heinz—who was now engineering manager—worked well together and formed a close and first-rate team. They all tried to keep the information on the operations to themselves, and found that by supporting each other, they could work well together without too much interference from others.

Eberhart asked for a copy of the planning system, saying he wanted to add some comments, and Rob handed him a copy.

During the morning meetings, both Brad and Abel made several attempts to interfere with their operation, often disputing the costs related to their wells. Nonetheless they kept a steady course based on their combined skills, planning and know-how.

Rob, Eberhart and Jurgen attended many extravagant company parties held at Jack and Abel's luxurious homes. One day Jurgen entered the names of the company Executives in the public U.S. tax data system. Jurgen discovered that the salaries and bonuses that these men were paid were completely off the scale, and informed Rob and Eberhart.

So that's why the CEO and his staff lived in such decadence! Rob thought. But he had to admit, life was also good for him. Rob enjoyed being home every night to see the kids grow up and become fluent in two languages, while Anne kept close contact with Dad and Agnes and her family, who looked after their house in Holland. Anne adapted easily to life in Texas and quickly found her way around, driving like a real trucker on the highways of Houston.

Bill Turner was now working at various offshore rigs, only too happy to be close to Texas, where he now had Carmen waiting for him.

Werner moved to the U.S. to work for Bernard Heumer. Together they started a turnkey company, drilling wells for a fixed rate. They had asked Rob to come and work for them, but he wanted to remain where he was for at least one year, and then make his decision. Besides, he was curious to know how far Abel and Brad would go to try and take over their operations and if the CEO would allow this to happen.

The first well was completed and the well testing results were above expectations. It seemed that the German geologist knew exactly which leases to pick, as every lease had so far produced oil or gas.

The order was given to the shipyard in Finland to modify the spare ship into an offshore production vessel. As this was a completely new technology, Rob consulted Gunther on how they should deal with it. They agreed to search the market to find a suitable candidate to be put in charge of the project.

One morning one of the service managers who had negotiated a contract with him for the fracking project called. 'Did you know that fracking at the other wells is being done without additional casing string? They've also increased the fracking pressures to optimize the production rate.'

Rob did not know, and he didn't want anything to do with such incredibly irresponsible and downright dangerous operations. Indignant, he questioned Moreland about it the next meeting. 'Are you aware of what's happening out there? Did you actually approve those changes in the program? What you're doing can be both harmful to the environment as well as dangerous because of channeling risks,' he argued.

'Yes, I am aware of the changes, and yes, I did approve,' Moreland said, vexed at being questioned. 'You'll just have to accept it, Rob. And if you have a problem with that, I suggest you start looking around for another job.'

Frustrated as he was, Rob would have handed in his notice right then and there, if it weren't for the fact that he had just received company stock that he wanted to sell over the weekend.

Chapter 11

One month later the CEO summoned him to his office. 'Very sorry, Rob,' Moreland began. 'The company has to cut costs, so I'm afraid we're going to have to terminate your contract with us. It's nothing personal,' he added with a polished smile. 'The same applies to everyone else who was transferred here from Germany.' Before Rob could even react, Moreland glibly went on to say, 'Abel will accompany you to your office. You are to leave everything behind, including your car, but of course you are allowed to collect your personal belongings. I'd like to inform you that the company will honor the transfer agreement. You'll find that the money has already been transferred to your bank account.'

Rob was completely stunned. He had seen American movies in which people went to work in the morning only to leave the place an hour later with only their personal belongings in a box. He had talked about the possibility of this happening with Eberhart and the others, but it turned out that the nightmare had become his reality.

He left Moreland's office, too astounded to speak, with Abel accompanying him to his office. From there he called Anne to pick him up, a gloating Abel standing within earshot. When she asked him why, he repeated his request irritably. 'Just please come and pick me up as soon as you can. I'll tell you why later.'

He quickly gathered his things, upon which Abel walked him to the lobby, where Rob was made to hand over the car and office keys.

As Rob turned around to leave the lobby, he heard Abel say to his back, 'This is payback time for what you did in Germany.'

It was then that he knew that somehow the octopus was involved. The mere thought of it made him feel like punching Abel between the eyes, but he kept his anger under control and left the office without a word.

When Anne came to pick him up, Rob was still feeling murderous. He threw the box with his things in the back, got in the seat next to her and slammed the door shut. 'I'll tell you when we get home,' he said, his face grim. From the tone of his voice Anne thought it wisest not to question him. But she already knew. Of course she already knew.

They sat down on the patio. 'Anne, everyone in the company knows that things always change if there's an acquisition or merger. A new owner will always use his own staff as much as possible in order to reduce cost. I know we took a risk accepting the U.S. transfer, but the risk was covered in the transfer agreement. This is why I insisted on those conditions. One year's salary, plus a lump sum to fly us and ship our furniture back to Holland. If you look at the past year, we gained new experiences, made new friends and did things that we wouldn't have missed for the world.' He turned to look at her and took her hand. 'The good news is that Werner has asked me to work for him.'

What was it that his mam said? "Things always happen for a reason." At that very moment the phone rang. It was Werner.

'I just heard the news, Rob,' Werner said. 'I wanted to say you're welcome to come and discuss working for us whenever you're ready. All you need to do is call. I already called Eberhart and Jurgen, I told them the same. Jurgen and I agreed to meet sometime next week, but Eberhart acted real strange. He told me he wasn't interested. He surprised me. I really didn't expect that.'

'Thanks, Werner, I appreciate this. I'll call you after the weekend. I still have to let this all sink in.'

He immediately dialed Eberhart, but it was his wife who answered. Somewhat embarrassed, she told him that Eberhart had been given strict instructions not to talk to him.

Crestfallen, he hung up the phone. It took a moment before it finally dawned on him. So Eberhart had played the game well. He had given his full cooperation and provided Buchanan & Ross Oil with all the information they wanted. Now he was being rewarded—he kept his job. Now he understood why Eberhart had wanted a copy of the planning system. It suddenly occurred to him that he never received it back, the comments and changes that he said he was going to make never made it back to his desk.

He couldn't believe that his intuition had let him down so much. So Eberhart had made his choice, and he could still keep his job with Buchanan & Ross Oil. It was obvious that the company still regarded him as useful.

He told Anne what he just learned. She, too, found it hard to believe.

'In Germany I knew instinctively that some of your colleagues were wolves in sheep's skins, but I never suspected that Eberhart would be one of them.' She shook her head in bewilderment. 'He has always been so friendly to us, at the company parties, and everything. I never expected anything like this.'

'Well, Anne. There it is. It turns out this is nothing but a ruthless battlefield where one is expected to take care of his own survival. In America it's "no job, no income". No unemployment benefits here as we have in Europe. And bills still need to be paid.'

'What will happen to us?'

'We'll know on Monday after I talk to Werner. Tell you what. Let's forget this horrible day for a while and drive to San Antonio. I'd really like to see the ruins of the Alamo. Some of my Western book heroes fought for their lives over there. We'll stay at a hotel as it's too far to travel in one day.

'I'll call Jurgen to see if he wants to join us. Maybe Bill is off duty, then my Cowboy friend can show us around, and we'll have time to talk.'

It turned out that Jurgen was also badly in need of some distraction, and Bill was off-duty, so they first drove up to Wimberley together, where Bill showed them part of 'his' Texas.

It was a marvelous weekend. Wimberley was a lovely town in the Hill Country, famous for its artists who settled there to perform all kinds of creative arts. They visited lavender farms and parked their car on a water bridge, where they stepped into the water of the overflowing Bravo River, the water cascading down. The children thought this quite a miracle.

They stayed in San Antonio for two nights, explored the river walk, went to the Mexican market and visited the Alamo, where they paid their respects to Rob's school time heroes and the inventor of Rob's bowie knife.

They returned on Sunday morning, when Bill took them to the San Marcos outlet mall, hoping to become the women's favorite. The mall was too big for seeing all shops in one day.

While the women went shopping, the men had a beer, looked after the kids and finally got to talking about everything that happened.

'Rob, we did not touch on the subject, but I told you to watch out. This is standard practice with takeovers. Will you be returnin' to Europe or trying your luck in the States? I could refer you to a lot of companies if you want.'

'Werner has asked me to join him at the turnkey company. I don't know yet. I'll talk to him on Monday.' He did not mention what Abel had said when he had left the office.

'Well, if you do need any help, just call me. You'll have to admit that the guided tour I organized this weekend was pretty damn good.' He winked.

'You did a great job, Bill. I think the women are especially grateful to you. But let's see if we can find them. I'm getting hungry.'

They found the women, smiling and loaded with shopping bags, and they finally returned to Houston to have dinner at a Mexican restaurant.

Chapter 12

On Monday morning he noticed that the separation money was transferred into his bank account, and he also received the shares that were due to him by mail. He sold the shares the very same day, as he never wanted to see the name of Buchanan & Ross Oil ever again.

After lunch he left to meet with Werner and Bernard Heumer. It was as if nothing had changed, only the office and country were different. Within an hour they had finalized the details surrounding his employment—he was to start work as Drilling Manager in the turnkey drilling business starting the following Monday.

They told him that Jurgen had also accepted their offer, and Rob suggested getting Joop on board, too.

He drove home, feeling great. It was good to be working for decent, honest people again.

Once he returned home, he immediately called Joop, asking if he wanted to work in the U.S. Joop wanted to discuss the offer with his wife and would get back to him within a week.

'It looks as if I'm back in business,' he told Anne. 'I've just gotten myself another job. I suggest we pack our swimming gear and shorts and head for the beach for five days.'

'But we were away last weekend! And now you want to go to the beach? What happened that changed your life style so drastically?'

'I can't remember ever having a holiday together. We should spend this week somewhere nice with the kids. I'll help you pack. We could be at Galveston beach in two hours.'

'You are crazy. But let's go anyway. I never know when you'll have time for us again.'

In Galveston they found a hotel on the beach and went for a late walk to watch the sunset. It was a wonderful week with only sun, water, wind, sand and love. He now knew where to go if he needed to clear his mind. He realized that this was their first holiday together, and when he saw how much fun the kids and Anne were having, it occurred to him that they were entitled to more of his time.

The last evening they watched the sunset and enjoyed the moment with everything, as it should be. That night Rob and Anne made love and slept on the balcony.

When they drove back to Katy, he promised Anne that he intended to take off more time to be with his family. She just looked at him.

'I'll remind you again in six months' time.'

That evening Joop called to say that he had accepted the job in Houston.

Chapter 13

It was strange, yet familiar, to hold a Monday morning meeting with Bernard Heumer, Werner Brandt and Jurgen to discuss turnkey drilling.

The turnkey concept was that operators who purchased a lease to drill and produce, but who didn't have the engineering and operational resources, could hire a turnkey company to plan and drill the well against a lump sum payment. The key to make money on these wells was tight planning and cost control.

It was Joop's job to prepare the drilling program and Rob's to drill the well.

Werner had already negotiated three turnkey wells with clients; Jurgen was responsible for logistics and procurement. With their tasks distributed, they went to work and drilled the first well.

Rob hired two drilling supervisors, and they proved to be an excellent team once again, as they completed the first well within six weeks, turned a neat profit and were ready to start on the next.

It was hard and precise work, as every mistake could result in loss or making profits. They discussed the purchase of their own rigs to avoid the fluctuating day rates of drilling contractors, and Rob asked Jurgen to search for available rigs. Rob did ask Bill if he wanted to join their team, but it seemed that Bill liked the new challenges and preferred the on/off schedule to have more time with Carmen.

Tom Lehmann called to inquire how he was doing. After the usual updates, Tom told him that he had talked about Buchanan & Ross Oil with some of his friends in the financial world, as their stock price had suddenly sky-rocketed. This concerned them, as they all thought the gas-earning reports to be unrealistic and overstated.

So that's why everyone was so secretive about the gas production rates, was Rob's first thought. They must have tampered with the production rates or reports!

'The CEO and his executives all sold their company stock,' Tom went on. 'That and the fact that they were paid exorbitant salaries and bonuses has probably ruined the company. Buchanan & Ross Oil is on the verge of bankruptcy, Rob. They'll have to take some drastic steps if they want to survive.'

Rob immediately contacted Werner and asked if he was aware of the situation. If Buchanan & Ross Oil was really about to go bankrupt, then it would give them the opportunity to purchase the drilling assets and joint venture agreement with the Russians.

'This is very interesting indeed,' Werner acceded. 'I'll talk to Bernard about it and let you know.'

Even though Rob had left Buchanan & Ross Oil, he was still furious whenever he thought about it. It seemed as if there was no place on earth where this money-grabbing had not gotten a hold of the industry. He had experienced how the European oil industry was being poisoned by greed and corruption, but this seemed an even bigger scandal.

The scenario was the same as in Europe. Once again, a group of arrogant suits had created their own policies, acted above the law and filled their pockets, bankrupting companies, causing the market to crash in the process.

Sure, the governments would step in and bail out the companies with taxpayer's money, after which the men in their smart suits would simply move on to the next company to start the process again, leaving people without their pension schemes, unemployment benefits and stock savings.

Taxpayers should really not accept this anymore and the news media should act as watchdog. People should stop buying products or services from any companies, hospitals or banks run by these white-collar criminals, at least until they are turned around and managed by decent, capable people. People like those in the previous management team, who were willing to invest in technology, new products or services. Managers like Bernard Heumer, who could steer companies into safe heavens should be an example to the new generation, and not a disgrace. White-collar criminals like Fritz Von Ritter should be forced to return earnings obtained illegally and treated like any other criminal.

He did not know exactly how it all happened, but somehow Bernard Heumer and Werner Brandt had, with the support of friends and financial institutions, in no time succeeded obtaining Buchanan & Ross Oil's U.S.

and European drilling leases, the Russian joint venture agreement and other drilling rigs.

Rob couldn't resist making one last call to Abel. 'Touché,' he said, very satisfied, and hung up the phone.

Chapter 14

Eventually they decided to stop turnkey drilling because of the financial risk involved, and to concentrate all their available resources on becoming an U.S. oil and gas company. Operations in Germany continued, and Gunther, the production manager, joined the U.S. team.

It was as if the short interlude that Hattenberg Oil had been acquired by Buchanan & Ross Oil never happened. Capable leadership, a steady course based on skills, planning, know-how and good teamwork made the company grow once more from a small startup to a respected, recognized oil company.

On numerous occasions Anne reminded Rob of his words while driving back from Galveston, when he said he would make more time for her and the kids.

And he would say, 'Next month when this project is finished' or 'Once that rig has been moved.'

Anne arranged for Dad with Agnes, Klaus and the kids to come visit them. Rob took time off to visit 'Houston Control' as Rob called NASA, and even surprised Anne by booking a cruise from Galveston to Mexico, Bahamas and Jamaica.

'Wow,' Anne said. 'I will ask them to come over every six months, if this is how you can make time for us.'

'Sorry, Anne. There's just too much work.'

'That will never change, because you are a worker.'

'One day this will change, and then you'll be my number one priority.'

'That will be the day!'

'I promise.'

The cruise was amazing. Everyone experienced it as if they were living in another world with all the luxury and entertainment on board. They went on excursions to see the dolphins and rays, and made a trip to a James Bond movie island. Both the children and adults had the time of their lives, and no one wanted to disembark, not wanting it to end.

After another two weeks Agnes and her family returned to Europe, but Dad stayed on for two more months to enjoy his grandchildren, daughter and the pleasant Texan weather.

Chapter 15

Then came a day Rob would remember forever, and it started with an early phone call from Hungary.

'Rob, thank you for changing some of my ideas into reality.'

'Laslo, is this you? Oh God, its good hearing from you, how are you doing?'

'I'm feeling fine hearing your voice and enjoying retirement in my home country. One of your secretaries called me yesterday, asked if I ever worked with you and gave me your phone number.'

'Laslo, thank you for sharing your ideas with me, because they brought important changes to the industry and helped me a lot in my career.'

'Then I'm glad you could handle the hurdles we discussed and I could assist you reaching your present position.'

'Laslo, do you enjoy your retirement or do you want to work in the USA?'

'Yes, that would be a dream come true.'

'Laslo, call me when you're ready to enjoy a few years in the States, and we'll see if we can come up with some good ideas.'

'See you in the States, Rob.'

But then disaster struck again. As Rob was driving to the office one morning, a news flash on the radio announced that a rig in the Gulf of Mexico had caught fire, and that people were killed.

The minute Rob got to the office he called Bill's home. He got a very distraught Carmen on the phone—Bill was in the Gulf working on that very same rig.

'Don't worry,' he told Carmen, his stomach turning. 'I'll do everything in my power to find him.'

But when he put down the phone, he felt a terrible sense of déjà vu. Not again! was his only thought.

But yes, Bill was on that same rig, the rig was on fire, and people were getting killed once more. It suddenly occurred to him that the rig belonged to the company where his American colleague worked, the man with whom he had discussed the planning system on the plane. He couldn't help but wonder if this had happened if he had used the system. The thought frustrated him terribly.

He used all his contacts to find out if the crew was evacuated and where the boats and helicopters would come in with the survivors. He closely followed the news on CNN and just prayed that his friend had somehow managed to escape.

Fortunately he did not have to wait so long this time. In the afternoon he received a call that Bill was one of the survivors and on his way to shore.

Feeling immensely relieved, he immediately called Carmen to tell her that Bill was okay.

That evening the phone rang. It was Bill.

'Rob, could you please pick me up? I just came ashore, but my car is parked at the heliport.'

'Thank God you're alive, Bill. I'll be there in one hour.'

He was there in thirty minutes. Seeing his friend wrapped up in an insulation blanket made him realize how much he meant to him. They just hugged, went to the car and drove off.

'You want to talk about it?' Rob asked casually.

'I need to talk about it. That's why I called you.' Bill took a deep breath before continuing. 'Rob, when you came on board and introduced the Look Ahead system, I knew straight away that it was a simple way to follow each step as laid down in the sequences necessary to drill a well for everyone on board.

'It made us communicate, learn, prevent previous accidents from happening again, to avoid lessons learned and above all, avoid mistakes that can kill people or harm the environment.

'I have seen my worst nightmare out there, Rob. Thank God that I'm alive and can hold my lady again. But I'm a drillin' man. I know what went wrong. I won't go into detail, but it's always the same. It all comes down to cost, experience, communications and last minute changes. And you know what else? Most people on the job are just plain ignorant. They don't even know what's happenin' half the time. The crew have to put their lives in the hands of engineers and supervisors, men who aren't even capable or don't know how to do their jobs properly.

'Rob, together we have one hundred years of experience. All the things that we've learned from that experience, that Mother Earth has taught us, they just weren't applied on that rig. I... couldn't take over command, Rob. I wasn't in a position to tell them what to do. I'm telling you, I'll never return to a rig again if I can't be in charge to watch over my own men.

'This is crazy, man! Governments join forces so that we can fly to the moon, but they're unable to avoid nightmares like these. Engineers invented safety cases and then believe they've found the solution. But it's not. The people on the job are the solution. They must be given simple tools to be involved and voice their concerns if necessary. God damn,' he swore beneath his breath, exhausted from his ordeal. 'Just take me home, Rob. I need time to get over this nightmare.'

'Listen, Bill. I'm not going to call you every day to see how you're doing. I know this will take time to heal. But if you're ready and want a different job, just let me know.'

He walked his friend to the front door and left him in the arms of a very relieved, sobbing Carmen.

While driving back there was one thing Bill had said that Rob could not get out of his mind. Why spend money flying to the moon when we cannot even avoid such disasters from happening in this world? The next one was bound to occur in the Caspian Sea, Mexico, Venezuela, Brazil, Russia, Indonesia or the North Sea within a matter of years.

He was convinced that written procedures and risk analysis were not the way to get people's attention. Visualization of the planning sequences and monitoring was. That would be a real step in the right direction. The procedures could be included in these visualized sequences, with the safety case measures clearly indicated. Proven risks and 'lost time' accidents could be included in the sequences so that no one needed to look at written reports or large data bases again.

People on board should realize that if they wanted to play an active role in the chain of events to avoid disasters, more efforts would be required on their part. Their time on board should be more dedicated how to do their jobs. The time spent watching television or movies should be used to prepare them for the next sequence. Generally, every spare hour should be spent learning and checking their work. Drilling operations are similar to car manufacturing, as most of the sequences are repetitive.

Drilling schools that provide well control courses and mandatory refreshment courses are financed by the drilling industry. The IADC has developed competence training courses, while the companies provide additional theoretical training courses.

But because of the on/off schedule, there are times that people on the job haven't carried out certain sequences for a while. They begin their work without refreshment, which is a sure recipe for mistakes.

When Rob asked the head of the German Department of Energy if his Department could play a leading role in taking the initiative to develop a system to avoid human error, he failed to take responsibility, leaving it to the industry instead.

Yet in every single country, governments are the biggest beneficiaries of oil and gas sales. They should take the initiative to protect its people, avoid disasters and protect the environment.

Drilling operations are often monitored on the rig and shown on large screens at the companies' offices. But governments and companies should combine the available resources and develop a standardized, visualized sequence system for everyone on board, so that anyone can constantly observe what's happening on large screens in the public areas, rig floor and offices. This way the rig and office staff are all kept involved and everyone can check which safety barriers are built in to avoid operational, engineering and marine disasters.

No operation should continue until safety conditions are complied with.

Fresh crews should be made to review the current and next sequences so that they are able to discuss all duties related to their jobs. And if that did not take place, then the system should signal this to the person in charge of that shift. Both supervisors and crews should be able to watch videos on how to carry out the sequences in a safe, correct way.

Rob knew that the operational-orientated men, just as his friend Bill, were thinking along the same lines. Yet they had to accept the risk analysis and engineering approach, as this was the lawful way to operate.

Each country where drilling disasters had taken place, as with the Alexander Kielland in Norway and the Piper Alpha in the U.K. had taken this approach.

But communication, know-how and experience are all equally important to break the chain of events. A group of drilling and production experts should work together with I.T. whizz kids to channel their wish list into a simple, more user-friendly planning and communication system to avoid disasters.

It takes leadership to look ahead and recognize the signs that a different approach is necessary. Having witnessed Bernard Heumer's swift action by using his network and forward thinking, Rob could only think of one person who could take a leading role.

After arriving at the office he told Werner and Bernard Heumer what had happened to Bill.

'Is there anything we can do for him?' Heumer asked, concerned.

'I offered him a job if he wants a change of scenery,' Rob told them. 'But there is something else I need your help with. I assume we'll have to go through the same methods as in Europe to complete the safety case before any drilling takes place. We have permits to drill in Europe because the safety case is approved, so they also apply to our U.S. rigs. When the oil industry starts discussions with the new Health and Safety Department, I suggest a new approach. One that requires more than just the standard safety case.'

He went on to explain his idea, outlining the monitoring system he had in mind. He turned to Heumer. 'Everyone in the industry knows and respects you. With your considerable network you could bring all the representatives from the government and the oil industry together. They could finally come to an agreement to finance the project. It's a learning process based on information technology, know-how, experience and teamwork. It's the only possible way to break the pattern. The only way to prevent the same disasters from happening again, and again.'

There was a long silence. Heumer pondered what Rob had just said, realizing all its implications and knowing the difficulties he would face.

Heumer looked at him with a twinkle in his eye, the challenge clearly appealing to him. 'Rob, I will do everything in my power to give it my best shot. I think we're in the right place here. Maybe Houston is the city where these changes can happen.'

THE END